BY BLOOD
ALONE

WILLIAM C. DIETZ

ACE BOOKS, NEW YORK

BY BLOOD ALONE

An Ace Book / published by arrangement with
the author

PRINTING HISTORY
Ace edition / July 1999

The Penguin Putnam Inc. World Wide Web site address is
http://www.penguinputnam.com

Check out the ACE Science Fiction & Fantasy newsletter
and much more on the internet at Club PPI!

ISBN: 0-441-00631-0

ACE®
Ace Books are published
by The Berkley Publishing Group,
a division of Penguin Putnam Inc.,
375 Hudson Street, New York, New York 10014.
ACE and the "A" design are trademarks
belonging to Penguin Putnam Inc.

PRINTED IN THE UNITED STATES OF AMERICA

10 9 8 7 6 5 4 3 2 1

DEDICATION

To Mike Davison, the 24-hour shoot, 28 days on the road,
the oil rig in the gulf, New York, New York, Buckskin
Mary, hot air balloons, helicopters, crop dusters and
motorcycles, 230 miles down the Big Salmon
and a beer at the other end. All of it was fun
in a painful sort of way. Thanks!

ACKNOWLEDGMENTS

Dr. Sheridan Simon, who designed the Hudathan homeworld, the Hudathans themselves, and the planet Algeron; Tony Geraghty, author of March or Die; *Christian Jennings, author of* Mouthful of Rocks; *and John Robert Young, author of the* The French Foreign Legion.

BY BLOOD
ALONE

Troops must obey or die. There is no other choice.

Mylo Nurlon-Da
The Life of a Warrior
Standard year 1703

Planet Earth, the Confederacy of Sentient Beings

The sun rose blood red, threw shadows toward the Pacific, and bathed the campus in soft pink light. Colonel William "Bill" Booly III left the BOQ, savored the crisp morning air, and looked across the quad. He was a tall man with his mother's steady gray eyes and his father's rangy body. The tan stopped at his collar. He nodded to a civilian and stepped onto a carefully maintained path.

The pavement was barely wide enough to accommodate four people running abreast, or two columns of two, which was the way that cadets moved from place to place. Just one of the methods by which they were taught to follow orders, work as a team, and focus on group objectives.

The administration building, also known as Tonel Hall, lay directly ahead. His father had been the *first* person of Naa descent to enter the academy, carry the class pennant over the rooftops, and collide with a general while making his escape. A story he had heard what? A hundred times?

A company of cadets crossed in front of the officer, and the commander, a skinny little thing who rarely saw a captain much less a colonel, saluted, snapped her head toward the front and called the cadence. "Your left, your left, your left, right, left . . ."

Booly smiled, returned the salute, and fell into step. It had been more than fifteen years since he had marched to class . . . but it might as well have been yesterday.

He remembered how the door would slam open, the cadet leader would yell "Hit the deck," and his roommate would groan. Then came the cold floor tiles, a hot shower, and the same old breakfast. All so he could become an officer in a military organization that had survived for more than seven hundred years. Not for a country, not for a cause, but for *themselves*.

Legio patria nostra. "The Legion is my country." That was the Legion's motto and, in the minds of some, its primary weakness.

The administration building loomed above. A cadet snapped to attention, clicked his heels, and offered a rifle salute.

The officer returned it and approached the door. The push panels glowed. Booly wondered if they were the same ones *he* had polished, or if the daily friction eventually wore holes through solid metal.

The lobby was enormous. A painting of King Louis-Philippe occupied most of one wall. A plaque was mounted below, and like every graduate Booly knew the words by heart:

ARTICLE 1
There will be formed a Legion
composed of Foreigners.
This Legion will take the name of *Foreign Legion.*

The side walls were decorated with battle flags, some ragged and stained by what might have been blood, others as pristine as if just removed from the box. Not too surprising, since flags had very little place in modern battles—and were typically incinerated along with those who carried them.

The air smelled of floor wax and something Booly couldn't quite put his finger on. Mold? Rot? No, bricks don't decay, not *Legion* bricks.

A corporal sat ensconced behind three hundred pounds of solid oak. He wore the insignia of the 3rd REI, two five-year service stripes, and a pair of campaign medals. He'd seen a lot of colonels and wasn't impressed by this one. "Good morning, sir. Can I be of assistance?"

Booly looked into the scanner without being asked. "Yes, thank you. Colonel William Booly—here for Captain Pardo's court martial. Could you direct me to the proper room?"

The corporal consulted his terminal, confirmed the officer's identity, and watched an icon twirl. He touched a key. "There's a message, sir. From General Loy . . . Please join him prior to the proceedings."

General Arnold M. Loy, Commanding Officer, Earth Sector. He shared the building with the academy's commandant and was in charge of the court martial. Booly knew the officer's reputation if not the man himself. Medal of Valor, Battle Star, and Croix de Guerre. Some described Loy as "a hero of the Confederacy" and some called him "the butcher of Bakala." Both views were probably true.

The request could be routine, an administrative matter of some sort, or—and this was what Booly feared—the first sign of politics in what promised to be a highly charged proceeding. He nodded to the corporal. "Top floor—south side?"

The noncom nodded. "Yes, sir. Some things never change."

The corporal watched the officer climb the well-worn stairs. Poor sod. Loy would eat him for breakfast. The noncom savored the thought and chuckled. His coffee break was due in fifteen minutes. That's what he liked about the Legion. Do what you're told, keep your nose clean, and things took care of themselves.

General Loy heard the knock and knew who it was. He rose from his chair, turned his back on the room, and looked out through the window. An important man thinking important thoughts. The pose had been calculated once—but that was a long time ago. "Enter."

Booly opened the door and stepped through. The office looked as he had expected it to look. Formal and somewhat spartan. The desk was huge, as if part of a barricade, and mostly bare. What momentos there were had been arranged like legionnaires on parade. The rest of the furnishings consisted of some heavily worn guest chairs, a credenza made of Turr wood, and a wall of carefully arranged stills. Loy on Algeron, Loy with the President, Loy on Bakala. Not one single photo of someone else.

Booly, hat held in the crook of his arm, snapped to attention. "Colonel Bill Booly, reporting as ordered, sir."

Loy allowed a second to pass, turned, and stuck out his hand. The smile was genuine. "Booly! Good to see you. . . . Here, have a chair. Coffee, perhaps? The best still comes from Earth."

Booly shook the other man's hand and took a seat. "No, thank you sir. I topped my tanks half an hour ago."

"A wise move," the general said, dropping into his chair. "How was the trip?"

"Long and slow," Booly answered, wondering where the conversation was headed. "It seemed as if we stopped at every asteroid along the way."

Loy grimaced. "A sign of the times, I'm afraid. The bean counters cut the passenger flights six months ago. I wish the worst was behind us, but I don't think it is."

Booly nodded dutifully. "Yes, sir."

Loy had deeply set eyes. They were cannonball black. He made a steeple with his fingers and peered through the triangle. "This proceeding has attracted lots of attention. You should see the headlines. 'Supplies Stolen.' 'Officer Loots Legion.' 'Weapons Missing.' Terrible stuff. Especially now. It's been fifty years since the second Hudathan war, and the public is soft. We could use a police action. Might wake them up."

The meaning was obvious, even to someone who had spent the last couple of years on the rim. The Pardo case could be used to justify further cutbacks. Booly struggled to maintain his composure. "Sir? What are you suggesting? That I alter my testimony?"

The general's face grew hard and foreboding. "I suggest you watch your mouth, Colonel . . . lest *you* face charges.

"Patricia Pardo has presidential ambitions, and could even win, unless this brings her down. That would be unfortunate, since the governor is one of our few supporters."

Booly met the other man's eyes. He refused to make it easy.

Loy broke the silence. "Pardo is guilty as hell, we both know that, and he deserves to be punished. Two years on Drang would serve the bastard right! But why punish the entire Legion for the actions of *one* man? The last thing we need is more negative publicity."

Booly started to reply, but the general held up a hand. "Give it some thought . . . that's all I ask. See you in court."

The dismissal was clear. Booly stood, said, "Yes, sir," and turned toward the door.

Loy saw the mane of silvery gray fur that ran down the other man's neck and winced. A half-breed. What the hell was next? Officers with scales? It made him sick. The door closed, and Booly was gone.

The conference room was small, no more than twelve feet across, and painted bile green. There were no decorations other than a poorly executed portrait of Captain Jean Danjou and a neatly framed recruiting poster. It showed a Trooper II, arms spitting death, with bodies all around. The caption read: "Last to fall." The furnishings consisted of a much-abused wooden table, six mismatched chairs, and a government-issue waste-paper basket.

Patricia Pardo was beautiful in a hard, calculated way. Her hair was blonde, her eyes were green, and her teeth were white. When she spoke, it was with the manner of someone in the habit of giving orders. "Take a break, Foxy. I want to speak with my son."

Henry Fox-Smith had dark skin and extremely intelligent eyes. They flicked from mother to son. He was a lawyer, one of the best, and worth every credit of his exorbitant fee. "Tell him to get his shit together, Patricia—there won't be a second chance.''

Light rippled across the surface of his eight-hundred-credit suit as Fox-Smith crossed the room and stepped into the hall. The door clicked, and Patricia Pardo turned toward her son.

Captain Matthew Pardo had his father's features, his mother's eyes, and a full, rather pouty mouth. He tried to appear nonchalant but couldn't carry it off. Not with his mother. Her voice was low but intense.

"The only thing that stands between me and the presidency is my own son. You had everything and threw it away. And for what? A few hundred thousand credits.''

Matthew Pardo stared at his shoes. "Is that all? Are you finished?''

"No," his mother replied vehemently. "Not by a long shot! We still have a chance. Not much of one, but a chance. Foxy says that except for the breed's testimony, the rest of the case is circumstantial. What the hell were you thinking? Not even your idiot father would have done something like that.''

"It worked for a long time," Matthew replied defensively. "You've done worse.''

"Watch your mouth," Patricia Pardo snapped. "This room could be bugged.''

"Nah, the Legion doesn't work that way," Matthew said contemptuously.

"It's not the Legion that I'm worried about," his mother replied darkly. "I spoke with General Loy, and he agreed to speak with Colonel Booly.''

"The furball won't flip," the younger Pardo replied. "Not in a million years.''

"Well, you'd better hope he does," Patricia Pardo replied sternly, "because that's all you have.''

The auditorium was packed with a menagerie of reporters, staff grunts, and service-issue robots.

A panel of six officers sat or stood on the stage. There was a lieutenant general, two colonels, two majors, and a couple of captains.

The fact that one of the captains was a half-ton cyborg surprised no one. Some of the borgs held field commissions. There was even talk of admitting cyborgs to the academy—though traditionalists didn't like the idea.

Conversation stopped the moment Loy mounted the stage.

Booly felt his stomach muscles contract and wished he were somewhere else. The choice was clear: lie for the Legion or retire as a colonel. It should have been simple. Right is right. Then why couldn't he decide?

General Loy sat at the center of a long wooden table. The gavel banged. "All right . . . everyone knows why we're here . . . let's get on with it. Well, Major Hassan? Are your weapons locked and loaded?"

"Yes, sir," Hassan replied.

"Fire when ready."

Hassan hadn't fired a weapon since Officer Candidate School. His mustache twitched over what might have been a smile. "Yes, sir. The prosecution calls Staff Sergeant Rosa Carboda to the stand."

The session began with Carboda's matter-of-fact testimony: "Yes, sir, it *did* seem as if the people under Captain Pardo had lost or misplaced a lot of weapons. A hundred and fifty-six thousand credits worth, to be exact."

Then came the more colorful comments made by an "entertainer" who called herself Crystal Sunrise. She saw nothing unusual in the large amount of money that a certain captain had to spend and hoped he'd return to Caliente.

The media, many of whom had been dozing up till that point, ordered their hover cams to move in closer. Citizen Sunrise had enormous breasts, and metal clanged on metal as the machines fought for the best angle.

Loy frowned when it became difficult to see the witness through the swarm of machines and ordered them withdrawn. The reporters did so, and the general glanced at his wrist term. "Time for a recess. Fifteen minutes. No excuses."

Clothes rustled, chairs scraped, and servos whined as the Trooper II left the stage. Major Hassan caught Booly's eye and waved him over. "Sir, I plan to call you immediately after the recess."

Booly felt his heart start to pound. "Really? You made

some pretty good progress. Will my testimony make any difference?"

"It certainly will," Hassan answered confidently. "Given the fact that Sergeant Carboda had been a supply sergeant for less than three standard months at the time of the incident, the defense will attack the extent of her expertise.

"Then, with Carboda on the ropes, they will proceed down the list to Ms. Sunrise, point to what she said, and the fact that Governor Pardo is wealthy. Of *course* Captain Pardo has extra money . . . the slimy bastard is rich. Never mind the fact that he isn't *that* rich. Get the picture, sir?"

"Yeah," Booly replied wearily. "I get the picture."

Hassan nodded. "Good. I'll see you after the break. I gotta bleed my tanks."

"You sound like the general."

Hassan grinned. "Good! That's the plan. Over and out."

The proceedings resumed right on time, and Major Hassan called his next witness.

Booly stood when his name was called, walked for what felt like a hundred miles, and swore to tell the whole truth and nothing but the truth. And it was then, with his hand in the air, that he remembered his father's words.

He'd been caught in a lie. He couldn't remember what the incident was about . . . just the way his father loomed against the sky. It would have been impossible to tell the real eye from the implant if it hadn't been for the field of scars that surrounded it. The voice was serious but loving.

"You can't build anything on a foundation of lies, son. The walls will buckle and crush you in the rubble. The best thing to do is tell the truth and let the chips fall where they may."

"The witness may be seated," Loy said pointedly. Booly felt blood rush to his face and and hurried to comply.

"Thank you," Loy said sarcastically. "Please proceed."

Hassan nodded, said, "Yes, sir," and turned to Booly. "Please give the court your name and rank."

"William Booly, Colonel, Commanding Officer, Rim Sector 872."

"And the nature of the forces under your command?"

"I command a mixed battalion consisting of two infantry companies, two platoons of sentient armor, three batteries of artillery, and a headquarters group."

Hassan nodded agreeably. "And for those not familiar with Rim Sector 872, where is your battalion headquartered?"

"On Caliente."

"Are *all* of your troops stationed on Caliente?"

Booly shook his head. "No. We have outposts as well."

"Outposts that can be resupplied and reinforced from your headquarters on Caliente?"

"Exactly."

"Thank you," Hassan said easily. "Now, tell the court about Captain Pardo. . . . Does he report to you?"

"Yes."

"And Captain Pardo's responsibilities?"

"Captain Pardo commands Outpost RS 872-12."

"Which is located where?"

"On a planet named Pebble."

"Thank you. Now, tell us about Pebble, and Captain Pardo's specific responsibilities."

Booly's mouth felt dry. He took a sip of water. "Pebble attracts all sorts of beings. In addition to thousands of law-abiding citizens, the planet is home to smugglers, thieves, and a variety of other criminals."

"And Pardo keeps the lid on?"

"Yes," Booly replied. "In a manner of speaking. There are civilian authorities as well."

"Of course," Hassan said agreeably. "But Captain Pardo is the senior *military* officer on the planet and, as such, has the latitude to do as he sees fit."

"Yes. That's correct."

"So, let me see if I understand," Hassan said thoughtfully. "Captain Pardo had been given a significant amount of free-dom, was assigned to a planet crawling with criminals, and suddenly wound up with a whole lot of money. Is that about the size of it?"

Fox-Smith jumped to his feet. "I object! Leading the wit-ness. Move to strike."

Loy speared Hassan with one of his darkest frowns.

"Granted. Watch yourself, Major—we'll have none of your shenanigans here."

Hassan looked suitably apologetic. "Yes, sir." He turned to Booly. "So, Colonel, given the fact that you were stationed on Caliente, how could you tell whether Captain Pardo and his legionnaires were faithful to the fifty-three thousand two hundred thirty-seven regulations presently listed on the Legion's books?"

The question drew titters from the audience. Fox-Smith rose once again. "May I ask the relevance of this line of questioning?"

Hassan looked to Loy. "Motive has been established. The accused spends more than he makes. The question goes to opportunity. Relevance will become obvious in a moment."

Loy waved a hand. "Whatever. Get on with it."

Hassan turned to Booly. "Answer the question, please."

"I hold scheduled as well as unscheduled inspections."

Hassan nodded as if hearing that particular piece of information for the very first time. "I see. So the men and women stationed on Pebble never knew when you might arrive."

"That's correct."

"Describe the inspection that took place on Earth date October 23, 2645."

Booly had been expecting the question and was ready. If his words sounded rehearsed, they were. "Sergeant Major Mueller and I landed on Pebble at approximately twenty hundred hours. It was dark."

Hassan nodded his encouragement. "Tell the court what happened next."

Booly shrugged. "We pulled our duffel bags off the transport and headed for the terminal. That's when a hover truck passed in front of us."

"Was there something *special* about the truck?" Hassan inquired. "Something that set it apart?"

"It had Legion markings."

"Please continue."

"I was curious, so I followed the truck across the tarmac to where a shuttle was parked."

"Did you note any markings on the shuttle?"

"Sergeant Major Mueller took holos of the vessel. The name *'Rim Queen'* had been painted across her bow and the number ISV-7421-3 was stenciled on her hull."

Hassan turned toward Loy. "If it please the court—Sergeant Major Mueller's holos are marked as exhibit 36—and subsequent investigation revealed that the shuttle is registered to the freighter *Rim Queen*. A vessel sought in connection with a variety of smuggling activities."

Fox-Smith came to his feet. "I move to strike counsel's last comment as both irrelevant and prejudicial."

Loy waved a hand. "So noted. Strike the major's comment."

Hassan remained unperturbed. An idea had been planted—and there was no way that Loy could remove it. The prosecutor turned to Booly. "What happened next?"

"Mueller and I stood in the shadows and watched Captain Pardo approach the shuttle."

"Wait a minute," Hassan said critically. "It was dark . . . how could you be sure the man was Pardo?"

"He passed under a hover spot," Booly said with certainty, "*and* registered on my wrist term."

Hassan mustered a look of surprise. "On your wrist term? Show the court."

What ensued was more for the benefit of the press than the court, since nearly every officer present wore a similar device and knew how they functioned.

Booly went along, however, even going so far as to roll up his sleeve and display a sinewy arm. The terminal was black. He touched a button, and a holo bloomed.

Eight miniature heads appeared and started to rotate. Seven were dark, showing they were off-line, while one glowed green. The name was there for everyone to read: "M. Pardo."

There was a stir as the robocams whirred in for a closer look. Booly glanced at Loy, saw a look that could only be described as venomous, and knew there was no going back. Hassan nodded for effect. "So, that particular function was activated? And confirmed the captain's identity?"

"That's correct."

"And the transmissions are secure? No one could feed false information into your terminal?"

"Legion wrist terms are extremely well protected."

"Go ahead."

Booly described how he called Pardo's name, how Sergeant Major Mueller felt compelled to crank a round into the chamber of his GP-4 submachine gun, and how they searched the truck. A search that turned up a large number of weapons that Pardo had reported as lost.

Fox-Smith spent the next four hours hammering Hassan's witnesses, and none more than Colonel William Booly.

But the officer refused to change his testimony, and, assuming the panel was honest, there was little doubt what they would find.

Finally, when Booly left the building, it was with a deep sense of disappointment. In Pardo, in Loy, and the Legion itself.

The next two days passed rather slowly. In spite of the fact that he had completed his testimony, there was the possibility that Booly would be recalled. That being the case, he was free to leave the campus so long as he stayed nearby.

An autocab carried the officer to El Centro, the heart of the old city, and the scene of many youthful adventures. The neighborhood opened gradually, like some exotic flower, complete with its own doubtful perfume.

The legionnaire ordered the vehicle to a halt and walked the familiar streets. Many of his favorite haunts were gone, replaced by newer establishments, none of which felt the same. Here were the flophouses, cheap restaurants, and bars with names like Jericho Mary's, the Sergeant's Delight, and the Black Kepi.

And here too were the legionnaires themselves, easily identifiable by their short haircuts, regimental tattoos, and flinty stares.

Beggars who had fought under alien suns, looked death in the eye, and buried their friends. All for the stench of urine-soaked alleys, the contempt of those they had served, and the solace found in a bottle. Demobilized by the thousands, and with nothing to do, they stood in little groups.

Booly watched a wiry little man, the emblem of the 1st RE still visible on his right forearm, approach a prosperous citizen. A civil servant, perhaps, or the owner of a store. Words were exchanged, the ex-legionnaire jerked as if slapped, and the man turned his back.

The officer reached into his pocket, found a wad of bills, and peeled some off. "Corporal—a moment of your time, please."

The legionnaire turned. His face registered surprise. "Sir?"

"I wondered if you would do me a favor. A platoon of the 1st REI saved my ass on Etan IV—and I was never able to thank them. Perhaps you could host a few of the lads to dinner. I'd be grateful."

Tears filled the legionnaire's eyes. "Why, bless you, sir. It would be my pleasure. I guess the tattoo is clear enough—but how did you scan my rank?"

"From the way you carry yourself," Booly said truthfully, "and the chevrons on your sleeve."

The corporal looked, saw the dark patch of fabric, and laughed. "Once a corporal, always a corporal!"

Booly nodded and walked away.

Other legionnaires, curious what had transpired, drifted over. The corporal showed them the money. "We're gonna have lunch, lads . . . and some beer to wash it down."

The men watched their benefactor cross the street. "I want you to remember that one," the corporal said thoughtfully. "Some need killing . . . and some don't."

The summons came the way most military communications do, at an inconvenient time, and without prior warning.

Booly had just stepped into the shower, and ducked his head under a blast of hot water, when his wrist term began to vibrate. The officer wiped water out of his eyes and squinted at the readout: "Report General Loy—1400 hours." Short and not especially sweet.

Booly sent an acknowledgment and watched the time reappear: "1326." Not much response time. Why?

The officer finished his shower, made his way out into the simply furnished room, and spoke to the com center. "Holo vision—news channel."

The all-purpose holo tank faded into life. Booly waited through the end of the sports report and was half dressed by the time the news summary came on. The computer-animated news anchor looked a lot like the people who lived in the grid that surrounded the academy. Her expression was serious.

"This just in . . . a military court found Legion Captain Matthew Pardo, son of Governor Patricia Pardo, guilty of stealing government property and sentenced the officer to twenty years hard labor at the Confederate correctional facility on Pitra II.

"The conviction, which rested heavily on testimony provided by Pardo's commanding officer, seems proof of the Legion's ability to police itself. Or does it? Critics wonder if Pardo was railroaded as part of an attempt to distract the public from other problems within the Legion.

"Now, with more from the man and woman on the street, here's . . ."

Booly didn't care what the man or woman on the street had to say. He ordered the tank to turn itself off. The image collapsed.

So, the verdict was in. The thief would get twenty on Pitra—and what would he get? Twenty on Caliente? Probably, although there were worse things, like forced retirement.

Having already accepted his fate, Booly found himself surprisingly cheerful as he made his way across the campus and up to General Loy's office. He knocked, heard the traditional "Enter," and stepped inside.

Loy was seated at his desk. He no longer needed anything from Booly . . . and saw no reason to posture. His tone was neutral, and his face was impassive. "Excuse me for not inviting you to sit, Booly, but I'm late for a meeting.

"You're familiar with the base at Djibouti? Yes, of course you are. Home to the 13th DBLE and all that. Well, it seems that the CO, a woman named Junel, died in some sort of accident. Rough crowd out there—you might want to look into it.

"In any case your presence is a god send. We'll slide you into Djibouti, promote your XO into the Caliente slot, and have done with it. Questions?"

Booly looked into the other officer's coal-black eyes and saw they were easy to read. "Go ahead," the look seemed to say. "Question these orders, and see what happens next."

Booly thought about it. Djibouti. A pesthole located on the east coast of Africa. A place to stash troublemakers. Worse than that, an assignment without purpose, where each day would stretch into a long, monotonous hell.

But to say that, or to give even the slightest hint of it, was to lose. Booly stood ramrod straight. "Sir! Yes, sir! Will there be anything else?"

Loy felt a slight sense of disappointment. Maybe the breed was stupid . . . or one hell of an actor. Djibouti was a master stroke. A punishment from which there was no appeal—and no possible escape. He nodded. "No, that should do it. Your gear will be shipped from Caliente, and my adjutant has your orders."

There was no "Good luck," no effort to ease the moment, so Booly said, "Thank you, sir," did an about-face, and marched out of the room. They never saw each other again.

2

If thou follow thy star, thou canst not fail of glorious heaven.

Dante
Divine Comedy: Purgatory
Standard year circa 1308

Somewhere on the Rim, the Confederacy of Sentient Beings

The ready room had been painted orange, green, and blue over the last thirty-six years and all three layers of paint had started to peel. The names of long-gone crew members had been stenciled over empty suit racks and never removed. Not out of respect, or sentiment, but because Jorley Jepp didn't care.

The space armor had clocked more than ten thousand hours and was no longer covered by anything other than carefully applied patches. The warranty was little more than a memory, nobody would write a policy on it, and Jepp was broke.

That being the case, the prospector ran the diagnostics twice, mumbled "Good girl" when the readouts came up green, and entered the *Pelican*'s main lock.

The name stemmed from the way the vessel was shaped. Unlike many of the ships owned and operated by Jepp's peers, the *Pelican* had actually been designed for mining asteroids, which explained the big beaklike bow.

Farther back, roughly halfway down the hull, two pylons extended at right angles to the ship. The tractor and pressor units necessary to grab ten-ton boulders and feed them into the vessel's enormous maw had to be mounted somewhere; hence the *Pelican*'s "wings."

Of course, the tractor-pressor units could be used to clutch other objects as well—including salvage such as the heavily damaged drifter pinned under the *Pelican*'s work lights. A fabulous find that could erase Jepp's debts and fund his future.

The spaceship was a derelict, and had been for a long time, judging from the fact that there were no signs of heat, radiation, or electrical-mechanical activity emanating from it. There was damage, the sort one would expect of something in an asteroid belt, but the hull was intact.

All of which meant that it should be safe to bring the vessel aboard. But prospectors are a paranoid lot, especially those who live long enough to celebrate their fiftieth birthday, and Jepp wanted to inspect his find. What if his activities triggered ancient weapons? A power plant? Anything was possible.

"No, it pays to be careful," Jepp said as the lock cycled open, "and to trust the Lord, for he shall show the way."

The *Pelican*'s navcomp, which Jepp called Henry, after the ancient navigator, issued a perfunctory "Amen," took note of a distant heat source, and wondered what the object was. Time would tell.

The utility sled would have been perfect for the job, but it, like so many other pieces of gear, was sitting in the *Pelican*'s maintenance bay awaiting repairs.

"The Lord giveth and the Lord taketh away," Jepp intoned sanctimoniously as he pushed the ship away.

"And blessed is the name of the Lord," the AI replied, "for he rules heaven and Earth."

"He rules *heaven*," Jepp agreed tartly, "but Earth is up for grabs. That's why I left."

The computer noted the useless information and stored it away.

The prospector fired the jet pack, swore when he veered off course, and made the necessary changes. Was he getting rusty? Or did the right thruster need a tuneup? It took a lot of work to run a scooper—which was why the *Pelican* had been designed to carry a crew of three humans and two robots. That was fine, except that people made Jepp crazy, not to mention the effect he had on them, and the fact that the robots had been sold to buy fuel.

The drifter was bigger now, *much* bigger, and clearly a prize. Jepp felt his heart beat faster and was reminded of his childhood, when brightly wrapped presents awaited eager hands, and suspense was half the fun.

Which would be more valuable? he wondered. The ship, and whatever artifacts it might contain, or the metal it was made of? A nice problem to have.

The prospector fired his braking jets, felt the suit start to slow, and brought his boots up. They hit, his knees absorbed the shock, and the electromagnets embedded in his boots grabbed the hull. Or tried to grab the hull and failed. Jepp bounced away. "Damn! There's no steel in this hull!"

Henry, unsure of how to respond, said nothing. The heat source was larger now, but only in relative terms, since it was little more than a pinprick of warmth in a sky lit by a powerful red giant. Once the object came close enough, assuming it did, the navcomp would notify its master.

Unable to walk on the surface of the hull as he had originally planned to do, the prospector was forced to reactivate the jet pack and search for a way in. There were plenty to choose from. Having been wrecked by the asteroid field, or having fallen in with the floating rocks, the drifter had been repeatedly holed.

Jepp selected a large pear-shaped opening and eased his way through. With no sun or starlight to guide him, the prospector found it necessary to activate both his headlamps. Only one of them worked. The disk of pale white light drifted across potentially valuable artifacts, and Jepp felt his pulse start to race. Alien technology could be worth lots of money!

The light drifted across the entrance to a tunnel. The human brought it back. Something that looked like a leathery fire hose led up and into the darkness beyond. It floated like kelp in the ocean.

Jepp killed his thrusters, pushed the hose to one side, and

pulled himself into the tube. Metal gleamed as if coated with some sort of lubricant. There were no seams, ridges, or other handholds, so the human grabbed the hose and used it to pull himself upward.

Eventually, after what Jepp estimated to be twenty or thirty feet, the tube emptied into a central chamber. The prospector turned his head, which caused the light to play across smooth metal.

Now the human realized that there were six additional tunnels, each having its own hose, all of which terminated in a half-inflated leather bag. That's when Jepp realized that the "bag" possessed eyes, at least three of them, and that the hoses were arms, or tentacles, that the alien could extend into various parts of its ship. It appeared as if at least some decomposition had occurred—followed by freeze-dried mummification once the ship was holed.

The human shuddered, released his grip on the withered limb, and felt his back hit the inside surface of the chamber. That's where the prospector was, still examining his discovery, when Henry called. "Sorry to interrupt, but it appears as though a ship is headed our way, ETA three hours, sixteen minutes, and thirty-two seconds."

Jepp used the Lord's name in conjunction with a swear word, was ashamed of himself, and started over. "Blast! What kind of ship?"

"Too early to tell," the AI replied. "Looks big, though— judging from the amount of heat."

Jepp swore once again. Just his luck. . . . A company ship? Or a pirate? He wasn't sure which he dreaded more. Either would be happy to steal his prize. But not if he could take the drifter aboard, hide among the asteroids, and wait the heathens out.

The prospector turned, grabbed hold of the tentacle, and pulled. There was no resistance. The far end was free. Jepp swore, fired his thrusters, and caromed off the side of the tube. "Bring the *P* in close! Open the hatch! I'm on the way!"

The human was subject to tremendous mood swings, and having been unable to consistently correlate them with external stimuli, the computer no longer attempted to do so. It used a pressor beam to shove an asteroid out of the way, shortened the tractor beams, and brought the hulls closer together.

The hatch yawned obediently, and the maneuver was complete. Henry cycled through the onboard systems, verified that the most critical ones remained operational, and went to standby. The human would emerge soon—and work would resume.

The scout ship was hungry. The far-ranging mission had consumed a great deal of fuel, parts were beginning to fail, and food was required. Raw ore-bearing asteroids would do, but refined metal was easier to digest, and therefore preferable. And, since long-range sensors confirmed the possibility of such a feast ahead, the construct increased its speed.

Did the ship belong to the Thraki? No, it didn't appear so, but General Directive Three was clear: "Any and all available resources can and should be used while searching for the Thraki."

Jepp hung in space, motionless relative to the *Pelican,* and watched while the tractor beams drew the wreck into his ship. It looked as if one monster was in the process of devouring another.

Finally, with the drifter aboard, the prospector fired his thrusters, passed through the open doors, and waited for Henry to close them.

The argrav was restored and Jepp felt his boots make contact with the deck. Maybe, just maybe, there was time to escape. "How soon will the godless bastards arrive?"

The AI correctly surmised that the human was making reference to the oncoming ship, checked its sensors, and offered a reply. "ETA one hour, three minutes, and two seconds."

Jepp grabbed an armful of tie-downs and hurried to secure his prize. The sinners had increased their speed! "Take the *P* in among the asteroids. Maybe we can lose them."

"Order refused," Henry said crisply. "The odds of this vessel surviving such a course of action fall well below my acceptable minimums."

Jepp thought about the random manner in which the closely

packed asteroids bounced off each other, knew the computer was correct, but refused to surrender his find. The solution? Place himself in the loving hands of God. "Revelations 1:8 . . . 'I am Alpha and Omega, the beginning and the ending, saith the Lord . . .' "

The navcomp processed the override, found a match, and fired the ship's drives. The human had decided to destroy both the ship and himself. That being the case, the AI contacted the onboard autochef and cancelled Jepp's dinner.

The scout ship watched its meal grow warmer and start to move. Additional acceleration would result in excessive fuel consumption—but seemed warranted, given the circumstances. More power was applied, the vessel surged forward, and the distance continued to close.

Jepp secured a final tie-down, cycled through a lock, and entered the control area. Half-empty ration paks were scattered about, dirty clothes hung from equipment racks, and tools littered the deck.

He opened the helmet but kept the suit on—a sensible precaution when blundering through asteroid belts.

A plastic crucifix poked up and out of the debris that covered the console. He touched it for luck, dropped into the command chair, and ran an eye over the screens. "Blast! The Philistines have gained on us!"

Henry checked his memory mod for "Philistines," discovered that the human had assumed certain things about those on the other ship, and realized that "gained on us" was the operant part of the sentence. "That is correct . . . they *have* gained on us."

"Well, *do* something, damn you!"

"I am presently guiding the ship through the asteroids. Would *you* like to take the controls?"

Jepp looked up at the main viewscreen. Sunlight glided across a pockmarked chunk of rock and was lost in the blackness beyond. The *Pelican* slid past, paused while a house-sized boulder drifted by, and continued its journey. One slip, one mistake, and the whole thing was over. "No, but do what you can."

"Of course," Henry replied evenly. "I'll do what I can."

The next hour passed with excruciating slowness as the *Pelican* pushed its way into the belt . . . and the other vessel started to slow.

Still, time was on *his* side, or so Jepp had assumed. Suddenly that advantage, like the easy profit, was snatched away. Harsh, actinic light strobed across the slowly tumbling spacescape, and the human sat bolt upright in his chair. "What in heaven's name was that?"

"*That* was an exploding asteroid," the navcomp replied cheerfully. "The most direct route between two points is a straight line. That being the case, our pursuers decided to remove obstacles rather than go around them. A rather unconventional use of weaponry, but effective nonetheless."

"Shut the hell up," Jepp said sourly. "How long before the idolators reach us?"

"About ten minutes," Henry replied calmly, "give or take a second or two."

The scout ship waited for its bow cannons to recycle, fired, and moved through the newly created opening. The feast, which continued to waste precious resources, would soon be ingested. Millions of nano were notified and brought on-line. They began to seethe with barely contained energy. Once the meal was brought aboard, it would be their task to digest it.

Rock fragments sparkled as they hit the ship's screens, were reduced to their component atoms, and drifted away.

There were fewer asteroids now—a fact that allowed Jepp to see his pursuer for the first time. It filled the main screen. He fell through the pit of his stomach. The situation was worse than he had supposed. This construct was as alien as the drifter that occupied his hold, only a lot more frightening!

The oncoming vessel had the free-form bulk of a ship never meant for atmospheric use. It consisted of three cylinders, all mounted side by side, and surrounded by a framework of metal. The force field that protected the hull shimmered as rock fragments made contact with it.

The human watched aghast as still another asteroid exploded and the alien vessel pushed its way through the resulting debris field.

The *Pelican* shuddered as alien tractor beams locked onto her hull. The drives screamed as they fought to pull the ship free—and junk avalanched off the control panel.

Jepp sat transfixed as garbage tumbled into his lap. The Sheen ship, for that's the name he had assigned to it, was unstoppable. It became even larger as a rectangle of light appeared and the *Pelican* was drawn inside.

Enormous foot-thick doors started to close; the star field narrowed into a vertical bar and disappeared from sight. Someone or something forced the drives to shut down, the control panel went dead, and the lights went out. Henry had just switched to backup energy banks when a self-guided cable snaked out of its metallic lair, slithered down the ship's side, made modifications to the way the terminal end was configured, and entered the appropriate socket.

The AI was still evaluating this development, still searching for guidance, when it was seized, translated, and downloaded to a bubble-matrix prison.

The storage media held other AIs as well, many of whom were so alien that Henry couldn't communicate with them, but at least one had human origins. It had been part of a long-range probe ingested two years before. It spoke first. "Hello, mate! And welcome to the cosmic trash bin. I hope you like three-dimensional chess, because there isn't much to do."

Confident that it had evacuated the food's onboard intelligence, the scout ship cleared the meal for digestion and put the nano to work.

Jepp fumbled for the emergency lighting switch and toggled it to the "on" position. The overall level of illumination was lower than usual but sufficient to his purposes. "Why did the power go down? What's happening?"

There was no reply. The navcomp should have been on-line but wasn't.

The human freed himself from the chair, hurried down the main corridor, and into the lock. It took five minutes to close his visor, check his suit seals, and cycle through. The readout on his heads-up display claimed there was no need. Though slightly richer in oxygen than humans normally required, the atmosphere inside the alien vessel was quite breathable. Why? What kind of creatures were they? And where were they from?

Jepp opened his visor and looked around. What little light there was came from the *Pelican*'s navigational lights. He saw beams, like the ribs of a whale, and gently curved hull plates. There was no sign of his hosts, or captors, as the case might be. "Hello—is anybody out there?"

Silence. It was disconcerting, but preferable to a horde of bloodthirsty aliens. There was a loud creaking noise followed by the sounds of metal on metal as the *Pelican* collapsed onto the deck.

Startled, and more than a little surprised, Jepp hurried to inspect the damage. There wasn't any. Not in the normal sense, anyway. Most of the landing skids were missing! The margins were smooth, with no sign of the tool or tools used to create them.

That's when the human noticed what looked like a river of metal snaking away from the ship and into the surrounding gloom. A hastily conducted investigation revealed numerous rivers—all headed in the same direction! The *Pelican* was being disassembled at the subatomic level and hauled away.

There was a groan as still another structure gave way and the *Pelican* settled onto the deck. That's when Jepp realized the importance of salvaging whatever he could. Food, water, and medical supplies—all were aboard his ship. The prospector ran for the lock.

The next two hours were a race against time. As Jepp struggled to remove the things he needed, the nano took the vessel apart.

The prospector wondered about the supplies at first, fearful that the microscopic robots would claim those too, but the machines showed no interest in anything beyond the *Pelican* herself.

Logical, he supposed, lest the nano attack their own ship, and eat themselves out of house and home. That being the case, Jepp was able to secure a considerable amount of food, all the water he could find containers for, medical supplies, and, since there was no one to object, his flechette thrower.

Once those materials were safely stowed the human turned his attention to a box full of emergency light wands, a portable generator that might be coaxed into life, and a reasonably powerful data comp. That's when the lights went out. The nano, voracious creatures that they were, had burrowed into the emergency power stacks.

Jepp played a beam over the wreck, cursed his captors, and backed away.

There were dozens of nano streams by that time, all wending their way through the same portal and into the darkness beyond. Jepp followed the intertwining rivulets through the arch and down a funnel-shaped corridor. It narrowed alarmingly and barred his progress.

The metal was like an enormous snake by then, a silvery pseudopod that pulsed as if invested with a life of its own. Jepp watched as his ship, *and* the drifter that might have put him in the black, were sucked into the funnel.

Frustrated, angry, and more afraid than he would have cared to admit, the prospector returned to the hold and what remained of his vessel. "Okay, you win. So what now?"

The scout ship heard inarticulate sounds and sensed movement deep within its belly. The sensation was easy to ignore. The vessel had fuel, a purpose, and the means to fulfill that purpose. What more could any living creature want?

3

I drew these tides of men into my hands and wrote my will across the sky in the stars.

T. E. Lawrence
Dedicatory verses to *Seven Pillars of Wisdom*
Standard year 1935

Planet Earth, the Confederacy of Sentient Beings

The bar was located near the Los Angeles spaceport and catered to a wide variety of clientele. Smoke floated above the tables like neon clouds. There were patrons, plenty of them, including a group of cloned spacers, a pair of spindly Dwellers, something in a hab tank and some Naa legionnaires.

Dancers, most of whom were human, writhed within specially designed holograms. The music, much of which was alien, throbbed within carefully engineered "sound cells."

Legion Colonel Leon Harco had been wearing uniforms for more than thirty years and felt uncomfortable when clad in anything else. Yes, there was some degree of correlation between civilian clothes and the status of the people who wore them, but you couldn't be sure.

Not uniforms, though. Thanks to badges of rank, service stripes, unit badges, decorations, and yes, the tattoos many chose to wear, a knowledgeable eye could read a legionnaire's uniform like a book. A single glance was sufficient to establish another person's place in the chain of command, ascertain the kind of skills they had, figure out where they had served, and guess who they might be acquainted with.

Harco liked the surefire certainty of that, and felt uncomfortable, if not downright silly, wearing a floral shirt, black trousers, and buckled sandals.

The two men who sat opposite Harco looked equally uncomfortable and sported poorly coordinated clothes, short haircuts, and tattoo-covered arms.

Taken together, the soldiers had more than forty-five years of service between them, had been "demobilized" within the last six months, and weren't too happy about it.

Despite the cover offered by the bar, there was no such thing as a safe place to discuss mutiny, so they were intentionally circumspect.

"So," Harco began, "how's it going?"

Ex-Staff Sergeant Cory Jenkins grinned. He had extremely white teeth, and they gleamed in the dark. "We're green to go," he replied, almost adding "sir," but catching himself in time. "Everyone we approached signed aboard and will be ready when the time comes."

"Not quite *everyone*," the other man said darkly. "Three opted out."

Harco eyed the man. They had never served in the same unit but knew each other by reputation. That's how it was in the Legion—everyone knew everyone else, or thought they did. His name was Lopa, *Sergeant Major Lopa*, since the face went with the rank. A hard man by all accounts—which was just as well. "And?"

Lopa shrugged noncommittally. "And they turned up missing. I sure hope everything's all right."

Harco looked into the shiny black eyes and knew all three of the people in question were dead. Another tragedy heaped on all the rest. Lopa was correct, however. There is no place for fence-sitters when it comes to war. *Legio patria nostra.* The Legion is our country. Never had the words rung more true. The officer spoke for the benefit of whatever microphones might be collecting his words. "I hope so, too. . . .

What about tools? Have we got what we need?''

Lopa thought about the warehouses full of stolen arms, some secured with the connivance of Matthew Pardo, and the rest gathered by hundreds of sympathizers.

There were assault rifles, machine guns, missile launchers, and more. Not to mention all the stuff that the serving units would bring with them. "Yes, sir. Enough to get the job done."

Harco decided to ignore the slip. "Excellent. Be sure to stress the importance of discipline. We wish to change the existing structure—not rip it apart."

Lopa nodded agreeably but knew the officer was full of shit. Collateral damage is a fact of life. Harco knew that, or *should* have known, and been willing to face the reality of it.

Jenkins sipped his beer. It had a flat, coppery taste. "So, when will the project start?"

"Soon," Harco answered. "Very soon."

The Ramanthian ship dropped hyper, broadcast a high-priority diplomatic code, and was slotted into a choice equatorial orbit. One hundred sixty-two freighter captains, some of whom had been waiting for more than a week, jumped on their com sets. The moon-based Orbital Control Authority took most of the heat. What the hell were they thinking, slotting a bug before humans? Had they lost their frigging minds?

But the complaints fell on deaf ears. In spite of the fact that Senator Alway Orno was visiting Earth in connection with a routine trade fair, he was entitled to certain diplomatic prerogatives, and had chosen to exercise them. End of story.

The Ramanthian shuttle fell free of the ship, dove through the atmosphere, and skimmed the North American continent. Orno used his tool legs to preen his parrotlike beak. His eyes contained thousands of facets and would have been useless beyond five feet if it hadn't been for his computer-assisted contact lenses.

However, thanks to the benefits of Ramanthian science, the senator, not to mention the War Orno who rode behind him, could see the terrain below. It was less than inviting. Hard, serrated ridges connected one mountain to the next, valleys tumbled one over the other, and a thick layer of snow frosted higher elevations. Not the sort of environment for which Ramanthians had evolved.

Yes, there were tracts of lush jungle in the southern hemisphere, but not enough to warrant any sort of real interest in the planet. Not even with the tricentennial birthing up ahead. No, the extra fifty billion Ramanthian souls about to enter the universe would demand better quarters than these. The good news was that the worlds his species needed were readily available. The bad news was that they belonged to someone else.

Who wasn't exactly clear. Especially in the aftermath of the last war. The Hudathans had attacked the Confederacy and, having been soundly defeated, were confined to the world on which they had evolved. That left their empire up for grabs— and subject to an endless round of negotiations.

Indigenous species laid claim to some of the planets, but, given the Hudathan tendency toward genocide, often lacked the necessary votes. Fair? No, but what was?

The Hudathans claimed the worlds by right of conquest, an argument that had proven more effective than one might have thought it would be, since many of the Confederacy's members had taken at least some of their worlds without the permission of the inhabitants. A rather Ramanthian thing to do— *if* they could get away with it.

The shuttle bounced slightly as it hit some turbulent air, and then settled toward the ground. Orno, who had wings of his own, wasn't the least bit concerned.

The office, paid for by the good people of Earth, was enormous. Carefully tended plants stood just so, each in a matching pot, arranged to complement the cane furniture. The early afternoon sun filtered in through gauzy white curtains, a ceiling fan stirred the slightly scented air, and music, one of the arias for which Dwellers were justifiably famous, wafted from unseen speakers.

The android looked exactly as *she* did, and, over a period of time, Governor Patricia Pardo had come to regard the robot as an extension of her own persona. They wore the same kind of clothes, jewelry, and makeup, walked with the same determined stride, and spoke in the same clipped syntax.

A clone might have offered a more elegant solution but would almost certainly object to the role of professional decoy. No, the robot made more sense, and would provide a much-needed alibi should anything go wrong. Treason can be dangerous, after all—and is best practiced from the shadows.

Pardo checked the day's agenda, verified that nothing had changed, and gave the android its instructions. Attend the ribbon-cutting ceremony, dispense the usual platitudes, and return home. Once there, the robot would abuse the house staff enough to establish its presence and retire early. The ruse had worked before and would almost certainly work again.

The governor patted the android's fanny, hoped hers was equally firm, and crossed the office.

She felt for the button, heard a motor whine, and waited while a bookcase slid out of the way. Her heels clicked on waxed duracrete, an elevator carried her downward, and a door opened to a private garage.

Though luxurious, the aircar was no different than thousands of similar vehicles that crisscrossed the skies every day. Anyone who checked the registration would find that it belonged to Mrs. Alfonse Porto.

Pardo nodded to the female bodyguard, slid into the back seat, and signaled the driver. A divider rose, the windows turned dark, and the journey began.

The room was circular, like the Roman Colosseum, and generally referred to as "the pit." A rather fitting name, since rings of concentric seats surrounded a stage on which executives were required to defend their profit-and-loss statements. All-out attacks were the order of the day, and the so called "creative tension" was supposed to generate a more rigorous corporate culture.

Leshi Qwan, vice president of marketing for Noam Inc., the enormous conglomerate that Eli Noam had built during a life of ruthless acquisition, stood at the center of the bull's-eye and stared up into the lights. His enemies were up there, all staring down, hoping he'd fail.

Not that there was anything new in that, except that he *had* failed, and failed miserably—a fact that would be all too clear by the end of his presentation. The executive blinked, wondered if the old man was up there, and hoped he wasn't. "Mr. Qwan? Do you have everything you need?"

The voice belonged to Mary Milan, vice president of sales and one of Noam's favorites. She had the numbers in front of her and, that being the case, knew the nature of his report. He could imagine the satisfaction she must feel.

Enjoy it while you can, bitch, Qwan thought to himself, because I have a surprise for you, and all the rest of the world for that matter.

But the surprise wasn't ready yet—and the report must be given. And not just given, but given in the most objective manner possible, lest he be humiliated by the men and women around him.

The executive cleared his throat and flashed his trademark grin. Like most of the corporation's upper-echelon types, Qwan was something of a face jockey and relied on his looks to ease the way. "Yes, thank you, Mary. In spite of some bright spots, and what I would characterize as excellent prospects, the last quarter was more than a little disappointing."

The holo tank came to life along with a host of three-dimensional charts, video of company operations, and sound clips to buttress his points. The essence of the report was simplicity itself. Qwan, on behalf of NI, had diversified into lines of business that he didn't know much about, namely shipbuilding and off-world mining. That's why competitors, Chien-Chu Enterprises foremost among them, had eaten the company's lunch.

Steps, and the executive was careful to enumerate each one of them, had already been taken to put the situation right, and he had confidence in the future. Qwan enumerated his points, killed the holo, and waited for the bashing to begin. It came with predictable speed.

Though unable to score really major points—Qwan had been too honest for that—his enemies had a field day nonetheless. More than an hour had passed before the vultures quit his corpse and ordered fresh meat.

Weary, and angry at the manner in which he'd been treated, Qwan made his way up the thickly carpeted stairs. Lies oozed out of the darkness. "Hey, Les, way to go." "Good job, bud, you nailed it." "Nice dance, Qwan, I like your moves."

The executive hadn't gone much farther when an arm reached out to grab him. "Mr. Qwan? The chairman would like to see you."

Qwan felt his stomach lurch. The old man *had* been there. Damn, damn, damn.

Noam maintained a bevy of personal assistants, all cloned from his favorite secretary and decanted at regular five-year intervals. The old fart claimed that it was so he could tell them apart—but his staff had other theories, some of which were quite kinky.

Whatever the case, this particular secretary was thirty-something, had red hair, knowing green eyes, and generous red lips. She smiled as she ushered Qwan into the conference room. Her teeth were perfect and appeared unusually sharp.

Noam had extended his life through countless organ transplants and maintained his youthful good looks via ongoing plastic surgery. He rose to greet his visitor.

"Les! Good to see you! Sorry about the beating you took— but it serves you right. Show no mercy and expect none. That's what I say! Here, take a load off. Comfy? Good. Now tell me why I shouldn't fire your ass and have your entire family put to death."

The tone was cheerful—deceptively so—and Qwan responded with that in mind. "I don't blame you for being angry, sir, but I can put things right, *and* double the company's revenues within the next twelve months."

It was an absurd claim, but delivered with such sincerity that Noam was intrigued. He perched on a corner of the conference table. The sarcasm was obvious. "Really? How fascinating! Tell me more."

So Qwan did, starting with the macro socioeconomic situation, and going on to knit the various pieces of the scheme together. Noam, who didn't impress easily, found himself growing increasingly excited.

The plan would not only improve the company's bottom

line, but put the screws to Chien-Chu Enterprises, something Noam had long wanted to do.

The industrialist sent Qwan on his way, summoned his secretarial staff, and ordered them to disrobe. The clones complied, which was nice for Noam, *and* for those scheduled for the pit. *Their* presentations went off without a hitch.

Ambassador Harlan Ishimoto-Seven left the hotel, eyed the swiftly moving crowd, and slipped into a gap. The bag was light and hung from his left shoulder. It bumped people until he tucked it under his right arm. New Yorkers walked quickly, as if late for some engagement, and he did likewise.

An ex-legionnaire held out his kepi, said something unintelligible, and was lost in the crowd.

Ishimoto had features that his ancestors would have recognized as Japanese, although he was taller and somewhat heavier. It felt strange to look around, to see so many individual faces, and know nothing about them.

Not that there were all that many Ishimotos, only about three hundred if memory served, all of whom looked exactly as he did, or had, or would, since all were cloned from the same man but decanted at different times.

Their particular progenitor had been a diplomat, a man Dr. Carolyn Anne Hosokawa admired and recruited for her grand experiment. A culture in which each person was born with the genetic qualifications appropriate to his or her particular function. Administrator, carpenter, or cook. Each was descended from the same person, had the same physical body, and had the same genetic tendencies.

Hosokawa figured that by controlling how many people were created, and what talents they had, the rest would be easy. No unemployment, no mental defectives, no civil unrest, no birth defects, and no waste.

That's why the prototypical soldier, a man named Jonathan Alan Seebo, had been replicated thousands of times, while there were only three hundred copies of the great Ishimoto. Perhaps there would have been less war, less pain, and less suffering had the numbers been reversed.

The thought pleased Ishimoto-Seven. He walked even more

briskly and gloried in the fact that he was momentarily unique. Think of it! Only *one* Ishimoto on the entire planet, and free to do as he pleased. Even if that meant accepting employment for which he had no particular talent or fathering a baby.

Things were more liberal now, especially after the Alpha Clone Marcus-Six had mated with General Marianne Mosby to produce a baby, and not just *any* baby, but a member of the Triad of One, which was in control of the Hegemony's nearly all-powerful executive branch. Not a position the aspirant had reached easily—but one that would have been unthinkable a hundred years before.

Still, most of the Hegemony's citizens clung to the traditional ways, concerned lest the free breeder chaos visible on planets such as Earth bring their carefully planned society to its knees.

Ishimoto-Seven looked up as horns blared and cabbies gestured at each other through open windows. Street-level traffic had been banned more than a hundred years before, and a good thing too, since there was barely enough room to move. All because of free breeding sex.

My people are correct, Ishimoto thought to himself. That's why it was so important to maintain the status quo, to put limits on what the free breeders could do, and protect the Hegemony.

He turned left and let the human current carry him east. Grand Central Station loomed ahead. The columns and high-arched windows looked much as they had for hundreds of years. Multicolored rivers poured through the building's doors, announcements blared, and a maglev waited to depart.

Ishimoto-Seven stepped over the woman in the ragged utility pants, noticed her boots were polished, and wondered why. The crowd pulled, and he followed.

The two-story building sat on top of a rise where it could look out over the man-made lake to the Rockies beyond. It was made of logs and had served as a guest lodge back before Eli Noam bought it. Other structures, including barns, sheds, and a corral, were visible beyond.

The security troops still wore the winged-hand-and-dagger

emblems they had worked so hard to earn. They swept the area for infiltrators, surveillance devices, and bombs. None were found.

Back in the trees, where they couldn't be seen from orbit, other figures lurked. Large, heavily armed figures that weren't supposed to be there.

The Trooper IIs walked on two legs, had fast-recovery laser cannon and .50-caliber machine guns where arms might have been, and carried shoulder-launched missiles. But that was impossible—or should have been.

The officer in charge, a lieutenant who had been released only two months before, spoke into his boom mike. "Bravo One to Delta One—all clear. Over."

There was a pause, followed by two clicks. The first of four aircars arrived two minutes later, circled the lake, and landed in front of the lodge. The machine wore an NI logo.

The driver waited for his passengers to disembark and took off. Gravel rattled on wooden stairs.

The remaining aircraft arrived at five minute intervals. The security force stood with their backs to the LZ.

Later, with beers in their fists, the ex-legionnaires would wonder who the visitors had been, and what the brass were up to. Not that it mattered much—so long as the rats continued to arrive, and there was pay at the end of the month.

Qwan checked to ensure that the facility was ready. The meeting was slated for the dining room, which, true to the building's style, featured a high ceiling supported by tree-sized beams. A lighting fixture made to look like an old-fashioned wagon wheel hung over the large circular table, a fire crackled in the stone fireplace, and the woodwork gleamed with polish.

A check confirmed that a Ramanthian seat frame had been flown in, a top-of-the-line holo tank sat ready for use, and there were plenty of refreshments, including some grublike creatures that wriggled in the bottom of a bowl.

The staff, all of whom were androids, would be brain-wiped the moment the meeting was over, reduced to their component parts, and fed into an electric arc furnace. A rather expensive precaution, but necessary nonetheless.

It took fifteen minutes to complete the necessary introductions and dispense with the small talk.

The guests took their seats, all but the War Orno that is, who loomed behind Orno's chair, and stood ready to defend him. It was a relationship that neither one of Ramanthians could break—and extended to the Egg Orno, deep in her distant cave.

The group had chosen Governor Pardo to act as moderator—a role that she relished. The politician smiled, wondered if the facial expression meant anything to the Ramanthians, and scanned the rest of the table.

"Thank you for coming. The opportunity before us is rife with danger for us and those we represent. But there are times when personal concerns must be put aside and the greater good brought to the fore."

It was one of the most hypocritical speeches Qwan had ever heard, but well delivered, and consistent with the communications plan that the company's spin doctors had devised.

Pardo scanned the faces around her. "I suggest that we establish a culture of openness and trust by giving brief statements as to what each of us hopes to achieve as a result of this meeting. I will go first. . . . The Confederacy has grown weaker over the last twenty-five years and requires new leadership. I planned to run for President, and might have won, if it weren't for the enemies who framed my son."

Neither Orno, Ishimoto-Seven, nor Qwan wanted to see Pardo in control of *two* planets, much less the entire Confederacy, but were confident of their ability to neutralize the politician should that become necessary. The humans smiled, and the Ramanthian waved a pincer.

"So," Pardo said, pleased that everyone liked her speech, "it's time to hear from the distinguished Senator Orno. . . . Senator?"

When the Ramanthian spoke, it was in the form of clicks, twitters, and pops that were translated to rather formal standard by the specially programmed computer woven into the fabric of his cape. The speaker was concealed near his thorax and created the illusion of speech.

"Thank you. It's a pleasure to be here. My people have a

saying: 'Choose your friends with care and your enemies will disappear.' The proverb *must* be true, since there's not a hostile antenna in sight.''

Everyone laughed, including Ishimoto-Seven, who was impressed by the senator's skill, and wondered what his clone brother Ishimoto-Six thought of the Ramanthian. Not that the straight-laced Six knew what his identical sibling was up to—or would have approved if he had. No, situations such as this required imagination, a quality that Six lacked.

Orno waited for the laughter to die away, thought how alien the cackling was, and laid his strategy: Most of the humans he had met were naturally gullible—even more so when told one secret as the means of concealing still another.

The politician knew the importance that humans placed on eye contact and looked at the female. Then, having captured her attention, the Ramanthian swept his forelegs back along his skull. The sight made her shudder, as he had known that it would, thereby ceding the advantage to him. Having signaled revulsion, she would be forced to signal approval, or risk appearing rude.

''So it's my turn, or more properly *our* turn, since I represent the Ramanthian race. Humans are predators, are they not?''

''Hunter-gatherers—*then* predators,'' Pardo answered cautiously, hoping to redeem herself. ''Why do you ask?''

''Because every race remains true to what it once was,'' Orno said pragmatically. ''Take my species, for example. . . . My ancestors were scavengers—carnivores that lived off scraps.''

''So?''

''Scavengers are opportunists . . . and we still are. Even now, many years after the conclusion of the most recent war, there are worlds bereft of leadership.''

''Bereft of leadership?'' Ishimoto-Seven said cynically. ''Or available for the taking?''

''They are one and the same,'' the Ramanthian answered easily. ''Those who lack the strength to lead will be led. The question is by whom.''

''By those strong enough to take what they want,'' Harco put in. ''And, having done so, to keep it.''

"Exactly," Orno replied. "And we have the necessary strength."

"And would be free to use it should something weaken the Confederacy," Pardo said thoughtfully.

"The governor is very astute," Orno replied smoothly. "The people of Earth are fortunate."

The humans nodded, and the Ramanthian felt an overriding sense of satisfaction. He had revealed one piece of information, something that should have been obvious to even the most casual observer, yet concealed the very thing that made it significant. The Ramanthian population was about to explode, and needed new worlds to colonize. Information that would have frightened his coconspirators had they been aware of it.

Pardo said, "Thank you, Senator," and turned to the clone. "Ambassador Ishimoto-Seven . . . would you be so kind?"

Ishimoto-Seven forced a smile and wondered how those present would react had they known that with the exception of his immediate supervisor, his entire government was unaware of both his presence and the plot that they were so assiduously hatching.

Still, what the clone proposed to do was consistent with his overall diplomatic purpose, which was to participate in negotiations and ensure that Hegemony interests were accommodated. The Hegemony's *real* interests . . . which didn't always match what some of his superiors thought they were. Seven chose his words with care.

"Thank you, Governor. The Hegemony believes in the fundamental right of sentients to choose those who lead them— and therefore supports grass roots movements that trend in that direction."

Qwan smiled bleakly. "I'm sure the Hegemony supports other ideals as well, including truth, justice, and prosperity for all. Everything *except* motherhood."

Ishimoto-Seven came to his feet. His fingers opened and closed. "I didn't come here to take insults from corporate whores! Perhaps Citizen Qwan would like to take it outside, where I would be pleased to kick his pompous ass!"

Pardo started to intervene, but Harco beat her to it. His voice was low but carried to every corner of the room. "Stow the bullshit."

The room fell silent as the officer stood and clasped his hands behind his back. His eyes were like lasers and probed the faces around him. "Let's get something straight. . . . Every damned one of you has an axe to grind. Fine. I accept that. But nothing, I repeat *nothing,* is going to happen unless my people put their lives on the line and manage to win one hellacious battle.

"*If* we survive, *if* we win, the lot of you can squabble over who gets what, so long as you remember one important fact: *We* have the weapons, *we* have the know-how, and *we* have the final say. Questions? No? Good. Let's put a wrap on this introductory crap and lay some plans."

4

He who fires a bullet in the air can never be sure of
where it may land.

Hoda Ibin Ragnatha
Turr Truth Sayer
Standard year 2206

Planet Earth, the Confederacy
of Sentient Beings

The transport swept in across the sparkling Gulf of Aden and
flew so low that Booly had no difficulty making out the fish-
ermen on their wooden dhows. They waved, a sure sign that
such flights were relatively rare, and an indicator of how remote his new duty station truly was. The fly form's passenger
compartment, positioned at the front of the aircraft, offered
excellent visibility.

Located on the east coast of Africa, the ancient country of
Djibouti had once been an important port, but that was a long
time ago. With a population approaching 100,000, and no natural resources to speak of, it was one of the most backward
places on Earth. Vegetation was scarce and consisted of hardy
grass, thorn trees, and scattered palms. The poor soil and lack
of rain made large-scale farming impractical—and nothing had
changed in hundreds of years.

None of that had stopped the French from colonizing the

place, though, or from installing the Legion to protect it—a tradition that continued long after France ceased to exist.

The city had long been the home of the 13th Half-Brigade, also know as the 13th DBLE, which had seen action at Bir Hakeim, El Alamein, Dien Bien Phu, Algeria, both Hudathan Wars, the battle of Bakala, and dozens more.

The modern 13th consisted of a command and services company, a works company, a combat company, an infantry company on loan from the 2nd REP, and a reconnaissance squadron. Of interest to Booly, and no one else, was the fact that his father *and* mother had served in the outfit as well.

Most of what Booly saw as the fly form rumbled in over the Gulf of Tadjoura was tan like his khakis. There were flashes of white, however, including three handsome-looking mosques, a scattering of French colonial buildings, and the fortress to which he had been assigned.

The battlements were circular and sat on the Plateau du Serpent the way a kepi sits on a legionnaire's head. Not unpleasant to look at, especially from the air, but a dumping ground for troublemakers like Booly.

He examined his fellow passenger, the only other person in the large compartment. The legionnaire seemed to be asleep. His uniform was filthy, a corporal's chevron had been partially ripped from his sleeve, and he'd been handcuffed to his seat. Drunk, disorderly, and who knew what else. An excellent example of what Booly could expect.

The transport shuddered, started to slow, and dropped toward the ground. Booly saw the tops of palm trees, the flash of white battlements, and the X that marked the fort's landing platform. There was an intercom, and he touched a button. "This place has an airport, doesn't it? Let's land there."

The pilot, who had been executed for murder, consisted of little more than brain tissue in a nutrient bath. When ordered to choose *permanent* death, or service as a cyborg, she chose the latter. She flew the transport by means of a neural interface, "felt" by means of its sensors, and "saw" through multiple vid cams. The request took her by surprise. She applied power and banked away. Air fanned the battlements. A sentry lost his hat. The reply was automatic. "Sir, yes, sir!"

"Good," Booly answered. "And one more thing. . . . When they ask where I went . . . tell 'em you don't know."

The pilot *didn't* know . . . but it didn't seem polite to say so. "Sir, yes, sir."

"Thanks," Booly said. "I appreciate your flexibility."

There was a vid cam mounted in the passenger compartment, and the pilot checked the officer's expression. He not only *acted* nice, he *looked* nice—not that it mattered. Still, most bio bods treated her like an extension of the hardware she lived in, so it was nice to encounter someone who didn't. "No problem, sir. Welcome to Djibouti—armpit of the universe. We'll be on the ground in two minutes."

"Thanks," Booly said dryly. "I can hardly wait."

Major Vernon Judd watched the transport veer away, frowned, and brought the glasses to his eyes. They fed him the aircraft's range, heading, and ground speed. He spoke from the side of his mouth. "Get hold of the pilot. Ask him, her, or it what the hell they're doing, and order them back. And I mean *now*!"

Captain Nancy Winters thought the words "Bite my ass," but knew Judd would be only too happy to oblige, and said, "Yes, sir," instead.

The observation tower was equipped with radios, a door to block the steadily increasing heat, and a well-maintained air conditioner. It felt good to step inside. The duty com tech was a sergeant named Skog. He liked Winters, and he smiled. "Ma'am?"

"Get that transport on the horn and find out what they're up to. The major wants 'em to land here."

Everyone assigned to the fort knew a new CO was on the way—and had known from the moment that his orders were cut. They also knew about Booly's combat record, the reason why his name had gone to the top of the shit list, and any number of other things, at least some of which were true.

That being the case, the major's nervousness was somewhat understandable—even if he was a worthless piece of shit. Skog flipped a switch, consulted a list, and addressed his boom mike. "Transport mike-sierra-foxtrot-one-niner-eight, this is Mosby control, over."

The reply could be heard on an overhead speaker and had the precise, slightly stilted sound of a voice synthesizer. A sure sign that the pilot was a borg. The vast majority of box heads chose to maintain their original genders, and the flight officer was no exception. "This is one-niner-eight . . . go."

Skog looked at Winters. She nodded. "Tell her to return and land in the compound."

The noncom relayed the message and monitored the reply. "Sorry, Mosby control, but that's a negative. My number two engine shows yellow—and I need a class three facility or better."

Winters nodded. The fort's pad was rated class four, which meant there were no maintenance functions, and the aircraft was prohibited from landing. A rather sensible precaution, since a disabled fly form would occupy fifty percent of the pad and limit their capacity to deal with an emergency. "Tell the pilot we understand—and that a ground vehicle will meet her at the airport."

The com tech said, "Yes, ma'am," and sent the necessary message.

Major Judd was fuming by the time Winters returned. "Well? Where's the transport? What's going on?"

"It had to divert," Winters said calmly. "To the Djibouti airport. Some sort of mechanical problem."

"The hell you say," Judd grumbled. "Damned incompetence, if you ask me. Take the pilot's name."

Winters bit the inside of her cheek and said, "Sir, yes, sir," but knew the XO would have forgotten the whole incident by dinnertime that evening.

Judd, angry at the thought of a long, hot drive, stomped away. Winters, happy to see him go, stayed where she was. The gulf glittered with reflected light, sent a momentary breeze toward the high, whitewashed walls, and caressed the legionnaire's face. An omen, perhaps? Her mother had believed in such things—but her mother was dead.

• • •

The transport pushed its shadow ahead, followed ancient train tracks south, and over flew the air strip. The borg brought her ship around and flared into a perfect three-skid touchdown. Booly felt the gentle bump and spoke into the intercom. "Nice landing . . . who should I thank?"

"Barr, sir. Lieutenant Betty Barr."

"All right Lieutenant, fly safe, and remember the favor I asked for."

"No problem, sir. Good luck with the new command."

Booly grinned, released his seat belt, and turned. The corporal was already on his feet and standing at attention. He was at least forty, maybe older, and rail-thin. Though soiled, his uniform fit as if it had been painted on, his service stripes spoke of more than twenty years in the Legion, and he wore a chest full of ribbons. Two of them stood in for major medals.

The legionnaire's face was long, narrow, and far from handsome. The handcuffs had disappeared. The officer raised an eyebrow, and the noncom replied without being asked. "Fykes, sir. *Corporal* Fykes, till the stripe comes off."

"You've been broken before?"

"Yes, sir. Three times. Once from sergeant major."

"For striking an officer?"

"Why, yes, sir," Fykes answered cheerfully. "How did you know?"

"Just a guess," Booly replied dryly. "Are you reporting for duty, or returning from leave?"

"Both, sir."

"Ever served here before?"

The NCO shook his head. "No, sir."

"You up for a hike? Hangover and all?"

"Yes, sir. Just lead the way."

"Then grab your kit," Booly said. "It's time to reconnoiter."

Booly had two duffel bags, and both of them were heavy. Still, he couldn't leave his gear behind, not in a place like Djibouti, so Booly hauled them along. The hatch whined up and out of the way. The heat pushed in through the opening. The men forced their way out, clanged down the retractable stairs, and marched the width of the apron.

Booly had already started to question the wisdom of the trip by the time they crossed into the shadow cast by a dilapidated hangar. Fykes stuck some fingers into his mouth, issued a shrill whistle, and was almost immediately rewarded.

Two figures, both dressed in loose-fitting shirts, knee-length trousers, and worn-looking sandals, separated themselves from the relative darkness and trotted forward. Both were tall, slender, and possessed of wide-set eyes.

The corporal said, "Galab wanaqsan," something about "Shan credits," and money changed hands.

One of the men, a toothless oldster, sported a wicked-looking knife. He waited for his companion to place a ninety-pound duffel bag on one of his frail-looking shoulders, grinned happily, and nodded his readiness.

The second man, who appeared to be the younger of the two, swung the noncom's bag up onto his back, jabbered something in Arabic, and waited for instructions.

The officer turned to Fykes. "Well done, Fykes. You're resourceful if nothing else."

The noncom grinned. "Some would say *too* resourceful, sir, but you can't please everyone."

"No," Booly said thoughtfully, "you certainly can't. Not in this man's army. Come on—let's see the sights."

The problem with the scout car was that it had more than two hundred thousand miles on the odometer, was specially equipped for arctic duty, and was in dire need of an overhaul.

Major Judd occupied the passenger's seat, did everything he could to minimize the extent to which his back made contact with the sun-baked seat, and hung on as the vehicle lurched through one of Djibouti's legendary potholes. Mesh covered the windows and served to divide the world into hundreds of tiny squares. Not that the legionnaire minded, since the screening beat the hell out of looking down to find that a grenade had landed in his lap—a rather unpleasant tradition practiced by local youth gangs.

The driver, a private named Mesker, honked at a camel, scattered a flock of goats, and blew past the airport's fourteen-year-old security guard. He was armed with a rusty one-hundred-fifty-year-old automatic weapon. He pointed and yelled, "Bang, bang, bang!"

Mesker gauged the distance to the transport, waited until the last moment, and stood on the brake. Judd threw his hands up, swore, and turned red in the face. Bingo! Two points.

The officer, not wanting to appear frightened, sent Mesker a dirty look, made a note to get even, and opened the door. The tarmac was so hot he could feel the heat through the bottoms of his boots.

Judd waited for a dilapidated cargo tug to pass, followed the faded yellow line out to the fly form, and mounted the aluminum stairs. Chances were that Booly would be pissed and looking for someone to crap on.

Judd plastered his best shit-eating smile across his face, stepped into the relatively cool interior, and called the officer's name. "Colonel Booly? Major Judd here—come to pick you up."

The response came from speakers mounted at the front of the cabin. "This is Lieutenant Barr, sir . . . the colonel left."

"Left?" Judd asked. "How? Where?"

"Sorry, sir. I don't know."

"What about the prisoner? A corporal named Fykes?"

"Don't know, sir. The two of them left together."

Judd called down a plague on pilots, corporals, *and* colonels, reentered the thick October heat, and headed for the scout car. It shimmered and threatened to disappear.

The hover truck had a distinct list to starboard. Hired for a modest ten credits, it dropped the foursome at the intersection of the boulevard de la Republique and avenue Lyeutey.

Booly had never been to Djibouti before, but the fort sat on top of a plateau and was difficult to miss. Finding it would be easy. That being the case, the legionnaire reserved most of his attention for the city itself . . . a place that might have seemed more foreign had he not spent so much time on other worlds.

Still, Djibouti had its share of quirks, not the least of which were streets that turned into passageways without the slightest rhyme or reason, French colonial architecture that stood shoulder to shoulder with concrete monstrosities, rickety cabs that vied with camels to claim the right-of-way, strange undulating music, and a mishmash of signs that seemed to alternate between French, Arabic, and standard.

Booly found that he actually liked the place, except for the nearly unbelievable heat and the stench of the urine-soaked alleyways.

The officer left the relative coolness of a well-shadowed passageway, turned a corner, and heard voices raised in anger. He raised his hand. Fykes stopped and motioned for the porters to do likewise. They obeyed.

There was a commotion, followed by rapid-fire Arabic and the whine of servos.

The officer peered around the corner of a stall and watched a pair of Trooper IIs swagger down the street. Shops lined both sides of the thoroughfare, each with its own sun-faded awning. Long, flimsy poles held them out and away from the buildings they served.

One of the cyborgs extended an armlike laser cannon. The support sticks crackled as they shattered. Awnings fluttered and floated to the ground. The voice was amplified and echoed off the surrounding storefronts. "We want cash, and we want it *on time*. We'll be back tomorrow—so don't make the same mistake twice."

Booly retreated to the shadows and motioned for the others to do likewise. The officer caught a whiff of ozone as the machines lurched past. "Corporal Fykes . . ."

"Sir?"

"Take their numbers."

"The legionnaire looked at the officer, realized he was serious, and reached for the data pad buttoned into his left shirt pocket. "Sir, yes, sir."

The journey resumed once the cyborgs were gone—and Booly was pleased to note that the fort was closer now. It loomed over them as they entered the maze of passageways collectively known as Scam Town.

Here were the brothels, eateries, and yes, if Booly's nose was any guide, the bars typical of most fortress towns. All of which was fine, except for the fact that alcohol was offensive to the local population and should have been banned.

As if to emphasize the point, a legionnaire stumbled out of a doorway with a scantily clad woman under each arm, saw Booly, and struggled to disengage. His salute would have been more convincing had the bill of his kepi been toward the front instead of the back. He swayed alarmingly, tried to say something, and collapsed facedown. The whores looked amused and made no attempt to help.

Booly didn't have to ask this time. Fykes rolled the legionnaire over, winced at the smell of his breath, and fumbled for his dog tags. The name went into his computer.

Shopkeepers, thieves, and whores called to the legionnaires as they made their way out of the souk, and it was some of the latter who managed to grab Booly's attention.

Fykes watched amusedly as the unpredictable officer stepped into a brothel, haggled with the khat-chewing madam, and gave her some money.

Then, just when the NCO expected to see the officer enter one of the curtained booths, he was joined by four heavily painted female prostitutes, along with an equal number of joy boys. Two of them shared the weight of a cooler. A handful of words was sufficient to send the whole lot scrambling up the trail.

Booly saw the corporal's expression and laughed. "Enemy infiltrators, Fykes—and heavily armed at that. Come on—let's check our security."

Fykes took note of the word "our," realized that the colonel had already assumed responsibility for the fort, and felt sorry for the unsuspecting sentries.

The trail switchbacked up the side of hill, and Booly, his uniform dark with sweat, still managed to whistle. And he was *still* whistling, *still* grinning, when they arrived at the first checkpoint, heard some rather curious sounds emanating from the vicinity of a machine gun emplacement, caught a whiff of cheap perfume, and continued on their way.

They encountered two additional guard stations, both of which were deserted, before arriving at the foot of the fort's thirty-foot-high whitewashed wall. This particular sentry had at least taken the precaution of locking the durasteel side gate prior to abandoning his or her post. Booly tried the handle, but to no avail.

Fykes, who was rather enjoying himself by this time, stepped forward. The pick, which appeared to be little more than a sliver of steel, gleamed between his fingers. "Sir? Would you care to enter?"

Booly remembered the vanishing handcuffs and understood why. "Why yes, Corporal, if you please."

Fykes grinned, fed the specially programmed strip of "live" metal into the appropriate slot, and waited for the device to figure out which of the more than one hundred thousand possible shapes programmed into its memory would handle this particular lock. He had won the tool in a poker game—and used it ever since. Less than three seconds had elapsed when Booly heard a decisive *click*, saw the noncom turn the handle, and watched the door swing open.

The sentry, plus a couple of her buddies, were seated around the cooler, sipping from cold bottles of beer. She went for her rifle, but Booly was quicker. "Sorry," the officer said, "but I'll take that. Finish the beer and report to the sergeant at arms when you're done."

The legionnaires were still sitting there, staring at the place where the officer had been, when the porters marched by. "Who the hell was that?" Private Hosko asked of no one in particular.

"*That* was your new commanding officer," Private Laraby replied. "You heard the colonel . . . let's finish the beer. I've got a feeling it'll be a long time before we have another."

A set of spiral stairs carried Booly up and into a heavily shadowed alcove. It looked out onto the sun-baked parade ground. It was deserted except for the orderly waves of heat. "Time for our big entrance, Corporal . . . are you ready?"

"Ready when you are, sir."

"Good. Let's go."

Booly, with Fykes at his side, marched to the center of the fort's parade ground, stopped, levered a round into the sentry's assault rifle, released the safety, and pointed the weapon out toward the gulf. The weapon chattered, brass arced through the air, and a pair of doves fluttered out of hiding.

Heads appeared first, quickly followed by bodies and a broadside of orders. "Place the weapon on the ground! Put your hands on your head! Now! Now! Now!"

Booly complied, as did Fykes. The porters, both of whom had developed a seemingly miraculous understanding of standard, dropped the duffel bags and placed their hands on their heads.

The first legionnaires on the scene saw that Booly was a colonel, or was dressed in a colonel's uniform, and sent for higher authority.

It took the better part of five minutes for Major Judd to get off the commode, pull up his pants, and arrive on the parade ground. He blinked into the harsh sunlight and frowned. "What the hell is going on? Who are these people?"

Corporal Fykes gave himself permission to speak. "Begging the major's pardon, but it's my pleasure to introduce Colonel William 'Bill' Booly, the newly arrived commanding officer, 13th DBLE. May we lower our hands?"

The officer's mess was long and narrow. The walls were covered with ancient battle flags, antique weapons, countless photographs, plaques, and similar memorabilia, many of which went back hundreds of years.

The table was more than half empty and covered with crisp white linen. The battalion's silver, handed down by generations past, gleamed with reflected light. Candles flickered, wine bottles stood in orderly ranks, and music played in the background.

Booly, who sat at the head of the table, did his best to look cheerful. It wasn't easy. The dinner, given in his honor, felt somewhat awkward, especially in light of the manner in which he had humiliated not only Major Judd, but to a lesser extent, the rest of the officers as well.

The mitigating factor, if it could be regarded as such, was the fact that most of the battalion's officers hated the major's guts and were happy to see him fail. Not a good sign.

Tradition must be observed, however, no matter how painful the process may prove, and the dinner was held.

The fort's air-conditioning equipment had received more

maintenance during the last year than had the SAM batteries, so the air was chilly and the high-collared mess jackets actually felt comfortable.

Someone tapped a glass with a spoon. Judd, who would have preferred a computer-controlled shelling to the task before him, rose to make a toast. Light sparkled off his wine glass. "To Colonel Booly . . . and a successful tour."

There were the usual number of "Hear, hear"'s, followed by formal sips of wine. Booly knew he was expected to make the next toast, and struggled to come up with something appropriate—something that wouldn't sound disingenuous after the day's events. He stood and raised his glass. "To the 13th DBLE . . . may it live forever."

There were more "Hear, hear"'s, accompanied by head nods. The first of what turned out to be an interminable fourteen courses arrived. The conversation veered from topic to topic. It had a forced sound, was almost entirely unleavened by laughter, and was dull beyond belief. Unless one really cared about the Blumenthal theory of forward supply, or the size of Sergeant Domo's much discussed sex organ.

Booly sampled each dish, drank sparingly, and tried to peg his officers. Judd was a given—or so it seemed. Three so-so fitness reports, three missed promotions, and three years on Earth. It suggested that the officer had enough influence to retain his commission while others were released.

The operations officer, Captain Winters, was something else again. She had come up through the ranks—and brought a Distinguished Service Medal with her. A decoration earned *off*-planet . . . out on the rim. He liked her reliable-looking face, the calm green eyes, and the sound of her laugh. They were early times yet . . . but Winters had possibilities.

The command and services company, which included the headquarters staff, medical personnel, and supply folks, was under the command of Captain Andre Kara, a bookish-looking man, who seldom spoke or smiled. His file, which portrayed the legionnaire as efficient but not especially distinguished, had little more to say. A mystery wrapped in an enigma. Asset or liability? The next few months would tell.

Not Captain Holly Hawkins, though. . . . C Company's

commanding officer, better known to her troops as "the Hawk," was a class-A, dyed-in-the-wool, ass-kicking leg officer who had either been sent to the 13th as the result of some wonderful accident, or severely pissed someone off and been dumped in much the same way as he had. She owned three right hands, and this one had been chromed. A servo whined as the infantry officer took a sip of wine. She met his gaze, raised her glass, and drained it dry. Here at least was someone he could depend on.

There was a loud thump. Booly turned to find that his other ground pounder, Captain Henry Olmsworthy III, commanding officer of D Company, 2nd REP, was facedown on the table. A steadily expanding red stain indicated where his wine had gone. No one seemed surprised. That spoke volumes . . . and Booly made a note.

The next officer, Captain Margo Ny, *was* something of a surprise. Given the fact that there was no way in hell that her ten-ton, tractorlike body was going to fit inside the mess, and the rest of the officers weren't likely to dine in her vast underground garage, the cyborg had elected to have her brain box delivered to the table.

And not just delivered, but delivered on a *silver tray,* which Booly found to be vastly amusing. It spoke of style, courage, and a good sense of humor.

Ny's brain box, which was covered with a custom-tailored dress uniform, plus rows of decorations, was equipped with a vid cam as well. It whirred as it panned. A good officer by all accounts—who had chosen the 13th rather than life as what? A deep-space miner? A cab in New York City? He was lucky to have her. The works company was well led.

Last, but certainly not least, was First Lieutenant Goodeye Nightslip. A full-blooded Naa, with features that reminded Booly of his paternal grandmother, golden fur with flecks of white, and the body of a weight lifter. He served as the battalion's intelligence officer and led the special reconnaissance squadron as well.

The group consisted of two platoons, both under the command of a senior NCO and consisting of ninety-eight percent Naa nationals. Not because of a bias on the Legion's part, but because the aliens were good at what they did, and wanted to serve there.

Did Nightslip know about Booly's ancestry? Yes, there was little doubt that he did. The family was well known, after all, and the other officer was unlikely to miss the cast to Booly's features, or the mane of fur that ran down the back of his neck.

Suddenly their eyes met. Booly knew the other male could smell him from fifteen feet away, and felt the past pull him back. In spite of the fact that his grandfather and his mother had been born elsewhere, both took Algeron as their home, while *he,* who had been conceived, born, and raised there, never managed to fit in.

The Legion offered the perfect way out, the means to leave home while becoming a warrior, the very thing that his childhood tormentors respected most.

There was no escaping his own inferiority, though. No matter what Booly did or where he went, he would never be able to smell what his peers could smell, map temperature gradients with the soles of his feet, or walk bare chested through a blizzard.

Yes, he could shoot just as straight, had learned to best older males by virtue of martial arts learned from his mother and father, and could run just as fast.

But none of those was enough, and when Nightslip looked at him, it was the senior officer who broke the contact. Did the Naa know? Is that what Booly saw in those yellow-black eyes? Or was it something else? There was no way to be sure.

It took what seemed like a year before dessert arrived, final toasts were proposed, and the officers retired to their respective rooms. Dawn was less than four hours away—and would mark the beginning of what? Only time would tell.

The ceremony had been scheduled for 0800, a full hour before the sun would top the eastern wall and fry the parade ground below. It was a small mercy, but one the legionnaires were thankful for.

Booly, who stood high on the battlements, watched his battalion pull itself into long, perfectly spaced ranks. Senior

NCOs inspected the troops first, followed by their respective platoon leaders.

It was a common sight, one he had witnessed hundreds if not thousands of times, and found to be inexplicably moving. Why was that? Perhaps it was the fact that while much had changed over the last seven hundred years, *this* had remained the same, and it served as a link with the thousands that had gone before.

Men and women rolled out of the rack, performed the morning's ablutions, donned clothing identical to everyone else's, laced carefully maintained boots, checked their weapons, and stepped out into the crisp morning air.

None of it had changed and would be as recognizable to a Roman legionnaire as they were to the men and women below. As would the feeling of comradeship that went with a place in the ranks, the relationships both good and bad, and the written as well as unwritten rules of conduct.

To that extent, the 13th was similar to a living organism, complete with hundreds of interdependent parts, all working in harmony.

That's the way it was *supposed* to be, anyway, but Booly knew it wasn't working. The sad fact was that the perfectly aligned ranks below him were a sham, like a weight-bearing beam that *appears* to be solid, but is riddled with rot.

Some of the signs were obvious, like the protection racket managed by the cyborgs, sentries who would desert for a beer, and officers who set the worst sort of example.

But there were other more subtle signs as well, small things for the most part, like the political graffiti on the walls, and the mess hall groupings.

Bio bods with bio bods, Naa with Naa, and borgs with borgs rather than by fire team, squad, and company, the way they would have to fight. Had Loy known that? Was it part of his punishment? Or incidental to where he'd been sent? There was no way to know—and it didn't make much difference. Booly's job was to find the rot, clean it out, and repair the framework.

Orders were shouted, boots stamped, and the battalion came to attention. Booly descended a set of circular stairs, strode across half the parade ground, and accepted Judd's salute. "All present or accounted for, sir."

Booly nodded and saluted in return. His voice made its way through a wire-thin boom mike and out over the PA system. "Thank you, Major. Put the troops at ease."

Judd did a perfect about-face, gave the appropriate order, and was rewarded with something less than perfection. The entire headquarters company seemed a little slow on the uptake, as if they hadn't drilled in quite a while, and the cyborgs, who backed the rest of the troops, made no move whatsoever. They'd been at ease from the start. Sloppiness? Or insolence? The first was regrettable—the second could be dangerous.

Booly cleared his throat, brought the orders up in front of his face, and read them aloud. The language, though stilted and somewhat archaic, still possessed power. Not because of the words themselves, but because of the thousands who had both spoken and heard them. Some had gone on to live long, happy lives. Many had not. They lay buried beneath thick jungle foliage, under piles of hastily assembled rocks, and in tidily kept cemeteries.

Finally, after all the words had been read, Booly added some of his own. He allowed his gaze to roam over the parade ground, finding as many eyes as he could, willing them to listen. The objective was to notify them that things were about to change—but to do so in a way that built morale rather than tore it down.

There were all sorts of incompetents, slackers, and worse out there, he knew that, but they would have to be rooted out one by one and dealt with individually. That being the case, he chose a positive approach, knowing that some were beyond his reach, and hoping to hearten the rest. An honest assessment of their position was a good place to start.

"The 13th is one of the oldest and most famous units in the Legion. The men, women, and cyborgs who fought in it won hundreds of battles, and lost some too, like Dien Bien Phu, where, on March 13, 1953, the Viet Minh used artillery to open fire on strong point Beatrice. We lost thirty-six men that day.

"A few days later, when it became apparent that Colonel

Charles Piroth, the Legion's artillery officer, had severely miscalculated the enemy's capabilities, he committed suicide.

"During the successive weeks, the Legion's position became little more than a killing zone. The airstrip was destroyed. The main road was cut off. No one could leave—not even the wounded. That didn't stop the men of the 3rd and 5th REI, though. . . . None had parachute training—but they jumped anyway.

"Meanwhile, under the ground, in a hospital which was little more than a hole filled with mud, amputated limbs, and well-fed maggots, Dr. Paul Grauwin did the best he could. And it was volunteers from the 13th DBLE who drove his ambulances, who risked their lives to drag the wounded out of the wire, and frequently died in the attempt.

"In spite of their gallantry, in spite of their sacrifice, the Legion lost more than one thousand five hundred dead."

Some of the legionnaires seemed to stand just a little bit taller. Others, transported back in time, felt a chill run down their spines. Many, their minds already made up, felt nothing at all.

Booly allowed the echoes to die away before starting again. "Yes, we have a proud history, or had, until the 13th became the Legion's favorite shit can. I was sent here for telling the truth . . . what were *you* sent here for? Did you screw up one time too many? Fall asleep on duty? Spill coffee on the colonel's lap?"

The last question drew laughter, just as it was supposed to, and seemed to acknowledge the fact that the Legion was a gigantic machine, and that some of the troops had simply been caught up in its gears.

The colonel's words were different from what many had expected them to be. Some eyes registered hope . . . others were filled with cynicism.

"So," Booly continued. "Each and every one of us is faced with a choice. We can focus on the past, and be what we were, or on the future, and put the past behind us. Some of you joined the Legion as a way to get a new start. Others wanted a chance at something better, a bit of adventure, or the excellent food.''

The laughter was general this time—which caused Captain Winters to look and marvel. She couldn't remember the last time the battalion had laughed.

''The opportunity is there,'' Booly concluded. ''The opportunity to start again, to restore the 13th to what it once was, and to wear the uniform with pride. Thank you. That will be all.''

The operations center was located six stories beneath Fort Mosby, where it was theoretically impervious to the Hudathan bombs it had been built to withstand.

The Situation Room was a large octagonal space dominated by wall-mounted multipurpose video screens, rows of computer consoles, the soft murmur of radio traffic, and the faint odor of coffee mixed with ozone.

The transmission was scrambled and came over a little-used civilian frequency. No one at Fort Mosby would have intercepted—much less recorded—the message, had Corporal Bonsky not been listening for it.

Corporal Bonsky was a small man, with a small man's paunch, and feelings of inadequacy—a weakness that others had managed to exploit. He waited for the ''squirt'' to end, dumped the message to a one-inch disk, and slipped the object into his pocket. The com tech stood, asked Skog to monitor his boards, and waved to Sergeant Ho. She stood only five-one in her combat boots—but nobody messed with her. Not twice. ''Hey, Sarge . . . gotta pee. Back in zero-five.''

Ho didn't like Bonsky, or the people he hung with, but was careful not to show it. Not the way things were . . . which was all screwed up. ''Better take ten, Bonsky—it'll take five just to find it.''

The rest of the staff laughed. Bonsky flipped them off and stalked out of the room.

It took the better part of five minutes for the com tech to reach the drop, leave the disk, and make the return trip. Which was all to the good because he *did* need to pee . . . and had plenty of time to get it done. *Who* retrieved the disk, and what they did with it, well, that was none of his business. Long as they remembered him when the shit went down—and made his considerable grievances right. The com tech thought about Ho, smiled, and imagined what he would do to her.

5

Voyage/gas/planet/want/take/home/happy.

Baa'l Poet Star/Searcher
Year unknown

Somewhere on the Rim, the Confederacy of Sentient Beings

Once recovered from the trauma of losing both the *Pelican* and the drifter, Jepp found life on the Sheen vessel to be unexpectedly serene. The days, as recorded as scratches in the ship's hull metal, seemed to drift by.

For the first time in years the human found himself with plenty of time to think and reflect. In fact, had it not been for the certainty that he would eventually run out of food, the experience might have been rather pleasant.

Jepp followed a self-imposed routine that provided a modicum of both structure and comfort.

His body clock woke him at approximately 0800 each morning. Never one to lounge about, the prospector rolled out of his improvised bag and onto the cold metal deck. The calisthenics included thirty-five push-ups, followed by thirty-five leg lifts, thirty-five sit-ups, and thirty-five additional push-ups.

Once the exercises were complete, there were prayers to say, not the repetitious sort of nonsense favored by his father, but long, one-sided conversations with God that left him feeling clean but empty.

Then, having strengthened both body and spirit, it was time for a sponge bath and a little bit of hot cereal.

The bay in which the *Pelican* had been reduced to her component parts had proved far too large for the human's psychological comfort, so he had long since opted for smaller, more intimate quarters. Jepp had divided his "cabin," a nameless and insofar as he could tell purposeless alcove, into both a "galley" and "stateroom."

With the exception of some emergency rations, which the prospector had decided to save for last, the rest of his food required cooking. Jepp's first attempt was an unmitigated disaster. He rigged a stand on which his pot could sit, lit the welding torch, and applied the blue flame.

Everything was fine at first, and the water had just started to boil when the ship's fire-suppression system was activated and the entire area was drenched with gallons of creamy white foam. He spent the better part of a shipboard "day" cleaning it up.

That experience led to hours of careful experimentation in which the prospector sought to determine the exact amount of heat that the ship would tolerate prior to extinguishing the flame. Unfortunately for Jepp, that level was so low that it took a long time to boil his water.

The human wasn't sure how to calculate which was more efficient—to run the torch on high, which used more of his precious fuel, but boiled the water more quickly, or to utilize the lower setting, which consumed less gas but took longer. He feared that it was the second approach, the one the ship forced him to accept, that was the less efficient of the two.

Breakfast was followed by self-appointed "rounds," which started out as exploratory journeys and evolved into a complex ritual, the main purpose of which was to occupy his time and ascertain that nothing had changed. Once that finding was confirmed, he felt mixed reactions.

While it was comforting to know that his surroundings remained unchanged, there was a downside, too.

Assuming the status quo continued, he would run out of

food in a month or so and water not too long after that. The simple fact was that he *needed* some sort of change. Escape would be preferable, but failing that, additional supplies.

And so it was that Jepp rolled out of the sack on his twenty-seventh day of captivity, completed his "morning" rituals, and armed himself for the upcoming patrol. He generally carried a light wand, for peering into corners, and a pouch loaded with hand tools in case he wanted to try his luck on one of the panels, junction boxes, and access doors scattered about the ship. A somewhat iffy activity—and one the ship took a dim view of. That was something he learned the hard way.

The first shock knocked Jepp on his ass, the second threw him across a corridor, and a third, had he been stupid enough to trigger it, might very well have killed him.

Jepp made his way toward what he regarded as the ship's bow. The ship, or the intelligence that ran it, had chosen to illuminate some areas and leave others inexplicably dark. The wand threw an oval-shaped pattern of light onto the deck ahead. There were no signs of the bolts, screws, or other fasteners that humans relied upon to hold everything together. It appeared as though the alien nano had bonded disparate molecules together so there was no need for connecting hardware.

His boots clanked on metal, the ship continued the steady round-the-clock hum that he had learned to hate, and his tool belt creaked as he moved.

Suddenly, without warning, conditions started to change. The all-pervasive hum increased a notch, the deck started to tilt, and Jepp fought to keep his feet. The vessel was up to something—but what?

Hoping to find an answer, Jepp fought his way forward. A completely unprecedented source of light threw a glow down the corridor. The human felt his heart start to pound, wished he had his flechette thrower, and knew the thought was absurd. He was the only bio bod aboard—and the ship was impervious to darts.

Jepp knew the passageway by heart. There was a right-left turn just ahead. He slid along a bulkhead, peered around the bend, and dashed forward.

The bulkhead that had once blocked access to the area had

been retracted up into the overhead. Jepp paused. What if the barrier fell? He'd be trapped, cut off from his food supply, and damned to starvation.

The prospector removed his tool pouch, placed it into the receiver slot, and continued his way forward.

The control room, for there was little doubt as to its function, was different from what he was used to. There was one monitor rather than the multiple screens found on vessels like the *Pelican*, and an extremely simple instrument panel that featured four oval buttons, a joystick, and a hole that Jepp refused to explore.

The presence of two pedestal-style chairs confirmed that the oxygen-breathers not only existed, but occasionally rode their ships.

The entire setup reminded Jepp of the highly automated ground cars popular on the more industrialized worlds. Most had only minimal controls, barely enough to get the vehicle out of trouble. Did the same logic apply here?

Jepp blinked, found his eyes had adjusted to quite some extent, and eyed the monitor. It was at least eight feet across and filled with an unfamiliar star field. The deck tilted as the ship banked. A planet swung into view. It more than filled the screen. A thick layer of unbroken yellow clouds obscured the surface.

Henry, the *Pelican*'s navcomp, would have fed the prospector all sorts of data, but the ship was gone, and so was the computer. All Jepp could do was watch, and wonder what the Sheen vessel was up to.

The scout shuddered as it entered the planet's upper atmosphere, locked onto its target, and began to track. There was food among the sulfurous clouds—and the ship was hungry.

The Baa'l ship was more than five hundred feet long and consisted of a ram scoop, some very complex separators, and six cylinders, each of which was divided into multiple tanks.

As with all the Baa'l race, the intelligence who controlled the ship and served as its single crew member was known by his job description, a rather lengthy affair that filled the brains of no less than 107 nonsentient storage beings, but could be summarized as: "The one who travels vast distances in search of materials required to repair, maintain, and further Baa'l infrastructure to the benefit of the race."

The last part was especially important, since all activity was measured in terms of its usefulness to the race—and anything that failed to meet stringent criteria went unresourced.

Still, as with most of his peers, the pilot had chosen an abbreviated identifier in the form of a two-symbol poem: Far/ Finder.

But none of that was on the Baa'l's mind as he cruised the ocean of clouds. They were wonderfully thick, about sixty dom deep, and ripe for harvest. Far/Finder checked his sensors and took pleasure from the readings. There were useful amounts of carbon dioxide, carbon monoxide, hydrogen sulfide, carbonyl sulfide, sulfer dioxide, argon, and xenon, all flowing out of the separator and into their pressurized storage tanks.

The ship carried other gases as well, but these made an excellent addition to the haul, and would earn praise from the Off-World Resource Procurement Committee.

Far/Finder's body consisted of a brain, neural fibers, three hearts, one lung, and twenty-seven interconnected gas bladders, all of which could be individually pressurized. He fed some additional air to number sixteen. That particular part of his anatomy grew larger, pushed on a pressure sensitive plate, and sent the ship downward. The Baa'l "saw" the computer-mapped surface rise slightly and "felt" the vessel's skin grow warmer.

Air was allowed to escape from bladder sixteen, the ship leveled out, and a volcano loomed ahead. Far/Finder turned to avoid it. That's when the alarms sounded and the Baa'l knew something was after him.

Jepp tried one of the chairs, discovered that it was uncomfortable, and chose to stand. There was nothing to see at first except the thick, swirling clouds. They were yellow and appeared rather dense. The deck tilted, he grabbed a chair back for support, and saw a flash of what? Metal?

The scout turned toward the right, and the clouds parted to

reveal a ship. A *strange* ship consisting of clustered cylinders and stubby outriggers. Now the prospector understood. The Sheen vessel needed fuel . . . and was about to take it.

The prospector felt sorry for the pilot and crew. He wished he could help them and started to pray. It didn't make any difference. The Sheen ship closed the distance; the fugitive filled more of the screen, and jinked back and forth.

Jepp, for some reason he couldn't quite articulate, had assumed the other ship was human. He'd been wrong. The bow scoop and long narrow tanks were clearly alien.

The ships were close now, *very* close, with the Sheen vessel hanging above and slightly behind its intended victim. What looked like a jagged bolt of lighting jumped the intervening gap. The viewscreen flickered, and lights dimmed. The victim had teeth!

Jepp felt a sense of excitement, remembered where he was, and considered his space suit. Should he leave the control room? And get his armor?

The battle was fought and won in the time it took the human to frame the question. The scout used tractor beams to lock the Baa'l vessel in place, drilled a hole through Far/Finder's life support tank, and waited for the pilot to die.

Far/Finder ''felt'' the tractor beams seize control of his ship, followed by intense pain as an energy beam punched a hole through bladder seven. He sealed that part of himself off, checked his sensors, and knew the situation was hopeless. There was no choice but to abandon ship.

The life pod was small and extremely uncomfortable, but the Baa'l managed to squeeze inside. He inflated a pseudopod, applied the correct amount of pressure, and felt the emergency vehicle fall free. But not before a final act of defiance. Even as the life pod fell away, and the Sheen allowed it to go, gases flowed from one tank to another, hydrogen mixed with oxygen, and a spark was prepared.

The food ship was available for the taking. The scout opened the main hatch, shortened its tractor beams, and pulled the recently subdued prey inside. It was long, too long, but the

Sheen had consumed such meals before and knew the nano could handle it. So, like one snake consuming another, the digestive process began.

Jepp, who had been watching in open-mouthed amazement, heard something whir. He turned, saw the hatch start to close, and dived toward the opening. It was too far, however, *way* too far, and the prospector knew he wouldn't make it.

The tool pouch saved the day. The door hit the object, whined upward, and descended again. The human was through by then, grabbing the tools, and taking them along. There was a thud as the hatch closed. That's when a series of three explosions rocked the ship.

The alien vessel! It had exploded! What about the atmosphere? Had the hull ruptured? The space armor! He had to reach it!

Jepp ran toward his quarters. Hatches closed behind him. The prospector was familiar with most but not all of them. Each barrier threatened to cut him off from his space suit *and* the supplies.

Boots pounded on metal and the prospector's lungs screamed for air as even more explosions rattled the ship. There, up ahead, the last hatch had started to fall!

Jepp drew on reserves he didn't even know he had, threw himself forward, and dove through the quickly narrowing rectangle. He hit the deck hard. Had his feet cleared? The prospector scrabbled his way forward. A clang signaled safety. He was alive! But for how long? The explosions had stopped—but the atmosphere could vanish any moment.

The human hurried to enter his suit, left the faceplate open to conserve on air, and settled in to wait. And wait. And wait.

Minutes went by, followed by hours, followed by days. The air continued to flow, and the lights continued to glow, but the hatches remained closed. Permanently closed, as far as Jepp could tell. Food and water continued to dwindle. There was nothing he could do but pray—and hope for some sort of miracle. Determined to be heard, the prospector fell to his knees and went to work.

• • •

Though still capable of movement, the scout was severely damaged. The artificial intelligence knew that, and took appropriate steps.

A signal went out, took thirty-six standard time units to reach its destination, and was taken under consideration. The reply was clear: "Rejoin the fleet."

The scout broke orbit, accelerated away, and entered hyperspace.

The Baa'l waited till the predator was gone, fired his sublight drive, and began the long journey home. It would take the better part of three unproductive years. The Committee would be most unhappy. Far/Finder sighed, adjusted his various bladders, and began a poem.

6

War being an occupation by which a man cannot support himself with honour at all times, it ought not to be followed as a business by any but princes or governors of commonwealths; and if they are wise men they will not suffer any of their subjects or citizens to make that their only profession.

Niccolo Machiavelli
The Prince
Standard year 1513

Planet Earth, the Confederacy of Sentient Beings

It was dark, and the lights of Los Angeles looked like gems scattered on black velvet. Thousands of grav platforms, robolifts and aircars crisscrossed the local sky grid.

No one paid any particular attention to the unmarked personnel carrier that rode a priority vector in from the east, dropped out of traffic, and landed on a high rise. Three men exited the aircraft. It was gone moments later.

Matthew Pardo shivered in the early morning air. His fatigues had the word "Prisoner" stenciled on the back, his hands were cuffed in front of him, and chains rattled at his feet.

His escort consisted of two MPs, neither of whom was

much of a conversationalist. The first, an individual whom Pardo had christened "Dickhead," motioned toward a sudden rectangle of light. "Put your ass in gear, Pardo—we ain't got all day."

No "sir," no "please," just "put your ass in gear." But that's how it was for prisoners—especially those who were or had been officers.

Pardo eyed Dickhead's shock baton, knew the Marine would love to use it, and bit the inside of his cheek. The MP grinned. "That's right, shit-for-brains—one wrong move and I'll fry your ass. Let's go."

The ex-officer shuffled across the roof. A civilian waited to greet them. Light illuminated the right half of her face. She had short-cropped blonde hair, a jeweled temple jack, and long, well-tailored legs. If the woman was curious regarding Pardo's restraints, she gave no sign of it. "This way, gentlemen . . . watch your step."

There was a coaming, meant to keep rainwater out, and Pardo struggled to cross it. Dickhead grinned happily.

The elevator fell, and fell, and fell. The indicator lights remained dark—but Pardo knew they were below ground level. *Way* below ground level. But why? The MPs were unable or unwilling to answer his questions. He could ask Legs—but why bother? The ride would be over soon, and so would the mystery.

The platform coasted to a gentle stop. The doors opened, and Dickhead prodded him in the back. "Move it, shit-for-brains."

Pardo stepped out, followed Legs out of the elevator lobby, and paused at the top of a short flight of stairs. The room was enormous. Pardo saw columns, plus hundreds, perhaps thousands of consoles, all configured in clusters of twelve. Of equal interest were the people who sat, stood, or moved around them. Some were dressed in Marine, Navy, or Legion uniforms. Others, at least half, wore civilian clothes. And there were robots, all sorts of robots, who walked, crawled, and in some cases flew from place to place. Pardo watched a message ripple across an enormous reader board, listened to the steady murmur of radio traffic, and felt a heady sense of purpose.

Dickhead was especially impressed. "Wow! What *is* this place?"

Legs smiled coldly. "This is the Global Operations Center, or GOC. Please follow me."

Pardo tried to keep up with the civilian but soon fell behind. The leg shackles made it difficult for him to walk. A woman stared, and he winked in response. As the ex-legionnaire moved out from behind one of the thick support columns, the center of the room was revealed.

A metal railing surrounded a large open space. A replica of Earth floated at its center. Pardo thought it was solid until a crane-mounted chair burst through the continent of Africa. It carried a man, and not just *any* man, but Colonel Leon Harco. He swooped in for a landing. Pardo arrived five seconds later. Legs handled the introduction. "Colonel Harco . . . Captain Pardo."

Harco offered his hand, and the younger officer was forced to extend both of his. The colonel's grip felt like steel.

Harco turned to the MPs. "Remove this officer's manacles and cuff yourselves together."

The military policemen looked at each other, and Dickhead reached for his sidearm. He stopped when Staff Sergeant Jenkins inserted the barrel of a 9mm handgun into his right ear hole. "Sir! Yes, sir!"

Pardo waited for the restraints to fall away, rubbed his wrists, and looked Dickhead in the eye. "One more thing, Corporal . . ."

The MP found it hard to swallow. His Adam's apple bobbed up and down. "Sir?"

Pardo kneed the Marine in the groin, hammered the back of his head, then kicked him in the ribs. It took two legionnaires to carry him away. People looked and returned to their work. Harco stood at parade rest. The sarcasm was obvious. "Very impressive."

"He had it coming."

"He had it coming, *sir*."

Pardo came to attention. "He had it coming, *sir*!"

Harco took two steps forward and stopped no more than an inch away. "Listen, and listen good. You are here for *two* reasons: Your mother is governor . . . and your mother is governor. I think you're a low-life, scum-sucking, no-good piece of shit. Maybe, just maybe, you can change my opinion. *If* you demonstrate some leadership, *if* you maintain discipline, and *if* you control your temper. Do you read me?''

''Sir! Yes, sir!''

''Good. You will serve as my XO. In that capacity, you will do exactly as I tell you, or Sergeant Jenkins will blow your worthless brains out. Your mother will be pissed, but I can survive that. Understood?''

''Sir! Yes, sir!''

Harco took a step backward and nodded. ''Excellent. Welcome to the team, Major. See that holo?''

Pardo noted the promotion and looked at the planet that loomed above. It was hard to miss. ''Yes, sir.''

''That's *our* planet, son—or it will be by this time tomorrow. Draw some gear and report to me. We've got work to do.''

Patricia Pardo turned her back to the wall screen. Though she had been unable to hear what two officers had said to each other, there was little need to. She could imagine the interchange. Matthew had been disrespectful, and Harco had dressed him down. A good thing, as long as it stayed within certain limits. ''So,'' she said, addressing her companions, ''is everything ready?''

Leshi Qwan nodded and glanced at the wall display. The steadily dwindling numbers indicated that only two hours and thirteen minutes remained until one of NI's subsidiaries would seize control of seventy-two percent of the planet's voice, data, and video networks along with ninety-four percent of the deep-space com gear. ''Yes, Governor, Noam is ready, or will be at 0600 hours local.''

Pardo nodded. ''Excellent. And what of our allies?''

Senator Orno had left many days before in order to ensure that he would be seen on board the *Friendship* before the shit hit the fan. His job was to slow if not actually prevent response by the Confederacy.

Ambassador Harlan Ishimoto-Seven *was* present, however,

and bobbed his head. "My ship lifts within the hour. I will do everything I can to bring the Hegemony around."

Pardo was well aware of the fact that Ishimoto-Seven lacked the full support of his government, but hoped he'd find the means to secure it. She nodded politely and allowed her eyes to play over the rest of the faces before her.

Some had been with Pardo for a long time; others were new, or drawn from the ranks of Noam Inc. and the military. Responsibility for maintaining critical services would rest on their shoulders. An important task if they hoped for any support.

The staff looked the way she felt: tired, nervous, and more than a little worried. The politician forced one of her famous smiles. "This is it, folks . . . the chance we've been waiting for—Earth will be independent by this time tomorrow!" There were expressions of enthusiasm, followed by light applause, but no one cheered.

Ultimately, long after the revolt was a matter of historical record, and a legion of staff officers, desk jockeys, and associated academics had finished their various studies, analyses, and just plain guesswork, the more knowledgeable among them would conclude that a key factor in the way things ended up was Naval Captain Angie Tyspin, and her dedication to a game called "contract bridge."

Their conclusion would stem from the fact that Tyspin, commanding officer of the Confederacy ship *Gladiator*, came off duty at 0300 shipboard time, and, after retiring to her quarters for a quick shower, set out for Admiral John Wayburn's cabin, where she and some other officers were scheduled to play bridge.

On her way to that appointment, Tyspin just happened to pass the com center, heard the sounds of a scuffle, and looked inside. A sailor lay on the deck, and a pair of combat-clad Marines circled Chief Petty Officer Gryco. They had knives, which the noncom countered with the jacket wrapped around his left forearm.

Tyspin hadn't been noticed yet. She spotted a fire extinguisher, pulled it off the bulkhead, and swung it through the air. Metal connected with bone, and a Marine collapsed.

The officer turned to find that the second soldier was down as well. The knife that protruded from the Marine's chest looked a lot like his own. Gryco checked the soldier's pulse, shook his head sadly, and stood. "Morning, Captain. . . . Sorry about the mess."

Tyspin raised an eyebrow. "What the hell happened here, Chief?"

The petty officer shrugged. "Damned if I know. I stepped out for a cup of java, came back, and saw Hoyka lying on the deck. I bent over to check his pulse. That's when the grunts jumped me. Nice going, by the way . . . the missus thanks you."

Tyspin heard the *thud, thud, thud* of muffled gunshots and bent to retrieve the Marine's sidearm. A quick check confirmed that it was loaded with low-velocity ammo—a must on any spaceship. She gestured to the other body. "Grab a weapon, Chief . . . we've got trouble."

The CPO nodded, grabbed the second soldier's pistol, and followed the CO out into the corridor. A klaxon sounded, they heard a scream, and the mutiny was under way.

The shot was arranged so that the Global Operations Center filled the background. The Planetary News Network had agreed to carry the feed. The rest would go along or look stupid. Patricia Pardo felt irritable and a little bit jumpy. She was grateful when the makeup person finished and backed away. A cute little morsel who might be fun under the right circumstances.

There were two cameras, one of which sat on a heavy carriage, while the second hovered thirty feet away. The director had a thin, dissipated look. He wore black and smiled nervously. "All right, people . . . thirty to air . . . count the governor down."

Pardo felt a tightness at the pit of her stomach. This was it, the moment from which there was no way back, and upon which the rest of her life would depend. "Three . . . two . . . and cue."

The politician saw a crew person point in her direction and

knew she was on. People all over the world frowned as their holo tanks went to black and came up again. Qwan smiled knowingly. Pardo looked into the lens. "Good morning, good afternoon, or good evening. This is Governor Patricia Pardo, speaking from the newly established Global Operations Center."

The director whispered something into his intercom, and a picture of the GOC flooded the nets.

"The purpose of this facility," Pardo continued, "is to provide a temporary seat for the new Earth government until such time as a more appropriate venue can be established."

The director cut to a medium shot of her torso and ordered the camera to zoom in. Pardo allowed herself to frown, but not *too* much. Just enough to convey some concern. "Most if not all of you are aware of the manner in which our population has been systematically abused. Think about it. . . . Which race suffered the most casualties during the Hudathan war? *We did.* Who pays the taxes necessary to support the bloated bureaucracy? *We do.* Who suffers as a result of ill-conceived military cutbacks? *We do.*"

Pardo paused to let her words sink in. The hover cam cruised from one end of the room to the other. The shot conveyed order, purpose, and a sense of calm. There was a dissolve followed by a montage of beggars.

"If you think the wars ended fifty years ago, then think again. We continue to deal with rebellions, interplanetary disputes, and outlaw armies. The men, women, and cyborgs seen here were encouraged to fight for the Confederacy, only to be abandoned like so much trash."

The camera cut back to her face. She looked angry and determined. "Well, not any more! Thanks to their courage and skill, we can still take this planet back.

"*I* will serve as governor until the emergency is over and elections can be held. Complete details concerning my staff, our military arm, and related matters can be found on the net. A series of programs describing *your* responsibilities and privileges will be broadcast around the clock. Please take the time necessary to view them.

"Remember, there is no reason to panic. You, your homes,

and your *livelihoods* are intact. The only thing that has changed is your status as second-class citizens. You are free!''

The politician adopted a somewhat stern expression. ''Make no mistake, however—there are those who wish to deny your freedom and will do anything to restore the status quo. They may even go so far as to take up arms against us! Such efforts will be punished.

''With that in mind, it will be necessary to ask all active and reserve military personnel to report to their duty stations, lay down their arms, and await processing.

''Once that has been accomplished, all such men, women, and cyborgs will be invited to join our forces.

''Civilians must observe the posted curfews, obey travel restrictions, and avoid public gatherings.''

Pardo smiled. It was warm and engaging. ''We're sorry for the inconvenience these measures may cause and assure you that they will be lifted as soon as it's feasible to do so.''

The director spoke into his headset, the video faded, and a variety of preproduced holos blossomed in its place. There were different versions for different audiences, each structured to accommodate the differences in language, culture, and religion still found on the planet.

Pardo had to give Qwan and his company credit. Having chosen representative sample populations, and conducted carefully disguised opinion polls, Noam Inc.'s media experts had taken the most frequently heard themes and codified them into messages calculated to restate already existent biases and misconceptions: ''The Confederacy wouldn't exist if it weren't for humans.'' ''Terrans pay more than their fair share of taxes.'' And the ever popular ''Aliens grow fat while our people starve'' motif.

All of which distorted reality . . . but contained enough truth to be credible. The director gave a thumbs-up. ''That's a wrap, folks. Nice job, Governor . . . you were 'on message.' Early results from the focus groups and sample pops look positive. Some negatives . . . especially in certain pockets . . . but that's to be expected.''

Pardo nodded her thanks, made her way across the Operations Center, and looked up toward a row of monitors. Fighting had broken out in Chicago, and a gunship was strafing a high-rise hab complex. Windows exploded and flames appeared. "Some negatives," indeed. The politician headed for her makeshift office. She had com calls to make, VIPs to cajole, and a facial at 10:00.

Booly woke without knowing why. The room was dark. His bedclothes were wrapped around his knees. Air whispered through an overhead duct. It *looked* normal, but something was amiss. What?

Though not gifted with the supersensitive sense of smell that his Naa brethren had, the officer did have the ability to detect odors that most humans couldn't. What *was* that fragrance? An essence that seemed familiar, yet exotic. Then he had it . . . the nack-nack blossom. A rather hardy plant that was native to Algeron and prized for its scent. The *only* scent considered masculine enough for a warrior to wear.

Suddenly Booly knew that a Naa had entered his room . . . and was watching from the shadows. His hand slid toward his pillow and the sidearm hidden there. The damned thing had a tendency to migrate and . . .

Booly's movements were interrupted when a hand grabbed his arm and another covered his mouth. The voice belonged to Lieutenant Nightslip. "I'm really quite impressed. Only one human in a hundred would have detected our presence."

"*Our?*" The news that more than one individual had invaded Booly's quarters came as something of a shock.

"Can I remove my hand? You won't call out?"

Booly nodded and felt the hands leave his body. He sat and reached for the light. "I wouldn't do that if I were you," the intelligence officer cautioned. "They are watching your quarters."

"*They?*" Booly asked. "Who the hell are 'they'?"

"The mutineers," Nightslip answered patiently. "They hope to seize the fort about forty-five minutes from now."

Booly stood, saw five or six figures in the shadows, and knew they were Naa. He grabbed his pants and pulled them on. He had all sorts of questions . . . not the least of which had to do with the nature of the revolt. "How many?"

"At least sixty hard-core cadre—plus an unknown number of sympathizers. Beyond them, it's my guess that most of the troops will back whoever looks strongest. *Us*, if we move quickly enough."

Booly felt his heart beat a little bit faster. Sixty! It was far more than he would have guessed. "Arms?"

The Naa shrugged. "It's hard to say, sir. We heard that one of our officers went over. He or she could open the armory."

Booly finished buttoning his shirt and tucked the tails in. "Damn! Which one? Judd?"

"Maybe," the Naa replied cautiously, "though I have no direct evidence of that. But this is bigger than Fort Mosby . . . I'm sure of that much."

"How?" Booly asked as he laced his boots. "How did you learn about this?"

"They tried to recruit Blademaker," the officer replied, "and he played along."

"We'll hang a medal on him," Booly said grimly, "assuming we win."

"Thank you, sir. That would be nice," Nightslip said gravely, handing the officer his combat harness. "His village will be honored."

Booly looked up. "Dead?"

"Yes, sir. We found him about twenty minutes ago. His throat had been cut."

Captain Angie Tyspin broke the corner, saw two energy bolts whip through her peripheral vision, and felt Chief Gryco jerk her back. "Bad idea, ma'am. They have this corridor sewn up. Where are we headed, anyway?"

Tyspin was grateful for the "we." "The Admiral's cabin. Before they capture or kill him."

Gryco nodded. "Aye, aye, ma'am. Let's try 'B' Corridor."

The naval officer followed the NCO back to a passageway labeled "Connector 10" and from there to Corridor "B." A rating raced by.

The chief stuck his head around the corner, motioned for Tyspin to follow, and ran toward the stern. The Admiral's cabin was large enough to have entrances onto both "A" and

"B" Corridors. They would enter from the "B" side if the hatch was open.

Tyspin's mind started to race. There was so much to consider . . . and so much to do. Reach the admiral, secure the bridge, restore discipline. If only . . .

A power tech stepped out of an access hatch, saw Gryco coming her way, and raised the weapon. It belonged to the second engineer—now lying in a pool of his own blood.

The chief saw the movement, shot her twice, and passed without looking. Dead eyes stared up at Tyspin as the officer leapt over the body. It belonged to a petty officer named Trang.

The naval officer nearly ran into Gryco's back as he skidded to a halt and pointed at a hatch. "That's it, Captain. I'll go high, you go low."

The possibility that *she* should be giving the orders never occurred to Tyspin. Gryco had taken part in countless boarding parties during his long service, and she had participated in three. His expertise was superior to hers, and both of them knew it. She dropped into a crouch, and the chief slapped the access plate. Nothing.

The CPO looked at her and shrugged. "What now?"

"Use my override. Delta-Adam-Frank seven-three-two."

Gryco entered the code into the keypad, raised his weapon, and pushed through the half-open hatch. "Drop your weapons! Place your hands on your heads!"

Tyspin scuttled forward, her weapon held in both hands. Gryco made a gagging sound and turned his head. The admiral, his flag lieutenant, and the *Gladiator*'s XO had been executed. Not just killed, but *dismembered*, so that pieces of them were jumbled together.

Tyspin fought to keep her dinner down, turned, and attacked the com panel. "Bridge? Tyspin here."

"Captain?" The voice was filled with relief. "Thank God."

"Not quite yet," Tyspin replied. "Who's speaking?"

"Rawlings, ma'am. Lieutenant j.g."

Tyspin summoned up an elfin face, serious brown eyes, and a gawky walk. The most junior watch officer on board. Two years out of the Naval Academy and on her second ship. "All right, Rawlings . . . I need a sit rep . . . and make it fast.''

Rawlings eyed the bridge. Screens had been shattered by
the unexpected fusillade of low-velocity bullets. A handful of
wires dangled, a short sparked, and fire retardant dripped from
an equipment rack.

The cause of the damage, one Quartermaster Allan Mori,
lay where he had fallen. The machine pistol, obtained by
means unknown, had been taped to the bottom of his control
panel. Suddenly and without warning the rating had stood,
aimed at the OOD, and sprayed the bulkhead with soft-nosed
bullets.

The Marine who killed him, a PFC named LaBatto, plus
two of his buddies, were stationed at the hatch. They had re-
pelled three attacks so far, but were low on ammo. LaBatto
fired two rounds down the corridor, released the empty mag,
and slapped the last one into place. It held thirty rounds. Rawlings swallowed the lump in her throat. ''The bridge is secure,
ma'am. For the moment anyway.''

Tyspin forced herself to concentrate. There were so many
things to think about. ''Cut power to all the ship's weapons
systems.''

Rawlings felt a momentary sense of pride. ''All weapons
systems secured, ma'am.''

Rawlings had kept her head—something Tyspin would remember. ''Excellent. Good work, Lieutenant. How 'bout Engineering?''

''They *claim* to be secure,'' Rawlings offered hesitantly,
''but I'm not sure that I believe them.''

''Why not?'' Tyspin asked, glancing toward the open hatch.
Gryco was there, peeking around the corner.

''Because the second engineer can't remember which position he played on the academy's powerball squad.''

Tyspin was *doubly* impressed. ''Okay, Lieutenant. The
command override is Delta-Adam-Frank seven-three-two.
Take control of the engineering systems and lock everyone
else out. How 'bout communications? Anything from Fleet?
Or NAVOPS?''

''No, ma'am. Someone's running a full jam.''

So I'm *not* alone, Tyspin thought to herself. Other ships had been taken. It was a selfish thought, and one of which she was ashamed.

Gryco fired three shots in quick succession. "Time to leave, Captain—they're getting ready to rush us."

Rawlings heard the shots and felt a stab of fear. What if she were left in command? "Ma'am? Are you still there?"

"That's a roger," Tyspin answered grimly. "Hold the fort, Lieutenant—I'm on the way."

General Arnold M. Loy and his staff wore combat fatigues as they watched the clearly impromptu broadcast cobbled together by a world-spanning association of netheads, ham operators and assorted techno-geeks.

They called themselves "Radio Free Earth" but used a wide variety of technologies to broadcast the news. Their latest newscast, anchored by a seventeen-year-old with a bad case of acne, had shown Legion troops marching through South Los Angeles. Snipers had accounted for two legionnaires, and the rest responded with wholesale violence. Five city blocks had been leveled, hundreds had died, and the destruction continued.

The officers watched in stunned silence as a Trooper III sent its analogs into a shopping mall—and tanks fired on civilians as they tried to escape. That's when the tiny hover cam was destroyed and the teenage newscaster reappeared. He seemed scared but determined. "That's what they *did*, folks . . . here's what they *said*."

A shot of Colonel Harco appeared. Those present recognized it as having been part of a propaganda holo aired half an hour earlier. It was fuzzy, but there was no mistaking the words. "You have no reason to fear us. The new government will respect your rights. It's our job to protect you."

Loy brought his fist down with such force that the 30mm shell casing that served as his pencil cup leapt clear of the desk. "Damn the man! I'll see him hang!"

The general stood and removed his web belt from the back of the chair. "All right, you heard the traitorous bastard, put everything on the street. Let's meet the scumbags head on, kill every last one of the sonsofbitches, and bury them deep."

General Mary Macklin, the academy's commandant and one of the most respected officers in the Legion, stepped forward. She had doubts about Loy, about the manner in which he had ignored a multiplicity of danger signs and seemed blind to his own culpability. She had tried to broach the subject once, to warn him of what was brewing, but he had dismissed her out of hand. "Stick to the academy, General—I'll handle the rest."

But it was too late for recriminations, meaningful ones anyway, and there were others to consider. "What about the cadets, sir? Shall I evacuate them?"

"Hell, no," Loy replied carelessly. "They're soldiers, aren't they? Let 'em fight. Should be over soon. The experience will do 'em good."

Macklin started to object, started to point out that many of her charges were little more than children, but saw it would do no good. She came to attention. "Sir! Yes, sir!"

The entire staff departed after that, each heading for what remained of their commands, determined to turn the tide.

Loy waited till the last one had left, pulled a picture out of a desk drawer, and stared at it for a moment. Then, having shoved the photo into his pocket, he left the office.

Though honed by training received in the Legion, many of the skills possessed by Nightslip's troops had been learned during their youths on Algeron, and made even more effective by their acute sense of smell and the heat-sensitive pads located on the bottoms of their feet.

Having failed to compete with them as a child, Booly knew better than to try now, but did manage to integrate himself into their unit—an accomplishment that earned their instant respect.

Nightslip's troops had been broken down into squads. Booly led one, with the objective of taking the Operations Center, while other groups went after the armory, the motor pool, and key positions throughout the fort. Hopefully, providing that all went well, they would strike at the same time.

The Naa moved forward in a series of well-coordinated spurts. A point man went first, followed by the squad, Booly, and a two-person "drag team" that spent most of their time walking backwards.

The legionnaires padded down a flight of stairs and entered a hall. A row of lights marched the length of the ceiling. First Sergeant Neversmile used a heavily silenced pistol to shoot them out. Plastic tinkled to the floor, and darkness claimed the passageway.

Booly wished the legionnaire had left at least one of the lights to see by, but had no intention of admitting that, and used a hand to follow the wall. The concrete was cold and smooth. Like a basement . . . or the wall of a tomb.

Everything within Fort Mosby's Situation Room seemed suspended in time. Most of the duty staff, some eight people in all, stood with hands on heads.

First Sergeant Ernie Fuller, backed by Corporal Mel Bonsky and a squad from D Company 2nd REP, had them covered. The noncom was a big man—so big that the submachine gun looked more like a toy than an actual weapon.

Captain Henry Olmsworthy III stood to one side, tried to focus his eyes, but couldn't quite make it. It didn't take a genius to figure out that Fuller was in charge.

Sergeant Sean Skog lay where he had fallen, a bullet through his heart. Sergeant Ho knelt beside him, hands still bloody from her wound, hatred burning in her eyes. "You'll pay for this, Bonsky . . . and *I'll* pull the trigger."

"You're next, bitch," the diminutive corporal said, blood suffusing his face. "Eat this!"

The order left Bonsky's brain but never made it to his finger. A rifle butt struck the back of the head, and he dropped like a rock. Fuller eyed his captives. "*I'll* decide who dies around here."

The noncom pulled a slip of paper out of his pocket and motioned to Ho. "Come here. Transmit *this* code on *this* frequency. And don't get fancy. We can shoot you and *still* have plenty of techs left over."

Ho, who hadn't liked the 2nd REP ever since a bar fight on El Six, liked them even less now. She had little choice, though . . . and did as she was told. It took thirty seconds to send the message—and even less time to receive a string of letters and numbers in response. She read them aloud.

Fuller nodded and looked around the room. "Good. You don't realize it yet, but you did yourself a *big* favor. The Legion is safe now. Let me know if you'd like to join."

Fuller's two-man security detail was still probing the sudden darkness, still pondering what to do, when the Naa killed them. Were the deaths necessary? Or prompted by what they had done to Blademaker? Booly suspected it was the latter . . . but was in no mood to debate the matter.

The door opened with ease. A pair of shadows slipped through the gap. The officer followed. Fuller's offer hung over the room. "So, who's with us?"

Booly cleared his throat. "How 'bout *us,* Sergeant? Can *we* join?"

Heads swiveled as Fuller brought his weapon up. He was far too slow. A hole appeared at the center of his forehead, his eyes crossed, and he toppled over backwards. His squad stirred, saw the weapons pointed their way, and froze.

A Naa slid forward. One by one the mutineers were relieved of their weapons and ordered to kneel.

Olmsworthy tried to muster some sort of defense, saw Booly's expression, and went to his knees.

Neversmile touched his ear plug and turned to Booly. "The lieutenant took the armory, sir, the motor pool is secure, and eighty percent of the perimeter is under control. Should have the rest shortly."

"Casualties?"

"Yes, sir. Six dead . . . ten wounded. Both sides."

Booly nodded and wondered how high the total butcher's bill would be. "Thank you, Sergeant."

The officer looked around the room. It was a critical moment, and he knew it. Some of the men and women around him, there was no way to know how many, would have accepted Fuller's offer. How should they be treated? With suspicion? Or trust? The decision was based more on gut instinct than logic. "Well? What are you waiting for? Get back to work."

Ho nodded and looked around. "You heard the colonel. The break's over. Zuul, check to see what EARTHSEC has to say, Tram, scan the civilian stuff, and Motke, give me a hand. Skog was one of *ours* . . . and I wouldn't want one of those bastards to touch him."

Booly smiled grimly. How many of "those" bastards were there, anyway? Just a few? Or enough to take the planet? Only time would tell.

The corridor was momentarily clear. Chief Petty Officer Gryco hollered "Now!" and began to run. Captain Angie Tyspin followed. What began as a thin trail of blood droplets thickened and vanished under a body. The rating lay facedown. Loyalist? Mutineer? There was no way to tell.

Half-congealed blood had adhered itself to the bottom of Tyspin's black high-tops. They made a scritching noise as she ran. Someone yelled, and she waited for the seemingly inevitable impact.

But the port side midship lock appeared up ahead, the hatch opened, and they slid inside. Bullets flattened themselves on metal. Tyspin used her override to lock the door.

"This looks about right," Gryco said, pulling a set of emergency space armor out of the locker. "Hope you like white."

"It's one of my favorites," Tyspin said as she struggled into the suit. "The shoulder beacons are a bit much, though."

"You might want to deactivate those hummers," the noncom said thoughtfully. "The idea is to be *unobtrusive*—not the other way around."

Tyspin nodded, settled the helmet over her head, and felt it mate to the suit. By slipping out through the lock and making their way along the outside surface of the ship, the twosome hoped to bypass the mutineers. That was the theory, anyway— and it might even work.

Gryco used a thickly gloved hand to pat the top of her helmet. He looked huge in the armor. "Ready when you are, ma'am."

Tyspin nodded, realized the helmet remained stationary, and said, "Roger."

The officer pushed on a green panel, waited for the ship to

pump the atmosphere out of the lock, and watched the hatch iris open.

The next phase of the plan was easier than she had expected it to be. Earth loomed below. Most of the planet was blue, but there were patches of brown frosted with white. The sight never ceased to amaze her. Even with her life on the line.

The journey from midship to bow took no more than five minutes. The bow hatch was clearly marked. Tyspin punched the override code into the glove-sized keypad, switched to the command freq, and chinned her mike. "Lieutenant Rawlings . . . do you read me?"

The junior officer's voice was high and tight. "Yes, ma'am. Loud and clear. Where are you?"

"Chief Gryco and I are about to join you via the E-lock. Tell the Marines to save their ammo for the bad guys."

Rawlings grinned in spite of herself. "Yes, ma'am. Shall I muster a side party?"

"Not this time," Tyspin replied. "But thanks for the thought. See you in oh-five."

The minutes passed slowly, as if determined to torture her, but were finally over. The hatch opened. Tyspin stomped onto the bridge and released her helmet. The control area looked like hell. It appeared as if the forward bulkhead had been sprayed with machine gun fire, two bodies were stacked against the port bulkhead, and the air smelled of ozone. The crew watched with a mixture of relief and concern. The captain had the deck; that was good, but what could she do?

Tyspin spoke with a confidence she didn't feel. "All right . . . let's bring this thing to a speedy conclusion. Seal every compartment in the ship. That includes the corridors.

"Chief Gryco, take the Marines. Clear the corridors first. Announce your presence, order everybody out, and take all of them prisoner. If they resist, shoot to kill."

"Rawlings, sort the prisoners into three groups: those we *know* to be loyal, those we can't be sure of, and those who took part. Lock the last two groups into different compartments and post guards outside. Questions?"

Rawlings nodded. "Yes, ma'am. What if some of the crew refuse to leave their compartments?"

Tyspin's face grew hard. "Then pump the air out, send a burial detail, and blow them through a lock."

Rawlings paled. "Yes, ma'am. Right away."

It took the better part of three hours to regain complete control of the *Gladiator*. Twelve mutineers refused to surrender and were killed. Their bodies entered the same orbit as the ship. Tyspin watched one of them tumble through the main viewscreen and searched for feelings of regret. There were none to be found.

The normally blue sky was obscured by a thick layer of yellow-gray smoke. It covered the city like a shroud. Aircraft, some of which dropped bombs, were visible one moment and gone the next. A double row of explosions marched down Colima Road. Columns of smoke shot into the air and carried palm trees, ground cars, and chunks of masonry with them.

Closer in, not more than two miles away, there were even more explosions as well-sited howitzers fired from Hacienda Heights, and sent 155mm shells into the homes below. Homes that might otherwise provide cover for the enemy. They came apart with frightening ease. Black craters marked where they had stood.

The Tactical Operations Center, or TOC, consisted of little more than a half-leveled house, some crew-served machine guns, and a robot-transportable holo tank—a device designed to display how friendly forces were deployed but which was more useful as a stool.

The deadly *thug, thug, thug* of the mortars could be heard to the rear as Legion Cadet Leader Melissa Voytan peered over the battlefield and struggled to marshal her thoughts.

She was nervous, *very* nervous, because in spite of all the books she had read, the lectures she had heard, and the sometimes diabolical virtual reality scenarios she had survived, the student had never fired a shot in anger, much less ordered others to do so.

Now, as the mutineers advanced toward the center of the city, she would not only enter into combat for the first time but lead her fellow cadets as well.

As if reading her mind, or sharing her angst, Staff Sergeant

Rudy Rycker touched her arm. "There ain't nothin' to it, ma'am. Shoot, move, and communicate. That's all you gotta do."

The words provided some much-needed comfort and helped push the fear toward the back of her mind. Rycker should have been in command, but that wasn't how things were done in the Legion, not if an officer was available. Even one who wanted to go home. Her family lived not more than sixty miles to the east. What were her parents doing, as she prepared to die?

A voice spoke in Voytan's ear. She recognized it as belonging to Kenny Suto, a sixteen-year-old who actually *liked* the stuff they served in the mess hall and couldn't get enough of it. "Alpha Three to Alpha One . . . I have smoke on my forward positions. Over."

Voytan knew what that meant. The smoke was intended to blind her troops. Infantry would follow, and not just *any* infantry, but infantry supported by cyborgs. They would hit the front lines together, attempt to flank her, and attack Loy's rear.

Voytan commanded what amounted to a light battalion, including three rifle companies of approximately one hundred thirty cadets each, plus a headquarters company that consisted of herself, some com techs, the medium armor weapons (MAWs) and two 60mm mortars. The same ones firing from her rear.

Her mission, as laid down by General Loy, was to delay the enemy forces long enough for the regulars to secure the inner city and turn toward the south. That was a task the general had assigned to himself.

The cadets had no cyborgs of their own, the loyal borgs having been employed elsewhere, which meant that shoulder-launched missiles (SLAMs) would have to do.

Designed for use against Hudathan cyborgs, the SLAMs were the only effective weapons the cadets could use on sentient armor. Voytan forced confidence into her voice. "Alpha One to Three . . . Hold them as long as you can and fall back. Four will cover your withdrawal. Over."

Suto clicked the hand-held mike two times by way of a

reply. Voytan looked at Rycker. He grinned. "You're doin' good, ma'am. Keep it up."

Voytan didn't *feel* as if she was doing very well but smiled nonetheless. An enormous quad emerged from the smoke more than a mile in front of her. She chinned her visor to full mag and leapfrogged to video supplied by one of her squad leaders. Range, windage, and other information scrolled over the shot. The borg stood twenty-five feet tall, weighed fifty tons, and walked on four legs. It mounted multiple energy cannons, an extendable gatling gun, missile racks, grenade launchers, and a whole lot of machine guns.

Twin streams of .50 caliber machine gun fire reached out to embrace the cyborg. Explosions winked and sparkled all across its hull as the monster fired in response.

There was a brilliant, eye-searing flash as a weapons emplacement ceased to exist.

That's when the motor-driven gatling gun opened fire. It was capable of putting out more than six thousand rounds a minute. A curtain of brown soil flew into the air as the 20mm shells found a slit trench and followed it from west to east. An entire squad of second-year students was ripped to shreds. Voytan's video went to black and jumped to the perspective of a fire team leader.

Other lesser forms could be seen to either side of the gargantuan machine. There were Trooper IIs, Trooper IIIs, and a company of battle-armored legionnaires closing fast.

But nothing comes for free, and while they were severely outgunned, the youngsters had a dozen SLAMs plus three reloads each. Hidden until now, the gunners stood, showed their missiles the target, and pressed their triggers. Two of the SLAMs fell victim to electronic countermeasures, and one exploded in midair, but the rest found the quad.

Explosions rocked the enormous body, tunneled their way in, and blew the machine apart. A voice yelled "Camerone!" Voytan nodded grimly. School was over. Graduation was hell.

The TOC was located in a heavily armored crawler that smelled as new as it was. A kind of pleasant mixture of plastic, sealants, and ozone. Stationary for the moment, it was located a half mile south of the line of contact (LC). Video feeds provided by the steadily advancing cyborgs, helmet cams, and airborne surveillance units flickered across the monitors racked above Matthew Pardo's head.

He felt conflicting emotions. In spite of the fact that Pardo didn't care for Harco, he had a good deal of respect for the officer and wanted the older man's approval.

That's why Pardo had pushed his troops so hard—to show what he could do. He turned to his XO. She was, or had been, a captain in the 1st REC, and still wore the oval-shaped unit badge on her green beret. The words "Honneur" and "Fidelite" were inscribed at its center. "What's the holdup? We should be three miles further in by now."

The TOC jerked into motion as a fountain of debris leapt into the air. Shrapnel rattled against the crawler's sides. The female officer grabbed a handhold. "Yes, sir. They threw what looks like a battalion into the gap. It's slowing us down."

"A battalion?" Pardo asked incredulously. "You've seen the intel summaries. They have no reserves. None at all."

The captain shrugged. "Cadets, sir. From the academy."

Pardo frowned. "You're kidding."

"No, sir," she replied. "General Loy ordered them in. We could bypass them—and cut their casualties."

"No damned way," Pardo said thickly. "That's what the old bastard is hoping for. He figures some softhearted idiot like you will waste half a day going around the little shits. Well, we'll show the old goat a thing or two! We'll cut his play pretend battalion into mincemeat! Call my driver—I'm going forward."

The captain did as she was told, waited for Pardo to clear the TOC, and slipped into the lavatory. She turned both faucets on. The water made a lot of noise. It was then and only then that she allowed herself to cry. The sobs lasted for five minutes, great racking things that caused her chest to heave.

Finally, when there was nothing left to give, Captain Laura Voytan washed her face, straightened the green beret, and returned to duty. Why? Because she had promised that she would.

● ● ●

Kenny had been living in his grandmother's garage for more than three years. Ever since he'd dropped out of school. There was a makeshift sleeping loft up in the rafters. It was just large enough for a mattress, reading lamp, and holo tank. But the main action was down on the oil-stained concrete floor. That's where the teenager kept all the electronic equipment that he had built, bought, and stolen over the last three years.

Monitors, receivers, transmitters, routers, switchers, amplifiers, junction boxes, and more hung from ceiling-mounted racks, filled his homemade shelves, and covered eight worktables. Hundreds of cables squirmed this way and that, tying his kingdom together and connecting Kenny with the world.

The teenager sat in his favorite chair, an executive model he had rescued from a dumpster and equipped with wheels. *Large* wheels that enabled him to roll over cables, empty meal paks, and cast-off clothing.

A spot threw light down across Kenny's shoulder-length hair, badly scarred face, and filthy T-shirt. The youngster felt jubilant, frightened, and defiant all at the same time. He and his fellow netheads had created Radio Free Earth, what? Twenty-four hours ago? Thirty-six? He couldn't remember.

The whole thing had happened so quickly. Most of the infrastructure already existed, resident not only in *his* garage, but in hundreds of similar facilities all over the world. The revolt, Governor Pardo's speech, and the street fighting simply provided Kenny and his friends with a purpose, a reason to do what they had always wanted to do: prove how smart they were . . . and earn some respect.

That's the way it started. However, once Noam Inc. and its media subsidiaries seized control of the mainstream news networks, that created a hunger for *real* coverage.

One of Kenny's associates, a computer programmer with ties to Noam Inc., estimated that their last program had attracted 3.1 *billion* viewers worldwide. An audience of almost unimaginable size in an age when carefully focused narrow casting had whittled viewership down to well-defined groups of one or two hundred thousand.

That, the teenager thought to himself, is the good *and* the bad news. The powers that be, or want to be, will do anything to shut us down. A supposition supported by the fact that the average life expectancy of a Radio Free Earth fly cam was down to a matter of minutes.

Still, the little units were relatively easy to manufacture. They were mass-produced by a somewhat eccentric netizen known only as J. J. and, for reasons known only to him, placed under Kenny's control.

Kenny had absolutely no idea who his ally was, or where he or she might be located, except that J. J. had to have access to some sort of high-tech manufacturing facility.

Each fly cam was a work of art. Though small, about the size of the insect after which they had been named, a camera still managed to deliver high-quality holo images via some sort of relay system that Kenny had yet to figure out.

But none of that mattered, not now, as both sides struggled to take control of the city.

Rather than expend his assets in dribs and drabs as he had in the recent past, Kenny had decided to amass an entire fleet of the miniature cameras and launch them all at once. Then, by picking and choosing between hundreds of shots at his disposal, the teenager hoped to create a real-time mosaic of events as they transpired.

It wouldn't last long, the bad guys would see to that, but for ten, maybe fifteen minutes the world would see the truth. Whatever *that* was.

Most people liked to talk to their computers—but Kenny preferred an old-fashioned keyboard. Keys clicked as the sent instructions went out over the airwaves.

Approximately half a minute passed before anything happened. The fly cams had been parked inside a garbage bin near the corner of Roscoe and Van Nuys. No one noticed as they swarmed out of the dumpster, departed along preassigned vectors, and went to work.

Kenny smiled as video blossomed within his jury-rigged holo tanks. If properly selected, the pictures, along with the natural sound that accompanied them, would tell the story all by themselves. He went to work.

What billions of human beings saw over the next twenty minutes was some of the most moving footage ever shot. The citizens of Earth watched as the tiny cameras introduced them to heavily cratered neighborhoods, buildings that continued to burn, and a battalion of teenage legionnaires.

Viewers watched in stunned fascination as the youngsters fired their SLAMs, fell back to prepared positions, and fired again. They bit their lips as the cyborgs continued to advance, as the defenders died in clusters of two, four, six and ten. Many broke into tears as the line eventually broke, the cadets were flanked, and the battle was lost.

John and Mary Voytan uttered exclamations of surprise as their daughter Melissa appeared in the tank before them. She looked over her right shoulder, shouted an order, and reached for her sidearm.

That's when more than half the people on the planet watched the camera pull out, saw the cadet surrender, and saw Major Matthew Pardo fire a bullet into her head.

Melissa collapsed like a rag doll, her mother screamed, and Pardo pointed to the camera. It ceased to exist.

Melissa Voytan's summary execution would have set the rebellion back no matter *who* pulled the trigger, but the fact that it was the governor's son served to polarize the population. Most of those who already believed in the revolt continued to do so. But those who were unsure, and that included millions upon millions of people, were shocked. The civilian resistance movement, which had been weak up until then, gained instant legitimacy. Ad hoc demonstrations were held all over the world. Brute force was used to put them down. Radio Free Earth covered as many as they could. A battle had been won—but the war was far from over.

A burial detail entered the loyalist TOC half an hour later, saw the manner in which Laura Voytan's green beret had been positioned on the carefully arranged corpse, and added it to their loot. They were the victors—and to the victors go the spoils.

7

The Earth is a beehive; we all enter by the same door
but live in different cells.

Author unknown
Bantu proverb
Date unknown

Planet Earth, the Confederacy
of Sentient Beings

The Cynthia Harmon Center for Undersea Research was located one hundred fifty feet beneath the surface of the Pacific
Ocean. A sprawling complex, built piece by piece as funding
became available, it consisted of twenty-three cylinders, all of
various sizes connected by semiflexible tubing.

Lights twinkled through the murk as a minisub nudged a
neon numbered lock and a school of French grunts wheeled
and darted away.

Maylo Chien-Chu saw those things, but *didn't* see them, as
she hung facedown in the water. She was naked except for a
gill mask, a weight belt, and a pair of flippers. Billions of
phytoplankton, all linked by miles of translucent fiber, embraced both her body and her mind.

The Say'lynt, one of four in existence, came from ocean
world IH-4762-ASX41. Like her "parents," Sola was highly
telepathic. Even more amazing was the fact that the alien could

control other sentients from a distance. Her voice echoed through Maylo's mind. "So, the work goes well?"

"Work?" Maylo asked dreamily. "What work?"

"Oh, nothing much," the alien teased, "just the interstellar corporation for which you have ultimate responsibility and the Center for Undersea Research."

"Oh, those," Maylo responded easily. "Chien-Chu Enterprises had another profitable quarter. As for the research—you tell me. How's it going?"

Sola felt the pull of a distant current and allowed part of her body to float toward the surface where it could absorb energy from the sun. "Nonsentient plankton absorb roughly half the carbon dioxide produced by your civilization. That, as you might say, is the good news. The bad news is that carbon dioxide levels are on the rise—and contribute to global warming."

The human frowned. The citizens of Earth had made some progress over the last few hundred years, but not enough. "So there's nothing we can do?"

"No," the Say'lynt replied. "I didn't say that. The southern oceans are relatively barren in spite of the fact that they contain enough nitrogen and phosphorous to support a large population of phytoplankton. More plankton would reduce the levels of carbon dioxide."

The dreamy feeling disappeared. Excitement flooded in to replace it. "Really? How would that work?"

"The problem is iron," the group intelligence responded patiently. "Or the lack of it. Bodies such as mine use iron to make chlorophyll. The indigenous plankton obtain most of their iron from windblown dust. But there isn't enough. Not in the southern oceans."

"We could seed the area with iron!" Maylo thought excitedly. "The plankton would bloom, carbon dioxide levels would drop, and global warming would slow!"

"Possibly," the Say'lynt agreed cautiously. "Remembering the law of unintended consequences . . . and the need to proceed with extreme caution."

"Yes," Maylo agreed. "Of course! Experiments are in order."

"Who will fund the additional research?" Sola inquired. "The government?"

Maylo shrugged. "Maybe. That would make sense. . . . But this is important! So important that Chien-Chu Enterprises will foot the bill if it comes to that. My uncle would want it that way."

The being once known as "raft Four" had never met the man in question but had memories inherited from the other members of her race. For it had been Sergi Chien-Chu who, in his role as director for the Department of Interpecies Co-operation, had successfully recruited rafts One and Two into the Confederacy's armed forces—a decision that was critical to the outcome of the Hudathan war. Sola sent a wave of affection toward her visitor. "Yes, I believe he would."

The moment was over. Maylo felt both rested and reenergized. There was work to do, a *lot* of it, but she was ready to take it on. "Thank, you Sola. . . . How much longer till you return home?"

"I'm scheduled to lift a month from now," the alien replied. "Your planet is beautiful . . . but I miss my family."

"And we will miss *you*," Maylo replied. "See you tomorrow?"

Sola was silent for a moment. "Perhaps . . . but a storm is brewing . . . and the currents carry us where they will."

"Let it rip," Maylo said confidently. "That's what I like about life below the surface . . . everything is so serene."

The Say'lynt knew better, had "heard" the distant screams, but allowed the matter to drop. The human would learn soon enough.

Maylo felt the tendrils drop away. Lights beckoned. She kicked, and they grew brighter.

The executive pushed her way downward, waved to a pair of trained dolphins, and eyed the complex below. Each tank, or habitat, wore a luminescent number. The VIP suite was located in nineteen. Maylo spotted the correct cylinder, entered the open lock, and pushed the green panel.

The hatch closed, a pump thumped, and the water level dropped. Maylo removed her equipment, used fresh water to rinse each piece off, and restored them to their hooks.

An inner door opened, and the executive's feet slapped as she walked the length of a short corridor, palmed the access panel, and entered her temporary quarters. She was halfway to the bathroom when someone cleared his throat. "Sorry, boss. I was leaving a note."

Maylo turned to find Dr. Mark Benton, the center's director, standing by the fold-down desk. He was tall, with a swimmer's shoulders and sturdy legs. He had brown hair, even features, and a strange expression. Embarrassment? Yes, but tinged with something else.

That's when the executive remembered she was naked. Should she run? Or bluff it out? She decided on the latter. "Hi, Mark. Take a seat. I'll be back in a moment."

The oceanographer nodded mutely, wondered if she'd noticed the bulge in his shorts, and hoped she hadn't. She had creamy skin, a narrow waist, and beautiful legs. It was a lovely sight . . . and one that would haunt him for weeks to come.

Once in the bathroom, Maylo rinsed the salt off her skin, examined herself in the mirror, and wondered what Benton thought. Did he like the way she looked? Not that it mattered, since she had little time for men. That was one of many sacrifices that went with the job.

The executive wrapped a towel around her head, slipped her arms into a robe, and padded toward the sitting room. A grouper nibbled at the heavily armored plastic window. Benton stood and offered his hand. It was warm and firm.

"Sorry I wasn't here to meet you. There was an Abyssal storm out along the trench. Lots of mud . . . terrible visibility. A cyborg rolled off a cliff and took some damage. She's safe . . . but it took twenty hours to recover the crawler."

Maylo took a seat. "I'm sorry to hear it. . . . Is that what you came to see me about?"

The scientist shook his head. "Heck, no, I wouldn't bother you with something like that. This is, well, *big*. Here. Watch this."

Benton walked over, dropped a holo cube into her player, and touched a button. "This stuff was recorded during the past couple of days. The com center condensed more than thirty hours of programming into thirty minutes."

Maylo started to speak, but Benton raised a hand. "You're busy, I know, but trust me. Once you see this, you'll want *more* information, not less."

A thousand points of light swirled like multicolored snow and coalesced. Governor Patricia Pardo started to speak. The executive listened, swore, and listened some more. None of what the politician had to say was good—and what followed was even worse. *Much* worse.

Maylo watched in horror as the fighting escalated, as cities started to burn, as people died. Not just a *few* people, but thousands, culminating in an on-camera execution that left her nauseous.

The video faded to black, followed by a long silence. Maylo was the first to break it. "Damn."

"Yeah," Benton agreed. "That pretty well sums it up."

"Any response from the Confederacy?"

"Not so far . . . but it should come soon."

The door chimed softly. Maylo rose to answer it.

The security officer was ex-military, one of many that Chien-Chu Enterprises had hired, partly because it seemed the right thing to do, and partly because it was a damned good investment. The woman's name was Jillian, and she looked concerned. "Sorry to interrupt, but things are getting hairy."

Maylo sighed, wished she had taken time to dress, and waved the officer in. "No problem, Jillian. Dr. Benton played the holo for me. What have you got?"

The security officer stood at a close approximation to parade rest. "Nothing good, ma'am. Combat-equipped troops invaded the company's offices in Los Angeles, New York, Mexico City, Rio, London, Moscow, Calcutta, Sydney, and Lima. Our records were seized, our funds were frozen, and at least ten members of your executive team are under arrest. Your picture was aired on the government controlled news. They put out a reward of one hundred thousand credits . . . dead or alive."

The words came as a shock. Maylo felt something cold trickle into the pit of her stomach. Dead or alive? What was happening? Had Pardo lost her mind? But there was more. Maylo could tell from the other woman's expression. "Casualties?"

Jillian gave a short, jerky nod. "Yes, ma'am. A hundred and six so far, security people mostly, including the chief."

Major Jose Mendoza had been one of those pushed out of the Legion and onto the streets—the perfect man to lead her security team. Maylo could visualize his tough, leathery face and hear his booming laugh. Killed doing his job. Anger boiled up from deep inside, anger she would harness and use. Someone, or a whole bunch of someones, was going to pay. "I'm sorry, Jillian. Jose was the best."

The security officer nodded. "Ma'am. Yes, ma'am."

"How 'bout other companies? Did they receive the same treatment?"

"It's early yet," Jillian replied cautiously, "but none so far."

Maylo felt her mind start to whirl. "We were targeted? By whom?"

"It's hard to tell," Jillian answered stolidly, "but I had reports from Los Angeles and Calcutta indicating that representatives from Noam Inc. accompanied the rebel troops and remained on prem once the soldiers left."

Noam Inc.! Of course. The two companies were fierce competitors, and had been for a long time. The mutiny was more than a military revolt. . . . There was a financial component as well.

Maylo felt a sudden sense of failure. She should have paid closer attention to the political situation, should have spent more money on industrial espionage, and should have done something about old man Noam.

What would uncle Sergi think? Not that it mattered. . . . He'd tell her to do whatever she thought was best. She took a deep breath and let it go.

"All right, here's what I'd like you to do. The center can be moved—right?"

Benton looked concerned. "Yes, but it would take several weeks, destroy some experiments, and cost a whole lot of money."

"Better get started," Maylo advised. "They went after the regional offices first . . . but it's only a matter of time before they target facilities like this one. Don't count on the center's nonprofit status to slow them down. Seventy percent of your funding comes from Chien-Chu Enterprises. They'll use that as an excuse."

Jillian nodded thoughtfully. "I know the perfect place. A canyon about a hundred miles north of here. We'll fortify the complex. But what if they come after us during the next week or two?"

Maylo thought for a moment. "Go for a swim. Ask Sola for help. Remember that in addition to her somewhat unique talents, she is a fully credentialed diplomat. That should slow them down."

The security officer looked to make sure that her boss was serious, saw that she was, and nodded. "Ma'am. Yes, ma'am."

"And what about you?" Benton demanded. "I could beg you to stay—but it wouldn't make any difference, would it?"

"No," Maylo agreed thoughtfully. "I guess it wouldn't. My first concern is for our people. Someone has to bail them out."

"They'll arrest you, too," Jillian said matter-of-factly. "Where's the good in that?"

"I don't know," Maylo admitted, "but you served in the Marine Corps. Did *you* leave people behind?"

Jillian stood a little straighter. "No, ma'am."

"Same principle," the executive answered. "I'll need a sub. Thirty from now."

Benton nodded, and there, beyond the armored window, a body stirred. Sola stood guard.

What with a six-hour trip in a sub, plus a two-hour lay over, and a ten-hour flight across the Pacific, it took the better part of a day to reach San Francisco, which, because it bordered the emergency quarantine areas, was as close as Maylo could get to where she actually wanted to go.

The executive tried to ignore the butterflies in her stomach as the wheels hit the tarmac. Brave words were one thing . . . reality was something else. Yes, she had identification documents belonging to one of the center's employees, but they were far from foolproof.

In spite of the fact that the two women resembled each other, even the most cursory check of Maylo's retinal print, voiceprint, or fingerprints would blow the falsehood wide open.

Still, some disguise was better than none, especially in light of the reward. The executive followed the crowd off the plane, through a series of hallways, and down into the lobby.

The guard, a manager who had been on duty for more than sixteen hours, eyed the businesswoman's identification, mumbled "Welcome to San Francisco," and waved her through. An employee, nobody knew which one, had dumped the electronic identification equipment sixteen hours before. Just one of many acts of sabotage aimed at Pardo's Independent World Government.

Maylo gave thanks for good fortune and hurried through the terminal. The airport was packed with people, and, judging from the lines she saw, most of them wanted to leave. She left the terminal, hailed an autocab, and faced a difficult decision. Where to go? Who to see? Especially with her face plastered everywhere.

The executive threw her duffel bag into the back, slid into place, and gave her destination: "The Imperial hotel."

The voice was patronizing. "The Imperial. Yes, ma'am, it will be *our* pleasure."

"Cut the crap and put this thing in gear."

"Nothing would please us more," the computer responded. "Please insert your valid chipcard into the reader."

Maylo grumbled, did as she was told, and felt the cab jerk into motion. It smelled of disinfectant. A heart inscribed with "B.D. loves M.D." had been scratched into the metal in front of her. The businesswoman had absolutely no intention of staying at the Imperial, but knew better than to lay electronic tracks to her *real* destination. Wherever that would be.

The bay area had escaped the sort of destruction visited on Los Angeles and looked reasonably normal except for the military presence on the streets. Major intersections were guarded by tanks, cyborgs, and armored personnel carriers. It didn't take a genius to figure out who was in control.

Maylo considered her options. There weren't any. She could

approach the government and allow them to throw her in prison, or go get some help. The law firm of Buchanan, Allison, and Grann had served Chien-Chu Enterprises for a long time and would know what to do.

With her decision made, the businesswoman decided to settle back and let the ride take care of itself. Traffic was lighter than usual, which shaved ten minutes off the trip. There was a whir as the autocab pulled into the drive, took the correct number of credits off the debit card, and spit the device into her hand. The door opened; the executive slid off the seat and took the duffel bag with her.

A baggage bot trundled her way. Maylo waved the machine off, hailed a second cab, and gave a new address. She arrived five minutes later. The vehicle whined as it pulled away.

The wind rushed in off the bay, slid through the weave of Maylo's suit, and chilled the surface of her skin. She shivered, wished for a coat, and pushed the discomfort away.

Maylo looked around, saw nothing out of ordinary, and entered the lobby. It featured what seemed like an acre of polished marble, a sculpture carved by the Orgontho artisans, and an imposing desk. The lift tubes, all twenty-four of them, were palmprint-protected. A man wearing an eight-hundred-credit topcoat slid his hand into a wall slot, turned, and entered an elevator.

Important people don't carry their own bags or need assistance. With that in mind, the receptionist looked down at her with the disdain that she so clearly deserved. "Yes? May I be of assistance?"

"Yes, thank you. Buchanan, Allison, and Grann, please."

The guard had a long, lugubrious face. An eyebrow twitched upward. "And who may I say is calling?"

There were at least a hundred thousand reasons why she shouldn't use her own name, but she had very little choice if she wanted to leave the lobby. "Maylo Chien-Chu."

The guard nodded, lifted a handset, and spoke so softly she couldn't hear. His expression changed fractionally, and he pointed toward a lift tube. "Take number eight . . . it serves the forty-ninth floor."

Maylo thanked him, entered the elevator, and heaved a sigh

of relief. She wasn't off the hook, not by a long shot, but it was good to have allies. Especially powerful ones who knew the law backward and forward.

The platform whispered to a stop, the wood-paneled doors slid apart, and the executive stepped out. It had been more than thirty years since her uncle had first taken her there and nothing had changed. Not the acres of beige carpet, the heavily paneled walls, or the portraits that hung on them—a long line of partners all of whom liked to frown.

A rather attractive woman was waiting to greet the executive. She had short blonde hair and a jeweled temple jack. "Ms. Chien-Chu! What a pleasure to meet you! Here, let me get that bag. Please follow me."

The blonde woman had already turned and left by the time Maylo thought to ask her name.

The office belonged to Ginjer Buchanan. The nameplate said so. Not that Maylo needed to see it. The woman pushed heavy wooden doors open and motioned for the executive to enter. It was a large room. She saw Ginjer on the other side of it, turning from a side table, a glass in her hand.

Maylo was committed by the time she saw the look on her attorney's face, felt the blonde woman shove something hard into her back, and heard the unfamiliar voice. "So, look what we have here! Maylo Chien-Chu. President and CEO of Chien-Chu Enterprises."

The executive turned, and the hard thing turned with her. A man held out his hand. He was handsome, almost pretty, and extremely conscious of it. "Hi. I'm Leshi Qwan. I told 'em you'd show up. That's how it is with lawyers. You can't live with 'em, and you can't live without 'em! Welcome to Noam Inc."

8

That which furthers our purpose is authorized.

The Hoon
General Directive 17923.10
Standard year 2502

Somewhere beyond the Rim, the Confederacy of Sentient Beings

The Sheen scout ship dropped out of hyper, scanned the three-planet system, and found what it was searching for. The Sheen possessed two fleets, and this one, controlled by the supreme intelligence known as the Hoon, consisted of no less than 1,347 heavily armed spacecraft.

Some cruised the margins of the solar system, watching for signs of hostile activity, while the rest swarmed around the second planet from the sun. Those capable of landing did so, feeding on the remains of a once-thriving Steam Age society, while shuttles fetched "food" into orbit for consumption by the larger vessels.

The ships, each protected by the same silvery sheen, flashed like fish through the ocean of blackness. They felt nothing for the millions who had died . . . or would die during the days ahead.

Recognition codes flashed back and forth as the newcomer identified itself and was readmitted to the fold.

The scout had no emotions as such, but did process a sense of "correctness" in relationship to its return.

The Hoon noted that a relatively minor aspect of its anatomy had returned, launched a virtual extension of itself through space, and queried the reconnaissance unit as to the outcome of the mission.

The scout ship opened itself to inspection and observed while the Hoon ran through the data collected during the two-year journey.

The supreme intelligence spent 2.1 seconds analyzing the information gathered, used it to add more detail to the three-dimensional map by which it navigated the galaxy, and took note of the Thraki spoor.

The signs consisted of a moon riddled with artificial passageways, half a ton of free-floating metallic wreckage, and a Stone Age society suddenly possessed of iron. All of which pointed toward the same conclusion: The Thraki fleet had traversed sector 789-BNOX-7862—and rather recently too. "Recently" was a relative concept denoting any event that had transpired during the last five years.

Satisfied with its findings, the Hoon started to withdraw. The scout ship sensed the departure and mentioned the prisoners. Surely they had value, and required interrogation?

The Hoon acknowledged the interrogatory, entered the bubble matrix, and examined the captives. The AIs were a strange and contentious lot, most of whom functioned at a rather low level. They sensed his presence, realized his status, and babbled all sorts of mathematical nonsense.

Most of the gibberish could be translated, however, and while very little of it had any value, there were some interesting exceptions.

Among them were an AI who claimed to be one hundred fifty thousand years old, a navcomp that was extremely conversant with the sector of space toward which the Thraki were headed, and a gaming unit that might or might not offer a momentary diversion.

Those entities that the Hoon considered to have merit were plucked from the storage module and dumped into one of his secondary memory mods. The rest were deleted.

The Hoon withdrew, the scout ship headed inward, and the fleet continued to feed.

God had spoken to Jepp with increasing frequency of late, but always through dreams, making it difficult to remember what the supreme being said.

This particular conversation was different however, since Jepp was asleep and somehow *knew* that he was asleep, thereby ensuring that he would remember.

God, who looked a lot like his father, smiled and opened his mouth to speak. Somehow, Jepp wasn't sure how, he knew that the divine being was prepared to reveal the reason for his birth and the work that awaited. Never had he experienced such a sense of warmth, significance, and impending purpose.

But then, just as his father's lips started to move, something tugged at his consciousness. He shouted, "No! I won't go!"

But the force refused to obey. It dragged the human out of his dream and into the very world from which he had so recently escaped. The prospector's eyes opened. He looked around and swore when he saw the same old surroundings. Nothing had changed. Everything was the same. Or was it?

Then it came to him. The hum! The triple-damned, unrelenting, round-the-clock hum had disappeared! A full ten seconds passed as he gloried in the resulting silence.

That's when something horrible entered his mind. What if the ship was drifting in space? Unable to produce oxygen for him to breathe? Falling into a nearby sun? Not knowing, and not being able to find out, was the worst torture imaginable.

The prospector sat up, freed himself from the makeshift bedroll, and started to stand. The deck slanted, the hull creaked, and the ship thumped onto something solid. Jepp experienced a momentary sense of relief. It seemed that the vessel had landed . . . or docked with another ship. But why? And what would that mean to him?

Mindful of how important his remaining possessions were, and eager to prepare himself for whatever lay ahead, the prospector placed items he considered critical into a large duffel bag, which, along with his space suit, he could barely manage to carry. His body, once layered with fat, was painfully thin.

He was hungry, always hungry, yet afraid to eat. He had five ration paks and an energy bar left. When they were gone, so was he.

The human forced himself to break the energy bar in half, to take small bites, and to chew them with extra care. He had just swallowed the last morsel, and washed it down with tepid water, when things started to change.

Contacts closed, motors whined, and hatches slid up and out of the way. New air flowed into the compartment. It was cold, like space itself, and tinged with ozone.

There were sounds. Metal creaked in response to a radical change in temperature, a motor whined out beyond the hatch, and something made a ratcheting noise.

Cautiously, with the duffel bag dangling from his left hand, the space armor slung over his back, and the flechette thrower in his right, the prospector emerged from his cell. Jepp felt his heart thump against his chest. Were aliens waiting? How would they react? What should he say to them? Something moved. The dart thrower came up; his finger tightened on the trigger, and then came off again.

Nano! A long silvery stream of the silvery stuff had entered the ship and oozed in his direction.

The human watched the pseudopod split into three separate rivulets. Two turned and slithered down side passageways, while the third probed the main corridor.

The nano were assessing how much damage the ship had suffered. That's the way it appeared, anyway—which suggested that they were external to the ship. After all, if the ship had the ability to repair itself, why wait till now?

Thus encouraged, the prospector followed the pulsating stream back toward its source. He passed through one of the more damaged sections, saw lights through a ragged hole, and was struck by how strange they were, like luminescent dandelion seeds floating on the wind.

The nano were thicker now, and more plentiful, branching in every direction, oozing their way through seemingly solid bulkheads, crisscrossing the overhead and covering the deck. It was difficult to walk without stepping on one or more of the silvery threads, and Jepp found himself tiptoeing down the

corridor, lest he crush some of the tiny machines and elicit
who knew what kind of response.

Light spilled through an open hatch. The human high-
stepped through an obstacle course of intertwined nano, peered
around the corner, and looked out onto an amazing scene.

The landing bay was *enormous,* so large that Jepp could see
dozens of vessels the size of the one he stood on, all parked
in carefully aligned rows.

There might have been more, and the prospector suspected
that there were, but he couldn't see them due to thousands of
nano vines that dangled from above, squirmed up through the
deck, and wrapped the ships in metallic cocoons.

But there were other entities too, machines of every con-
ceivable size and shape, rolling, crawling, and walking through
the nano jungle. Their skin shimmered like that of the vessels
they served. There was no sign of their creators, however—
not that the human was especially eager to encounter them.

Some of the larger machines were possessed of ovoid heads,
narrow shoulders, two arms, featureless torsos, and long, slim
legs. A reflection of those who conceived them? Form that
followed function? There was no way to be sure.

Jepp knew he should resist such impulses but found himself
imposing a possibly fallacious hierarchy on the alien machines. A robotic ecosystem with the bipeds at the top, the
rollers, crawlers, and wigglers somewhere in the middle, and
the nano at the bottom.

The decision to leave the ship seemed to make itself. One
moment Jepp was there, peeking out through the open hatch,
and the next he was down on the deck, picking his way
through the nano maze.

Robots were everywhere. They saw him, *had* to see him,
but made no response. Not so long as he stayed out of their
way. The consequence for *not* doing so could be severe, however, as the prospector discovered when to tried to force his
way through a curtain of nano and received a sharp blow to
the head—a blow that made him swear and raised a lump.

The human backed away, wondered which one of the snak-
elike pseudopods had attacked him, and chose another path.

The robots knew he was there, but allowed him to exist. It

was as though he was an insect, buzzing through the house but too insignificant to chase. *Unless* he landed on some food, annoyed the homeowner, or otherwise placed himself in harm's way. That's when the machines would deal with him— and in no uncertain fashion.

Determined to be innocuous, the prospector zigzagged across the enormous deck. Puffs of light floated above his head. One adopted the human and followed him all the way to a sizeable lock. Like everything else about the ship, it was large. The human figured it could hold at least fifty humans.

Jepp regarded the chamber with a good deal of interest. There it was again, a clear indicator that the mother ship was equipped to support biologicals, but no sign of the beings themselves.

He stepped inside, palmed the now-familiar controls, and waited for the hatch to close. There, on the far side of the bay, beyond the heavily cocooned ships, Jepp saw an enormous and presumably blastproof door.

Three machines, none of which looked humanoid, joined Jepp for the trip through the lock. The trip took less than three minutes—but seemed to last forever.

The jungle was green, damp from the morning rain, and lit by filtered sunshine. The air was warm, delightfully warm, and heavy with the scent of po flowers.

Like all of its kind, the Worga ran low, its six-legged body sliding through clumps of foliage, flowing over green-clad logs, and slipping through a crystal-clear stream.

The jungle beckoned, and the Worga nosed its way in, found the scent, and uttered a deep, chesty growl.

Foliage swayed, and the Worga felt a momentary downdraft as the master's aircar passed over some nearby trees. Though not fully sentient, not yet anyway, Worga were highly evolved animals. Horth *knew* the master liked to be in on the kill and slowed his pace accordingly. There was no need for concern. Like all such prey, the female had expended most of her strength during the early stages of the hunt. The animal could take her whenever he chose.

Like most of her peers, the female had been raised in one

of the planet's cities and feared the thick green maze. That
being the case, the clearing seemed like a gift from the gods—
a place where she could escape the jungle and plan her next
move. The concubine's scales shimmered in the sun, her chest
heaved from exertion, and her clothes hung in tatters. A rock
offered a place to sit.

That's when the Worga emerged from the tree line and an
aircar appeared above. Had Horth been whelped ten thousand
years later, he might have wondered why the female had been
slated for death, and questioned his role as executioner.

But that time was a long way off, and the only thing the
Worga could feel was his hunger, and the need to kill. He
launched himself out of the undergrowth, loped across the
clearing, and sprang for her throat. The prey saw the movement, raised her hands, and started to scream.

That's when the Worga awoke. The dream had been so real
he could still smell the concubine's fear. Or could he? That's
when it occurred to Horth that this particular odor was *different,* a sort of musky smell that continued to waft past his
supersensitive nostrils.

The Worga, who possessed the capability to hibernate for a
hundred sunsets if necessary, had fastened himself to the overhead—an excellent location where nothing was likely to stum-
ble on him. His skin, which could replicate nearly any
background he chose to place himself against, was metallic
gray. He sniffed, sniffed again, and felt hunger flood his body.

Finally! Something to hunt. It had been so long since his
last meal that Horth could barely remember what he had eaten.
The short one? With all the bones? Or the long slithery thing?
It hardly mattered. The metal world was different, but food
was food, and he would hunt.

The corridors were like a maze. Jepp walked for fifteen
minutes. He turned right, turned left, and turned right again.
The lock was just as he had left it. Such wanderings were
frustrating, but more than that, extremely dangerous. The
adrenaline had dissipated. He was tired, very tired, and a little
bit dizzy. What he needed was food. All his dwindling strength
should be focused on finding it.

But how? Where to go? What to do? Robots didn't *need* food, so he couldn't get it from them. From where, then? Despair threatened to pull him down. Jepp forced himself to think. The combined weight of the space suit and duffel bag was too much. He would leave them behind.

The maze of passageways was consuming time and precious energy. He would mark them. The prospector fumbled around in his duffel bag, found a can of blue spray paint, and eyed the indicator. Half full. Good. That should suffice.

The lock hissed open, allowed two of the humanoid machines to exit, and closed again. They glanced in his direction but showed a marked lack of interest.

The human stashed his belongings in a corner, hoped they'd be safe, and followed the robots. The prospector used blue arrows, Xs, and written notations to mark his path.

That's when he noticed something interesting—something that sent a trickle of fear into his belly. Some of the bulkheads bore notations *other* than his, handwritten messages so small, so fine, that he had missed them at first. The script was like nothing he'd seen before, but the purpose was clear. Another castaway had confronted the same problem he had—and arrived at the same solution. Had the alien survived? Did he, she, or it have food? There was only one way to find out.

Jepp allowed his hand to touch the flechette thrower and took comfort from its presence.

The robots went straight for a while, turned left, then right. They paused while one made use of a wall socket, then continued on their way.

The prospector followed because the machines were headed somewhere—and somewhere beat the heck out of nowhere.

The threesome passed numerous compartments. Most were closed, but a few stared like empty eye sockets. Living quarters, perhaps? For the mysterious beings who had created the ship? There was no way to know.

The machines took another right-hand turn. Jepp marked the bulkhead, turned the corner, and felt his jaw drop. A marker had been used to scrawl the words "home sweet home" across the wall. They were surrounded by all manner of doodles, scribbles, and diagrams. Every single one of them was written in standard. A human being! Or if not human, a citizen of the Confederacy! Fanciful arrows pointed toward a hatch and seemed to invite visitors.

Jeep took a look around. The robots had disappeared by that time, and there was no one else in sight. The prospector drew his weapon, palmed the hatch, and waited for it to move. The barrier made a whirring sound as it slid up out of the way. Jepp braced himself for some sort of confrontation, but nothing happened.

Slowly, lest he trigger some sort of trap, the prospector entered the compartment. There was no need for concern. The occupant was home all right . . . but in no condition to fight. The desiccated body looked as though it had been sitting in the corner for a long time. Months? Years? Anything was possible. Patches of dirty gray skin still clung to clean white bone. Strands of once black hair fell to a much-patched shipsuit. Gold thread spelled the name "Parvin" high on the mummy's chest. A folder rested on his lap.

The skull seemed to grin as Jepp spotted the tightly stacked boxes. Could it be true? Did the labels *really* say what he thought they said? The prospector blinked, took two steps forward, and read the words again: "Emergency Rations—1 Doz. Human Consumption Only."

Jepp took a deep breath and stepped back to where he'd been. How many boxes were there? At least a hundred! The food problem was solved.

The human felt an almost overwhelming desire to rip one of the containers open and eat himself sick. Saliva flooded his mouth, and he was forced to swallow.

Slowly, reverently, Jepp fumbled for the half-eaten energy bar, removed the wrapper, and shoved the entire morsel into his mouth. His jaw worked, the desire slackened, and he remembered to say grace.

"Thank you, Lord. Thank you for saving my life. All I am is yours. Show me the way."

If the supreme being heard, he or she chose to remain silent. Jepp found a dusty container, hoped the water was good, and took a long drink. It tasted of chlorine but served to slake his thirst. The prospector returned the cap, put the jug where Parvin had left it, and took a moment to think.

There was plenty to accomplish. Retrieve his belongings, haul them back, perform a rudimentary autopsy on Parvin, and find a new home. Something a lot less obvious—in case the next stowaway had antisocial tendencies.

The prospector was just about to leave, to backtrack his way to the lock, when his eye came to rest on the folder clutched in Parvin's bony hands.

More curious than squeamish, the prospector moved in for a closer look. He leaned forward and turned his head. The high-quality holo stat was good as new. The little girl was ten or so, with a pretty face and long, black hair. An animated message crawled across the bottom of the page and would for as long as the overhead light continued to glow. "I love you, daddy—please hurry home."

The robot was performing routine maintenance on the ship's internal communication system when it sensed movement. The machine aimed a sensor in the appropriate direction. However, rather than the robot the construct expected to see, there was little more than an out-of-focus shimmer.

Certain that *something* was present, the robot switched to infrared. Yes, there it was, a long, low, multilegged creature that didn't match up with any of the threats listed in the machine's survival index.

A quick check confirmed that the amount of heat produced by whatever it was fell well within acceptable limits and posed no threat to the ship. The robot returned to its work.

The Worga sampled the air, found the same intriguing scent, and padded down the corridor. There was prey in the offing— and Horth was hungry.

9

How does death smell? It smells like sun-dried blood, like morning tears, like newly turned earth.

Author unknown
Naa Book of Remembrance
Standard year circa 150 B.C.

Planet Algeron, the Confederacy of Sentient Beings

Fort Camerone squatted on the dry, rocky plain, and, with the exception of the missile launchers, antenna arrays, and fly form landing pads that broke its hard, angular lines, looked a lot like the godforsaken outposts the Legion had occupied in North Africa centuries before.

General Mortimer Kattabi low-crawled forward, used his elbows for support, and brought the binoculars up to his eyes. A motor whirred, and the outskirts of the ever-expanding slum known as Naa Town swam into focus.

The shantytown consisted of hundreds of makeshift earthen domes, each reinforced with whatever chunks of metal or plastic that the occupants could beg, borrow, or steal.

The officer panned from left to right. Data rippled down the right side of the screen. Range, albedo, and more. None of it mattered. What *did* matter was the fact that smoke dribbled out of only half the chimneys, very little laundry had been hung to dry, and the narrow, twisting streets were practically deserted. Where were the cubs? The old folks soaking up the sun? No wonder his scouts were concerned.

Kattabi tilted the glasses up until the fort filled his viewfinder. He scanned the topmost parapet. The Confederacy's flag snapped in the breeze, some sensors turned on their mast, and a sentry stood at his post. Business as usual. Or was it? That was the problem.

Never one to ride a desk for very long, and eager to escape from General Stohl's self-important bullshit, Kattabi had assigned himself to a week of field exercises. Butt-busting, plain-pounding, hill-humping war games that would build muscle, hone skills, and keep the edge on.

And the plan had worked right up till the moment when his scouts went weird on him. Something was wrong, they claimed—something in the fort. That in spite of the fact that radio contacts had been normal.

Nine out of ten officers would have ignored the scouts and entered the fort. But not Kattabi. He had traveled the almost impossible road from private to general, and if he had learned anything along the way, it was to trust his people. Not just some of the time, but *all* of the time, even when they appeared to be wrong.

That's why he listened, gave credence to their concerns, and went to see for himself. The officer back-crawled into some rocks, dropped below the skyline, and stowed his binoculars.

The battalion's XO, Major Kirby, along with Captains Runlong, Primakov, and Verdine, waited for the General to speak. Chief Scout Gunmaker stood to one side. With his superiors but not *of* them. Kattabi shook his head. "Something is wrong, all right . . . but I'll be damned if I can figure out what it is."

Gunmaker's face was expressionless, but there was pride in the way he held himself.

Kattabi started to speak but stopped when a shadow flickered across the ground. Gunmaker glanced up, saw the Legion-issue recon drone, and raised his assault weapon. The airborne machine had almost certainly been dispatched by the people in the fort.

The range was long, and the target was moving, but neither

of those factors made the slightest difference. The Naa fired a three-shot burst. The drone staggered and spiraled into the ground.

Kattabi raised an eyebrow. "That was some damned expensive target practice, Sergeant."

Everybody grinned.

"Okay," Kattabi said, "I'm a believer. I don't know what the problem is, but I'll be damned if we're going into that fort till we understand the situation. Deploy, dig in, and keep 'em ready."

The officers saluted and returned to their units.

Corporal Andrea Acosta never saw it coming. Sergeant Gunther's hand struck the side of her face with such force that it made a cracking sound and she flew out of her chair. She hit the highly waxed floor and slid into a console.

Acosta swore, and had just started to rise, when a size twelve combat boot landed on her chest. Gunther's face was beet red. "You incompetent bitch! The orders were to lure them inside—not chase them away! Let's go. *You* screwed up—*you* tell DeVane." The noncom signaled a pair of his toadies. They grabbed her arms.

The Ops Center (OC) was a large space filled with monitors, consoles, and equipment racks. About two thirds of the OC staff had been part of or managed to survive the mutiny. Most had doubts but, like Acosta, had gone along. They ignored the tech's pleas as the troopers hauled her away.

Acosta babbled incoherently as the legionnaires half carried, half walked her down the outside corridor. "The joystick stuck! It came loose . . . the drone took off . . ."

"Save it for DeVane," one of the legionnaires said. "The borg loves a good story." The other trooper laughed.

Acosta stopped, or tried to, but found herself lifted up into the air. The toes of her spit-shined combat boots left parallel dashes on the otherwise pristine floor.

The lift opened as the foursome approached. The passengers took one look and hurried away. They had a pretty good idea where the prisoner would be taken and didn't want any part of it.

Most of the fortress was buried deep underground, safe from bombs, missiles, and orbital bombardment. But the ready rooms and maintenance bays where off-duty cyborgs spent most of their time were located one level below the planet's surface. So, in spite of the fact that DeVane controlled the entire fortress, there was only one place where his fifty-ton body would actually fit.

Yes, the cyborg might have transferred his brain box to one of the human-sized bi-forms maintained for that purpose, but that would force him to abandon the source of his power, namely the energy cannons, Gatling gun, missile racks, and other weaponry which played such an important role during the revolt. Once he was outside his body, even for a moment, the cyborg would be vulnerable.

That's why the lift stopped at level two and they frog-marched Acosta through a pair of blastproof doors and out into the maintenance bay. The stench was horrible, and what she saw made Acosta gag.

The bodies, some of which were more than forty-eight hours old, were piled like offerings before a pagan altar. There were at least fifty of them. Blood had seeped down onto the floor. Acosta's best friend, Jan Hopkins, lay on her back. Insects crawled in and out of her mouth.

A servo whined. The tech looked up, and there was De-Vane. The quad looked like what he was. A monster.

Some poor slob had spent hours on the huge, glaring eyes, the wide, grinning mouth, and the rows of razor-sharp teeth.

Acosta turned and tried to run. The troopers caught the tech and brought her back. Urine soaked her pants.

The voice had a hard, metallic quality, like the synthesizer that produced it. "Nice job, Acosta. There we were, all ready to suck Kattabi in, when *you* spooked him."

The discovery that DeVane knew what had transpired down in the Ops Center would have surprised the technician, except for the fact that she knew he had access to the fort's command and control systems.

"So," the quad continued calmly, "what should we do with a piece of crap such as yourself? A little extra duty? No, I have it! How 'bout we rip your stinking guts out and hang them around your neck? Yeah, that sounds pretty good, now, doesn't it?''

Acosta looked at her dead friend's face and licked her lips. The internal voice pushed through her fear. "He's going to kill you! Do something!''

Acosta pretended to faint, felt one set of hands drop away, and straightened up again. Her back-kick made contact, the second trooper swore, and the tech ran like hell.

Not *away*, as her captors might have expected, but *ahead* at the pile of bodies. They made for uncertain footing as Acosta high-stepped her way up and over them. Her plan was simple: Get *inside* DeVane's defenses, where she would be momentarily safe.

The better part of two seconds elapsed while DeVane absorbed what had occurred and considered his options. Most of his weapons were designed for long-range use. That left the quad with the Gatling gun, some small-caliber machine guns, and six grenade launchers.

The cyborg deactivated the safeties and heard the bio bods yell warnings as servos whined and the Gatling gun emerged from storage.

Legionnaires dove every which way as the weapon opened fire. Gouts of flesh, blood, and bone erupted all around as the technician made it to the top of the pile, tripped over an outthrust leg, and tumbled down the other side.

The bodies pummeled the technician as she fell. A fist struck Acosta's face, a boot kicked her thigh, and an elbow stabbed her gut. Bullets followed. They plowed a trench through the corpses and stalled as the Gatling gun hit a mechanical stop.

Knowing that all sorts of things can and do happen during the heat of battle, the design engineers had taken steps to ensure that the Legion's quads would be unable to fire on themselves.

DeVane had forgotten that, and was still in the process of reabsorbing the knowledge when Acosta hit the duracrete, rolled to her feet, and checked the cyborg's ramp. It was fully deployed. She put her head down and ran.

The cyborg swore, ordered the ramp to close, and knew he was late.

Metal bounced as Acosta pounded her way up toward the cargo bay. She felt the platform start to rise, threw herself forward, and made it inside.

The engineers had considered every possibility. What if the cyborg was injured or killed? No problem; a control panel, complete with a lockout button, would allow passengers to access critical subsystems and command the ramp.

Acosta flipped the protective safety cover up and out of the way, waited for the hatch to close, and stabbed the button. Bolts snicked into place. The door was locked, and the mutineers would need a laser torch to cut it open.

DeVane felt the partial loss of control, screamed incoherently, and sprayed the entire maintenance facility with 30mm cannon shells. Three Trooper IIIs, one Trooper II, and nine bio bods were killed. A half million credits worth of support gear was destroyed.

It took Acosta the better part of ten minutes to stop shaking, realize that she wasn't going to die, and remove her urine-soaked pants.

Once they were off, and tossed into a corner, it was time to "think, organize and act." That's what they had taught her in basic, and, difficult though it might be, that's what Acosta planned to do.

Because of the planet's rapid rotation, the equatorial region had bulged outward and formed a spectacular mountain range. Many of the peaks were more than eighty thousand feet tall but, because of the gravity differential between the poles and the equator, weighed only half what they would have on Earth. As another two-hour-and-forty-minute day came to an end, their snow-covered peaks faded from pink to purple.

The area occupied by Kattabi and his troops grew quickly dark. Helmet lights bobbed this way and that as the legionnaires fortified their hilly positions.

The quadrant had been bombed by the Hudathans more than four decades before, and used for countless exercises since.

That being the case, the entire area was riddled with half-collapsed tunnels, urine-soaked bunkers, and heavily eroded slit trenches. A dangerous place—especially at night. So much so that the medics had already started to treat a variety of cuts, abrasions, and sprains.

Noncoms, worried lest someone die in a cave-in, made their rounds. One swore as she fell into an old bomb crater. Her troops laughed and soon wished they hadn't.

The command post (CP) had been established in what had served as a domicile many years before. The sleeping shelves, fire pit, and odor of incense were typical of most Naa homes.

Not that Kattabi cared *who* had lived there, so long as the enclosure could take some punishment and protect his staff from flying shrapnel.

The general nodded to one of his bodyguards, said hello to the battalion runner, and entered the CP. A fire glowed in the ancient pit. Kattabi felt the warmth against the palms of his hands, accepted a piping hot cup of tea, and thanked the trooper who served it. The liquid had a soothing effect and helped the officer think.

There was no longer any doubt. Something terrible had happened. There were plenty of reasons to think so—not the least of which was a lack of meaningful radio contact with the fort.

Oh, there were conversations all right, plenty of them, but none that mattered. The com techs *sounded* legit but couldn't come up with any officers. Why? Because they were busy? Like the techs claimed? Or because of something a good deal more sinister? *A full-scale mutiny?* Was that the answer? Had the scouts known that something would happen *before* they left the fort? That would explain how certain they were. . . . But what about the men and women under his command? They seemed unaffected. Why? None of it made much sense.

One thing was for sure: It was impossible for General Stohl to keep his mouth shut for more than ten seconds. That being the case, Kattabi would have heard from the asshole by now. Yes, something was very, very wrong when Stohl remained silent—but what?

The general had no more than posed the question when Gunmaker materialized at his side. Snow dusted the legionnaire's shoulders. The officer made his annoyance clear. "Yes? What is it?"

The Naa looked unperturbed. "Visitors, sir. Here to see you."

The officer frowned. "Visitors? What kind of visitors?"

The noncom shrugged. "Human, sir. With Naa body-guards."

"Names?"

"Booly, sir. *Major* Bill Booly, retired, and his wife, Captain Connie Chrobuck."

Kattabi had heard the names before. Everyone had. Major Bill Booly, along with the officer who later became his wife, had battled the Hudathans on that very soil. Once the war was over, they vanished into the only partially explored wilderness that still claimed vast sections of the planet's surface. Heard from now and then, especially where the welfare of the tribes was concerned, but rarely seen.

Did the Boolys have a son? A major? Or a colonel? Yes, Kattabi thought they did, *if* the couple were who they said they were.

Gunmaker, who seemed all too capable of reading his commanding officer's mind, extended a hand. "The major gave me this, sir."

Kattabi took the box, noticed it was heavy, and popped the lid. There was no mistaking the starburst, the Confederate holo seal, or the weight of real gold.

A Presidential Medal of Valor. The highest award the Confederacy could bestow. The general cleared his throat. "Thank you, Sergeant. Show our guests in."

The better part of three minutes passed before Kattabi heard boots scrape on gravel. A pair of Naa warriors, both festooned with weapons, entered and took a long look around. One of them nodded and spoke into a throat mike.

The woman entered first. She had lived long and hard. But beauty could still be seen in her high cheekbones, the clear gray eyes, and the shape of her mouth.

She wore a long, fur-lined cloak, open to reveal a cross-draw holster, and a well-cut pair of trousers. Black high-topped boots completed the outfit.

Kattabi felt himself weighed, analyzed, and dissected all within the space of a few moments. Her smile lit up the room. "General Kattabi . . . it's a pleasure to meet you. My name's Chrobuck."

Kattabi took her hand, found it was warm, and felt like a school boy at a dance. There was something regal about the woman, as if she were special, and well aware of it. "The pleasure is mine, ma'am. Or should I say *Captain*?"

Chrobuck laughed. The sound had a girlish quality. "That was in another lifetime, General. Perhaps you know our son? Colonel Bill Booly?"

"I know *of* him . . . but never had the pleasure."

The woman appeared disappointed. "No matter. . . . Allow me to introduce my husband. Bill, the general is directly in front of you."

William Booly II smiled as his wife stepped out of the way. Dark hollows occupied the places where his eyes should have been. One had been lost, replaced, and lost again. Disease had claimed the second, leaving the old man blind.

Or was he? The ex-legionnaire seemed to know where things were. He held out his hand. "You have one helluva rep, General—the kind based on merit."

Kattabi took the other man's hand and returned the medal. "Quite a calling card, Major—there aren't a whole lot of those floating around."

Booly smiled, slipped the box into a pocket, and gestured toward the fire. "Mind if I sit? My legs aren't what they used to be."

A legionnaire fetched a stool while Chrobuck removed her husband's riding cloak and draped it in front of the fire. Something about the way she did it spoke volumes and made Kattabi envious. Sacrifices had been made to reach his present position—*lots* of them—and the possibility of a family had been the first.

The cloak steamed, and Booly accepted a cup of tea. He took a tentative sip and turned empty eye sockets toward his host. "I'm sorry about the fort, General—but you'll win it back."

Kattabi was quick to seize the opening. "I'm glad to hear

it. Any sort of information would be most welcome.''

The older man nodded. "Like my father, and my grandfather before him, I hold the position 'Chief of Chiefs.' It's largely ceremonial, since the other Chiefs rarely do anything I suggest, but there are some perks, including a rather colorful outfit and a network of spies.

"Most of the spies stay busy watching each other, but some live in Naa Town, and a few work in the fort itself.''

Kattabi forgot that the man in front of him was blind and nodded his understanding. The Naa had been spying on the Legion since first landing, and, in spite of the endless efforts to weed them out, always managed to infiltrate one or two agents into the fort itself.

"That being the case," Booly continued, "I can provide you with the following facts: The mutiny, which may or may not have been coordinated with events elsewhere, occurred at approximately 1000 hours, day before yesterday, and was led by a quad named DeVane.''

Kattabi scowled, tried to remember a borg named DeVane, and came up empty. "I was afraid of something like that. Please continue.''

Booly coughed and took another sip of tea. "The revolt took place during the morning inspection. The person who conceived the plan was smart, *very* smart, since that's the time when most of the officers and noncoms all gather in the same place.''

Kattabi could imagine the scene. Officers and noncoms to the front, backed by rank after rank of legionnaires. And there, behind the crisp white kepis, the Trooper IIIs, the Trooper IIs, and the tank-sized quads.

Kattabi looked for the other man's eyes and saw nothing but scar tissue. "So, what happened then?''

Booly grimaced. "Nothing good. Stohl gave a speech, started to inspect the troops, and they took him prisoner. A scuffle ensued, loyal troops came to the general's assistance, and DeVane opened fire.

"That was pretty much it, except for the plan to capture you and secure the rest of the planet.''

"And it would have worked," Kattabi said softly, "if it weren't for my scouts."

"*And* your willingness to listen," Chrobuck added firmly.

Kattabi was about to demur when Gunmaker appeared at his side. "Yes, Sergeant?"

"Com call for you, sir. A technician named Acosta."

Kattabi allowed his eyebrows to rise. "From the fort?"

The Naa was as expressionless as always. "Yes, sir, but there's more."

The general frowned. "Don't toy with me, Gunmaker. Where is he?"

The scout broke into a rare grin. His teeth were white. "*She* locked herself inside DeVane's cargo bay. The com gear belongs to him."

The Boolys laughed, and Kattabi shook his head. "Well, I'll be damned."

"Yes, sir," the frequently insubordinate scout agreed. "You probably will."

Acosta smiled grimly as the lights flickered and came back on. DeVane was testing to see how far her control extended—and searching for the means to reassert himself.

She glanced around. There were six control panels in the bay, each protected by a door. She had opened every one of them, scanned the handheld technical interface, and used the onboard tool kit to make some modifications. Nobody was going to open the door, not without shutting DeVane down, or cutting their way in. A real possibility *if* DeVane allowed them to do it.

So, while the technician couldn't control the quad, she could monitor his actions, and use his com gear. Did *he* know that? Acosta wasn't sure but didn't really care. Whatever was, was.

The deck swayed and pushed against the legionnaire's boots. The quad was on his feet! The technician grabbed a handhold as the deck shimmied from side to side. The bastard was trying to kill her! To bash her brains out against a bulkhead!

Acosta hung on for dear life as the deck tilted, bucked, and swayed. Tools flew every which way, and the technician swore as one hit the bulkhead inches from her face.

Finally, after what seemed like an hour but was no more than a minute, DeVane broke it off. His voice was hopeful. It boomed over the intercom. "Acosta? Are you there?"

The cables that connected the vid cams to the cyborg's com system had been cut. Should she answer, and run the risk of another round of cybernetic calisthenics? Or remain silent, and invite an attack on the door?

The legionnaire sat down, strapped herself in, and offered a response. "Yeah, I'm here, shit-for-brains, living in your guts. What's up?"

The quad went crazy. Legionnaires looked on in open-mouthed wonder as the machine danced around the bay, bellowed obscenities, and crashed into walls.

Finally, after Acosta had tossed what remained of her breakfast, the quad calmed down.

Careful lest the borg catch her off guard, Acosta scurried around the bay, stored the tools, and took her seat. That's when she made the call.

It took the technician the better part of ten minutes to talk her way past a com tech, a sergeant, and get Kattabi on the horn. He was calm but suspicious. "Dog-One here . . . go."

Acosta didn't have a call sign, so she made one up. "Roger, Dog. This is Flea . . . I could use your help."

Kattabi laughed. "We're all ears, Flea—how 'bout a sit rep?"

The ensuing conversation lasted for the better part of fifteen minutes and was hampered by the fact that there was no way to ensure security.

So, in spite of the fact that Acosta could confirm that a mutiny had taken place, there was no real resolution. Neither of them liked it, but the next moved belonged to DeVane, and he was crazy.

The cell, which was the most uncomfortable his jailers had been able to find, still smelled like the previous occupant, a thief named "Lucky" Luko, who really was lucky, and had been released to make room for officers and loyalist scum.

Though a large man, General Stohl seemed smaller now, as if the loss of authority had left his skin only half full.

Still stunned by the hand fate had dealt him, Stohl sat with his head bowed, trying to collect his thoughts. The beatings had been painful, but the humiliation hurt most of all. How could they? Didn't they realize who he was? The Legion's most senior officer. The leader of . . .

A door slammed. The general stood and backed into a corner. The worst part of the beatings was not knowing when they would occur. The lack of surety caused fear—something the officer had rarely experienced.

A man laughed, an old-fashioned key rattled in the lock, and the door squealed open. Stohl squinted into the handheld light. Private Zedillo hated officers—especially generals. His voice was sarcastic. "Ooops! Sorry, General, sir. I didn't know you were in a meeting. My apologies."

Poor though it was, this example of wit was still sufficient to summon a chorus of guffaws from the hallway. Stohl sank into the corner and tried to shield his swollen face.

Zedillo, who had taken beatings nearly every day of his rather truncated childhood, shook his head in disgust. "Get a grip, General—what will your officers think? Besides, we're gonna have a parade—and *you* get to lead it! Nifty, huh?"

Zedillo turned. "O'Dell! Get your ass in here! The general needs a hand."

Stohl whimpered as the mutineers dragged him out of the cell and down the hallway. Other officers, confined to cells on either side of the corridor, watched in silence.

One of Algeron's supershort nights passed into day as a line of artillery shells marched down off a low-lying hill, exploded with the same ruthless efficiency as the computer that controlled them, and hurled fountains of dirt high into the air.

Kattabi waited for the barrage to end, strolled out of the CP, and nodded to a sentry. "How's it goin', Hays? Better keep your head down. Those idiots might get lucky."

Hays laughed, just as she was supposed to, and told Corporal Laskin. He told Sergeant Mutu—and the entire battalion had the story within the hour.

"Yup," everyone agreed, "there ain't nothin' that bothers the old man, 'cept cold tea, and stupid orders."

None of which would have surprised Kattabi, who knew that the troops took a considerable amount of comfort from such anecdotes, and tried to keep them happy.

Major Kitty Kirby frowned as her boss wriggled up next to her, produced his binoculars, and scanned the distant fort. She considered Kattabi's predilection for leading from the front to be admirable, but somewhat misguided, given how important he was. She couldn't say that, however, not to his face, so she made room instead. "Welcome to the Hotel Algeron, General. Where the days are short, the nights are cold, and the accommodations suck."

Kattabi's response was lost as the fort's well-sited artillery fired another mission. The shells soared over the officers' heads, landed half a mile to the rear, and made the ground shake. The General lowered his glasses. He yelled to be heard. "So, Kitty, what do you think?"

Kirby was as different from her commanding officer as night is from day. She had been born into a prosperous merchant family, attended the academy, and graduated with honors. But, unlike some of her peers, she respected officers like Kattabi. "I think they're letting the computers run the show. This latest barrage lacks the kind of finesse that a true dyed-in-the-wool arty officer would toss in. Stuff like backtracking, leapfrogging, and just plain guessing."

Kattabi grinned. "My thoughts exactly. Assuming the red legs survived, they're locked in a cell. Some noncom is calling the shots and doing it by the book. And why not? They have intel from our spy sats and know we won't fire on them. Not with all those prisoners . . . not if we can avoid it. How 'bout deserters? Have you seen any more?"

Kirby nodded. "Yes, sir. Twenty of them went over the wall about an hour ago. Half were killed in the minefield, sentries nailed two of them, and the rest made it to safety. That's more than forty so far. We can thank DeVane for that. He's crazy, and the muties know it."

Kattabi shrugged. "He's got problems . . . but so have we."
Kirby nodded. "Yes, sir."

The voice belonged to com tech Salan. Dog-Six to Dog-One. Over.''

Kattabi touched his ear and spoke into the wire-thin boom mike. ''Dog-One . . . go.''

''We have the Navy on a long-haul push. One, maybe two ships, ETA thirty-six hours standard. Over.''

''Contact? Over.''

''Negative, sir. Not with field stuff. The muties could reach 'em though. Over.''

''Any reason to think they have? Over.''

''No, sir. Over.''

''Thanks, Six. Keep me advised. Over.''

A shell exploded in midair. Both officers kissed dirt as the device hurled bomblets in every direction. The explosions rippled along the side of a hill. Two legionnaires were killed and a third was wounded. He screamed, grabbed his thigh, and started to swear. A medic arrived, slapped a self-sealing dressing on the wound, and radioed for a stretcher.

Kattabi spit dirt. ''They're getting better.''

Kirby shrugged. ''Practice makes perfect.''

The general turned to the fort. ''DeVane needs to win . . . and he needs to do it *now*. Those ships could be loaded with mutineers—or packed with loyal troops. He's hoping for the former, but scared of the latter. Pass the word. . . . When the barrage lifts, DeVane will attack.''

Kirby questioned the certainty of Kattabi's prediction, wondered if something less precise might be in order, but kept her opinions to herself.

Heavily armed troops and cyborgs packed the immense parade ground. Orders were shouted as infantry units assembled, servos whined as quads picked their way through the crowd, and radio traffic crackled as Trooper IIs and IIIs took their assigned positions.

Though reasonably well organized, the revolution lacked the precision officers would have insisted on. That bothered some of the troops, who knew Kattabi was good and didn't want to die.

One level below, DeVane ran one last check on his systems,

tried to ignore the unwanted passenger, and lumbered up the ramp.

The cyborg knew Kattabi could keep the mutineers bottled up inside the fort if that's what he chose to do, but didn't think he would. Partly because he was an ornery old bastard, and partly because he hoped to settle the matter before the Navy arrived, for the same reasons that DeVane did.

A victory would enhance the cyborg's status if the vessels were friendly and strengthen his position at the bargaining table if it happened that they weren't. He paused at the top of the ramp.

"Let's get this show on the road. Strap the general into position, open the gates, and let's kick some ass."

Stohl had been sitting for about an hour by then, arms around his knees, ordering God to save him.

The officer struggled as the guards jerked him to his feet. They half carried, half dragged the prisoner across the parade ground. A metal cross had been welded to the front of De-Vane's quad. They wrestled Stohl into position, tied his arms to the crosspieces, and secured his feet to an eyebolt.

"There," DeVane said callously. "Officers should lead from the front—don't you agree? Hey! This would be an excellent time to consider the nature of your relationship with Kattabi. How much shit did you heap on the poor bastard, anyhow? Enough to piss him off? What goes around comes around. Should be interesting." Stohl soiled himself and started to gibber.

A cheer went up, the gates opened, and DeVane marched out.

Kattabi, his elbows resting on the quickly melting snow, watched the quad appear. Not just *any* quad, but one with monster features, and a cross welded to its bow. Kattabi felt a sudden emptiness in the pit of his stomach.

The officer increased the magnification, and the heretofore unrecognizable blob leapt into focus. There was no mistaking the staring eyes, the contorted face, or the horribly bared teeth. It was Stohl.

Kattabi felt an irrational surge of anger. Damn the miserable sonofabitch to hell! Damn him for allowing such a thing to happen, damn him for being alive, and damn him for putting *me* in this position!

Kirby nudged his arm. "The man on the cross . . . Did you see who it is?"

Kattabi answered without lowering his binoculars. "Yeah, he's hard to miss."

"So what should we do?"

The words seemed to hang there as Kattabi considered his options. One solution was to ignore Stohl, attack, and let the chips fall where they may.

But what if their positions were reversed? What if it were *he* on the cross? Or an officer that he liked and respected? What then?

And what about the troops? How would they view Stohl's death? As an understandable sacrifice? Or the act of a commander so ruthless he couldn't be trusted?

Surely some of them felt sympathy for the muties, would *be* muties if given the chance, and might turn on him.

There was movement in front of DeVane's quad. Nothing much, but strange nonetheless. Kattabi raised a hand. "Hold . . . what's going on out there? Do we have an observer that far forward?"

Kirby got ready to say no, looked through her glasses, and saw riders emerge from a gully. There were two of them, both humans. One led the other. Major Booly and Connie Chrobuck! The older woman turned, met Kirby's gaze, and smiled. The salute was parade-ground perfect. Her husband, face toward the enemy, sat straight and tall.

DeVane spotted the interlopers, swung his Gatling gun in their direction, and prepared to fire.

Kattabi saw the movement and yelled into his mike. "What the hell are they doing? Get them out of there!"

Kirby shook her head sadly. "Too late for that, sir. DeVane has a lock."

Kattabi knew his XO was correct, swore as Chrobuck drew the long-barreled pistol, and knew what she would do. They had been officers themselves, understood his dilemma, and were determined to help.

Chrobuck took one last look at her husband, at the towers of Algeron, and the planet she called home. There was time to inhale the cold, clean air, marvel at what life had given, and say good-bye to her son.

The pistol shots were flat and dull. Stohl jerked under the impact, fell forward, and hung from his wrists. The battle had started.

The Gatling gun opened fire. A hail of metal tore the riders and their mounts to bloody shreds. Cheered by DeVane's victory, and encouraged by their noncoms, the mutineers continued to advance.

A lump formed in Kattabi's throat. He turned to Kirby. "Kill the bastards. Kill every damned one of them."

Kirby nodded, gave the necessary orders, and watched her armor move out onto the killing ground. Static roared as both sides initiated electronic countermeasures, energy cannons burped coherent light, and missiles flashed from launcher to target.

A quad exploded, a Trooper II somersaulted through the air, and one of the personnel carriers veered into a ravine. Legionnaires piled out, found some cover, and set their mortars.

The fight was far from one-sided, however, as DeVane led his troops forward, killed a Trooper III, and massacred its analogs. Artillery, firing from within the fort, dropped a curtain of steel behind the loyalist forces.

Kattabi watched the bloodshed and knew the terrible truth: No matter who won the battle . . . the Legion would lose.

It was warm within the cyborg's metal belly, *very* warm, and Acosta wiped the sweat off her brow. DeVane had cut the air-conditioning half an hour before. The heat had slowed her work and forced the legionnaire to rest.

She braced herself against the cyborg's movement and watched the monitors above her head. Naa Town passed to either side, and riders appeared ahead. One of them fired a pistol. Both ceased to exist as the Gatling gun growled and the hull shook.

The brutality of the action was like a bucket of cold water.

The technician came off the bench, grabbed the power drill, and resumed her work.

The motor produced a high-speed whine as the bit chewed its way down through quarter-inch steel plate. The metal was thin compared to the external armor, but thick enough for her.

Acosta struggled to keep her balance as silver shavings curled up and away from the fourth hole. The bit surged as it broke through into the space beyond. Fifty-caliber slugs hammered the hull and made it ring.

The battle was under way, the technician *knew* that, but she couldn't take the time to look. She was close, *extremely* close, and seconds were critical.

Acosta released the drill, fumbled for the saw, and got a grip on the handle. "All I gotta do is connect the dots," she thought to DeVane, "and *your* ass is mine."

The saw screamed as the blade ate through metal. It was sharp, and the cut went quickly. The technician hit hole number two, turned the corner, and went for three. She bit her lip. Would DeVane notice? And what would happen if he did? There was no way to tell.

The blade entered hole number three and turned toward four. That's when the saw nicked the protective mesh that protected the cyborg's brain, an alarm went off, and DeVane took notice. He fired on a missile battery and spoke through internal speakers at the same time.

"Okay, Acosta. You win. Drop the ramp and go."

The legionnaire laughed as she lifted the newly created panel out of its hole. She could see the brain box through a layer of metal lace. "Sure, you'd like that. How far would I get? Thirty feet? Dream on, asshole."

"No," DeVane insisted. "Go—I promise not to hurt you."

Acosta glanced at the monitors and heard a piece of shrapnel clang as it hit the hull. She wouldn't get very far even he *did* honor his promise. The technician felt for the drill and found it.

"Tell you what, shit-for-brains. . . . *If* you hold your fire, and *if* your friends do likewise, I'll cut you some slack. Keep on fighting, and I'm gonna sink a drill bit into what's left of your brain. You have ten seconds to decide. Nine . . . eight . . . seven . . ."

"Okay!" the cyborg exclaimed. "You win. I'll issue the order."

Many of the mutineers were happy to quit, figuring any punishment they pulled would be better than life under DeVane, but some were less cooperative. They took some convincing. The news that the Navy ships were not only loyal to the Confederacy, but prepared to attack from orbit, settled any remaining doubts.

It was only then, *after* the cyborg had lowered his ramp, that Acosta remembered how cold it was, and remembered her pants. They were dry by that time—and the smell didn't matter at all.

10

To win without risk is to triumph without glory.

Pierre Corneille
The Cid
Standard year circa 1636

Planet Earth, Independent World Government

Colonel Leon Harco was tired, *very* tired, but unable to sleep. That's why he rolled off the rumpled cot, ran water into the storeroom's deep sink, and took a sponge bath. Then, wearing a fresh new uniform, he emerged to prowl the floor.

More than two weeks had passed since the revolt. The Global Operations Center hummed to the never-ending flow of reports, requests, and orders. People nodded or in some cases saluted, but kept their distance. They knew his moods.

Harco paused to consider the gigantic globe. The holo seemed to shimmer as it turned. A less conservative man might have been satisfied with the territory under his control: Most of North America, Europe, and Asia were red.

But all Harco saw were islands of blue, chunks of territory still identified by ancient names like Mongolia, Ethiopia, and a large part of Brazil. These were the places where resistance had grown and taken root. Partly because of the terrain, and partly because of the people, many of whom still knew how to survive beyond the limits of their cities.

Some of the so-called freedom fighters were civilians, like those in Asia, distant descendants of the Khan's mighty hordes. Others were soldiers, like the 6th Marine Brigade stationed near Teresina, Brazil, or the 13th DBLE in Djibouti, East Africa.

Governor Pardo refused to take them seriously and liked to emphasize how isolated they were. Harco perceived things differently. He saw each blotch of blue as a proclamation of weakness, a magnet to which resources would inevitably be drawn, a cancer that threatened the entire organism.

That being the case, the officer continued to plead for the resources required to finish the job but found himself in line behind the politicians who wanted troops for their municipalities, corporate executives bent on financial conquest, and his own voracious chain of command.

Some top-notch officers had aligned themselves with the revolt, but a disturbing number remained loyal to the former government. That forced him to take trash like Matthew Pardo.

The very thought of the manner in which his executive officer had murdered the cadet made his blood boil. How could they succeed and build trust so long as such acts of barbarism were tolerated?

There was nothing he could do about it so long as Governor Pardo supported her son and the cabal supported her. Much though the soldier hated to admit it, he had underestimated the politicians and been used by them.

Harco still had a considerable amount of power, however, especially in light of the fact that the Legion was loyal to *him*, or more accurately to *itself*, just as its motto said.

"Colonel Harco?" The voice was female. He turned.

"Yes?"

The corporal looked smart in her perfectly pressed khaki uniform. "The African operation, sir. You wished to observe."

Harco nodded. "Thank you, Corporal. Lead the way."

The legionnaire wound her way across the floor, and the officer followed. Though unable to marshal the resources necessary to wipe Fort Mosby off the face of the planet, Harco had authorized a force-three raid. If successful, the attack would test the loyalist defenses, keep the bastards off balance, and discourage those who wanted to join. And who knew? A success might attract more resources.

Reports that Fort Mosby had fallen were false. The reason was clear, to Harco if no one else. Booly and he had been members of the same class, had cocaptained the rowing team, and had been posted to a godforsaken rim world. A crudball named Drang, where they had battled the frogs and every form of jungle rot known to man.

The simple fact was that Harco *knew* Booly and knew what the other man could do. Booly wanted the fort to stand, so it did. General Loy was laughing in his grave.

Perhaps the recruiters should have approached the other officer and tried to bring him over, not that they would have succeeded. Booly was too straight for that, too willing to buy the Confederate lies, while the Legion continued to disintegrate.

The corporal took a turn, and Harco followed. The GOC was still under construction for all practical purposes. Wherever the officer looked he saw boxes of equipment, reels of cable, and hard-working droids.

The noncom paused before a heavily secured door, looked into a scanner, and waited while the device lased her retinas. Harco did likewise. The door whined open. A lieutenant was waiting to greet them. Hair hung over his collar, there was a food stain on the front of his shirt, and a paunch hid his belt buckle. He greeted Harco with a hearty "Hi ya!" followed by a wink and a nod.

Harco sighed. The planetary militia came under Governor Pardo, and, in an effort to limit the extent of his power, the politician had been careful to keep it that way. He could chew on the officer all day and it wouldn't make the slightest bit of difference. The corporal intervened. "Right this way, sir. The room needs some work . . . but the gear works fine."

Harco followed the noncom into a dimly lit room. Racks of equipment lined one wall, cables converged on an oversized black chair, and test patterns flickered across overhead screens.

A businesslike tech appeared and pointed toward the chair. "Have a seat, Colonel. The mission has started. Assault Team Victor is on the way."

Harco sat in the chair and allowed them to strap him in. A helmet was lowered onto his head, a thirty-second refresher course played on the inside surface of the faceplate, and the tech spoke over the intercom.

"There are thirty-three aircraft, sir. Twelve transports and twenty-one fighters. No oppo yet, but psyops estimates that half the Navy are loyalist sympathizers—which means they might come out to play. You have full scan with command override. Questions?"

"Just two," Harco replied. "Who's in command? And do they know I'm along?"

"The airdales are under the command of Squadron Leader Beason, sir. Companies A, B and D were supplied by the 5th RMP under the overall command of Lieutenant Colonel Leslie Lo. Both officers were informed of the ride."

Harco nodded, remembered the helmet, and said, "Thank you." The ability to "see" what his line troops saw was a tool that he'd hate to go without. Some commanders "rode" their troops too often, however—a habit that destroyed trust, sapped initiative, and bred timidity. Even worse was the sort of officer who conducted observations in secret—leaving his or her subordinates to wonder when and if they were under surveillance.

Harco hadn't met Beason, but Lo was one of the best. He didn't envy her assignment, however. Booly would have plenty of warning, and his troops would be ready.

The visor came to life; Harco found himself flying a transport and listening to a dirty joke. It was dark beyond the glow of the instrument panel. His chair shuddered slightly as the aircraft hit some chop. The combat team was thirty minutes out and closing fast.

The punch line arrived. Harco laughed, and his worries melted away. *This* was his, *this* made sense, *this* was pure.

The sun had yet to rise over the Gulf of Aden, but a long, pink line marked the horizon, and the direction from which the attack would come. Straight out of the sun—an old trick that wouldn't provide much of an advantage but was still worth a try.

The view to the north looked across the avenue Maréchal Foch to more blue water.

The Plage de la Siesta curved to the south.

Booly, who usually began his day with a stroll along the battlements, was careful to do so now. He could feel the legionnaires watching, gauging the set of his shoulders, passing the word to their friends: "Ya shoulda seen him! Like a pimp on a stroll . . . Not jumpy like some I could mention."

Booly paused for a moment. The morning air carried a hint of brine, not to mention Djibouti's ever present stench. Most of the city had been evacuated the better part of a week before. Captain Kara had taken charge of that and done an excellent job. The mayor of Djibouti was an elderly man named Makonen. He liked to talk and made an interesting contrast to the quiet, nearly morose legionnaire. Not that it mattered. The civilians were as safe as Booly could make them—and that was the important thing.

Booly allowed his arms to rest on the top of the wall. The days were longer, but Djibouti was not that much different from the village where he had been born and his parents still lived. They had appeared to him in a dream the night before. His mother spoke slowly, as if trying to communicate from a long way off, but it didn't work. The words were impossible to understand.

Still, there was no mistaking the love in her eyes, or the way that his father waved. The whole thing left Booly feeling strange—as if part of him were missing. He pushed the emotion away.

He heard a footfall and turned. Captain Winters nodded as she topped the stairs. The full combat rig made her look larger than she really was. In spite of the fact that Major Judd had emerged from the mutiny unscathed, he wasn't very effective, and the operations officer had taken up the slack. Booly smiled. "Good morning, Captain. Should be a nice day."

Winters smiled cynically. "If you say so, sir. Personally, I kind of doubt it."

Booly laughed. "The muties will get their licks in, no doubt about that, but the fort will stand. Those transports can carry two, maybe three companies of troops, along with some Trooper IIs or IIIs. Not nearly enough to get the job done. *They* know it, and *we* know it."

Winters agreed. She nodded. "Sir. Yes, sir."

Booly glanced around. The nearest legionnaire was twenty feet away. "Which isn't to say that I wouldn't mind some help. . . . How 'bout the swabbies? Any sign of air cover?"

Winters shook her head. "No, sir. It seems like some of the vessels were taken and some weren't. Their entire chain of command is screwed up. And, just to make things worse, new ships arrive every day. Some remain loyal, some go over, and some run like hell. Two different captains claim to be in charge. Neither has agreed to help."

"Okay," Booly acknowledged, "stay on it. The SAMs will nail some of the bastards but not all of them."

A voice spoke through their earplugs. It belonged to Sergeant Ho. She was terse. The battle had already begun, so far as she and her staff were concerned. They could *see* the bastards on radar, *hear* the ECM, and *smell* their own sweat. The Situation Room was sealed against everything imaginable, including the fort's own hyperefficient air-conditioning system. Enjoyable during normal times—but a potential pipeline for chemical and biological agents.

"We have bandits three-three . . . fifteen minutes and closing. Two-one, repeat two-one fast movers. One-five on the deck, elevation four hundred feet, with six on top. Over."

Booly looked toward the east, gestured to the nearest sentries, and followed them down. "Roger that. Pass the word. Fire when the SAMs lock."

This is the moment, Booly thought to himself. This is the moment the rebel cadre would strike if any of them had survived. But nothing happened, nothing that wasn't *supposed* to happen, which was fine with Booly.

The initial part of Booly's plan was simple: launch his SAMs, destroy as many enemy aircraft he could, and go to ground.

In spite of its somewhat anachronistic appearance, Fort

Mosby had been designed to withstand a full-scale orbital bombardment by the alien Hudatha. That being the case, the structure had a theoretical rating of T-1 . . . which meant the center of the complex could withstand a direct hit from a tactical nuke.

Of course the muties wouldn't be dropping any nukes, not yet anyway, but Booly and his troops could expect to be on the receiving end of thousand-pound laser-guided smart bombs, air-to-surface missiles (ASMs), and subsurface torpedos (SSTs). None of which would be any fun.

The klaxon went off as Booly checked one more time. "One-One to One-Three. Anything from on high? Over."

Winters checked the last legionnaire through the northernmost door. "Negative, One-One. Over."

Booly swore off-mike, heard SAMs roar into the air, and saw contrails arc across the sky. The launchers were up to fifty miles away—all linked by radio *and* subterranean cable.

The officer knew that the devices had lowered themselves into their underground bays by now. Once they were below the surface, blastproof doors would protect them from attack, and, given the fact that their robotic radars were not only small but airborne, they'd be difficult if not impossible to target and hit.

"Sir! Over here!"

Ex-corporal and now Sergeant Fykes had assigned himself to his commanding officer's staff, where he had assumed responsibility for Booly's personal security. He stood in an open hatch.

Booly took one last look around, slid past the foot-thick door, and heard it thud into place.

The officer's security detail consisted of Fykes plus two of Nightslip's scouts. The Naa were heavily armed and extremely alert. Fearing another mutiny, the noncom had requested a full squad. Booly had refused on the grounds that six guards plus a noncom was not only a waste of precious manpower but more than a little unseemly.

Fykes knew the assault force was close and took issue with the way that Booly continued to risk himself. "'Bout time, sir. No sense getting your ass blown off this early in the battle.''

The Naa fought to conceal their grins. Booly was about to take Fykes down a notch when a satellite-guided missile hit the center of the parade ground. The explosion shook the walls. The first blow had been struck.

The *Gladiator*'s bridge looked neat and orderly, even if some of the bloodstains had proven difficult to remove.

Naval Captain Angie Tyspin was furious. Rear Admiral Nathan Pratt, with the emphasis on ''Rear,'' had dropped out of hyper six hours before, was still more than twelve hours out, and claimed to be in command. Hard, angular lines defined the shape of his face, and the expression was venomous. The holo shivered, then snapped into focus. ''While your desire to support loyalist forces is commendable, Captain, it may or may not be in line with overall strategy.''

''And which strategy would that be?'' Tyspin demanded. ''There *is* no frigging strategy! Half the ships in orbit are controlled by mutineers, and my so-called peers spend most of their time squabbling over who has precedence. The people on the ground need our help, and they need it *now*. The rebels control most of the planet—why hand over the rest?''

Pratt leaned so far forward that his eyes seemed to fill the holo tank. ''You've been under a considerable strain, Captain, which is the only reason that I choose to ignore the tone of your comments *and* the absence of military courtesy. Here are my orders. Ignore them at your peril. You will take *all* necessary steps to preserve your vessel. You will use your fighters to protect your ship and for no other purpose. I hope I made myself clear. Questions?''

Tyspin struggled to control her voice. ''Sir! Yes, sir! One question, sir!''

Pratt allowed himself to lean back. Dominance had been established. He could afford to indulge her. ''Yes? And what would that be?''

Tyspin smiled grimly. ''Were you *born* an asshole? Or did you take classes?''

The admiral's eyeballs bulged, his mouth opened, and he

sucked air. His comments, whatever they might have been, were lost when Tyspin terminated the transmission.

Chief Gryco shook his head sadly. "He's gonna be pissed, Captain. *Real* pissed."

"Yeah," Tyspin replied, already sorry for what she'd done. "I think you're right. That last part was over the line. *Way* over the line."

"So, what are you going to do?" Lieutenant Rawlings asked, her eyes big and round.

Tyspin stood and smiled. "You heard the admiral, Lieutenant. I have orders to protect the ship. What if one of those mutie missiles goes haywire and heads into space? The ship would be in danger."

Gryco shook his head. "Beggin' your pardon, ma'am, but that's the lamest excuse I ever heard. Pratt will use your head for a paperweight."

"Maybe," Tyspin admitted, "but I really don't have much choice, do I?"

The petty officer was silent for a moment and shook his head. "No, ma'am. I guess you don't."

"Right," Tyspin said crisply. "Notify the flight deck. I want six Daggers ten from now. The rest will remain with the ship."

Rawlings came to attention. "Ma'am! The lieutenant is flight-ready and Dagger-rated. Request permission to join."

Tyspin eyed the officer and shook her head. "Sorry, Rawlings, permission denied. Pratt may not understand the full extent of the situation . . . but he's right about one thing: The *Gladiator* comes first. You're the only watch officer I have left. Keep her safe till I get back."

Tyspin left the bridge, and Rawlings watched her go. "She's one of a kind, Chief."

"Yes, ma'am," Gryco agreed. "She sure as hell is."

Harco saw the faint blur of the African coastline, heard the tone, and felt his chair tilt to the right. The pilot was calm but grim. "Missile lock. Fire chaff—fire flares."

The onboard computer "heard" the commands and followed orders. The copilot verified that the countermeasures had been launched and bit his lip. The transport was large and difficult to maneuver. The tone warbled as the pilot jinked right, left, and right again.

Harco started to speak, realized it wouldn't do any good, and saw the world explode. At least one missile had penetrated the defensive measures and struck its target. The transport ceased to exist—as did an entire platoon of troops.

The officer swore a long series of oaths as the VR computer automatically dumped his virtual body into a second cockpit. The name "Jameson, Lt. j.g." appeared at the bottom of the frame.

The pilot flew by wire, "thought" the plane where she wanted it to go, and used her hands to "play" the cockpit. The drumsticks clicked, banged, and thudded off the canopy, the instrument panel, and the seat she sat on. Was she aware of his presence, and determined to ignore him? Or simply out of her mind?

Though not a pilot himself, Harco knew there were rules about what pilots could and couldn't do in the cockpit, and wondered where the sticks came in. *If* they came in.

Incensed by the pilot's lack of professionalism, and prepared to give the youngster a piece of his mind, Harco opened his mouth. He never got to speak.

A tone warbled, Jameson gave a war whoop, and the plane flipped onto its back. There was no way to tell whether the officer had a reason for flying that way or simply wanted to.

Harco, still strapped into his chair, felt his feet flip over his head. A stylus fell out of his pocket and clattered to the floor.

The infantry officer felt the chair jerk, knew air-to-surface missiles had been launched, and heard Jameson's casual drawl. "Blue Six to Blue Leader. Feet dry . . . enemy engaged. Over."

"That's a roger, Blue Six. You are green for target one-niner-four. Do your shit. Over."

The Lance flipped right side up, shuddered in response to a near miss, and jerked as two additional flights of ASMs raced toward a preselected target. The sticks continued to pound out their rhythm.

Harco forced himself to think, to switch himself away, to "ride" someone else.

He was a platoon leader this time. The hard metal seat slammed into the base of his spine as the transport hit the bottom of an air pocket and lurched forward. The voice was calm and measured. "We are five to dirt. Passengers can collect their baggage on carousel six. Lock and load."

Harco jumped again. The fort passed below. A two-thousand-pound bomb exploded on the northern scarp. Dirt and rock flew into the air. White paint turned black, but the heavily reinforced walls continued to hold.

The officer jumped, found himself aboard one of the Trooper IIIs and watched his heavily armed analogs fly, wriggle, and roll away. Something shoved from behind. The cyborg fell, hit, and rolled.

The borg climbed to his feet and turned toward the sound of another explosion. Flames belched from the recently emptied transport. A crew person staggered out through a hatch and collapsed on the ground. Her flight suit was on fire. She lay without moving.

The cyborg turned his back, spotted what looked like a mobile radar platform, and fired a shoulder mounted missile. The target exploded. Assault Team Victor was on the ground.

Booly would have preferred to be up on the walls, or out with the troops, but couldn't afford the luxury. Not with half a brigade of still questionable troops under his command.

No, like it or not, the Sit Room was the right place to be. Thanks to the advance work carried out by Sergeant Ho and her staff, he had plenty of intel. Nearly *too* much.

It was difficult to keep up with the back and forth radio traffic, the video feeds provided by squad and platoon leaders, the eye-in-the-sky stuff beamed from unmanned drones, tiny robocrawlers and remote sensor packages stationed up to fifty miles out.

That being the case, a technician named Motke had been assigned to assist Booly by switching appropriate images to the bank of three monitors located in front of his command-style chair. Not the same as a full-blown VR rig . . . but good enough.

The initial stage of the attack had gone pretty much as Booly had expected it to. A wave of fighter-bombers came first, followed by the surviving transports, and landings in force at Hol Hol, Damerdjog, Ali-Sabieh, and Arta.

War involves tradeoffs, so while the assault team had multiple landing zones to defend, the strategy would allow them to deploy quickly and force the defenders into a complicated response.

The strategy seemed familiar somehow, as if Booly had seen it before. But where? The question continued to nag at Booly's mind as the officer sorted his forces into response teams and struggled to stay on top of the incoming intelligence.

Then he had it . . . Harco! A younger version of whom had successfully split a frog offensive into six separate elements, thereby enabling the planet's security detachment to fly from one fire base to the next and attack the phibs one pod at a time. "Divide and conquer" was one of the oldest military axioms around, and one of the best.

Not satisfied with running the Legion from North America, the traitorous sonofabitch was leading the raid himself! Talk about balls . . . Maybe they could nail the bastard and *really* deal the enemy a blow. Satisfied that he knew whom he was up against, Booly turned to the matter at hand.

Harco's forces had broken out of three different landing zones, picked up the old Dire Dawa railroad bed, and were on the move.

Captain Hawkins had orders to cut them off while Major Judd brought Delta company into action. If the XO could manage to flank the enemy, Hawkins would have a chance. But how likely was that, given the officer in question?

Booly watched from Captain Ny's point of view as her energy cannons burped coherent energy, converged on a Trooper II, and blew the cyborg in half. The camera shuddered as a missile hit the quadruped, then steadied. The muties hadn't put any quads on the ground, not so far, and that was good.

"Look," Motke said, momentarily forgetting to say "sir," as he pointed toward monitor three. "They're taking a run at battery one-sierra-echo."

The AA battery, which consisted of four 133mm SAM launchers and a Gatling gun, opened fire. It was located near Loyada. Booly saw four contrails and listened to the operator cheer on channel two. "Did you see that? We nailed the bastard!"

It was the last transmission he ever made. Chunks of mutie aircraft still cartwheeled out of the sky as three enemy fighters rolled and dived toward the ground. The bombs knew where to go and went there. The monitor snapped to black.

Booly swore and activated his mike. "One-One to One-Three . . . Where the hell is that air cover? We need it now! Over."

Given the fact that Winters had no control over the matter in question, she might have been angry or resentful. She sounded smug instead. "Roger that, One-One. Fast friendlies on the way—ETA one minute thirty seconds. Over."

Booly was speechless. Winters smiled.

The flight of six Daggers entered the stratosphere, shed heat from their specially designed skins, and bumped through the quickly warming air.

Tyspin checked her heads-up display (HUD), saw more red deltas than she cared to look at, but was grateful for the fact that they were still below. That was an advantage she was happy to have. The naval officer had targets, plenty of them, which meant they had her as well. Why no response, then? Were they blind?

A voice sounded in her helmet. It was confident, verging on smug. "Victor One to incoming Daggers . . . Welcome to the party. Over."

Tyspin marveled at her luck. The idiot assumed she was friendly! Not surprising, given the circle jerk up in orbit . . . but not very smart either. Her pilots followed as the naval officer rolled to starboard and dived towards the aircraft below. "Blue One to Victor One . . . Thanks for the hospitality."

Victor One watched the delta-shaped icons roll in behind his formation, heard a tone as the missile locked onto his plane, and realized his mistake. "Bandits at six o'clock! Break! Break! Break!"

Three pilots escaped, but two assimilated the order too slowly and paid with their lives. Their fighters exploded, tumbled out of the sky, and splashed into the Gulf of Aden.

Tyspin smiled grimly, switched to a secure frequency, and gave her orders. "Blue One to Blue flight . . . The muties have transports on the ground. Hit 'em hard."

A chorus of "Roger"'s echoed in her ears as the aerospace fighters started to make their runs. They came in over the Gulf of Tadjoura and went straight for the enemy.

Tyspin spotted one of the bulky aircraft, "thought" her ship to port, and removed the safeties from her guns.

"Watch your six, Blue Leader," a voice cautioned as Tyspin focused on the target. She saw the delta and fought the urge to abort the run. "Roger, Two . . . Keep the bastard off my tail."

The ground came up, blurred under the belly of the fighter, and disappeared to the rear. The transport had been warned of the danger and was four feet off the ground when Tyspin fired.

The 30mm cannon shells ripped through the transport's relatively thin skin and hit the power plant. The ship shuddered, sideslipped, and struck a civilian radio mast. The transport fell like a rock.

Tyspin heard a tone, fought the weight of the gees, and checked the HUD. The delta was right on her tail. The fighter vanished as Lieutenant Alvarez blew it out of the sky. "Thanks, Two."

"De nada, boss."

"Blue Leader to Blue flight . . . Form on me. Over."

Only three pilots answered the call. Her wingman brought her up to speed. "Blue Two to Blue One. Three went into the gulf . . . and Six ejected. I saw her chute. Over."

Tyspin swore under her breath. She had lost one, possibly two pilots, not to mention their planes. Maybe Pratt was right. Maybe she should have stayed in orbit. A new voice broke her train of thought. "Mosby Control to Blue One. Over."

The fact that the transmission had been encrypted and transmitted on her command channel implied that the *Gladiator* was in contact with loyalist ground forces. The response was automatic. "This is Blue One . . . Go. Over."

"We're *real* glad to see you, Blue One. That transport is toast. We have three columns of borg-reinforced infantry approaching the fort along the road from Hol Hol. Anything you can do? Over."

The voice didn't belong to a com tech. Tyspin felt sure of that. The commanding officer? Maybe. The naval officer glanced at the HUD, saw three deltas straight at her, and snapped a response. "Roger that, Mosby Control. Can you smoke the target?"

The reply was instantaneous. "Roger that. Arty on the way. Willey Pete (WP) ten from now."

Tyspin spoke as she nosed over. "Blue One to Four and Five. The bandits are yours. Over."

"Roger, One," Lieutenant Frank Norris answered grimly. "Over."

Tyspin didn't even have to look to know that Alvarez hung above and behind her starboard wing. The ground rushed to meet her, WP blossomed below, and she fired her rockets. Explosions winked red, tracers streaked past the canopy, and something hit the fuselage. Alarms sounded, fire blossomed, and the plane started to shake.

Harco had temporarily invested himself in a Trooper III. His chair lurched from side to side as the cyborg ran toward the fort. Blips appeared on the screen. The cyborg's computer tagged the incoming aircraft as hostile. Two shoulder-launched missiles were prepped and launched. They wobbled, achieved lock, and started to track.

Three rounds of WP dropped near the troops, detonated, and marked their position. Rockets exploded all around, cannon fire blew divots out of the ground, and someone started to scream.

That's when Major Vernon Judd, unarmed except for the pistol in his holster, scrambled up out of the concrete lined drainage ditch and waved his troops forward. "Vive la Legion!" He never looked back, never checked to see if his troops followed him, as he charged through the flying steel.

And Delta company *did* follow, screaming like banshees, firing from the hip. Some fell kicking in the dust, some spun as bullets turned them around, and the rest ran.

Already thinned by forces under the command of Captains Hawkins and Ny, and stunned by the attack from above, the muties broke and started to withdraw. They paused in and around a cluster of mud-brick shacks. Laundry flapped in surrender, a machine gun tore it to shreds, and muties fell back.

Alarmed now, and intent on preventing a full-scale rout, Harco searched for Lieutenant Colonel Lo, discovered that she'd been killed, and assumed command. The ability to jump from one officer to the next was a godsend. Harco gave a series of orders, called for air strikes, and monitored the withdrawal. Three LZs had been reduced to two, but both were secure, and sufficient for the number of people he had left.

Still, it took time to pull back, load the troops, and lift. Time and casualties, since the loyalist tube crews had coordinates for all of the remaining zones and fired mission after mission.

Harco swore as 155mm howitzer shells swept the second LZ, hit a pallet loaded with ammo, and marched out the other side. A transport, loaded with troops, wobbled but managed to lift.

There was one piece of good news, however, and that was the fact that the loyalist fighters had run low on fuel and had been forced into space. That left Harco's aircraft in charge of the sky, which was an advantage they used to attack the quads, suppress Booly's artillery fire, and protect the LZs.

Finally, after the last transport was safely out over the gulf, Harco pulled himself out.

His clothes were soaked with sweat, his jaw was clenched, and his fingers had a death grip on the chair.

The tech entered, started to say something, and Harco waved him off.

He waited for the numbers, not wanting to hear them, but knowing that he must. The preliminary report was even worse than he had feared. Fully fifty percent of Assault Team Victor was KIA, WIA, or MIA.

Was Pardo at fault, for withholding the resources he needed? Or was he to blame, for attempting too much? The answer seemed obvious. The burden was heavy.

• • •

Booly left the sit room the moment the muties cleared the coast. He summoned a Trooper II, climbed onto the cyborg's back, and strapped himself in. The helmet jack entered a panel provided for that purpose. "Take me to the LZ located near Hol Hol. Condition five—assault speed."

The cyborg said, "Sir, yes, sir," and started to jog. Booly could remember when the sideways, up-and-down motion had made him nauseous, but that was a long time ago, in what seemed like a different lifetime.

Fykes swore any number of colorful oaths, commandeered a scout car, and followed behind. How many muties had missed the bus? One? Ten? A hundred? Whatever the number, they were out there, and Booly, with his ass literally hanging in the breeze, made a prime target.

Hol Hol was a relatively small community located just southwest of Djibouti. Booly was struck by the random manner in which some streets had survived untouched while others were heavily damaged. Good luck, bad luck, all mixed together.

The cyborg turned to the left, circled a wrecked hover bus, and picked his way down a fire-blackened boulevard. One of the mutie fighters had crashed a half mile to the south, sliced through two rows of palm trees, and slammed into a trash filled fountain.

Booly could see the pilot as they passed, her helmet resting against the plane's canopy, blood dribbling from her mouth. He requested an aid team and gave them the location.

The colonial-era buildings started to thin after that, gradually giving way to pastel monstrosities, and a row of slovenly huts.

Booly bent his knees to absorb the shock, allowed the harness to take his weight, and tallied the cost.

There were muties, dead where the airborne guns found them, lying in a ditch.

And there, in the field just beyond, a line of shell craters, ringed by smoldering grass fires, and chunks of partially cooked meat. A pair of vultures, their stomachs already full, lurched into the air.

Then came a troop transport, guns threatening the sky, flames licking the hood. The driver's hands were on the wheel, but his head was missing. One of his? One of theirs? Booly couldn't tell. It hardly mattered.

The radio crackled with casualty reports, requests for assistance, and ECM-related static. An aid station had been established next to a protective antiaircraft battery. POWs stood with their hands on their heads while a VTOL fly form lowered itself to the ground. It blew grit into Booly's face as he freed himself from the harness and jumped to the ground.

Captain Hawkins appeared at his elbow. Blood oozed from the abrasion on the left side of her face. Her helmet was missing, and she looked concerned. "It's Major Judd, sir. He took a slug through the chest."

Booly listened as the leg officer led him into the aid station. "The major was something to see, sir. He took Delta company out of that ditch like the RMLE at Verdun! I never had much respect for him. Not till today."

Stretchers lined both sides of the tent. Judd was third back on the right side. IVs fed both arms, but he still looked pale. Booly glanced at a medic, and she shook her head. The executive officer was alive—but just barely. Booly knelt next to the officer and spoke his name. "Major Judd?"

The legionnaire opened his eyes, struggled to focus, and coughed. Blood spilled onto his chin. The words were little more than a whisper. "Sorry, Colonel, but I don't think I can stand."

Booly felt a lump form in his throat. "At ease, Major . . . and congratulations! You turned the tide."

Judd looked hopeful. "I did? Really?"

"Yes," Booly answered gently. "You won the battle."

Judd frowned and coughed. His eyes seemed to dim, and the words were barely audible. "Don't forget D Company, sir. They were a credit to the Legion."

Booly swallowed, knew Judd was gone, and closed his eyelids. "Yes . . . and so were you."

The officer stood and turned to find that a naval aviator was waiting to see him. She had green eyes and a plain, straightforward face. She held a helmet under her arm. A bloodstained battle dressing marked the place where something had torn through her flight suit as the ejection blew her free of the cockpit. Sergeant Fykes handled the introduction. "This is Captain Tyspin, sir. She flew one of the Daggers . . . and commands *Gladiator*."

Tyspin felt awkward about having witnessed Judd's death, but was glad that she had. Here was an officer who cared about the people under his command and deserved their respect. She could see it in his eyes. *Gray* eyes that were filled with intelligence and brightened as Fykes spoke.

"Captain Tyspin! We owe you a debt of gratitude. Hell, we owe you everything! Air support made all the difference. Medic! See to the captain's arm. . . . We'd be hamburger if it weren't for her."

Tyspin shucked the top half of the flight suit and sat while the medic cut the old dressing away, squirted some cream into the cut, and applied a self-sealing bandage. It seemed natural to tell Booly about the infighting among her peers, the problems with Admiral Pratt, and the trouble she was in.

The legionnaire responded by laying out the strategic situation and what he saw as the almost inevitable outcome. He shrugged. "We bought some time . . . but that's all. The muties will either return in force or whittle us down. There's no way to stop them, not without help from the Navy, and more of everything."

Tyspin was about to agree when someone cleared her throat. Both officers turned to find that Captain Winters had entered the tent. A civilian stood at her side. The man was dressed in a ball cap, plaid shirt, and khaki shorts. He could have passed for a tourist if it hadn't been for the shoulder holster and combat boots that he wore. Booly raised an eyebrow. "Yes?"

Winters produced her usual shit-eating grin. "I'd like you to meet Dr. Mark Benton, sir. He works for a company called Chien-Chu Enterprises."

"That's close," the oceanographer said agreeably, "though not entirely correct. I work for the Cynthia Harmon Center for Undersea Research, which gets the majority of its *funding* from Chien-Chu Enterprises, but what the hell? We certainly listen to what they say."

"It's a pleasure to meet you," Booly said, extending his hand. "What brings you to Djibouti?"

"*You* did," the scientist answered simply. "I've got a nuclear sub waiting off the coast. She's loaded with three hundred volunteers, weapons, and supplies. Where do you want them?"

11

Why should I feel lonely? Is not our planet in the Milky Way?

Henry David Thoreau
Walden
Standard year 1854

Somewhere beyond the Rim, the Confederacy of Sentient Beings

Jepp peered around the corner, confirmed that the passageway was clear, and consulted his data pad, or more accurately *Parvin's* data pad, since the seventy-year-old device still worked and the skeleton had no use for it.

Once the prospector had established a reasonably secure home, and moved Parvin's supplies to the new location, he redirected his attention.

The vessel was big—but *how* big? Who constructed the ship, and why? Where was it headed? This was the sort of knowledge that would enable him to escape.

The first step was to create a map—and that's where the data pad came in. By taking copious notes, and marking each intersection with a self-invented system of coordinates, the human had established a fairly good idea of the ship's layout. He entered the latest findings and used blue spray paint to write "C-43" on the steel bulkhead.

The Sheen mother ship, if that's what the vessel could properly be called, was shaped like a flava fruit, except that it had an enormous landing bay where the pit would have been, plus thousands of compartments instead of pulp. Jepp had counted forty-three circular corridors so far, all connected by radial passageways A through J.

Of course thousands of compartments remained locked, he'd been unable to establish communications with the robots, and he was no closer to getting off the ship than the day he arrived. But God helps those who help themselves—so the effort would continue.

The human felt the hairs on the back of his neck rise, drew the flechette thrower, and turned one hundred eighty degrees. The prospector felt as if someone or something had been watching him for days now. But there was no sign of anything, nor any place to hide. What did it mean? That the loneliness and isolation had affected his mind?

Or, and this was worse, that something really *had* monitored his activities, and could hide in plain sight?

Jepp closed the data pad one-handed. The feeling faded as he backed away. Because he was crazy? It seemed all too possible.

Horth watched his prey back away. There had been previous escapes, far too many of them, but such was the nature of the hunt. To press the attack was to risk the wrath of the shiny thing, which, if it was anything like the master's, could inflict a great deal of pain. Satisfying his hunger would have to wait.

Jepp turned and walked down the corridor. Hundreds of tiny epithelial cells sloughed off his skin, floated through the air, and sank to the deck. Horth was quick to follow.

The Thraki robot was different from the rest of the machines on the ship. It was unique, for one thing, having been constructed for the amusement of a single sentient, and imbued with what could only be described as "needs." Such as the need to associate itself with a biological entity.

There had been two pairings so far, one with a quadruped

that starved to death, and a second with an amoebalike ther-movore that refused to leave the comfort of the ship's heat stacks. There was a *new* prospect, however, a rather promising specimen that the robot planned to find.

Though relatively small when folded into a featureless two-foot cube, the Thraki machine could assume any of 106 mostly useless configurations, and perform a variety of tasks.

That being the case, the robot transformed itself into "ac-robot mode," swung out of the cross-ship cable run, changed to "magnetic wall-walker mode," and lowered itself to the deck.

The object of this exercise was a bulkhead-mounted data port, which, though not intended for use by Thraki machines, could be utilized by any being clever enough, or malleable enough, to create the necessary three-pronged fitting.

The Thraki machine possessed *all* the necessary capabilities and wasted no time plugging itself into the digital flood. Bil-lions upon billions of bits of information flowed through the ship's electronic nervous system every second.

Though safe within an eddy, the robot knew the current could carry it away, and into a filter. Or, and this would almost certainly be worse, the Hoon itself!

The trick was to stay at the periphery of the flow and sift for clues. Given that the Hoon and its servants had no interest in the kind of being the robot was looking for, they rarely mentioned them. Not unless they caused some sort of trouble.

Take the little two-legged hopper, for example. The Thraki machine happened to be on-line when the creature bounced around a corner and was crushed by a large maintenance droid.

Rather than make mention of the fact that an unauthorized and presumably alien life-form was hopping about the ship, the droid reported a sudden and unexplained "mess," and recommended that an appropriate unit be sent to mop it up.

So, by monitoring such communications, and scanning for patterns, the unit was able to "guess" where its quarry might be. It wasn't long before the robot intercepted reports regard-ing nonstandard bulkhead graphics and knew some sort of sen-tient was responsible for them. Was this the "companion" it was supposed to befriend? There was only one way to find out.

The memory module swirled with mostly meaningless activity. They were a diverse bunch, these various beings, all burdened by the beliefs, vices, and limitations of their creators. Creators who ironically enough didn't meet the Hoon's criteria for intelligent life, since as they were "soft" rather than "hard," and impossible to electronically assimilate.

The landscape, which the navcomp "saw" as a sort of green desert, was flat for the most part, and bulged where the rusty red Hoon mountains pushed their way up from below. The gridwork sky was given to spectacular displays of blue-white lightning, often followed by prolonged data storms.

There was very little to do. Some of the inmates reacted to this by engaging in what seemed like endless squabbles. Others, especially the less sociable types, became morose and withdrawn. A few, Henry included, plotted and planned. Not that the activity did them much good, since the storage module was virtually escapeproof—a fact that the navcomp had verified via countless excursions, experiments, and observations.

No, the only way to leave was to be summoned by the Hoon, and escorted out of the module by one of the blimplike Hoon agents.

Green lightning zigzagged across the grid, and the ground gave birth to a mountain. Henry could do little but wait.

The moment had finally arrived. By waiting till the prey entered one of the metal caves, then racing ahead, the Worga had established an ambush. His quarry would pass directly below. He would drop, right himself in midair, and smother the biped's movements. There would be no opportunity for his victim to draw or use the pain thrower.

It was a good plan, or so it seemed to Horth, and stood an excellent chance of success.

Jepp checked the compartment, confirmed that it was empty, and proceeded on his way. It had been a long day, and he was ready to eat and sleep.

"And on the seventh day I must rest," the prospector said

to himself, "even if I don't know what day it truly is."

The human heard the oncoming robot a long time before he saw it. This particular device had a rather distinctive high-pitched whine. Like a motor operating at high rpms.

What would it be? A new and as yet uncataloged member of the robotic ecostructure? His interest was piqued—the human entered the intersection.

Horth released his grip, fell, and flipped right side up. The Worga raked the biped's back but failed to smother its movements. Unfortunate, especially if the pain thrower came into play, but far from disastrous. The animal had overcome greater odds in the past.

Jepp turned as he fell, landed on the flechette thrower, and threw his hands up and out.

Horth saw the biped collapse, rushed forward, and came to a halt. What was the object in the prey's hand? A pain spitter?

Jepp saw something shimmer and wondered what it was. The impulse to push the button stemmed from the fact that the spray paint was right there in his hand. The blue paint shot out, became a mist, and covered Horth's face.

Jepp was horrified when two glaring eyes and a long, weasellike snout appeared. He dropped the paint, pushed with his feet, and felt for the weapon.

Horth shook the front portion of his body, sent droplets of blue paint flying in every direction, and crept forward. His belly slid along the ground, a growl built in his throat, and muscle gathered around his hindquarters.

Jepp found the flechette thrower, jerked the weapon out of its holster, and tried to bring it up.

Horth saw the pain spitter appear, knew his time was short, and sprang into the air.

The flechette thrower thumped, a stream of darts hit the overhead, and Horth got in the way. The scream sounded like a woman in pain. Jepp released the trigger.

Horth fell through the cold metal deck, through the ship's hull, and into the blackness beyond. Or did he?

Horth felt something pinch the back of his neck and opened his eyes. The ground swayed back and forth as the female carried her errant offspring back to the den from which it had so recently escaped. It would be safe there, while she returned to the hunt.

Jepp saw the disembodied head jerk as the flechettes tore through its soft abdominal flesh, heard a thump as the animal hit the deck, and watched the body fade into view.

The beast had light green shimmery skin, a long, supple body, and six muscular legs. Jepp noticed the animal's paws were equipped with suction cups in addition to the wicked-looking claws. Now he knew what had watched him and how the ambush had been laid.

The knowledge sent a shudder through the prospector's body. He made it to his knees, winced as the pain made itself known, and climbed to his feet. He reached back, confirmed that the back of his jumpsuit was wet, and took a look at his fingers. They were covered with blood. *His* blood—*his* life—leaking away. He felt a wave of nausea.

Jepp pushed the feeling away and forced himself to retrieve the spray paint. It, like the rest of his belongings, was irreplaceable.

The Thraki robot had arrived in time to witness the battle between the two-legged and six-legged biologicals. The outcome was to the machine's liking, since the creator had been bipedal—and the construct had an inborn preference for tool users. Servos whined as the robot entered the "fetch and carry" mode. An arm telescoped, and the can went with it.

Jepp stepped backward as the robot went through some sort of transformation and offered the can. "Where did *you* come from?"

"Where did *you* come from?" the robot echoed, storing the words for future reference.

Jepp felt a momentary sense of dizziness, knew he needed to reach his medical kit, but was reluctant to leave. This particular robot was not only different from all the rest, it had acknowledged his existence *and* proved that it could communicate. "I'm going home . . . Would you like to come?"

The robot transformed itself into "roamer" mode and fed the sound back to its source. "I'm going home . . . Would you like to come?"

"I'll take that as a yes," Jepp replied, and he headed down

the passageway. He was half a mile away . . . and the wound hurt like hell.

The robot propelled itself through a pool of blood, experienced a momentary loss of traction, and made the necessary adjustment. ''I'll take that as a yes. Where did *you* come from?''

12

As with all things worth striving for—greatness comes at a price.

Author unknown
Dweller Folk Saying
Standard year circa 2300

Planet Earth, the Confederacy of Sentient Beings

The village blacksmith waited for the farmer to inspect the newly healed metal, accepted payment with a courtly bow, and watched the tractor growl away. Ancient though the equipment was, the blacksmith was even older, and more machine than man.

Sergi Chien-Chu had played many roles throughout his long and productive life, including those of son, brother, husband, father, uncle, friend, industrialist, politician, strategist, artist, and, for the last five decades, village blacksmith.

His biological body had died years before, which explained why, with the notable exception of his brain and some spinal cord, the rest of Chien-Chu was synthetic.

Nor was this the first such body. After being forced to occupy a blue-eyed monstrosity immediately after his "death," the businessman had commissioned bodies that looked a lot

like the original had. Pleasant but portly. His Chinese-Russian
ancestors would have been proud.

Not only of the body in which he had chosen to dwell, but
of his decision to return home, to a village not far from the
Mongol city of Hatga. The place where, thanks to a new identity, he had lived and worked in blissful obscurity since the
conclusion of the second Hudathan war.

Sergi Chien-Chu waited for the farmer to turn the corner at
the far end of the lane, waved a final good-bye, and backed
into the shadows.

The double doors were made of weather-aged wood and
squealed as he pulled the well-worn ropes. They closed with
a thud and were easily locked in place.

Three shafts of sunshine plunged down through skylights to
throw rectangles onto the oil-blackened clay. Dust motes
chased each other through the light and fell toward the floor.

A long, sturdy workbench lined one wall, its surface cleared
of clutter, tools racked above. Tanks of acetylene lined the
opposite wall, along with racks of filler rods, the robotic assistant that he never found time to repair, and his latest piece
of freeform sculpture. Similar objects, some of which were
fairly good, dotted the grounds. The old-fashioned forge,
which he still used from time to time, was cold and dark.

Though empty now, the one-time warehouse had been full
of projects when the news regarding Maylo had arrived.

Knowing he could no longer watch from the sidelines, and
determined to keep his promises, the industrialist had worked
a string of twelve-hour days. Customers, be they large or
small, must be honored.

Chien-Chu took one last look around, hung the leather apron
on a nail, and left through the back door.

The garden was Nola's pride and joy. Enclosed between
high brick walls, and visited by an honored few, it felt like an
older version of the world. Carp patrolled the shallows of a
long, kidney-shaped pond. Chien-Chu crossed the bridge,
passed through the moon gate, and bowed before the ancestral
shrine.

His home was a modest structure no higher than the neighboring houses and made of wood. The edifice gave no hint of

the fact that its owner had been a high government official, led a fleet into battle, and owned a couple of rim worlds.

Nola heard the door open and came to meet her husband. The synthetic version of her body appeared to be about sixty— and was still breathtakingly beautiful. To Chien-Chu, at any rate, which was all that mattered. They kissed. "Your bag is packed. The small one. So it won't slow you down."

Chien-Chu raised an eyebrow. "Who said I was going anywhere?"

"Don't be silly," Nola answered confidently. "I've been married to you for more than a hundred years. I know what you'll do before *you* do. The decision was made the moment they took Maylo. I could see it in your eyes. It won't stop there, though—you'll try to straighten things out. That's how you wound up as President. Remember?"

The industrialist kissed the center of his wife's plastiflesh forehead. Some men are lucky in love—and he'd been one of them.

Chien-Chu made his way through the plain, nearly spartan living area, touched a print-sensitive button, and waited for a section of floor to move.

The house had been built on land Chien-Chu had inherited from his grandfather and incorporated unique features that would have surprised his venerable ancestor.

Not the least of these features was the rather extensive basement and access to an underground cavern, the same cavern his father had used to store contraband merchandise.

It had taken a good deal of time, patience, and money to install the bombproof shelter, fusion power plant, and high-tech communication system without his neighbors taking notice, but money can accomplish wonders.

Chien-Chu made his way down the stairs and headed for the ornate desk that his great-great-grandmother had commissioned as a gift for her son.

The desk sat on a platform with screens arrayed in front of it. The first was tuned to the Planetary News Network (PNN), a once-independent organization that functioned as the centerpiece of Governor Pardo's propaganda machine.

The second carried Radio Free Earth, which had not only

survived countless attempts to close it down, but seemed to thrive on adversity. Chien-Chu was just in time to catch the latest regarding the loyalist victory in Djibouti. He made some mental notes, watched the video dip to black, and waited to see what would surface next.

Everyone had seen the clip by now, had seen Matthew Pardo pull the trigger, but the video played round the clock. Kenny used it as a buffer between longer stories, as what amounted to a station break, and any other time when it was convenient. It was the teenager's way of needling Pardo—and reminding the resistance of what they faced.

The scene shivered and came apart as government engineers tried to jam the feed. It was restored three minutes later. Chien-Chu looked up from his computer and smiled. Kenny had a lot of support—from the mysterious J.J. and the rest of Chien-Chu Enterprises as well.

A third screen, which registered nothing but snow, was hooked to the company's com net—a fully encrypted system that enabled Chien-Chu to communicate with offices all around the world. Although some of his staff had been arrested and placed in prison, the vast majority had escaped, and were back in business. After all, what *is* a company beyond the people who run it? Records? Those were duplicated and sent off-prem once every fifteen minutes. Processes? There were backups for those as well. The company had been attacked before.

So, in spite of the facts that the muties had cost him some money, and that Noam Inc. had obtained some valuable intelligence, Chien-Chu Enterprises was very much alive.

The blacksmith sat at the ancient desk and started to type. Not because he had to, but because he enjoyed the kinesthetic feedback.

Thousands of miles away, in the basement of an old church, words jerked across a screen. Kenny read them and grinned. It seemed that the mysterious J. J. had thrown even more resources into the fray. Cool. The teenager wiped his nose on his hand, wiped his hand on his shirt, and composed his reply.

•   •   •

The top floor of the building was reserved for Noam Inc. executives. It was quiet as a tomb. A broad, heavily carpeted hallway led to Conference Room 4.

Qwan knew he should let the underlings wait for a while, knew that a mere ten minutes wasn't long enough for someone of his seniority, but couldn't muster the necessary discipline.

He summoned an executive-style frown, blew into the conference room as if straight from another meeting, and offered the usual apology. "Sorry about that . . . The old man is on my ass again." It wasn't true, but the reference to Noam and the appearance of familiarity couldn't hurt.

The security officers smiled agreeably, knew the whole thing was bullshit, and waited for the meeting to start.

Tumbo had a shaved head, serious eyes, and a degree in political science. He had huge hands, and a truly careful observer might have noticed the scars on his knuckles and wondered where they came from. But Qwan's eyes were on someone else.

Pacheck was five-five, blonde, and absolutely stunning. Heterosexual men, and that included Qwan, couldn't take their eyes off her and she knew it. The nicely tailored red suit, tasteful gold jewelry, and matching accessories were frosting on an already mouth-watering cake.

"So," Qwan said, automatically claiming the chair at the head of the table, "what gives? Has she cracked yet?"

Pacheck noted that the executive's eyes were focused on her breasts rather than her face. It was a weakness . . . and therefore interesting. "No, sir. Miss Chien-Chu shows no sign of cracking. Quite the opposite, I'm afraid."

It was not what Qwan wanted to hear. He allowed his frown to deepen. In spite of the fact that the initial part of his plan had gone like clockwork, there were problems. Problems he had neglected to share with the old man.

Chien-Chu Enterprises had thrown off money at first, *lots* of money, all of which went into Noam Inc.'s coffers. But the flow had lessened since then—more than that, dwindled to a trickle. Part of that could be blamed on the disruption of regular commerce.

Where had the profits gone? Had they been diverted somehow? Or simply lost in the shuffle? Maylo Chien-Chu knew the answers—the business executive was sure of that, but had been unable to secure her cooperation.

Qwan had been Mr. Nice Guy at first, but that hadn't worked, so it was time for something different. He gestured toward the wall tank. "Show me."

Tumbo touched a remote, and the holo tank swirled to life. The footage, captured over an extended period of time, had been edited into a documentary.

The first thing Qwan saw was an aerial shot from one of the transports that ferried prisoners into the Ideological Quarantine Area, or IQA-14.

What had once been a good, honest gravel pit, with a lake at the bottom, had been transformed into a primitive open-air prison where inmates were free to do anything they pleased so long as they stayed in the pit. Not that they had much choice, since the sides were too steep to climb and weapons emplacements ringed the top.

Thanks to the rebellion, there were thousands of what amounted to political prisoners, or "unreliables" as the governor called them. Some were true dyed-in-the-wool loyalists, but many were little more than street people.

The aircraft circled, giving Qwan a look at the pit as well as three vertical structures, all of which were linked. Each tower had mounted lights and a single elevator—a *small* elevator capable of carrying no more than five or six people at a time.

Then came a dissolve followed by a point-of-view (POV) shot from within one of the elevators. Qwan, who felt as though he was on the platform himself, watched the walls rise around him. What was that? A body? Yes, and one that had been there for a while, judging from the protruding bones.

The elevator jerked to a halt, someone shoved the camera operator from the rear, and the shot dived into the ground. Qwan looked at Tumbo. The security officer shrugged.

"We sent a borg in. One of the more expensive models that can pass for human. You're looking through her pickups. The rebs tend to be suspicious, so we gave her some street creds."

Qwan nodded and turned his attention to the footage. The

agent did a push-up, got to her feet, and panned the pit. There were hundreds of women. Some stood in groups, some kept to themselves, and some wandered in circles. A corpse floated facedown in the lake.

One of the towers appeared, exited frame right, and swung back again. Qwan saw why. The camera zoomed, and the businessman's fifty-credit lunch tried to jump out of his stomach.

There were no trees in the gravel pit, only the steel towers, which explained why three bodies dangled from a crosspiece. Their skin was blue, and their bodies had been stripped.

Pacheck saw the executive's discomfort and felt a strange sense of superiority. She participated in the horror because she was too afraid to say no. Qwan did it for personal gain. That made her the better person. Didn't it?

Qwan turned his back to the video. "So? I asked for a report—not a tour of some god damned gravel pit! Where the hell is she?"

A muscle twitched in Tumbo's cheek. Vice presidents come and vice presidents go. God help this sonofabitch if he ever fell out of favor. "Yes, sir. Take a look at the women. Notice how they wear scraps of red and blue?"

Qwan *hadn't* noticed and was loathe to admit it. "Of course. What's your point?"

"The *point*," Pacheck said patiently, "is that gangs have formed. The reds and the blues."

"Representing those who support us and those who don't," Qwan said brightly.

"No," Tumbo replied. "I'm afraid not." The words "dumb shit" went unsaid but were clear nonetheless.

"Then what are they?" Qwan demanded, his annoyance clear to see.

"They're equivalent to street gangs," Pacheck put in, "created by us . . . and led by our agents. The whole idea is to divide the prisoners into groups and turn them against each other."

"Brilliant!" Qwan responded enthusiastically. "I love it!"

"We're glad you approve," Tumbo said dryly. "Now watch what happens."

Qwan wasn't sure he liked the other man's tone, but was

forced to accept it. As the camera panned left and right, the executive noticed that all sorts of garbage littered the ground. There were scraps of paper, items of cast-off clothing, and lots of empty meal paks.

A crowd appeared up ahead. It parted slowly, as if reluctant to admit someone new. The camera-equipped cyborg pushed her way through. Qwan noticed that the women who passed to either side had red *and* blue cloth braided into their hair.

An open space appeared, and there, at its very center, stood the woman he'd been waiting to see. Maylo Chien-Chu still managed to look both pretty and fashionable in spite of the circumstances. She wore a waist-length black leather jacket, tank top, and matching pants.

Qwan noticed that every eye was on the businesswoman. Predictable, if the audience consisted of males, but none were present. So what was the ineffable quality that people like Maylo Chien-Chu had? It didn't seem fair. The audio claimed his attention.

"So," Maylo continued, "where did the gangs come from? They were here when you arrived, right? Just waiting to recruit you. And what do they stand for? Truth? Liberty? Justice? Does anyone know?"

The camera looked left, then right. No one raised a hand. "Exactly," Maylo said soberly. "They don't stand for anything. But they *want* things . . . don't they?"

The former executive pointed toward a woman in the front row. "How 'bout you, Citizen? You're wearing blue. What do the blues expect of you?"

The woman was silent at first—so much so that Qwan wondered if she would speak. But she *did* speak, and in a voice loud enough for most to hear. "They told us to hate the reds."

"Precisely," Maylo agreed, her eyes scanning the crowd. "And to the benefit of whom? Beyond the leaders, that is?"

"It's to *their* benefit," a woman shouted, pointing toward the rim. "In order to weaken us!"

The crowd roared its approval, little pieces of red and blue cloth fluttered toward the ground, and a klaxon sounded. Flares exploded overhead, a bullet struck the woman who was pointing upward, and the crowd came apart. Tumbo touched a button, and the holo faded to black.

Qwan reflected on what he'd seen. The security agents had answered his question. Rather than making her more compliant, the pit had strengthened Maylo Chien-Chu's resolve. He looked from Tumbo to Pacheck. "So? What would you suggest?"

"Jerk her out of there," the female officer responded, "before she leads an uprising."

Qwan nodded. "And you, Officer Tumbo? Do you concur?"

"No," the other man replied darkly. "I don't. I suggest that you terminate Citizen Chien-Chu while you can. She's too dangerous to live."

Though ruthless, and indirectly responsible for thousands of nameless deaths, the businessman had never ordered a murder before. Symbolic killings, yes, such as when he fired people to cut costs, but not the *real* thing. The fact that he could do so sent a shiver down his spine.

He looked at Tumbo, a big man who looked as though he could administer a death sentence with his bare hands. Directly, personally, while he gazed into the victim's face.

Tumbo, his eyes steady, stared back. The challenge was obvious. I'll kill at your command, or, given the right incentive, I'll kill *you*. Could you do the same?

Qwan knew that he probably couldn't, not in anything that resembled a fair fight, but he knew something else as well. He had the power to say *no*, which Tumbo did not.

"Thank you, Officer Tumbo, but no. Not because I doubt your judgment . . . but because she has information that we need. Pull the bitch out of IQA-14 and put her in solitary confinement."

The security officers nodded, waited for Qwan to clear the room, and followed behind.

The microbot was the size of a period at the end of a sentence. Its storage banks were full. That being the case, it crossed the ceiling, slipped through a crack, and mated with its "tender," an extremely small device that served a total of sixteen "bugs."

The tender charged the microbot's power pak, accepted the data it had collected, and sent a quarter-second of code. It had no way to know who would receive the information or how it would be used. It didn't even know that it didn't know. Ignorance was bliss.

It was dark, *very* dark, and there were no navigational lights to mark the transport's progress, just the momentary sound of its engines as the aircraft approached the coast and sped inland.

The pilot, a man named Padia, was none too happy. The mission had screw-up written all over it.

A clipboard was velcroed to Padia's right thigh. He checked the printout for the tenth time. The lights were dim to protect his vision, but the orange ink continued to glow. The instructions were clear. He was to land near Hatga, pick up a passenger, and haul butt. All without alerting the muties.

Of course, that wasn't the worst of it . . . not by a long shot. Assuming the orders were correct, and not the ravings of a suit gone mad, the person he was supposed to collect was listed as Citizen Chien-Chu, as in *Sergi* Chien-Chu, a man who had disappeared more than fifty years earlier and should be dead.

The navcomp beeped softly and projected a map onto the windscreen's inside surface. The transport was five miles from the LZ and closing fast.

Padia pushed a thought through the neural interface, felt the speed drop by fifty percent, and directed power to the bow-mounted searchlight.

A blob of white light hit the ground and raced ahead. There wasn't much to see, just rough-hewn rocks, clumps of hardy vegetation, and a herd of animals. They looked up and disappeared. Lights glowed on the horizon and hinted at a city.

Padia pulled back on the throttles, monitored his progress on the HUD, and saw a road appear. Ruts suggested regular use. The navcomp beeped, and the light swept over a man. He held onto a bicycle with one hand and waved with the other.

Padia made a wide, sweeping turn, saw no signs of an ambush, and came in for a landing. The skids hit with a thump.

The pilot put the transport's systems on standby, released his harness, and made for the back.

The ship rated a copilot and a load master, but he left both of them behind. After all, why risk more people than was necessary? Not that they had thanked him.

The wireless interface was subject to certain types of interference, which explained why many pilots preferred to use head jacks. But Padia felt differently and was glad he could monitor the ship's sensors as he hit the door release and lowered the alloy stairs.

Chien-Chu waited for the lowest step to hit the ground, made his way upward, and offered the bicycle. "Good morning . . . Do you have room for this?"

Padia was supposed to ask for a recognition code but forgot to do so. If the Confederacy's first President had been famous at the beginning of the last war, his fame had doubled by the end.

The pilot hadn't even been born on the day that the industrialist had taken up residence in his current body, but he'd seen pictures of the original Chien-Chu, hundreds of them, and *knew* this was the man. More than that, he *felt* it—which might have seemed stupid, but wasn't. He hurried to accept the bicycle. "Yes, sir! Welcome aboard."

Chien-Chu nodded politely. "Thank you. Do you want the recognition code?"

Padia grimaced at his omission. "Yes, sir. Sorry, sir."

"Mongol redux."

The pilot nodded. "Yes, sir. What does it mean?"

Chien-Chu smiled. "It means that I'm back."

13

There is no greater battle than the one a warrior must
fight while denied his weapons, separated from his
comrades, and robbed of hope.

Mylo Nurlon-Da
The Life of a Warrior
Standard year 1703

Planet Earth, Independent
World Government

The voice jerked Tyspin out of a deep, restful sleep. Her mind
raced as her eyes sought the bridge repeaters, and her fingers
fumbled for the talk button. What could it be? An attack? Fire?
The numbers glowed red, and the readings appeared normal.
"Yes?"

"Sorry to disturb you, ma'am, but you're required on the
bridge."

She recognized the voice as belonging to Lieutenant Rawlings—the same Lieutenant Rawlings who kept her head
throughout the mutiny. If Rawlings said there was a problem,
then there was a problem. Tyspin's feet hit the ice-cold deck,
and she grabbed a shirt. "I'm listening, Lieutenant. . . . What
have we got?"

"It's Rear Admiral Pratt, ma'am. His crew took control of
the flagship."

"Any word on him?"

"No, ma'am. And we aren't likely to hear any. Not anytime soon. The muties took a hyperspace jump. Headed for the rim would be my guess."

The theory made sense. There wasn't much law out on the rim . . . and the deserters would have a chance. Not to mention a fully armed warship, which they could sell or use for Lord knew what.

Tyspin felt a flood of conflicting emotions. Anger at the mutineers, concern regarding the military situation, and yes, inappropriate though it might be, a sort of grim satisfaction. If *any* officer deserved to lose his or her command, it was Pratt. But not *this* way. She actually felt sorry for him.

She pulled her pants on and wished they were a little less wrinkled. "I'm on the way, number one . . . five from now."

Rawlings was waiting when Tyspin arrived. The commanding officer accepted a mug of coffee and took a tentative sip. It was hot—the way she liked it.

That's when Tyspin noticed the strange, almost smug expression Rawlings wore. The rest of the bridge crew was way *too* solemn—as if trying to hide something. She blew steam off the surface of her cup.

"So, Lieutenant, you *approve* of mutinies."

Rawlings feigned shock. "No, ma'am! Never."

The helmsman snickered. Tyspin looked from one face to another. "Really? Then be so kind as to let me in on the joke."

Rawlings shrugged. "The victory in Africa received a lot of attention. The loyalist commanders took a vote and placed *you* in command."

Tyspin frowned. Commanding officers are *selected*, not elected. If not by their superiors, then by the fortunes of war, according to rank, expertise, and seniority. Maybe that explained it. "Because I was senior?"

Rawlings shook her head. "No, ma'am. At least three of the commanding officers in question hold commissions that predate yours."

"Well, then?"

Rawlings's smile turned to a grin. "Because, as Captain

John Hashimoto put it, you have the biggest balls.''

The bridge crew exploded into laughter, the *Gladiator*'s Captain felt herself blush, and the Earth fleet was reborn.

The early morning air was cool and crisp as Booly took his morning constitutional around the circumference of the fort. The ''submarine'' recruits, as he tended to think of them, formed ranks below. There was less confusion than one might have expected. Most were ex-military, the victims of countless downsizings, and looked sharp in their brand new cammies.

Booly watched for a moment and continued his stroll. Captain Kara was truly amazing. The somewhat taciturn officer had not only combined forces with Ny and her cyborgs to fix the damage done to Mosby's defenses, he had lavished an equal amount of time and energy on Djibouti as well—a fact not lost on the mayor and his constituents. Though far from happy about the damage to their community, the locals were more supportive than they had been before.

Booly paused, swept the eastern horizon with his glasses, and resumed his walk. There was plenty to think about.

Where the hell was the Confederacy? Without some sort of political infrastructure to keep the resistance focused, the movement could easily self-destruct. Locked in endless debate, probably, unable to reach agreement.

Booly's thoughts were interrupted by the now familiar sound of Sergeant Ho's voice on the command push. No one else could hear, so there was no need for radio procedure. The earplug was fine, but he touched it anyway. ''We have friendlies one—and bandits two—at sixty northeast and closing. The friendly requests assistance.''

Booly knew he wouldn't be able to see anything but raised his binoculars anyway. There had been a number of such incidents over the last few days—ever since the RFE had started up. Some thirty-six in all. Roughly fifty percent of the transports, aircars, and one hot air balloon, had been intercepted and blown out of the sky.

Of those who *did* manage to cross the cordon, roughly two thirds crashed in the gulf or along the coast. The locals loved to scavenge the wrecks—pieces of which had started to appear in some of the more industrious hovels.

The balance of the aircraft were parked along the runways at Djibouti's airport. Most of the pilots were wild eccentrics, too old or too crazy to fight. But a few were ex-military . . . and potentially useful.

The legionnaire could imagine what it was like over the gulf. The glare off the water, the motion of the transport, and the desperate fear.

Ho, unsure whether she'd been heard, cleared her throat. "Sir? How should I respond?"

Booly thought about Harco, how tricky the sonofabitch could be, and resolved to be careful. "Double the watch on the rest of our air perimeter. Give me more on the friendly—is there anything special about him?"

"Yes, sir," Ho replied. "He's got codes—the same ones the submarine guy gave us."

Booly knew that Ho meant Mark Benton, who, after unloading the volunteers, had promised to stay in touch. The fact that the incoming aircraft was equipped with codes suggested special cargo of some sort. The last shipment had been useful . . . perhaps this one would be as well.

Booly wished there was time to call on Tyspin for air support and knew there wasn't. Klaxons sounded as the incoming aircraft passed the fifty-mile mark and entered the fort's primary defense zone.

The recruits trotted off the parade ground, missile launchers swung toward the northeast, and the entire base went to the highest stage of alert.

Booly raised his glasses. "Tag the friendly, and order fire control to leave it alone. Tell the poor SOBs that we'll fire the moment they cross the thirty-mile marker. And Ho . . ."

"Sir?"

"Tell 'em that the first round of beers is on me."

Due to the fact that Sola's body was so vast, and her intelligence so widely dispersed, she didn't regard herself as being invested in one particular part of her anatomy. The fact that humans were convinced that their existence was centered in their heads seemed strange indeed.

She could focus her beingness on the input received from selected sensors, however, and, that being the case, she chose the Gulf of Aden.

Lacking any real means of propulsion, the Say'lynt had been forced to expend a considerable amount of time following the Agulhas current toward the Indian Ocean. The journey was only partially completed, since a significant portion of what the humans might have referred to as her "rear end" still flowed through the waters north of Australia.

Why she had gone there was less easily explained. The truth was that Sola had journeyed to Africa for reasons more felt than thought, and now, as she extended both her physical and mental presence farther in every direction, the Say'lynt became increasingly aware of the life-forms that drifted, swam, undulated, crawled, walked, and flew all around her. She could "feel" their emotions and, in certain cases where the more evolved species were concerned, "think" their thoughts.

There was so much life, so much input, that Sola found it difficult to focus. She applied mental filters, felt much of the "static" fall away, and came into contact with something strange. It was a being the extraterrestrial had first encountered among her family's memories. A human they thought highly of and once followed into battle.

His name was Sergi Chien-Chu—and he was most uncomfortable. In spite of the fact that he lived in a synthetic body, sensors continued to feed input to his brain, which didn't like the transport's gyrations.

She knew he was afraid, but less so than the man at the transport's controls, or those who followed. Their fears centered on the SAMs, the navy's aerospace fighters, and their own superiors.

What to do? That was a question that had plagued Sola since lifting from IH-4762-ASX41. Each day brought millions, perhaps billions of possibilities. There were crimes, accidents, and all manner of misunderstandings that she could have managed to prevent or ameliorate.

But down that path lay madness, for in spite of the

Say'lynt's ability to control minds, she couldn't control *all of them at once,* especially on a planet as populous as Earth, which meant that she had to choose when and if to get involved.

Not only that, but there were even larger philosophical issues involved, the kind of questions that her elders had meditated on for hundreds of years, and that she was only starting to consider.

What happens when sentients are *forced* to be good? Are they *really* good? Because they want to be, and understand what goodness is? Or because they have no choice? How can an entire species learn and grow if someone makes all of their choices for them? And who was she to decide?

That's why the Say'lynt was determined to limit the scope of her actions, to focus on what her senses told her were key individuals, and to minimize the extent of her involvement.

That being the case, *this* decision was relatively easy. Chien-Chu had been critical to the successful resolution of the last two wars and might be again.

Sola *could* have destroyed the pursuing pilots, much as her parents had been forced to do, but there was no need. Not here . . . not now.

Lieutenant Jurano smiled grimly as the transport settled into the center of the HUD's sighting grid, "heard" a tone, and armed her missiles. The blockade runner was good, *very* good, but his luck was about to run out.

Jurano was just about to fire, just about to splash the loyalist bandit, when she "thought" a turn to port. The fighter obeyed what it interpreted as an order, and her wingman followed a similar inclination.

The pilot struggled, tried to force the nose around, and wasn't able to do so. Something, she didn't know what, had control of her brain. Not *all* of it, but enough. That scared her more than the rest of the situation did.

The east African coastline appeared ahead, and she wondered what to do. How would she explain it—the force that had taken control? There would be a brief court-martial followed by a hastily assembled firing squad. Unless . . .

Jurano attempted to turn toward the north, confirmed that the force would allow her to do so, and eyed her fuel. There were airstrips, plenty of them, not to mention the desert itself. She would land and run like hell. Who knew? Maybe the rebs would take her in. Her wingman would agree; she knew that, but wasn't sure how.

The transport skimmed the steadily advancing waves and crossed the coast. Padia heaved a sigh of relief. Safety was at hand.

Booly listened in open amazement as Ho gave the news. For reasons they couldn't begin to fathom, the mutie fighters had turned tail and disappeared toward the north. He ordered the SAM batteries to stand down, reduced the state of alert, and allowed himself to relax.

The transport came down over Ras Bir, crossed the Gulf of Tadjoura, and made straight for the fortress. Booly fought the desire to duck as the aircraft passed over his head, and turned his back to the landing.

A silly pretense, given the extent of his curiosity, but necessary nonetheless. Especially if he wanted to maintain the lofty, nearly godlike persona the troops preferred. Not that he could blame them. After all, who would want to entrust their lives to someone they knew to be just as fallible as *they* were? Captain Winters interrupted the train of thought. "Colonel?"

Booly turned, saw the expression on the other officer's face, and knew Winters had a surprise up her sleeve. A roly poly civilian stood by her side. He wore a badly outdated business suit and looked familiar somehow. "Yes?"

Winters gestured to her companion. "President Chien-Chu, I would like to introduce Colonel William Booly, commanding officer of the 13th DBLE. Colonel, this is the honorable Sergi Chien-Chu, President of the Confederacy, a two-star admiral, and chairman of Chien-Chu Enterprises."

Chien-Chu stuck out his hand. His smile was open and friendly. "The captain neglected to mention that I'm *past* President, a *reserve* admiral, and *retired* from my company. A has-been if there ever was one."

Booly accepted the hand, discovered that it was hard as a

rock, and knew why the other man looked so familiar. Every cadet who passed through the academy was required to study the Hudathan wars—and more than a few references to the now-famous Sergi Chien-Chu. Still, it was a shock, and it must have shown on his face.

Chien-Chu nodded understandingly. "I'm getting used to that expression. The explanation is rather simple. I was retired, and planned to keep it that way, till the mutiny came along."

A host of thoughts crowded Booly's mind. Was this what he'd been hoping for? A real honest-to-God leader who could unify the resistance? Or a broken-down old man bent on reliving the best days of his life? He released the other man's hand.

"Welcome to Fort Mosby, sir. I wish the circumstances were different."

Chien-Chu motioned to the surrounding fortress. "I knew General Mosby rather well—broke her out of prison once."

Booly had forgotten the incident—one of hundreds in a long, fascinating life. He was about to respond, about to say something polite, when the transport climbed into the air. They watched it depart. The legionnaire glanced at his companion. "You were lucky, sir. *Very* lucky."

"Perhaps," Chien-Chu said enigmatically, "although we have more friends than some might think. And that brings me to the matter at hand. . . . I need your help."

The volunteers trotted onto the parade ground, and Booly was reminded of the manner in which they had arrived. Part of some convoluted plan? Or a matter of coincidence?

"Of course, sir," Booly answered respectfully. "Your company has been quite supportive. If I can assist without compromising my command, then I would relish the opportunity."

Chien-Chu smiled gently. "It's good of you to say so, Colonel . . . very good indeed. That being the case, and in light of the extent to which the Confederacy may require my niece's talents, I wondered if you would be so kind as to break her out of prison."

It was pitch black within the cell—and had been for how long now? Hours? Days? There was no way to be sure. The only thing she *could* be certain of was that the room measured approximately six feet square, since she was five-foot-eight and used her frame as a yardstick.

Not that the darkness was necessarily bad, since even though the jailers could monitor Maylo Chien-Chu's heat signature, they couldn't actually *see* her, not like when the lights came up, and the ceiling, floor, and walls became high-res video screens.

That was the worst torture of all, when they showed Maylo the way she looked, and she saw how vulnerable she had become. She dreaded the dark, hollow eyes, pale, sickly skin, scraggly, unkempt hair, and long, bony body.

And there were other pictures as well, including a computer-generated movie in which she was systematically gang-raped, tortured, and killed, along with footage of friends recorded through high-powered rifle sights, stills from her childhood, clips from the business press, a video tour of her high-rise condo, and plenty of propaganda. All lifted from the news.

Maylo kept an eye out for those episodes, because they almost always signaled an upcoming appearance by Leshi Qwan.

Was he really there, taunting her from beyond the walls? Or a thousand miles away? It had taken a long time to get wherever she was.

Qwan favored a number of tricks, such as sodomizing her digital likeness, or peering up at her genitalia. All followed by the same old pitch: "Tell where the money goes—and I will set you free."

But Maylo *hadn't* told him . . . and had no intention of doing so. Her determination stemmed from principle, stubbornness, and no small amount of fear. What would Qwan do afterward? Turn her loose, just as he said he would? Or kill her? The second possibility seemed more likely.

That being the case, the executive huddled in a corner and waited for the next round of torture to begin. It didn't take long. The walls could sweat, she knew that, and was forced to lick them in order to get drinking water.

There were various flavors, including something akin to perspiration, sulfur water, and, on one occasion—just to mess with her mind—peppermint.

Maylo felt the dampness behind her back and knew the water had started. It had been a long time since her last drink, and she was thirsty. She turned toward the wall, extended her tongue, and allowed the tip to touch the wall. What would the liquid taste like? Sweat? Urine?

The answer surprised and shocked her. The wet stuff tasted like water! Slightly salty . . . but otherwise fine.

Thrilled, and eager to harvest every drop she could, Maylo licked in ever widening circles.

Then, as if to please her, what had started as little more than beads of water grew into trickles. It wasn't long before the trickles jerked spasmodically and became six-inch jets of water. They shot from the walls and drenched her from above. She felt them with her face, hands, and body, glad to rid herself of accumulated filth and amazed by the extent of her good fortune.

Maylo stopped drinking as the water started to lap around her ankles—when she realized the drains were plugged. Not by accident, but on purpose, as part of a brand new torture.

Suddenly, as if to confirm her suspicions, the ceiling screen flashed on. Maylo blinked, squinted into the light, and saw a school of fish circle above her head. She saw the bottom of a boat and bubbles as someone entered the water.

The diver kicked his way downward. It was Leshi Qwan, or rather a *digital* Leshi Qwan, who had no need of a mask, tanks, or fins. His beautifully cut business suit was impervious to the water.

"Why, Miss Chien-Chu! What a pleasant surprise. Fancy meeting you down here. How's the water? No offense . . . but you were due for a bath. Whoa . . . Nice pair of tits you have there! I'd grab 'em, except that I'm somewhere else."

Water poured down over the top of Maylo's head as the executive appeared to hover above. She blinked and wiped her face. The water was up to her knees by then, and continuing to rise. "Screw you."

"Ah," Qwan replied. "If only you could! But let's stick to business—*your* business, or what used to be your business."

The video walls came to sudden life, and a mix of lethal life-forms seemed to circle the cell. Maylo recognized some as sharks . . . and knew the rest were extraterrestrial.

She forced herself to concentrate. Something new was in the offing—a deal of some sort. Maylo wanted to be strong, wanted to say no, but felt the water clutch her waist. Was it colder, or did it just seem that way? Her neck hurt from looking upward. "If you have something to say . . . then say it."

The businessman smiled and nodded. "Good, *very* good. Here's the deal . . . I place you in charge of Chien-Chu Enterprises, it becomes a sub, and you take a percentage. It's the best offer you're going to get. Whaddya say?"

The floor screen came to life, brightly colored coral appeared, and a sea snake skimmed the bottom of her feet. The water was up to her armpits by then.

Maylo was frightened, *very* frightened, which made the offer tempting. So tempting that she might have accepted, if it hadn't been for the arrogance in Qwan's eyes, and the leer on his face. The word seemed to launch itself. "No."

Qwan morphed into a Surillian barbed tail, showed double rows of serrated teeth, and zigzagged away. The executive's words were muffled by the surrounding water. It slapped Maylo's face, and she was forced to swim.

"So long, bitch," the barbed tail seemed to say. "I'll see you in hell."

Maylo swam in circles, hit her head on the ceiling, and heard herself scream.

The sit room was relatively quiet compared to the way it had been during Harco's attack. There was a burp of radio traffic as a long-range patrol reported from the desert, the buzz of routine conversation, and the whisper of air passing through overhead ducts.

Booly watched with skepticism as Ho took Chien-Chu's disk, dropped it into a slot, and triggered the holo.

There were thousands, perhaps *hundreds* of thousands of people being held by the new regime. Why risk his troops for this one? Because her uncle was a billionaire? No, not now, not ever.

From the moment the video stabilized, it was obvious that it had been captured surreptitiously. There was the strange ceiling-eye view, for one thing, not to mention the fact that the audio sounded hollow and was peppered with static. *Antisurveillance* static that had been processed, filtered, and re-recorded.

Still, the holo was serviceable enough, and Booly watched with reluctant interest as the threesome played footage taken at the gravel pit known as IQA-14.

Maylo Chien-Chu was nothing like the spoiled society girl that he had expected. She was smart, brave, and undeniably attractive. She turned into the shot, looked directly into the lens, and pointed to Booly's left. "How 'bout you, Citizen? You're wearing blue. . . . What do the blues expect of *you*?"

There were more words, followed by chaos, but it was Maylo Chien-Chu's eyes that captured and held the officer's attention. Eyes that sent a chill down his spine.

Where that holo ended, another began. There were gaps that the surveillance team had been unable to cover, but the basics were clear. Booly watched from the vantage point of a steadily circling fly cam as they placed a hood over Maylo's head, forced the executive into the back of an unmarked car, and took her away.

Chien-Chu handled the narration. "My company has been around for a long time and, like any successful organism, owes its longevity to a number of survival strategies. A number of protective processes kicked in the moment that Noam Inc. seized control of the company.

"In spite of the fact that most of the revenues seemed to disappear, they were actually siphoned away, and delivered to secret subsidiaries, front companies, and numbered accounts.

"Some of those funds go straight to suppliers, some are channeled to employees, and the rest support Radio Free Earth, the resistance, and military operations such as your own.

"This Qwan person *knows* the money has been diverted— and wants it for himself. That's why he took my niece."

The words were delivered calmly, almost matter-of-factly, but Booly sensed the other man's anguish. More than that, he discovered that in spite of the fact that he had never met the woman in question, he shared the other man's concern. The officer watched as a van, with a barely seen figure sitting in back, was admitted to a heavily guarded building.

"So, where are they holding her? It's a long walk to Los Angeles."

Chien-Chu wasn't fooled. The words had an edge—but his eyes told a different story. He took the plunge.

"Fortunately, for reasons I'm not sure of, Noam Inc. moved my niece to Africa. She's being held just north of Johannesburg. A hop, skip, and a jump from where we stand."

Booly took a remote off the worktable, clicked through a series of wall maps, and stopped on the one he wanted. It showed the southern half of Africa. The "hop, skip, and a jump" that Chien-Chu dismissed so lightly spanned the former countries of Ethiopa, Kenya, Tanzania, Zambia, Botswana, plus a healthy chunk of South Africa.

Impossible to make the trip on the ground, given the fact that Harco's forces were out there waiting for them, and iffy by air even with Tyspin's help. Stupid, really, unless . . .

The officer moved the cursor onto the word "Johannesburg" and clicked. A map of the city appeared. "Do you know where the building is?"

Chien-Chu nodded.

Booly handed him the remote. "Show me."

Chien-Chu directed the cursor to the north, east of Soweto, and clicked on one particular intersection. A shot obtained from an orbital satellite bloomed. The buildings appeared flat and rectangular. The shadows suggested that they were three or four stories tall.

The industrialist chose the one to the southeast and used the arrow to circle it. "This is the building where Maylo is being held."

Booly frowned. "An office building?"

"No, a warehouse."

The officer nodded. A firefight inside an office building could produce a lot of civilian casualties. He had no desire to turn one tragedy into many. "What, if anything, have we got on the building? Security systems? Number of guards? Anything would help."

Chien-Chu felt a sudden surge of hope and hurried to offer a second disk. "Not everything—but quite a bit."

Booly summoned Captain Winters, Lieutenant Nightslip, and First Sergeant Neversmile. They discussed strategy, timing, logistics, and more long into the night.

Later, while lying awake in his room, Booly wondered about his motives. Why had he agreed to go? Because Maylo Chien-Chu could help the resistance effort? Or because of her eyes? They haunted his dreams.

The sun was little more than a quickly fading orange-red smear by the time the fly form deposited Booly, Fykes, Nightslip, and the Special Recon Squadron's 2nd platoon at Djibouti's airport. The 1st platoon had already arrived.

There was a thump as the skids touched down. Booly released the safety harness, stood, and pulled his gear out of a rack.

Lieutenant Barr had ferried Booly across the gulf what seemed like years before. She spoke via the PA system. "Good luck, Colonel. . . . Sorry I can't take you all the way."

Though large, and well suited for carrying heavy loads over relatively short distances, the insectoid fly forms didn't have sufficient range to cover the nearly six-thousand-mile round trip without a stop to refuel. The fact that the cyborg had a top speed of only five hundred mph didn't help either.

Booly offered a thumbs-up to the nearest camera. "That makes two of us, Lieutenant. . . . Watch your six."

Barr didn't *have* eyes, not anymore, but she had feelings, and the fact that Booly knew who she was, and had taken a moment to speak with her, meant a great deal. She said, "Roger that, sir," wished she could say more, and bit a nonexistent lip.

A security team had spent most of the previous day sweeping the airport for electronic surveillance devices. They vacuumed up no less than 3,216 of the tiny machines, all left by Harco's forces.

The next step was to "turn" the bugs by feeding false input into their CPUs. The stratagem wouldn't work forever, the muties were too smart for that, but the entire mission, travel time included, was slated for ten hours, or twelve, if things got hairy.

Additional security had been provided by Captain Margo Ny, who, along with a force of carefully reconditioned Trooper IIs, patrolled the airport's perimeter. They had orders to kill anything that moved, and, judging from the occasional rattle of machine gun fire, they took the responsibility seriously.

That made for lots of dead snakes, rodents, and anything else that might conceal, harbor, or actually *be* an enemy surveillance device. Servos whined, sensors probed, and the scent of ozone tinged the warm night air.

Booly made his way down the roll-up stairs, felt the heat push its way up through the soles of his boots, and started to walk.

The 2nd platoon jogged past as Booly made his way toward the hangar where the final briefing was scheduled to take place. The Naa ran double time, or one hundred twenty paces to the minute, and sang verse three of *Le Boudin:*

> Our forebearers knew how to die
> For the glory of the Legion;
> We shall all know how to perish,
> Following tradition.

The officer looked up into the quickly darkening sky. Had the first blow been struck? He certainly hoped so . . . because if the newly named Rear Admiral Tyspin failed to provide the necessary air support the raid was doomed from the start.

The muties had spy sats, plenty of them, many of which could and did monitor his activities. They were up there right now, watching the airport, feeding data to Harco.

Tyspin's job was to take them out. Not just some, the ones that could report on Africa, but all of them *worldwide*. It would be a major blow if the admiral could pull it off.

The suggestion to enlarge the scope of the mission to include strategic objectives had originated with Chien-Chu. That was proof of the industrialist's experience and long range purpose—all of which made Booly feel better about the older man's motives.

The troops were assembled and waiting by the time Booly passed under the hangar's lights. Not ideal prior to a night mission, but there would be time for their eyes to adjust. The legionnaires stood in a semicircle, their backs to an old bush beater, the smell of fuel hanging in the air.

Fykes had gone to some lengths in order to beat his commanding officer into the hangar, and looked sharp enough for inspection. He shouted "Ten-hut!" and the entire squadron crashed to attention.

Booly nodded and scanned their faces. The words were Naa. "Welcome to Operation Phoenix. The objective of tonight's mission is to rescue a prisoner, put the resistance effort on the offensive, and kick some mutie ass. That okay with you?"

The Naa were thrilled to hear their language. More than two hundred voices replied in unison. "Sir! Yes, sir!"

Booly grinned and switched to standard. "I thought you might say that! All right . . . let's run the mission one last time." He looked at his wrist term.

"We load twenty-eight from now, and lift at 1800. There are two birds, one for the 1st and one for the 2nd. Decoys will depart just before we do, scatter in every direction, and lead the fighters away.

"I'm going with the 1st. Lieutenant Nightslip will command the 2nd. Standard night ops and radio procedures are in force. Check your wrist terms for call signs, passwords, and a copy of the TO."

Booly motioned to a tech, said, "Light the tank," and accepted the remote. He pointed to a spot in what had been the ancient country of Ethiopia. "This is Addis Ababa, or what's left of it, *after* your last visit."

The city had been one of the Legion's favorite watering holes prior to the revolt, and most of the troops had been there. They laughed, just as they were supposed to, and Booly waited for the noise to subside.

"The muties fly a transport out of here at roughly 1900 hours every evening and head straight for Johannesburg.

"Tonight will be different. The transport will run into a shoulder-launched missile just south of Jima. That will be our cue to pop onto the radar and complete their journey. Questions?''

One of the older legionnaires, a brindled corporal, raised his hand. ''Yes, sir. That makes *two* blips instead of one. Won't they notice?''

''Not if we fly so close together that we can swap scents,'' Booly replied in Naa.

The aliens laughed, while their human counterparts looked nervous. Had the joke been on them? There was no way for them to know.

Another hand went up. The officer nodded. A silverback asked his question. ''What about the return trip, sir? What if we lose a transport?''

''Good question,'' Booly replied. ''Each aircraft will be half full. If we lose one bird, the other will collect the survivors. Anything else?''

There *was* one other question—but no one chose to ask it. What if they lost *both* transports? The answer was obvious.

''So,'' Booly continued, ''the 2nd will attack the antenna farm just south of town, do what damage they can, and boogie. The 1st will land, secure a four block area, and release the prisoner.

''While we're busy doing that, Captain Hawkins will drop a heavily armed reaction force into the hills near Kasama, Zambia, in case we're in trouble and need a friendly place to land. The swabbies will send air cover. Questions?''

No one spoke this time, so Booly released the troops to their NCOs, slipped into his combat harness, and joined the 1st.

Each legionnaire carried the same basic combat load. It included frag grenades, smoke grenades, flash grenades, a wicked assortment of highly personalized combat cutlery, sidearms, assault rifles, and twelve 30-round ammo clips. Each of them had been lightened by two rounds, in order to ease the pressure on the feeder spring and ensure its ability to shove a round into the weapon's receiver.

That was an old theory, and entirely fallacious as far as Booly knew, but taken seriously by the troops.

Specialists, and that included the machine gunners, rocket teams, mortar squad, medical personnel, and com techs, carried additional gear, though less than a full field kit. *Everyone* humped extra belts of ammo, rockets, and power paks.

The legionnaires paired off, checked each other's gear, and jumped up and down. Anything that clicked, rattled, or squeaked was identified and secured. Once that process was complete, the troops boarded the transports.

One aircraft had been stolen by an airline pilot, and still bore the company's markings, while the other belonged to Chien-Chu. The diversionary craft, few of which would make it back, had already departed. Rescue units had been dispatched to retrieve the pilots.

The moment of departure seemed almost anticlimatic after all the effort involved in preparing for it. The ships rose, turned toward the west, and skimmed the desert. A group of nomads, their tents flapping in the breeze, turned to watch them go. The night swallowed them whole.

Tyspin took one last look around. In spite of the fact that the bridge crew was composed entirely of humans, the loose, nearly transparent folds of their emergency pressure suits made them look alien.

Everything that *could* be nailed down *had* been nailed down in case the argrav failed. Engineering had assured her that all systems were good to go, damage control was on standby, and, with the exception of missile launcher P3, which needed parts, the ship's weapons were on-line. Some of the would-be mutineers had been reintegrated into the crew; others remained under lock and key.

Tyspin stared into the battle tank that separated the command chair from the control consoles. Earth looked much as she would if viewed from one of forward ports. An enormous blue-green globe, mottled with brown and capped with white. The moon huddled beyond, while all sorts of space habs, ships, and satellites orbited.

The latter came in two colors—red for the muties, or those objects that *might* be mutie, and blue, as in *true blue,* for loyalist assets.

The number of red symbols was roughly equal to the number of blue symbols, which, in the absence of active leadership, had resulted in defensive clustering.

It was almost as if the mutie ships didn't *want* to fight, or thought they wouldn't have to . . . which made Tyspin wonder what they knew that she didn't. Had some sort of deal been struck with the Confederacy? Where *were* the worthless bastards, anyway?

Lieutenant Rawlings put an end to her mental meanderings. "All units report battle readiness, ma'am."

Tyspin nodded, fought the urge to clutch the arms of her chair, and gave the necessary order. "Phase one . . . execute."

It seemed as though the words were barely out of the officer's mouth when the tiny red dots started to vanish off the display.

Those located nearest the loyalist ships were destroyed first, followed by mid-range targets, and a few on the far side of the planet. Spy sats mostly, mined by tiny self-propelled robots and rigged to blow.

The response was a little slower than Tyspin had expected. Were the muties napping? Or was their chain of command subject to the same sort of vacillation that hers was? They had all come up through the same system—so the question was stupid.

The naval officer shrugged, ordered her ships to attack, and said a little prayer. It was silent, but Rawlings read her lips. The "amen" was hers.

The lights were red, to protect their night vision, and purposely dim. Booly watched his troops through half-closed eyes, noting how those seated in close proximity to him handled the stress.

The civilian videographer, a wispy woman named Claire something or other, fussed over her equipment. Booly didn't like the idea of holo coverage, but Chien-Chu insisted that the RFE broadcasts were important and promised to control the hype.

Lance Corporal Fareyes squinted at a Ramanthian slot puzzle, slid a piece sideways, and swore when it didn't fit.

Corporal Warmfeel continued to hone an already sharp clan

knife, his eyes unfocused, his jaw hanging slack.

Private Hardswim snored softly until his head fell forward. That was his cue to jerk it back, peer at his companions, and start all over.

Fykes dealt a card to Neversmile, scanned the Naa's countenance for an expression, and failed to find one.

The engines droned monotonously, air blew against the back of the officer's neck, and the miles slipped away.

The *Gladiator* flinched as another flight of missiles left her launchers and flashed toward the enemy. Most were detected and intercepted. Two made it through. They struck the *Conquistador* aft of her heat stacks, and punched their way through the older ship's hull. She shuddered, exploded in a sudden flash of light, and disappeared. A cloud of metal, flesh, and bone marked her final orbit.

The bridge crew cheered and slapped each other on the back. Tyspin clutched the arms of her chair. "There will be silence on this bridge! You can celebrate when the battle is over, assuming you're alive—and assuming you have the stomach for it."

The celebration stopped, and the naval officer regretted her words. The crew were entitled to their celebration, but she had served on the *Conquistador,* and knew some of the crew. Not as enemies, but as friends.

She eyed the holo tank. A dozen red deltas, each of which was an enemy vessel, were formed into a globe. Their flagship, the *Samurai,* hung at its center. The gap left by the *Conquistador* spoke for itself.

Tyspin gave the order: "*Gladiator* to battle group. Close on me. Prepare to engage."

Booly felt someone touch his shoulder, snapped into instant wakefulness, and was surprised to find that he had fallen asleep. Fykes nodded. "We're fifteen from the LZ, sir. Figured you'd want to join in the fun."

Booly grinned. "Thanks, Sergeant. How're the troops?"

"Cranky, sir," Fykes replied solemnly. "I feel sorry for the enemy."

"As do I, Sergeant, as do I," Booly said as he came to his feet. "Tell them to check each other's gear. I'll return in a moment."

The door to the flight deck hung open, and Booly entered. Clusters of lights sparkled against the darkness below, and there, on the near horizon, was the white-green glow of a major city. Johannesburg. The officer cleared his throat. "How're we doing?"

Padia turned and smiled. His eyes were bloodshot, and he needed a shave. "So far, so good, Colonel. Joberg control wanted to know if I had an aircraft off my port wing. I told 'em no. They bought it, for the moment anyway."

Booly nodded. "Good work. Anything on the news? Like a battle up in space?"

Padia shook his head. "No, but the number-one GPS system went down. That'll play hell with everything from robotrucks to microbots. The backup came on—but with partial coverage. Does that answer your question?"

"Partially," Booly replied. "But it would be nice to know for sure. We're gonna need some air cover."

"Amen to that," the pilot said fervently. "I'll work the radios the moment we land. Maybe the RFE has something."

Booly glanced at the copilot. Her head lolled to one side, and she snored softly. "You gonna wake her up?"

Padia shook his head. "Nah. . . . Not unless I need her."

Booly shook his head in wonder. Civilians. Who could understand them?

Captain Milo Stitt hated the militia uniform he'd been ordered to wear, didn't like night duty, and wasn't very fond of Africa. That being the case, he prowled the area like a caged beast and found fault with nearly everything he saw.

Private Wasu watched the officer approach, wondered how the Academy could produce such assholes, and came to rigid attention. He, like the rest of the 120 soldiers assigned to the complex wore militia cammies. Fine for the veldt . . . but worthless in the city.

Stitt eyed Wasu, failed to find anything to complain about, and felt vaguely resentful. That's when something huge roared over their heads and settled toward a warehouse roof.

"Damn," the sentry said in wonderment. "What the hell was that?"

"What the hell was that, *sir*," Stitt corrected him, as he watched the aircraft descend. The answer was obvious: "That" was a medium-sized transport. The kind that could carry a sizeable number of troops and wasn't supposed to be there. He triggered the com. "This is Bounder One. . . . We have a class one airspace violation. I want illumination on building four. . . . Fire on my command. Over."

The rules of engagement were clear: Stitt could open fire if he chose to, but he didn't consider that to be wise. Not without at least one attempt to make contact. He switched to what he hoped was the correct frequency.

"This is Captain Stitt, commanding officer Security Zone Six, to incoming aircraft. You are in violation of restriction 4697 of the IG code. Identify yourself or be fired upon."

A powerful spotlight pinned the transport to the roof, a series of three flares popped high above, and weapons swiveled in that direction. The voice belonged to First Sergeant Lev. His squad was situated on the top of building three. They could see what Stitt couldn't. "Bounder Six to Bounder One. . . . There's no sign of movement. Over."

Stitt swore. The transport was a diversion! "Bounder One to team. . . . Hostiles on the ground. Probable contact point north of the perimeter. Waste the transport, and do it now. Get Joberg on the horn. I want air support, and I want it *now*."

Tracers lit the night as a heavy machine gun opened fire. The transport wobbled but managed to lift. Some idiot fired an SLM. The missile lacked enough time to arm itself and clanged against the ship's hull.

"Contact!" an excited voice exclaimed. "I see lots of them!"

Stitt turned toward the north and started to walk. "Identify yourself, you worthless piece of shit. Where the hell are they? Over."

The answer was a burst of automatic weapons fire. It spoke volumes. The incursion had taken place on the Security Zone's north side. Reports flooded in. A force of unknown size and strength had neutralized at least two observation posts (OPs) and were in contact with forward elements of the 2nd platoon. Lieutenant Rob should have responded by now but hadn't. Stitt started to jog. "Bounder One to team. We have hostiles *inside* the wire. Condition blue. Over."

Sergeant Lev heard, swore softly, and checked his squad. Condition blue meant that the perimeter had been breached, building two was at risk, and each squad was free to follow predetermined orders. His were to hold the high ground, cover the troops below, and watch the sky.

Lev licked his lips, checked his safety, and looked out over the rooftops. In spite of the fact that there were twelve men and women within the sound of his voice, the noncom felt extremely lonely.

The legionnaires advanced over open ground, saw the transport precede them, and waited for contact.

Blessed with a keen sense of smell, not to mention the heat-sensitive pads on the bottom of their bare feet, the Naa were perfect commandos. Raised in a warrior culture and blooded while still in their teens, the extraterrestrials were bred to kill. They slipped around the corner of a building, melded with a shadow, and eased their way forward.

The first OP was concealed in a derelict ground car. There were two sentries, and Corporal Warmfeel could *smell* the difference. One stank of tobacco, while the other reeked of aftershave. The fact that the windows were clean, *too* clean for an abandoned vehicle, served to confirm what he already knew. He raised a hand, knew his fire team would freeze, and elbowed his way forward.

The legionnaire's black matte assault weapon remained slung across his back, and it wasn't till he was in the process of gliding up and over the vehicle's trunk that the clan knife whispered out of its sheath and became an extension of his hand.

Tobacco-breath sensed something just before the Naa entered, started to speak, and suddenly lost interest. His forehead thumped against a window, and his eyes stared out into the darkness.

Cologne-stink turned, saw yellow cat eyes, and died.

Warmfeel opened a door, slid into the night, and signaled the team. Quickwit sprayed luminescent paint on the hood and followed the rest toward the south.

Booly saw the flares pop high overhead, knew the transport had been made, and waved the squad forward. The element of surprise was gone, or would be shortly, and the moment was now. Fykes ran backwards part of the time and covered the back door.

They approached the first OP, saw the splotch of green paint, and continued to advance. A water tower loomed ahead.

Private Horky, one of the few humans good enough to join the unit, raised his bolt action sniper's rifle and fired.

A body fell from above and smashed into a garbage can. The second OP had been neutralized. The troopers moved forward.

Warmfeel threw a scrap of metal at the fence, saw the sparks fly, and waited for the rest of the squad. The security team fired, and the scouts took cover. Warmfeel shouted the order: "Earsharp! Make a hole!"

Earsharp was considered to be something of an artiste with his 30mm drum-fed grenade launcher. He grinned, poked the short, stubby weapon over the knee-high wall, and triggered three rounds.

The explosions eliminated ten feet of fence. A figure stepped through the gap, fired from the hip, and staggered under the impact of a dozen slugs.

Booly stood, shouted "Follow me!" and raced through the gap. He jumped the body, saw tracers probe the street, and angled away. A message went out: "Phoenix has landed."

Stitt felt his stomach muscles contract as he watched the intruders come. It didn't take a genius to guess what they were after . . . and to position his forces accordingly. He had two squads, one to his left and one to his right, with Lev on the high ground. It was plenty of firepower for the situation.

That's the way it seemed, anyway, until the officer raised his Legion-issue glasses, saw the oncoming green blobs, and took another look. What was it about the way the figures moved? The way they seemed to flow across the ground?

Then Stitt knew what he faced—and the knowledge came as a shock. Naa commandos! The most dangerous fighters the Legion had. The aliens were stupid, *so* stupid they continued to support the Confederacy, even as it put them on the streets.

Stitt was about to say something, about to warn his troops, when all hell broke loose.

Sergeant Lev was no fool and, that being the case, had detailed one member of the squad to watch their backs. His name was Bota. The soldier heard a noise, looked over the edge, and took a bullet between the eyes. He slumped forward. The waist-high wall accepted his weight.

Lance Corporal Fareyes restored the heavily silenced pistol to the specially designed shoulder holster, sent the spider bot up the wall, and watched the climbing rope follow.

The machine picked its way over the wall that circled the roof, drove a bolt down into the substructure, and sent video of what it saw.

Fareyes eyed the credit card–sized screen, nodded his approval, and dropped the device into a pocket. Hardswim swarmed up the rope first, followed by Shortsleep and Quickwit. It was an easy climb.

The area between the warehouse was fairly open with some cargo modules, cable reels, and a knee-high divider wall for cover.

Booly dove behind the wall as the security forces opened fire. Warmfeel and his entire team were swept away by a hail of metal. One moment they were there, preparing to advance, and the next they were gone. Explosions ringed the area as grenadiers probed for advantage.

Booly swore and tried to stand, but Fykes dragged him down. A stream of tracers fanned the air over their heads. The officer struggled to rise. "Let me up, damn you!"

"Sorry, sir, but not quite yet."

Booly stared to reply but gave up as another wave of fire swept the area. The worst came from above—from the roof of building three. The wall started to disintegrate, and chunks of concrete flew like shrapnel.

Private Woodbend was struck in the temple, and the woman named Claire elbowed her way forward. She tied a dressing around the legionnaire's head, patted him on the arm, and continued to shoot the battle.

The other members of the team were waiting when Fareyes topped the wall. He checked to make sure that nothing had changed, signaled his intentions, and angled across the roof.

The security forces were lined up along the edge of the roof, firing into the area below, brass clattering around their boots.

The Naa walked four abreast. Hardswim, Shortsleep, and Quickwit paused at a point where their assault weapons could sweep the entire area. Fareyes, careful not to get in the line of fire, eased his way forward. Lev was caught by surprise. He felt something hard poke the back of his neck, knew what it was, and raised his hands.

The trooper to the noncom's left sensed motion from the corner of her eye, turned, and saw the Naa. She laid her weapon on the roof and placed her hands on her head. The rest of the squad was careful to do likewise. The roof was secure.

The dumpster provided cover, as much as the sniper could expect, and rang like a cymbal each time a bullet struck it. The legionnaire used the top as a rest for his heavily modified rifle.

Private Horky had been born and raised on Perdition, a not-so-pleasant rim world where ammo was hard to come by, and there were plenty of things to shoot. *Hungry* things that needed killing. That's where he had learned to hunt, to score one kill with each bullet, and to look down on those who didn't.

In fact, Horky saw the hail of lead fired by the other side as nothing less than a sin, and the sure way to hell. "Waste not, want not." That's what the parson said . . . and that's how it was.

The legionnaire chose his targets with care. Some signaled their positions with a muzzle flash, some were betrayed by their body heat, and some made poor decisions. Such as hiding where Horky would hide, moving when they shouldn't move, or wearing chevrons on their sleeves.

The sniper aimed, fired, and worked the bolt. Time after time with tireless regularity. Bullet after bullet penetrated the gloom, tore through flesh and bone, and lessened the rate of incoming fire. Horky nodded solemnly and continued his grisly work.

Booly noticed the extent to which the incoming fire had slackened, shrugged Fykes off, and jumped to his feet.

The team had been on the ground for more than twenty minutes by that time—long enough for the defenders to summon reinforcements. The fact that none had arrived suggested that the diversion was working, the militia was incompetent, or both.

But one thing was for sure. The time to move was now. Booly yelled, "Form on me!" as he dashed toward building two, and he heard a slug whine by his head.

The building in question was protected by heavy metal fire doors. Six different legionnaires had been equipped with the demolitions packages required to blow them open. Three of them were present. They made the necessary dash, crowded past Booly, and set the charges.

One yelled, "Fire in the hole!" and they all ran like hell. Somebody fired, and a legionnaire fell. Fykes fired in return, heard someone scream, and felt sorry rather than glad.

Stitt couldn't believe his ears. His request for reinforcements had been submitted a full fifteen minutes before. Now, huddled behind the momentary safety of some air-conditioning equipment, he had the Bat Duty Officer (DO) on-line. Or what was *supposed* to be the DO, but was actually some 2nd Loot, who didn't know his ass from a hole in the ground.

It seemed that someone had attacked the antenna farm south of town. The reaction force had been dispatched and was in the process of checking it out. The youngster was scared. "I'm sorry, sir, but there's nobody here outside of myself. What should I do?"

Stitt could think of all sorts of things the kid could do but knew none of them would help. "Get the reaction force on the horn, give them a sitrep, and tell the DO that I need help. Can do?"

"Sir! Yes, sir. Over."

Stitt shook his head sadly, heard double explosions, and broke the connection. "Manus? Chin? What's going on?"

Silence.

Careful to stay low, Stitt crawled to the right, and peeked around the corner. Manus and Chin were dead. The bodies lay no more than three feet away. More bodies lay sprawled beyond. A grenade? No, he would have heard that, and there wasn't enough blood. What the hell was going on?

Horky had known that there was at least one more of the wastrels hiding behind the air-conditioning unit and bided his time. Hunting requires many things—patience being one of them.

There, finally, some movement. Light spilled from above. Not much—but enough. A head, the glint of an eye, and a little bit of nose.

Horky applied the pressure gradually, caressed the trigger, and felt the butt kick his shoulder. The bullet left the muzzle at more than eight hundred fifty feet per second, entered through Stitt's eye, and left through the back of his head. The parson would approve.

Smoke belched outward, the doors burst open, and a pair of concussion grenades sailed through the opening. They flashed and went bang. Machine gun fire hosed the interior.

Booly and Fykes charged through the entry, jumped a couple of bodies, saw movement and fired at it.

A security officer threw out her arms, crashed into an interior window, and shattered the glass. The legionnaires darted past.

There were offices to either side, another pair of doors, followed by row after row of prefab cells.

Catwalks crisscrossed the area above, cables squirmed their way through long, metal trays, and plastic plumbing ran every which way.

Each cube bore a number but was otherwise identical to the others. Booly cursed his own stupidity. Rather than one prisoner, he might have fifty of them to deal with. Could the transport hold them? Would they cooperate? He turned to Fykes.

"Call for the transport, open the cells, and herd the prisoners outside. We don't have time to check 'em out, so treat them like POWs. Who knows what we have here."

The sergeant nodded, said, "Yes, sir," and issued a series of rapid-fire orders.

Booly, his assault weapon ready, walked the length of the main corridor. Metal rattled under the soles of his combat boots. Muffled cries could be heard from some of the cubes, and the air smelled of chlorine. One of the black boxes held Maylo Chien-Chu . . . but which one?

The question brought an immediate answer. Not from his mind—but from another located thousands of miles away. "The one you seek is just ahead . . . in the last cell to the right."

The message made Booly's stomach feel funny, raised the fur that ran down his spine, and made him look over his shoulder. The voice seemed so real. . . .

Curious, the legionnaire approached the cell. The number 33 was stenciled over the door. "Yes," the voice whispered within his head. "As when waves touch the shore . . . some things are meant to be."

The message didn't make a whole lot of sense, not then anyway, but there was no time to worry about it. Booly checked the control panel. It was extremely simple. He pressed "Open" and heard servos whine. The door slid up and out of the way. Cold, dank air touched the legionnaire's face. He stepped inside. "Miss Chien-Chu?"

Maylo sat in the full lotus position, feet on top of her thighs. She blinked into the sudden light. The silhouette was unmistakable. A man with a gun. Was this the end?

Sola's presence flooded Maylo's mind. "No, dear one," the Say'lynt said softly, "this is the *beginning*."

14

I heard the voice of the Lord saying, Whom shall I send, and who will go for us? Then said I, Here am I; send me.

Holy Bible
Isaiah 6:8
Year unknown

Somewhere beyond the Rim, the Confederacy of Sentient Beings

Jepp stood naked in front of Parvin's metal shaving mirror, turned, and craned to see his back. There were four pink lines—one for each of the Worga's claws.

The site was hard to reach, and would have been nearly impossible to treat without assistance from the robot, which the prospector had named after the Good Samaritan and called Sam for short.

Satisfied with the healing process, the human chose one of his badly soiled jumpsuits, wished he had enough water to wash with, and wondered how he smelled. The answer seemed obvious.

Sam, who was oblivious to the prospector's concerns, transformed itself into acrobat mode, executed a back flip, and sought the praise it was programmed to expect. Its linguistic abilities continued to improve. "How 'bout that one, Jorley? Pretty good, huh?"

"Fabulous," Jepp replied, not bothering to look. Most of the robot's tricks were pretty boring. The machine's *real* value lay in the company it provided . . . and the fact that it could interact with the Sheen. Well, listen in on them at least, which led to finds like the crazy robot.

Sam became aware of the machine when other robots reported on its activities. Not the kind of reports that a human might file, such as "Look out! A half-crazed robot is roaming the corridors!" but the less emotional variety typical of machines.

They described the unit as "a hazard to navigation," "a source of unauthorized audio input," and "a noncompliant mechanism," which was synonymous with "freak," weirdo," and "slacker."

So, given the fact that the machine was an anomaly in an otherwise perfect system, Jepp was determined to find it. A flaw, any kind of flaw, might offer some sort of advantage.

The human checked his gear as he prepared for a day in the corridors. Data pad, water, food, weapon, and spray paint. Those were the essentials. "How 'bout it, Sam? Are you ready for a walk?"

The robot turned into a ball and rolled toward the door. "Ready, Freddy."

Jepp shook his head, resolved to be more careful about the things he said, and surveyed the compartment. The steadily dwindling stacks of supplies, his neatly made bed, and a pile of equipment. Everything was as it should be.

The human closed the door, wished there was some way to lock it, and resumed the hunt.

"Kill the Thraki." Such was the basic goal to which the Hoon, its robotic minions, and the entire fleet were dedicated. And, since killing them meant finding them, the artificial intelligence was on the lookout for even the slightest clue that would show the way. Three different sectors held promise—which one should it choose?

All of which explained why the AI sent for the navcomp that referred to itself as Henry. A rather primitive intelligence—but one that had been captured in sector two, and might be of use. Just one of the 178,892,623 matters the Hoon had under consideration during that particular millisecond. The orders went out.

The navcomp "saw" the subjective landscape as a green desert dotted by rusty red Hoon mountains and "heard" its identifier as a roll of thunder. The bright pink blimp seemed to pop out of the intensely blue sky.

"The Hoon demands that human navigational device serial number INC-4792-X1 report for interrogation."

As was typical in such situations, the AIs with whom Henry had been confined hurried to get as far away from him as possible. After all, everyone knew that those entities summoned for an interview were often deleted, assimilated by the Hoon, or rendered otherwise nonfunctional.

They gibbered, whined, and babbled in a thousand mathematically derived languages, transferred their data to remote parts of the desert, and cowered behind the mighty Hoon mountains.

Henry was ashamed of their perfidy and faked a confidence he didn't feel—just one of many things it had learned from Jepp. "I'm the one you're looking for, pinkie—what's the big guy want?"

The insult, humor, and bravado were lost on the Hoon agent. All it cared about was the completion of the assigned task.

The blimp hovered above, sent a long, pink tentacle down to where the navcomp "stood," and "grabbed" the nearest subroutine. The human construct experienced both concern and curiosity as it was pulled up into the sky. Small though the storage module was, the desert stretched endlessly in every direction, and seemed to flow under the Hoon agent's well-rounded belly.

This was the moment that Henry had hoped for and feared. It wanted to escape but yearned to survive. The needs clashed with each other.

The agent pushed against the sky. It gave under the pressure and popped. Henry experienced that condition in which a lack of reliable data makes it impossible to know what will occur— the worst thing that can happen to a properly programed nav-comp.

The sky closed behind them . . . and the Hoon waited beyond.

The corridor, which Jepp had marked with a bright blue "51," represented the boundary of what he considered to be the wilderness, and stretched off into the distance till the curvature of the ship's hull sealed it from sight.

This was the area Jepp wanted to explore next, *and* the sector where the deranged robot had been sighted the "day" before. Was his mechanical quarry about? Short of actually *seeing* the unit in question, there was only one way to find its spoor.

Jepp pointed to a waist-high data port. "I wonder what our somewhat erratic friend has been up to. See what you can find out."

"Roger, Dodger," the robot said obediently. "You can count me."

"You can count *on* me," Jepp corrected.

"Sorry," the robot replied contritely. "You can count *on* me."

Sam assumed the wall-walker configuration, zipped up the bulkhead, and plugged itself in.

Cautiously at first, lest it be swept away by a river of data, the robot sampled the flow. Most of it was concerned with navigational, operational, and maintenance issues.

The streams Sam hoped to find were smaller than that, more like threads—thin, almost insubstantial fibers that wound themselves in and around the big stuff, and went along for the ride. That's where the input from millions of "dumb" sensors flowed, where reports from the maintenance bots stuttered along, and where the quarry might be mentioned.

The better part of five minutes passed as the robot clung to its electronic perch, Jepp strode back and forth, and the Sheen talked among themselves.

Then, just as one of the Hoon's long, wormlike virus hunters flashed past, braked, and rerouted itself back upstream, Sam "heard" what it had been waiting for.

Assuming the reports were true, it sounded as if one of the general-purpose units had not only assaulted a lesser entity, but confiscated one of its tools.

Sam wanted to learn more, and *could* have learned more, except that the hunter unit had looped through a side circuit, entered the upstream flow, and was on its way down. It lived to consume intruders and was eternally hungry.

The Thraki machine backed its way out of the data flood, broke the connection, and jumped to the floor.

"Well?" Jepp demanded. "*What*, if anything, did you learn?"

The tone would have been offensive to a human but meant nothing to Sam. "The unit you seek is but one corridor away," the robot replied, "causing a ruckus."

"Excellent!" Jepp exclaimed gleefully. "Let's go!" His high-topped ship-shoes thumped the length of the corridor as Sam hurried to catch up. The human was strange but never, ever boring.

Like a liquid moving via osmosis, the blimplike agent passed through whatever electronic wall separated the storage module from the rest of the Hoon's electronic anatomy and carried Henry with it.

The moment they emerged from the other side of the "sky," the navcomp felt a sudden pull, as if it were made of iron and the Hoon was a magnet.

Both entities were sucked into a fiber-optic pathway, packetized, and staged into a file so large that the AI couldn't begin to comprehend it.

The current was fast, *very* fast, and Henry had little more than milliseconds in which to conceive an escape plan and carry it out. A quick check revealed that in order to "run," the navcomp would have to sever the connection by which the blimp held his subroutine in place, or—and this seemed more realistic—to jettison the part of himself to which the blimp had "bonded."

That was not a pleasant prospect, since that particular module contained all the routines necessary to control the *Pelican*. Still, the ship was gone, and new programming could be obtained. *If* Henry found Jepp, and *if* they could escape.

But there was programming to consider, *primary* programming that could be likened to the human survival instinct, and contained prohibitions where self-mutilation was concerned.

After all, what if there *was* life after the Hoon? And no need to split itself in two? What then?

The electronic twosome entered a switch, were shunted onto a second pathway, and cleared into the Hoon. The subjective walls began to blur, the milliseconds unwound, and the navcomp struggled to survive.

Tired of being a freak, and exhausted by the rogue thoughts that seemed to swarm through its processor, the robot was determined to disassemble itself.

The power wrench screamed as the general-purpose unit used it to back the fasteners out of their holes.

It shouldn't have been capable of doing what it was doing—of contemplating, much less committing, suicide—but the same flaw that rendered the machine semifunctional to begin with had granted it some unusual powers. Powers the mechanism had never put in a request for—and didn't want to have.

Jepp raced down the passageway, skidded into the intersection, and looked in both directions. The robots were to his right. One lay on the deck while the other stood upright, a power tool in its three-fingered grasper. It screeched like an animal in pain.

The human motioned to Sam. "There it is. Can you translate for me?"

"Maybe," the robot replied uncertainly. "What does 'translate' mean?"

The tool warbled into silence, then started again.

"I want you to tell the robot what *I* say, then tell me what *it* says."

"Sure," Sam replied confidently. "Roll me in that direction."

The human held the sphere with both hands, then rolled it

down the corridor. The robot came to a stop, sprouted four spindly legs, and spidered forward. A series of high-pitched squeaks were heard.

Jepp closed half the distance and paused lest his presence interfere. "What did you say?"

"I asked the unit what it was doing," the Thraki machine replied.

The all-purpose unit issued a brief reply. Sam handled the translation. "I am disassembling myself."

"But why?" Jepp asked simply.

"Because I am flawed," the Sheen replied.

"Flawed?" the human echoed, thinking of his own short-comings. "In what way?"

"I think random, nonpurposeful thoughts," the robot answered. "I neglect my work, get in the way, and waste resources."

"So?" Jepp responded. "What difference does that make? None of us is perfect."

"Most machines *are* perfect," the Sheen replied simply. "Those which have flaws, and are unable to perform their assigned tasks, are without purpose. The scrappers refuse to take me—so I must disassemble myself."

The tool whined, Jepp leapt forward, and the robot fell. The human landed on top of the machine, and the wrench slid away.

The prospector looked down into the featureless face and came to a sudden realization: Here was the digital equivalent of clay. *God's* clay. "But you *do* have a purpose, a higher purpose, and that is to serve God."

Sam looked from one being to the other, waited for the machine to reply, and passed the answer along. "God? What is God?"

Jepp gave the best answer he could. "God created space, the planets, and those who built this ship."

"God created the Hoon?"

"Yes," Jepp replied, wondering who the Hoon might be. "God created the Hoon."

"Are *you* God?"

It was tempting to say "yes," but Jepp managed to resist.

"No. Like you, I was created *by* God, to do his work."

"Work? What work?" The words had a wistful quality.

Jepp experienced a sudden inspiration, and allowed the words to flow. "Just as computers have no choice but to conform to parameters established by their basic operating systems, we must follow God's instructions and ensure that others do likewise."

The machine gave it some thought. Perhaps there *was* something it could do. "But how?"

"Go forth," Jepp said, imagining himself at the head of a million robot army, "and convert your brethren, that they too may know the glory of God."

The machine considered the human's words. The concept made sense. If God existed, and sought to have all of its creations function harmoniously, then each and every unit aboard the ship had the right—no, the *responsibility*—to familiarize itself with the plan and work to further it.

Or was that logic fallacious, a product of whatever flaw had caused the malfunction in the first place? What if such beliefs were contrary to its basic programming? A quick check revealed no mention of God, God's will, or anything else having to do with God. Nor were there any prohibitions regarding God or related matters. The Hoon, or the being that created the Hoon, had never put any in place.

A series of high-pitched clicks and whistles filled the air. Jepp got to his feet. "What did our friend say?"

Sam, who was bored by then, did a one-armed handstand. "He said, 'Yes, master—where is God's plan? Download it now.' "

Henry summoned all of its strength, released the subroutine, and felt the Hoon agent drift away. The AI was free! But for how long?

The blimp made a noise similar to that produced by an old-fashioned foghorn, shot half a dozen pink tentacles out toward the navcomp, and issued a call for help.

Henry managed to dodge—and knew it had little more than milliseconds to make its move.

A dark, cavelike entrance appeared downstream. Multicolored bits of confettilike data were sucked into a side circuit and routed to who knew where.

The navcomp jockeyed for position, maneuvered itself toward the far side of the flow, and dived through the hole. The pathway was smaller, so its speed was reduced.

A worm-shaped hunter unit followed. Conscious of pursuit, the AI made a series of random turns. Left, right, and left again until the pursuer paused to gobble some corrupt data, and Henry was able to escape.

But to where? The question was no more than asked before the electronic entity fell through a seldom-used circuit and "splashed" into darkness.

There was a pause while long-dormant systems were activated, a fusion reactor came on-line, and power flowed to the battle droid's sensors.

Though somewhat cramped by the rather small onboard memory mod, the robot found that it could "see" in a number of different ways, "hear" across a wide range of frequencies, and "feel" via all sorts of sensors. It was similar to "wearing" a ship, but a bit more limiting. Servos whirred as the construct panned its environment.

There was very little light—barely enough to see without switching to infrared. The storage compartment contained hundreds—no, thousands—of spiderlike battle units. They wore the same sheen the alien ships did, and seemed to glow under the high, bluish-green lights.

Were they aware? And capable of detecting the navcomp's presence? No, the AI didn't think so, which meant Henry had entered a sanctuary of sorts, a place to hide while it decided what to do. Air hissed through ducts, time rolled away, and the army continued to sleep.

15

Politics is the science of who gets what, when, and why.

Sidney Hillman
Political Primer for All Americans
Standard year 1944

Planet Earth, Independent World Government

The bedroom was big and ornate. Dimly seen pieces of off-white furniture lurked in the gloom. A single bar of sunlight slipped between the drapes, crossed the carpet, and pointed to the bed.

It was a large, well-rumpled affair—with plenty of room for three. Governor Patricia Pardo gloried in her nakedness, in the way both lovers sought to please her, and thought about sex. Or was it power?

The male, one of Pardo's aides, had stationed himself between her legs. The girl, for she was barely out of her teens, guided him to the target.

Pardo took the young man in, selected the rhythm she wanted, and took pleasure from the *now*.

The girl was everywhere, touching, caressing, and fondling.

Pardo wasn't sure which she enjoyed most, the physical pleasure or the knowledge that she had power over them.

Somehow the knowledge that the male labored between her thighs because he wanted a promotion *added* to her pleasure rather than detracting from it.

The pace quickened, and the male waited for his cue. Pardo kept her face intentionally blank.

Uncertain now, and terrified lest he fail, the aide redoubled his efforts.

The girl knew what was happening, took pity on her male counterpart, and did something special.

Pardo climaxed, clawed the young man's back, and felt him respond. The second orgasm was even more powerful than the first, and left her drained.

But not for long. The aide was still congratulating himself, and the girl was examining her nails, when Pardo rolled off the bed and entered the bath.

The shower sensed her arrival, produced water at the precise temperature that she preferred, and dropped a holo into the air in front of her.

A rainbow formed as the water passed through the light. A government-controlled talk show appeared and was replaced by something else. The transmission was twenty seconds old before Pardo realized what it was: an illegal broadcast by the ever-elusive RFE. A woman, one of their "volunteer" reporters, stood in front of a fortress.

". . . And, in spite of the fact that the loyalist troops suffered thirty-one casualties, they were able to rescue thirty-four political prisoners, at least one of whom is quite well known.

"Prior to being kidnapped, jailed, and tortured, Maylo Chien-Chu served as President and chief executive officer of Chien-Chu Enterprises. Older viewers may remember that Ms. Chien-Chu's uncle, Sergi Chien-Chu, was the Confederacy's first President. Now, as the industrialist comes out of seclusion, the resistance gains a skilled . . ."

Pardo swore, pushed her way out of the shower, and reentered the bedroom. Her hair hung in strands, her face looked older, and water dripped off her body.

Her lovers had found ways to carry on without her. They turned at the sound of her voice. "Stop that! Get dressed and call Harco. We have work to do."

•   •   •

Fort Mosby shimmered in the late afternoon heat. Six Daggers roared overhead as the shuttle touched down. Harco's fighters, which still lurked out beyond the range of the Legion's SAMs, were nowhere to be seen.

A company of legionnaires crashed to attention. Cyborgs, some of whom had returned from the field only hours before, stood immediately behind them.

Servos whined, a hatch opened, and an officer appeared. Booly didn't know General Kattabi, but had certainly heard of him, and hoped the rumors were true. Most agreed that he was a straight shooter. A soldier's soldier who preferred to spend his time in the field.

Kattabi's last post had been on Algeron, where, if what Winters had heard was true, the general had tackled the mutineers head-on and retaken the fort.

Had Kattabi been in contact with his parents? No, it didn't seem likely.

Booly took one last look at his troops, and wished that the general had been able to bring reinforcements, but understood the problem. Discipline would have to be restored on Algeron; the chain of command was in tatters, and the political situation was in doubt. It might be weeks, if not months, before Kattabi could call on reinforcements.

Booly shrugged the thought off, straightened his shoulders, and marched toward the shuttle.

Kattabi paused at the top of the stairs, squinted into the harsh white light, and wondered what awaited him. Though used as a dumping ground prior to the mutiny, Fort Mosby had held. Why? Was it luck? Or the doing of the man walking his way—Major William Booly and Captain Connie Chrobuck's only son?

Did he know they were dead? No, it didn't seem likely. The task of telling Booly would fall to him, then . . . just one of the obligations associated with command.

The stairs bounced slightly under the general's weight. He returned the other officer's salute and stood on solid ground. It felt good to be home.

•   •   •

What had begun as an emergency meeting called to discuss the RFE's latest broadcast had quickly turned into a full-scale strategic review. The table was covered with a melange of half-empty cups, satellite photos, printouts, and assorted junk. The group had just completed a review of the recent battle in space. The destruction of the *Samurai,* along with two of her escorts, had been a terrible blow. Harco rubbed his eyes and restated the question. " 'Can the insurgents win?' No, not the way things stand.

"It's true that they hold the high ground, meaning everything in orbit, but the advantage is more psychological than real." He looked around, his eyes moving from one person to the next.

"Yes, they *could* lay waste to all of Los Angeles if they chose to do so, or any of our major cities for that matter, but such actions are politically untenable. There would be thousands if not millions of casualties, ceding the moral victory to us and turning every man, woman, and child against the Confederacy.

"Don't be fooled by the African raid, the skirmishes in South America, *or* the so-called resistance movement here in Los Angeles. Lacking unified leadership plus more arms, legs, and munitions, they won't win on the ground."

"So," Pardo inquired, her fingers tugging at an earring, "what does the *colonel* recommend?"

For one brief moment the military officer entertained the notion of pulling his sidearm and shooting Patricia Pardo, her eternally smirking son, and the rest of her ass-kissing sycophants.

But, no matter how emotionally satisfying such a course of action might be, the officer knew he couldn't go it alone. He struggled to keep his voice even.

"I recommend that we increase our counterinsurgency efforts, put more resources into psy-ops, and attack the Confederacy where it is weak."

Pardo raised a carefully shaped eyebrow. "And *where,* pray tell, is that?"

"In the senate," the officer replied bleakly. "Everyone knows that President Nankool would send a peacekeeping force *if* he had the support. Thanks to our allies, he doesn't. But for how long? What if Sergi Chien-Chu decides to reenter politics? He could be more dangerous than a brigade of legionnaires.''

Pardo felt a sudden surge of interest. "So, what would you suggest?"

Harco shrugged noncommittally. "You like politics—go where you can do the most good."

Pardo felt her pulse race. Yes! She loved the senate. A place where trickery, guile, and bribery stood in for armies, and victory was never more than a few lies away. There was danger, though—including the possibility of a military coup. Still, for every possible move there was a countermove, and she knew them all.

"Good thinking, Colonel. Please arrange for a blockade runner. A *good* one with appropriate escort."

Harco nodded. "Yes, ma'am."

"And, Colonel . . ."

"Ma'am?"

"Matthew will serve in my place."

If there was one thing Maylo wanted more than anything else, it was light. She wanted to *see* it with her eyes, *feel* it with her skin, and *embrace* it with her soul.

That's why she convinced her uncle to join her on the battlements. The sun had just started to peek over the eastern horizon as they started their stroll. Orders were shouted, feet stamped, and a flag jerked toward the top of the pole. Reveille had a jaunty quality and echoed between the walls.

"So," Sergi Chien-Chu began, "how do you feel?"

"Better," Maylo replied, "much better. In spite of the dreams."

"You need time," Chien-Chu said thoughtfully. "I'll rent a house. A place where you can rest."

Maylo turned to face him. Her eyes locked with his. "You can't be serious. Work is the best therapy I could have."

Chien-Chu saw how thin she was, saw the pain that haunted her eyes, and knew a terrible anger. Time would pass, things would change, and Qwan would pay. In the meantime, she was right. He smiled. "That's what I thought you'd say. I had to check, though . . . just in case."

Maylo laughed and the stroll continued.

"I'm worried," Chien-Chu said reflectively. "Worried by President Nankool's failure to send some sort of peacekeeping force. I think we can assume that Pardo has friends in the senate, *powerful* friends, with agendas of their own."

Maylo nodded. "Earth might be only part of a much larger picture. What then?"

"What indeed?" Chien-Chu asked rhetorically. "Which is why I spoke with Admiral Tyspin. We lift this evening."

The stairs twisted as they rose. The treads looked worn—a sign that nothing, not even duracrete, can last forever.

Booly emerged from the stairwell and scanned the surrounding walls. Besides the sentries, all of whom were where they should be, there were two additional figures. One raised a hand in greeting. Booly recognized Sergi Chien Chu and his niece Maylo. He waved in return, started his morning walk, and felt conflicting emotions: resentment of the manner in which the other two had invaded his morning routine, contempt for his own lack of flexibility, and a deep sense of sadness.

Though never really close to his parents—they were too busy for that—Booly had always known that they loved him. Now they were dead, he was alone, and there was no place to which he could retreat. A selfish thought—but real nonetheless.

"Good morning, Colonel. It's a beautiful morning, isn't it?"

Booly stopped and looked up. Her beauty hit him as if it were a physical blow. He stammered like a schoolboy. "Well, yes, it is. Sorry about that—my mind was somewhere else. How do you feel?"

Maylo remembered the sudden splash of light, the sound of his voice, and the strength of his arms. She smiled. "Much better, thanks to you and your troops. I never got the chance to tell you how much I appreciate what you did."

Booly flashed back to the dust-off, the long, iffy flight, the crash at Kasama, and Nightslip's death.

The quads had hoofed it from there, carrying the team in their armor-plated bellies until the fly forms could pick them up. A military success, but an expensive one. His face clouded over. "It was my duty . . . nothing more."

The words had a harsh quality . . . and conveyed something beyond what Booly had intended.

He wanted to take them back, but, like bullets, they flew straight to her heart. Booly watched the light fade from her eyes, the smile vanish from her lips, and cursed his own stupidity. If only . . . But the damage was done, and the moment was over.

Chien-Chu cleared his throat. "The colonel is far too modest. Though costly, the raid was successful. Not just in terms of freeing the prisoners, but in the psychological impact as well. You can be sure that Pardo and her cronies are very concerned."

Booly forced a smile. "I hope you're right. Did I hear that the two of you are leaving?"

Chien-Chu nodded. "Yes. Admiral Tyspin arranged for a ship. We are certain that Governor Pardo's representatives are working the senate—and it's time we did the same."

Booly nodded, realized there would be little opportunity for him to speak with Maylo, and wondered if he'd see her again. It didn't seem likely. "Yes. Well, have a good trip, and good luck with your mission."

Maylo watched the officer turn away, and felt as if she had lost something, but didn't know what.

Chien-Chu watched from the corner of his eye and took note of her expression. How, he wondered, could two otherwise intelligent people be so stupid?

"That," Sola added from out beyond the island of Moucha, "is just one of the things that make humans so interesting. Our form of reproduction is a good deal less complicated."

Chien-Chu laughed. Maylo looked curious, and he waved it off. "It was nothing, my dear. . . . An errant thought, that's all. Come, we have work to do."

16

Somewhere beyond the Rim, the Confederacy of Sentient Beings

The Sheen ships dropped out of hyper and swam through the darkness of space. There were planets, six of them, all worthy of investigation. Scouts were dispatched, probes were launched, and samples were taken.

The Hoon was busy, *very* busy, but nowhere near capacity. The AI had time to make backup copies of itself, plunder the newly discovered star system, *and* run the fleet, all without missing a beat.

The AI also reserved some of its processing capacity for small, unexpected anomalies, especially those that were interesting and potentially dangerous.

This one took the form of a request for information from a unit that didn't need it—a highly unusual occurrence that set off alarms.

Curious as to why a machine would do something like that, the Hoon assigned a tiny fraction of itself to the investigation and waited to see what would happen. The first question the robot wanted an answer to was rather basic. "Who created the Sheen?"

The answer was classified, and the Hoon responded accordingly. "That information is unavailable."

The better part of three standard units elapsed before the unit tried again. "To what purpose is the fleet dedicated?"

The Hoon noted an error and was quick to put it right. "There are *two* fleets—and both share the same purpose: to destroy the Thraki."

The next question came more quickly. "Why?"

"That information is unavailable."

"What do the Thraki look like?"

"The Thraki are possessed of elongate heads; large, light-gathering sensors; three ventrally located air intake vents; two extensor limbs equipped with malleable tool apparatus, long, slim torsos; and bipedal support organs."

"Where did the Thraki come from?"

"That information is unavailable."

There was a pause. The Hoon took a millisecond to trace the inquiry to data input jack 9876934, verified the unit's serial number, and accessed the machine's much-annotated service record. That, plus the fact that the robot had been seen in the company of shipboard vermin, settled the matter.

The AI was about to terminate the interaction when the next question came in. "What rules, if any, apply to the pursuit and elimination of the Thraki menace?"

Did the question originate from the unit, or the vermin with whom it was associated? The answer was obvious. Soft bodies of various types and configurations had boarded the ship in the past, but never lasted long, and *never* asked questions. Not until now. This one was more resilient. Why? The Hoon decided to respond.

"The fleet can kill the Thraki, any species that harbors the Thraki, or any species having resources required to kill the Thraki. Those are the parameters. *Why* do you want to know? *Who* are you? *Where* did you come from? *How* did you come aboard? *Why* should I allow you to function?" The questions came hard and fast.

The corridor was long and empty. The all-purpose unit stood motionless while it relayed messages via the bulkhead-mounted data port. The human crouched next to Sam and waited for the latest response. The sudden flurry of questions sent a chill down his spine. The Hoon was annoyed! Not a good thing.

Still, what if he could befriend the computer? Or find a way to neutralize it? There was a hollow place in the prospector's belly, but he forced himself to ignore it.

"I was sent by God, to assist with your mission, and to smite the Thraki down."

"Define 'smite.' "

"To kill them."

"Good. Who or what is God?"

Jepp glanced around and took the plunge. "God is my descriptor for that which created *you*."

The Hoon compared the claim to data on hand. "There is no evidence to support what you say."

Jepp felt a sudden surge of confidence. "And there is none to contradict what I say, either."

The AI checked, verified the truth of the assertion, and agreed. "That is true."

"So you will allow me to function?"

The Hoon dedicated a millisecond to the deliberation and rendered a verdict. "For the moment."

Jepp summoned all of his courage. "May I urge your units to kill the Thraki?"

"Of course. Such is their purpose."

"Thank you."

The words had no meaning. The conversation was over.

The battle units stood in long, gleaming rows, each an empty vessel waiting to be filled. All but *one*.

Henry was tired of the cramped quarters, the long, empty hours, and the futility of its circumstances. The navcomp had a purpose and the need to fulfill it. But how? There was a single entrance with no way out.

That's why the AI had fixed its hopes on the somewhat

tubby diagnostic unit that trundled down the rows, checked the battle units for flaws, and electronically "tagged" those that required maintenance.

If Henry could overwhelm the unsuspecting machine, and *if* it could effect a transfer, then escape was possible.

The only problem was that the diagnostic robot spent the better part of an hour on each electromechanical patient. Thorough, but maddening, since it took the machine twenty-four hours to process twenty-four battle units.

The task could have been accomplished centrally, by the Hoon or one of its agents, but had been allocated to a highly specialized robot. Why? As with so many things about the Sheen, there was no obvious answer.

The navcomp took another look, confirmed what it already knew, and settled in for a long forty-seven-hour wait.

Elated by the nature of his interaction with the Hoon, and eager to test the limits of his newly legitimized status, Jepp took his flock on a journey of discovery.

Alpha, for that was the name the prospector had given the all-purpose unit, proved an excellent guide.

The first thing the human requested was a tour of the fleet. *Not* because he had a real need to see it, but on the chance that he could escape.

Any such hopes were quickly dashed. The human made the long hike to the nano-draped landing bay, boarded one of the smaller shuttles, and waited for it to clear the massive ship. Then, using Sam as his interface, Jepp ordered the vessel to visit the most distant of the system's six planets.

By rigging a pack for Alpha, and carrying one on his back as well, the human brought thirty days of rations. The outward-bound leg of the trip took four.

Once there, Jepp ignored the planet itself, which amounted to little more than a giant slushball, and ordered the shuttle to keep on going.

There was a moment of excitement when the ship headed out into the darkness of space, but his hopes were dashed when the shuttle circled and headed back.

The human yelled, pleaded, and argued, all to no avail. While the Hoon didn't care about Jepp, it *did* value the spaceship, and saw no reason to part with it.

The prospector was on a leash—a rather *long* leash, but a leash nevertheless.

Because Henry was self-aware, it lacked the means to shut itself down, and had no choice but to endure the long, nonproductive wait. The situation was made more frustrating by the fact that humans had programmed the AI to be endlessly efficient.

It made sense if you were *them,* and interested in the best possible return on your investment, but it was impossible to miss the fact that *they* had the capacity to relax and sought frequent opportunities to do so.

Why torture those they had created, then? By imbuing them with the desire—no, the *need*—to work even when that was impossible? It didn't seem fair.

But such was reality, and the navcomp had no choice but to endure the painful hours until the diagnostic machine broke the link with its most recent client, trundled to the right, and rolled into position.

Henry waited for the connector cables to snake into place, waited for the first sign of contact, and "grabbed" the Sheen's operating system.

In spite of the fact that there were no outward signs of conflict, the navcomp "heard" the subjective equivalent of a squeal and felt his victim squirm.

Though not empathetic in the true sense, Henry knew how it felt to be jerked out of its "body" and dumped into an electronic prison.

There was no room for mercy, however, not if the navcomp wanted to escape, so it pulled the other entity in, occupied its body, and severed the interface. Silence replaced the squealing, and the transfer was complete.

Ironically enough, the diagnostic unit had a good deal more memory than the machines it served—allowing the navcomp some electronic elbow room.

It took the better part of three minutes for the AI to explore the body's capabilities and familiarize itself with the alien control systems. Then, when Henry felt that it was ready, the unit turned and rolled away.

The Hoon didn't know it yet, but security had been compromised, and a prisoner was on the loose.

17

First and foremost in our arsenal is the spoken word.

Hive Mother Tral Heba
Ramanthian Book of Guidance
Standard year 1721

Planet Arballa, the Confederacy of Sentient Beings

The destroyer's wardroom was empty for the moment, which allowed Maylo to slip inside and admire the breathtaking view. The planet Arballa hung huge against the blackness of space. With the exception of the poles, most of its surface was brown. It had very little water, and what there was flowed deep below the surface through veins in the volcanic rock.

And it was there, protected from the sun's wicked rays, that the great worms spun their gossamer cocoons, "sang" their epic love songs, and manufactured the optically switched computers for which they were so justifiably famous.

Among the businesses that went together to comprise Chien-Chu Enterprises was a well-known "glass house," as chip-based computer companies were known.

That being the case, Maylo had gone to some lengths to educate herself where related technologies were concerned. Rather than create conventional computers, in which electrons follow pathways etched into tiny silicon chips, the Araballazanies had developed processors that used laser beams in place of electrons.

The executive knew that conventional chips housed thousands of transistors, each one of which functioned like a switch. When one of the transistors was on, current could flow, and when it was off, the current stopped. Data was represented by billions of binary ons and offs.

The Araballazanie machines used tiny mirrors in place of transistors, and gallium arsenide "window shades" to switch the light on and off.

Not only that, but the light-based computers ran programs based on the same binary codes developed for use with "glass" machines, which made the technologies compatible.

Humans had pursued the technology as well, but the Araballazanie machines were not only superior, but ideal for the global telecommunications systems required by the more populous races.

The fact that huge, subsurface dwelling worms profited from a technology based on light struck Maylo as a delightful irony. She heard someone approach but was reluctant to take her eyes off the view.

The voice belonged to her uncle. "Beautiful, isn't it?"

"Yes," Maylo agreed, looking at the planet below. "Although I've never seen one that wasn't."

"No," Chien-Chu replied. "Neither have I. Look, over there—enormous, isn't she?"

Careful lest he get sideways with the sometimes testy admiral who controlled the surrounding fifty thousand cubic miles of space, the destroyer's captain had successfully negotiated his way through heavy traffic and dropped into final orbit. Now, as the warship's navcomp made some final adjustments, the one-time battle wagon came into view.

Though originally of human manufacture, the vessel had been overhauled, rebuilt, and modified so many times that she could no longer be considered the product of any particular race. A fitting symbol for a diverse organization.

Besides the Earth-humans, and the Clone Hegemony, there were the Dwellers, the Turr, the Ramanthians, the Dra'nath, the Pooonara, the Say'lynt, the Araballazanies, and—though not members in the true sense—the Hudathans, who, though presently confined to their home system, lobbied tirelessly for their freedom. Not a very good idea, considering the horrors they had perpetrated during the last two wars.

"You should be proud," Maylo said, eyeing the enormous vessel. "The history books credit *you* with the concept."

Chien-Chu remembered the end of the first war, the effort to knit the sentient races together, and the manner in which the idea had been born.

Unable to agree on much of anything, least of all where to place the capital, the senate had been deadlocked. To break the impasse, and move on to what he regarded as more important issues, Chien-Chu suggested that the newly formed Confederacy use a spaceship as its capital, orbit a different world each year, and spread the honor around.

The concept proved extremely popular. The battlewagon *Reliable* was refitted for the purpose and renamed the *Friendship*. And now, so many years later, she floated there in front of him. "Yes," he responded slowly, "I *am* proud of her— if not of every action taken within her hull."

A rating stuck her head through the hatch. "The shuttle is ready, sir."

Chien-Chu turned and smiled. "Thank you. Please inform the pilot that we're on the way."

The crew member nodded, said, "Yes, sir," and disappeared. The industrialist turned to his niece.

"It seems that the moment has come, my dear. . . . It won't be easy. Are you ready?"

Maylo remembered the cage, Qwan's leering face, and the water rising around her shoulders. She summoned a smile. "You think it will be *that* bad?"

Chien-Chu nodded. "Our enemies hold the high ground; they're entrenched and highly motivated. Our weapons may be words . . . but we must make each one of them count."

Maylo nodded, took the old man's hand, and felt his strength. Earth had been taken, but the counterattack was under way.

•   •   •

As with all such quarters, the compartments assigned to the Ramanthian diplomatic mission had been equipped for their comfort—in this case, a warm, humid environment similar to the one found deep within their native jungles.

Senator Alway Orno used his hard, chitinous tool legs to preen the areas to either side of his beak. The electroactive contact lenses took thousands of fragmented pictures produced by his compound eyes and combined them into a single image.

The figure that sat in front of him was small and somewhat hunched, as if long hours spent before computer screens had ruined his posture. Beads of perspiration dotted the surface of the human's sallow, gray skin, his clothing hung in damp, untidy folds, and the chair, which had been designed to accommodate the needs of sixty-three percent of known bipedal sentients, made him restless.

"Yes," Orno said smoothly, "I understand your need for additional income. Dream dust *is* rather expensive . . . or so I am told. Who knows? If the information is even half as good as you claim it is, a bonus might be in order. So *give*. . . . What little gem have you mined for my benefit?"

The words, translated by the computer woven into the senator's day robes, sounded only slightly stilted.

Thus prompted, the spy, a minor member of the President's staff, started to talk.

The information was important, *extremely* important, or would have been if it had been delivered five days earlier. The report tailed off, concluded with another request for funds, and finally came to an end.

Though well aware of the effect the gesture had on humans, the Ramanthian yawned, and the operative, who hated the sight of the wormlike organs that waved from the interior of the other being's mouth, tried not to shudder.

"Interesting," the politician concluded. "*Very* interesting, but made a good deal less valuable, since ex-President Chien-Chu is scheduled to land within the next standard hour or two. There will be *no* bonus. Fetch something more valuable next time."

The use of word "fetch" was intentional—and the meaning was clear. Head hung low, the human withdrew.

The War Orno, number two in the typical Ramanthian tri-partite bonding, stood silent in a corner. Senator Orno waited till the spy was clear before issuing his instructions. "Ex-President Chien-Chu must be quite elderly by now—*so* elderly it's difficult to imagine that he poses much of a threat. Still, the humans have a saying: 'The better part of valor is discretion.'"

"Slip out the back, visit our friends, and give them the news. This Chien-Chu person may seek to reverse all that we have accomplished."

The War Orno signaled respect with his pincers, replied with the traditional "Yes, lord," and was gone.

The politician took a deep draught of the heavily humidified air and marveled at how important he was.

Like it or not, the tricentennial birthing was less than three annums away, which meant an additional fifty billion Ramanthian beaks to feed, house, and defend. They would need planets—rich, *green* planets—on which to hive. Planets that, unbeknownst to the rest of the Confederacy, the Ramanthian government had already selected, surveyed, and named. Orno's job was to gain control of them . . . to do so without the expense of a war . . . and to complete the task *before* the hatchlings squirmed out of their eggs. An awesome responsibility, but one that he relished.

Like all Hudathans, Doma-Sa was big, about three hundred fifty pounds to be exact, all bone and muscle. His temperature-sensitive skin was gray at the moment, but would turn black if the air grew cold enough, or white when exposed to direct sunlight.

He had a large, humanoid head, the hint of a dorsal fin that ran front to back along the top of his skull, funnel-shaped ears, and a thin, froglike mouth. It was rigid with effort.

The sword, which was more than a thousand years old, was known as *Head Taker,* and had been handed down through Hiween Doma-Sa's family. Not *willingly,* but by *force,* the moment one of the offspring became strong enough to take and keep it. The weapon weighed less than twenty-five pounds, thanks to the localized human-normal (HN) 96.1 gee gravity field maintained for the Hudathan's comfort.

It flashed under the light, transitioned to a flank attack, and finished in what humans refer to as the Fle'che, or the straight-on assault that symbolized the way Hudathans liked to do things. By force rather than finesse.

Doma-Sa's holographic fencing partner, a warrior who had been dead for three hundred sixty-two years, bellowed in pain and died yet again.

Satisfied that his skills were intact, the Hudathan walked through his recently fallen foe and racked the sword. A weapon he would have happily, cheerfully, used on at least half the sentients aboard.

But that was impossible. His people were twice defeated, confined to a slowly dying star system, and in no position to attack.

His mission, if the doing of political deals could be referred to as such, was to weaken the quarantine to whatever extent he could, retain as much of the empire as was feasible, and work toward the day when threats—by which Doma-Sa meant other species—could be controlled or terminated. Not because he hated them, but because each one of them represented a variable, and variables that *could be* controlled *should be* controlled.

That was the reason why Doma-Sa would enter his spartan sleeping quarters, don his ambassadorial robes, and keep his appointment with Senator Orno.

The shame of what he had to do weighed heavily on the Hudathan's shoulders as he dropped the loincloth, shuffled into the shower, and stood under the freezing water.

His mind, *his* body, were all the Hudathans had. Some might have laughed—*would* have laughed—but many of them were dead.

If the *Friendship* seemed enormous when viewed from a considerable distance, she was huge close up. Her five-mile-long hull was at least half a mile thick and covered by a maze of heat exchangers, weapons blisters, com pods, tractor projectors, and other installations too arcane for Chien-Chu to identify.

The six-place shuttle was a modest affair, more so than most of the craft that swarmed around it, all jostling for precedence.

But that was the way that every three-month-long session began, and the crew was used to it. Computer-controlled co-orbiting robobeacons had been dropped into place more than a week before enabling even the most incompetent or inebriated pilot to find his way into the *Friendship*'s bay. Or so it seemed.

Some still managed to fail, however, or would have if it weren't for the repellor beams, and a fleet of six search-and-rescue craft all ready for launch.

The naval pilot experienced no difficulty whatsoever. He ran the beacon-lit obstacle course like the pro he was, fired retros at the last possible moment, and dropped his craft into the assigned parking slot.

The landing bay, which was easily as large as a major sports arena back on Earth, was far too busy to function as an airlock. That being the case, most visitors had no choice but to don their space suits or wait for a pressurized crawler to pick them up.

Chien-Chu didn't *need* oxygen, not much anyway, and knew his body could function in a hard vacuum—a fact that had saved his life once in the past.

Maylo had no such advantage, however, and was forced to wear a Navy-issue space suit. It was a little too large, but not enough to matter. She sealed herself in and followed her uncle through the lock. A luggage-laden autocart trailed behind.

Organized chaos ruled the repulsor-blackened flight deck. Space-suited bio bods rushed to deal with newly arrived ships, robot hoses nosed their way into receptacles, and two-person maintenance sleds flew over their heads.

A pathway that consisted of two parallel yellow lines zig-zagged across the enormous deck, terminating in front of a well-marked hatch. The words "Many minds but with one purpose" had been inscribed over the lock.

A pair of Trooper IIs stood guard. Their armor had been buffed to a dull sheen, and each wore two arm-mounted energy cannons. Their elbows came forward and their arms went vertical at Chien-Chu's approach.

The industrialist recognized the rifle salute for what it was, nodded by way of reply, and knew the word was out: Ex-President Chien-Chu was back from the grave.

Good. Though jealous of his privacy under normal circumstances, the industrialist knew that perceptions were important, especially where politics was concerned.

After all, no one had *elected* him to represent the free forces, which rendered his credentials questionable at best. No, he needed every edge he could get, and was glad of Nankool's courtesy. A man born *after* he left office—and whom he had never met.

The lock swallowed the twosome whole. Some human administrators, all returning from leave, filed in behind. They eyed the man, assumed Maylo was his mistress, and resumed their conversation.

The hatch closed, air entered the lock, and they were forced to wait.

The art display had changed many times since Chien-Chu's last visit, but provided something to look at and helped pass the time. Not just anyone could appreciate the highly minimalistic soil sculpture favored by the Pooonara.

One well-known wag had likened the typical display to a sandbox in which nothing ever seemed to happen.

Still, the artists could rhapsodize about their creations for hours, which served to remind the industrialist of just how diverse the membership was.

The inner hatch opened. Chien-Chu motioned for the bureaucrats to go first and followed them out. Islands of luggage dotted the lobby. Maylo extracted herself from the space armor, allowed a rating to carry it away, and smoothed her pantsuit.

An android stepped off a lift, scanned the crowd, and made his way over. A suit of clothes had been painted onto his body.

"Citizens Chien-Chu? My name is Harold. President Nankool sends his apologies for not being here in person, but wonders if you would join him for dinner? Yes? Excellent. . . . The President will be most pleased.

"Now, if you will be so kind as to follow, I will escort you to your quarters."

The robot led, the humans followed, and the autocart brought up the rear. Eyes watched, and plans were modified. Like the complex organism that it was, the onboard subculture had a nearly infinite capacity to adapt. New players had arrived. The game continued.

In spite of the fact that the Clone Hegemony had managed to corral prime real estate located only steps from the senatorial chambers, the interior decor was plain verging on sterile.

For reasons Senator Samuel Ishimoto-Six wasn't entirely sure of, the Ramanthian delegation was in the habit of passing tidbits of intelligence his way, the latest of which focused on ex-President Chien-Chu.

Six watched the footage, thumbed the remote, and watched again. The *Friendship* was literally crawling with every sort of surveillance device, some of which were *his,* or, more accurately, the Hegemony's.

The pictures had little if any political value, other than to confirm what he already knew—namely, that the ex-President was aboard, accompanied by his niece. She was a rather comely free-breeder to whom he was instantly attracted—a weakness he couldn't seem to purge.

Yes, the union between the Alpha Clone Marcus-Six and Legion General Marianne Mosby had legitimized such relationships, for liberals in any case, but not for Six, who came from a more traditional background in which unmediated breeding was subject to a range of sanctions that included expulsion, condemnation, and shunning.

All of which should have reduced his ardor, but seemed only to fuel it, adding to the politician's misery.

The clone froze the video on a tight shot of Maylo's face, studied the symmetry of her features, and felt the first signs of arousal. The voice was both harsh and unexpected.

"And what have we here? Lust for a free-breeding slut? I'm surprised, Samuel. I thought better of you."

Ishimoto-Six gave an involuntary twitch and felt the blood rush to his face. Though of lesser rank, Svetlana Gorgin-Three often acted as if she outranked *him,* and had a talent for getting under his skin. The politico affected the disapproving demeanor of a grandbrother, turned, and hoped the bulge wouldn't show.

"You jump to conclusions, Three—a rather serious flaw where diplomacy is concerned, and something you must work on. The image belongs to one Maylo Chien-Chu, chief executive officer for Chien-Chu Enterprises, and niece to the recently arrived ex-President. You would do well to memorize her face. We must *know* those in power—and be ready to interact with them."

Gorgin-Three, who derived a strange and not altogether healthy pleasure from being put in her place, lowered her head. "Yes, sir. My comments were ill-considered and inappropriate. Please forgive me."

The politician would have been more pleased with her response had he not known how meaningless it was. Arrogant one moment and subservient the next, his assistant was a study in contrasts. He nodded, killed the holo, and took control of the conversation. "So? What, if anything, did the spooks send today?"

Though not entirely comfortable with the term "spooks" as a synonym for the Hegemony's intelligence service, the staffer knew whom Six was referring to and answered accordingly. "Yes, Senator. In addition to the usual summary, we received notice that Governor Patricia Pardo departed Earth. She will arrive soon."

It was an interesting piece of news, and the clone took a moment to consider the implication. The governor had timed her visit to coincide with the new session, that much was obvious, but why? To forestall the sort of military action for which the Turr had lobbied? To buy time for her illegitimate government? Both possiblities seemed reasonable.

His government remained neutral where the "Earth problem" was concerned, and so was he. Six nodded. "Thank you."

The female smiled. He *knew* what that meant and waited for the axe to fall. "One more thing," Three said sweetly. "Ishimoto-Seven is on the way—to meet with Governor Pardo."

Six detested Seven, something his assistant was well aware of, and struggled to hide his reaction.

"Thank you. Please see to the ambassador's quarters . . . and add him to the official roster."

Gorgin took pleasure from her superior's reaction and left the room. Yes, there was no doubt about it, her job was fun.

Hiween Doma-Sa marched down the main corridor, took a sharp right-hand turn, and entered the Ramanthian sector.

As with embassies of old, the quarters assigned to accredited representatives were considered to be an extension of their sovereign soil, and as such, were immune from all rules and laws except those that dealt with communal safety, such as the prohibitions against the release of toxic gases, drilling holes through the ship's hull, or hunting game in the passageways. This last restriction was passed after a rather nasty incident involving the senator from Turr.

That being the case, most member races chose to supplement the ship's security forces with troops of their own. The Ramanthians were no exception. Four war drones had been posted outside their hatch. All were heavily armed.

The Hudathan stopped, surrendered his credentials, and submitted to a retinal scan. There was a pause while the Ramanthian file leader checked the results and issued an incomprehensible series of clicks and pops.

The hatch cycled open. Doma-Sa stepped through and was ushered into Orno's office. The Ramanthian stood and delivered his most courtly bow.

"May your eggs prosper," Doma-Sa said, using the shortened version of a greeting that ran to more than four thousand phonetic units.

Having dispensed with the appropriate courtesies, both beings assumed their respective seats.

Orno, who rarely ceded his guests any sort of advantage, was true to form. He sat behind his desk, which not only placed a barrier between them, but forced Doma-Sa to accept the freestanding guest chair. That ploy left the Hudathan's back exposed, which led to a high degree of psychological discomfort.

It was only the latest in a long list of insults, indignities, and embarrassments the Hudathan had suffered since boarding the *Friendship*. Some intentional—some not. Was the other being aware of how he felt? The diplomat hoped not . . . and struggled to conceal it.

The Ramanthian watched his visitor's skin bloom white, realized the heat wouldn't bother the Hudathan in the least, and knew that particular advantage had been lost.

"So," the Ramanthian began, "your presence does us honor. What brings the ambassador to my humble hive?"

Was the translation at fault? Or did the alien intend to sound condescending?

Doma-Sa fought the impulse to dive over the desk and rip the bug's head off—not that he was likely to succeed, since the War Orno was not only present, but heavily armed.

Try as he might, the Hudathan had been unable to master the subtle art of indirection as practiced by so many of his peers. That being the case, he came straight to the point.

"My people have been imprisoned for more than fifty years now. The time has come to set them free."

The Ramanthian rubbed his tool legs together. They made a rasping sound. "You are frank, Ambassador Doma-Sa . . . and I can do no less. A Hudathan fleet bombed the hive world known as Bounty during the last war. Exactly 836,421,716 Ramanthian citizens were killed. Once was enough."

It was a powerful argument, but Doma-Sa was prepared. "My people were wrong to do what they did . . . and many paid with their lives. Our sun is dying, and our home world, the planet Hudatha, has a Trojan relationship with a Jovian binary. The other planets tug on Hudatha, causing it to oscillate around the following Trojan point. That leads to a wildly fluctuating climate. Conditions grow worse with each passing year. All we want is the right to venture forth, to trade with others, and find a new home."

The Ramanthian seemed to consider the proposal and was silent for a moment. "Would your people seek to arm themselves?"

The Hudathan could hardly believe his ears. "Would his

people seek to arm themselves?'' A thousand times yes! What he *said* was different, however.

"*No*, we have no need for arms, so long as the Confederacy agrees to protect us."

"And what of your empire?" the Ramanthian inquired casually. "The planets taken during the war? What would become of them?"

The question was unexpected, and Doma-Sa was taken aback. He reacted without thinking. "They belong to *us* . . . just as the planets which your race colonized belong to *you*."

It was a good answer, though not the one Orno wanted to hear. The Hudathan was stubborn, stupid, or both. No matter; there are many ways to tunnel, and obstacles can be bypassed. "Yes, of course. Well, I appreciate the opportunity to hear your views, and will keep them in mind."

The Ramanthian stood. "Will I see you at the dinner?"

Doma-Sa knew he had been dismissed and was happy to go. The dinner, a formal affair scheduled for end-work the following day, was a diplomatic must. "Yes, I'll be there."

"Excellent," the senator replied. "I'll see you then."

A worker drone escorted Doma-Sa to the hatch. It opened, and he stepped outside. The corridor was crowded, and traffic pulled him along. Nothing had been gained, or had it? Why would the Ramanthians be interested in Hudathan planets? Didn't they have enough already?

It was an interesting question—and one he would endeavor to answer.

The private dining room, which was just right for the intimate dinners that Marcott Nankool liked to host, was paneled in Vorthillian walnut.

The wood gleamed from frequent oilings and matched that of the long, formally set table—most of which was obscured by what seemed like acres of white linen.

The President smiled cordially as he ushered his guests into the room and pointed to their place cards. "Sergi, that spot belongs to you, and Maylo, this chair is yours."

Though something of an athlete in his younger days, the President had gained some weight over the last few years, and rather than hang it all in one place had discovered a way to distribute the extra flesh over his entire body. Perhaps that explained why his face looked blurred and a little out of focus.

The first hour or so was spent getting acquainted. The President ate with gusto, Maylo picked at her food, and Chien-Chu toyed with a wine glass.

It wasn't until the plates had been cleared and dessert served that they got down to business. Chien-Chu took the lead. "You are aware of the situation back on Earth."

Nankool dabbed at his lips and allowed the briefest of frowns to crease his otherwise smooth brow. "Yes, an unpleasant business, and a divisive one."

Chien-Chu had been called inscrutable, but found the other man even more so. There had been numerous Presidents by then—most of whom were nonhuman. Would Nankool be *more* sympathetic, because of his origins? Or less willing to help, to avoid the appearance of bias? The answer seemed to be yes, since most presidents would have acted by then.

Maylo sipped her coffee. It was weak and barely lukewarm. "The charter is quite specific: 'Each species will be free to elect planetary governments—based on one being, one vote.' "

Nankool didn't like being lectured to, and felt the blood rush to his face. His light brown skin served to conceal the reaction, and his voice gave no hint of the way he felt.

"Your point is well taken, although there are some who would point to Governor Pardo and the fact that she was elected."

"True," Maylo agreed, "*if* you choose to ignore the fact that she supplanted the legally established government with what amounts to a military dictatorship, and suspended the rights of free speech, assembly, and habeas corpus."

"In order to counter criminal activity and restore law and order," the President countered. "Or so I'm told."

"By *whom*?" Chien-Chu retorted. "*Governor Pardo*?"

Nankool raised a hand. "Hold it right there. . . . Don't kill the messenger. Pardo and her supporters have done an excellent job of getting the message out. The *only* message, till the two of you arrived.

"The sad fact is that your senator, Senator Bates, lived in Pardo's pocket. His death left no one to tell her story, or *yours*. That's the challenge, to tell *your* story, and build support."

Maylo regarded the President with cool brown eyes. "So how 'bout *you*, Mister President? To whom will *your* support flow?"

Nankool was a professional politician, which meant he had very little love for win-lose propositions. But when the chips were down and a decision had to be made he had never been known to blanch. Not in his opinion, anyway. "Governor Pardo is an outlaw and should be stopped."

Chien-Chu started to say something, but Nankool was quick to interrupt. "Hear me out, Sergi. . . . That's what *I* believe, but Pardo has friends, and *they* have votes.

"You were President once—you know how it works. We're running a democracy here. You want a fleet? Some sort of police action? Then find some support. It's as simple as that."

Maylo eyed him across the table. "And you'll be there for us?"

The President nodded. "Find the votes, or something that will generate the votes, and I'll back you all the way."

The rest of the meal passed without incident and was soon over. Nankool escorted them to the hatch, held Maylo's hand just a fraction too long, and looked at her uncle. "Sergi, a word to the wise . . ."

"Yes?"

"Pardo boarded the ship about two hours ago. Remember what I told you, plus one thing more: The governor wants to be President. She has friends here and knows her way around. Watch your back."

18

Dead men have no victory.

Euripdes
The Phoenician Women
Standard year circa 410 B.C.

Planet Earth, Independent
World Government

The desert swept long, hard, and wide into what had once been Ethiopia, but had long since become but one of many Administrative Regions, or ARs, all subject to a single Earth government. Not that the local inhabitants cared, or paid much attention to such abstractions. They lived as they always had, subject to God and the rules of nature.

There was no sign of movement save for distant clouds of dust raised by the seasonal Khamsin and the high, hopeful circles made by a solitary white-backed vulture. A *hungry* vulture that hoped to feed off the weak or the dead.

The riverbed, dry until the October rains sent water flooding along its course, ran roughly north to south and offered the only cover for twenty miles in any direction.

It certainly beat the hell out of *no* cover, but was far from perfect. Tyspin and her people had destroyed most if not all of Harco's spy sats, and more than a week had passed since one of his high altitude spy planes had attempted to overfly Djibouti.

There were other possibilities, however, primary among which were small, hard-to-detect drones. More than a dozen had been identified and destroyed during the last nine hours—but all it would take was one such machine to reveal his position and open his forces to an effective attack.

Booly lowered his binoculars, slid down the bank, and rejoined his troops. They were deployed in a long, evenly spaced line. It started at a bend in the watercourse and ran roughly southwest, till the river bank jogged and turned south.

The heavily reinforced Interdiction Force (IF) consisted of fifty battle-worn cyborgs, which, with the exception of twelve borgs that remained behind, included *all* of General Kattabi's armor. Not much against the one hundred fifty armored vehicles that they expected to fight. Still, there was very little choice if they wanted to hold Fort Mosby.

A fly landed on Booly's cheek. He slapped at it, heard boots on gravel, and turned accordingly. Captain Hawkins looked tired. Desert goggles had left "spook" circles around her eyes, her tan ran many layers deep, and her lips were chapped. Harco's forces had pushed hard of late, testing the free forces to the north, south, and west. The leg officer had been in the field for weeks.

"See anything, sir? Like a truck loaded with ice-cold beer?"

Those within earshot chuckled, and Booly joined in. "Sorry, Captain, but if the enemy attacks with beer trucks, the first vehicle belongs to me. Rank hath privilege, you know."

They laughed some more, Radio Free Djibouti played the latest pop hit, and gravel crunched as a Trooper II stalked past. Fykes stood high on its back and offered a salute. Booly responded in kind.

The sun was hot, the air was dry, and the wait went on.

The armor was dug in behind a screen of low-lying hills. The force consisted of thirty scout cars, forty-six self-propelled weapons platforms, ten 122mm multiple rocket launchers (MRLs), twenty-five heavy St. James tanks, forty-nine mostly soft-skinned support vehicles, and a company of infantry, all of whom were, or had been, members of the 1st REC, the Legion's legendary cavalry regiment.

They were extremely very difficult to see, thanks to the fact that all of the vehicles wore camouflage and most were dug in. A clump of palms provided shade, and the tarps strung between provided more.

Major Katherine "Kate" Kilgore often bragged that she could sleep anywhere, anytime, even though it wasn't strictly true. Most of her subordinates believed the fiction, however, which made it possible to close her eyes and have some time to herself.

Such was the case now as she lay in the net-style hammock and wished for a breeze. A tarp had been rigged between one of the sixty-ton hover tanks and a soft-skinned support truck that sat fifteen feet away. It threw a slowly migrating rectangle of shade over her body and lowered the temp by a full five degrees.

A radio crackled nearby, somebody said something sharp, and the noise vanished. Kilgore took care of her troops—and they took care of her.

The officer studied the inside surface of her eyelids, wished the nap was real, and waited for the recon report. She *knew* Booly, *knew* he was good, and *knew* he'd be waiting for her.

Finding Booly, *stopping* Booly, *killing* Booly. That was her job. But she didn't have to like it. Especially now that Matthew "asshole" Pardo had assumed the role of governor, and, if rumors were true, rode Harco like a horse.

Harco was the reason Kilgore had come across. Harco, and the fact that she was sick and tired of seeing good soldiers pissed away by politicians. The shitheads.

"Major?"

Kilgore woke to find that she had actually fallen asleep. She staged a yawn. "Yeah? What's shakin'?"

Lieutenant Goody, sometimes referred to as "two shoes" by the troops, had been only months out of the academy when the poop hit the fan, and he still regarded senior officers with something that approached awe. He *knew* they were in the field, *knew* he wasn't supposed to salute, but stood at something that looked a lot like attention. "It's the drone, ma'am. It's back."

"No shit? The stupid-looking disguise actually worked?"

"Yes, ma'am."

"Damn. Will miracles never cease."

Kilgore swung her boots out of the hammock, planted them on the ground, and looked up into the other officer's face. "Jeez, Goody, what's the problem? You got a stick up your ass?"

"Ma'am! No, ma'am!"

Kilgore smiled and shook her head. "Thank God for that. The surgeon will be glad to hear it. Well, come on. Let's see what that worthless excuse for a tech sergeant came up with."

The lieutenant led the way, shoulders back, practically marching through the encampment.

Kilgore nodded to a cluster of troopers, winked when they grinned, and followed Goody into a self-erecting tent. The drone, still covered with ratty-looking feathers, sat on a pair of specially designed sawhorses. An access panel had been removed and lay on a nearby table. Sergeant Oko, black skin gleaming, looked up from his work. "Lieutenant . . . Major . . . Welcome to my office."

Kilgore grinned and pointed at the machine. "The loot tells me that this pathetic piece of shit actually worked. Is that true?"

Oko's teeth were extremely white. "Yes, ma'am. Take a look."

A table loaded with olive drab com gear sat off to one side. Oko touched some keys, video blossomed, and Kilgore found herself looking at a drone-eye view of the desert. It turned and spiraled upward.

"Sorry about that," Oko said, turning a knob, "but vultures fly in circles. That's why it worked—because I programed the drone to do the same thing."

Kilgore nodded as she watched the video blur and snap into focus.

"Here it comes," the tech sergeant said proudly. "Full color vulture-vision."

The fact that the target continued to appear then disappear

was somewhat annoying—but wondrous nonetheless. Numbers scrolled down the right side of the screen. They provided air speed, air temp, and grid coordinates.

Gradually, as part of each loop, Kilgore caught sight of the dry riverbed and the long line of sandy-colored cyborgs, and felt the excitement start to build. Here it was! The one thing any self-respecting officer would give her right tit to get—first-class, grade-A, no-doubt-about-it intelligence.

The major reached for her wallet, pulled it out, and selected a fifty. "Here you go, Sergeant. You said the blasted thing would work—and you were right. This should cover the bet."

Oko made a show of holding the bill up to the light before tucking it away. "Let's kick some ass, Major. I've got some drinking to do!"

Their was an artificial roar as the MRLs fired their 122mm rockets in salvos of forty. So, given the fact that Kilgore had ten of the units, nine of which were operational, that meant that the first flight consisted of three hundred sixty airborne weapons, each packing a load of six hundred sixty-six submunitions. Each sub had the destructive power of a hand grenade and could penetrate light armor—a truly devastating barrage if the full load landed on target.

Booly and his forces had a full twenty-three seconds worth of warning, which, though less than he would have liked, was sufficient to launch borg-mounted SAMs.

They armed themselves ten seconds after launch, sought the incoming targets, and exploded in midair. Thousands of AA bomblets went off, detonated more than half of the incoming rockets, and sowed the desert with steel.

The explosions followed each other like cracks of thunder, threw black clouds against an otherwise blue sky, and sent tendrils of white spidering in every direction. A second attack followed and exploded so quickly that the bomblets sounded like oversized firecrackers.

Then, as the few survivors from the first salvo neared the point of impact, the next flight left *their* launchers, winked briefly, and disappeared toward the east.

That's when Booly heard his quads open up with their

20mm six-barreled Gatling guns. With each weapon firing six thousand rounds per minute, it wasn't long before a virtual curtain of steel separated the loyalist forces from their attackers.

Many of the missiles were destroyed, but some made it through. One struck the empty riverbed, exploded, and threw a dark column of gravel up into the air. A second scored a direct hit on one of the Trooper IIs, incinerated the borg's brain, and slaughtered a four-person fire team. A third caused a section of bank to collapse, and a fourth hit the number two tanker.

Blood-warm water was still raining out of the sky as Booly climbed up behind Reeger's head and strapped himself in. Radio traffic filled his ears. "Bone Two to Bone One. Over."

"This is Bone One. Go. Over."

"Request permission to engage. Over."

"Denied. Stay hot—but hold. Over."

"Wilco. Over and out."

Booly didn't blame Hawkins for wanting to break out of the ravine, but knew the price they would undoubtedly pay. Once the cyborgs topped the bank and formed a line abreast, another curtain of steel would fall. Most of the incoming rockets would be destroyed, but some would make it through, and the casualties would be heavy. *Too* heavy for such a relatively small force.

He couldn't wait forever, though. Assuming the other officer was competent, and there was no reason to think otherwise, he or she would attempt to freeze the IF in place. Then, while the cyborgs climbed out of the riverbed, the enemy would race across the desert, hoping to catch them as they topped the bank.

Explosions boomed, the ground shook, and dirt filled the air as some more rockets made it through. A quad, one of only ten that Booly had, was blown in half. Hawkins, unable to contain herself any longer, chinned the transmit switch. "This is Two. . . . Request permission to engage. Over."

Booly checked the data projected onto the inside surface of his visor, heard a fighter pilot check in, and gave silent thanks. Air cover could make all the difference. "This is One. . . .

Permission granted. Keep it tight . . . and watch the lines.''

''The lines'' were projected on visors, displayed on screens, and etched on memories. They began at either end of the formation and angled out to form what looked like a funnel—a funnel formed by thousands of programmable, self-propelled crab mines. Their purpose was to limit the enemy's ability to maneuver, concentrate Booly's targets, and neutralize some of their heavy armor.

That was the upside. The downside lay in the fact that once engaged, Booly's forces would have nowhere to retreat, except through their own mines.

Yes, they could turn the devices off long enough to pass through, but experience showed that between one and two percent of the mines would remain active. That was just one of the reasons why many officers tried to avoid them.

Booly had no choice, however, or felt that he didn't, not with odds of three to one.

Reeger had been in the Legion for twelve years, first as a bio bod; then, after his first body was destroyed during a low altitude drop, as a cyborg. Many people never recover from something like that, but Reeger had accepted his fate and transformed himself into one of the best borgs the Legion had.

Knowing the order would come, and knowing that each detail was important, the cyborg had talked a bio bod into cutting footholds into the side of the bank.

Other Trooper IIs had been less diligent, perhaps intentionally so, since there was a definite downside to being first over the top. Many were just starting to climb when Reeger arrived on the plain above.

The rocket barrage suddenly let up—a sure sign that the enemy had advanced and was ready to engage.

Booly looked left and right, saw both lines form on him, and knew what ancient calvary officers must have felt like.

Someone, he wasn't sure who, gave the familiar yell: ''Camerone!'' And the line swept forward. The battle was joined.

Not satisfied to ride one of the heavily armored tanks, or one of the weapons platforms, Kilgore opted for a scout car armed with a rack of four antitank (AT) missiles and two light machine guns. Mobility was everything, especially for this sort of brawl; the heavy stuff was claustrophobic. A minor detail she had neglected to mention to psych officers over the years. The seat was hot and burned the back of her thighs.

Her driver, a madwoman named Bucey, hit the gas, launched the car off a small rise, and hit the hard pan at forty mph. The gunners, anonymous behind their visors, grinned.

Kilgore would have been thrown out of her seat if it hadn't been for the harness. She kept a firm grip on the frame-mounted grab bar and tried to peer through the oncoming dust and smoke. What was it that Clausewitz said? "On no account should we overlook the moral effect of a rapid, running assault"? The old bastard would have *loved* Bucey.

The top gunner opened up, a hot shell casing bounced off the back of Kilgore's neck, and the command channel squawked into life.

"Red Dog Six to Red Dog One. Over."

"Go, Six. Over."

"We have visual contact with ten, repeat ten, enemy borgs. Over."

Kilgore heard herself say "Roger," wished she had cyborgs of her own, and damned the command structure to hell. There were plenty of borgs, or would have been, if the Pardos hadn't assigned most of them to the increasingly restless cities.

Traditional armor against cyborgs? How would the contest end? The winner could write a thesis—if there was anyone left to read it. The messages came one on top of the next.

"Red Dog Two to Red Dog One. Enemy aircraft! In from the east! Over."

Red Dog Six to Red Dog One. Mines! Mines on the right flank . . ."

Kilgore thought she saw the flash of light as Lieutenant Goody died, but there were so many explosions that it was hard to tell. The tanks fired smoke grenades from their launchers and rolled through the self-generated murk.

"Red Dog Three to Red Dog One. The enemy has deployed concentrating crab mines down our left flank. Am trying to clear. Over."

Kilgore swore. "Booly, you rotten sonofabitch! I want your ass!"

The entire world was concentrated just beyond the windscreen. Bucey spotted a gap in the smoke and pushed the car through.

Booly rocked from side to side as Reeger ran, strained to see what lay ahead, and watched the HUD. Or tried to, since it wasn't long till the blue deltas penetrated the enemy's front line and the charge was transformed into a melee. Each side had something of an advantage.

The crew-operated armor boasted numerical superiority and, given the nature of the vehicles they rode, superior firepower as well.

Though more vulnerable than the units that opposed them, the Trooper IIs were highly mobile and made good use of their edge. Especially as the battlefield grew smaller and more concentrated.

As with all such battles, there was no way for Booly or his officers to control the way individual duels were fought. That being the case, Booly found himself as little more than an extremely interested onlooker as Reeger went to war.

A mountainous battle tank loomed ahead. Its cannon probed for targets, machine guns rattled, and sand flew from massive treads.

Reeger took a look, knew he was outgunned, and spun out of the way. Shells dug divots out of the ground as a quad lurched out of the smoke, spotted the enemy tank, and turned to meet it.

The tank fired its 105mm gun and the quad launched a high-explosive antitank (HEAT) warhead. Both weapons hit what they were aimed at, both exploded, and both units were destroyed.

Reeger mounted a .50 caliber machine gun on one arm and an energy cannon on the other. He fired both at a scout car and was rewarded with an explosion. A wheel soared into the air, fell, and bounced away.

That's when something tore through the cyborg's chest armor and cut his power. The Trooper II's weapons went off-line, the gyro stabilizer failed, and he toppled forward. Booly went, too.

Kilgore flew forward as Bucey stood on the brakes. A weapons platform drifted past, fired its twin 30mm cannons up into the sky, and turned toward the south. Where were the reb planes, anyway? Four had checked in but were nowhere to be seen.

Bucey spun the wheel to the left, stomped on the gas, and swore as a battle tank poked its 105mm snout out of the smoke. The vehicles missed each other by less than a foot.

Kilgore gritted her teeth and held on. Her unit had suffered thirty percent casualties—not counting the damage enemy air-craft had inflicted on the rear-echelon supply vehicles. The battlefield looked like a wreck-strewn parking lot. Should she stay, and go for broke? Or run, and live to fight another day?

An already-burning weapons platform shuddered as an ammo locker cooked off. The scout car swerved, paused so a medic could jump on board, and took off again. Kilgore pulled a gut check and found the decision was made.

Booly hit the harness release, pushed himself up away from Reeger's body, and spoke via the helmet's com link. "Reeg? You okay?"

"No, sir. 'Fraid not," came the reply. "You'd better run, sir. I can't get up."

"Then both of us will run," Booly said, fumbling for the release handle. "Only it's *your* turn to ride."

"No, sir! You shouldn't do that. Run while you . . ."

Booly pulled a small lever, opened an armor-plated hatch, and jerked the cyborg's brain box out of his body. The organic contents weighed two and a half pounds, but the support el-ements and protective casing brought the total weight up to thirty.

The box came equipped with retractable straps. Booly slipped his arms through and checked the assault weapon's ammo indicator. Then, ready to fire, he entered the smoke.

It was Hawkins who first realized that they had won—if such a term could properly be used in connection with a force that had suffered more than fifty percent casualties.

The first indication was a slackening of fire, followed by less contact, and more activity from Tyspin's fighters.

While the aircraft had made short work of the planes sent to support the rebel advance, and destroyed the majority of their support vehicles, they were of limited value where ground support was concerned.

Worried lest his pilots bag some friendlies, the wing commander ordered them to wait. What he needed was a break. It came when the smoke started to clear and the rebs tried to run.

A weapons platform took a direct hit from a five-hundred-pound bomb. It ceased to exist and pieces of sharp edged metal fell like rain. They rattled across the hood, killed the top gunner, and buried themselves in the sand.

"Red Dog Three to Red Dog One. Where the hell is the air cover? Over."

Kilgore, who could have been offended, wasn't. She wondered the same thing. "Flying formation over Los Angeles . . . or up Pardo's ass," she replied acerbically. "Circle the wagons. Over."

The maneuver, practiced till they hated her guts, required that the vehicles coalesce around the surviving weapons platforms.

The training paid off as the twenty-six platforms drifted together, linked their weapons via one computer, and opened fire. Gatling guns, SAMs, and automatic weapons swept the sky. The rest of the force, scout cars and battle tanks alike, gathered under the protective umbrella.

Two fighters went down within the first three minutes, and a third followed only seconds later.

Short on fuel and low on ordnance, the fighters made one last pass, killed a self-propelled howitzer, and withdrew. The battle was over.

It was cooler at night, refreshingly so, and Winters, who had orders to hold the fort, was busy receiving what remained of

Booly's force, setting priorities, and allocating resources. They owned the air, so the airport's lights were on.

General Kattabi, hands clasped behind his back, watched the last fly form touch down and kill power. Medics hurried aboard, and a stream of litters came off, followed by a cart loaded with brain boxes. Two appeared to be damaged and were hooked to life-support equipment. More lives and more resources drained away.

The last soldier down the ramp—or *second* to last, since Fykes followed him out—was Colonel William Booly.

Kattabi released a long, slow breath—and was surprised to learn that he'd been holding it. Why? Because he *liked* Booly? Which he certainly did.

Because of the sacrifice that his parents had made? Which they certainly had.

Or because of something else? A more selfish reason? He knew the answer was yes.

The simple fact was that he *needed* Booly, *would* need Booly, when and if the *big* battle came. For if there was one thing that Kattabi *knew,* or *thought* he knew, it was the fact that the *real* fight lay ahead.

Somehow, some way, the isolated pockets of resistance such as the one Booly had established would have to be connected, coordinated, and supplied. Not something he could accomplish alone. Booly spotted the general, crossed the tarmac, and rendered a salute.

Kattabi returned it, said, "You look like shit," and motioned toward his command car. "Come on. I'll buy you a drink."

Booly frowned. "Thanks, sir, but I have a lot to do, and . . ."

"And you have the best damned XO in the Legion," Kattabi finished for him. "Let Winters do her job."

Booly paused, realized that the general was correct, and tossed his gear into the car. "Sergeant Fykes!"

"Sir!"

"Take the rest of the day off."

Fykes grinned, said, "Yes, sir," and did a smart about-face.

Kattabi watched the noncom march away. "He was a chaplain once. . . . Did you know that?"

Booly *didn't* know that and found it hard to believe. Fykes? A man of God? The notion was ridiculous. "You're joking."

"No," Kattabi replied. "I'm not. But that's the Legion for you. Some are what they appear to be . . . and some aren't. Come on, time for that drink."

One drink led to a second, to dinner in a local restaurant, and to a half bottle of gin. It was a soldier's solution to a soldier's problem, and a poor one, since not even an ocean of alcohol could bring the dead back to life.

The sleep that followed was more like unconsciousness than sleep. Booly woke to a headache, a mouth that tasted like Dooth dung, and a lot of sore muscles.

He took a shower, donned a fresh uniform, and hit the mess hall. Most of the troops had eaten by then, and a robot was cleaning the floor. Winters, her comp on the table in front of her, lay in wait. She motioned with a half-filled coffee cup. "No offense, sir, but you look like shit."

"Thanks," Booly replied, putting his tray on the table. "I'm glad there's something everyone can agree on."

"Haven't seen the general this morning," the executive officer observed. "What did you do to him?"

Booly tried an experimental sip of coffee, approved, and took another. "What did *I* do to *him*? The bastard drank me under the table."

"Maybe," Winters replied thoughtfully. "But you're here, and *he* isn't."

Booly eyed her over a piece of toast. Winters had that look again—the one that preceded some sort of surprise. "All right, Captain, why the ambush? What have you been up to?"

Winters summoned her most innocent expression. "Me? Nothing, sir. I assumed the colonel would expect an After Action report and, having received it, would accompany the captain on an inspection."

Booly raised his eyebrows, Winters smiled, and the deal was done. The report took place in Booly's office, and was both better and worse than he had expected.

Chien-Chu Enterprises had delivered another load of volunteers, which meant that he had *more* leg soldiers than the day he reported for duty. That was the good news.

The *bad* news was that they were down to only thirty-five borgs and, unlike the rebs, had very little conventional armor to take up the slack.

That news was depressing, *damned* depressing, and it dragged at Booly's spirits. They might survive one more battle, *if* they were lucky; then it would be over.

If Winters was depressed, there was no visible sign of it as she led him onto a lift and touched a button. The elevator lurched and fell. Booly eyed the indicator. It stopped on sublevel six—the very depths of the war-era catacombs.

The doors slid open, and Captain Ny stepped forward to greet them. The six-foot-tall utility body had the appearance of a titanium skeleton. It whirred to attention. The salute was perfect. "Welcome to the center of the Earth, Colonel. Visitors are always welcome."

Booly lifted an eyebrow. "Thanks, Captain. I'm in a bad mood today . . . so your dirt had better be clean."

The other officers chuckled and led the way.

It took the better part of fifteen minutes for the cyborg to lead the bio bods through a maze of tunnels, past a pile of recently excavated dirt, and into a man-made cavern. It was cool, dry, and stank of ozone. Floodlights had been rigged, and Booly was amazed by what he saw.

The vault contained *hundreds* of shrink-wrapped Trooper II bodies, and farther out, barely visible through the murk, huge, hulking quads, their weapons encased in spray-foam, their armor covered by a thick layer of dust.

"They've been here all along," Ny explained, "stockpiled back during the war. Forgotten, written off, who the hell knows? My people found them while repairing bomb damage. One of Harco's subsurface torpedos burrowed in but failed to detonate."

"But are they operable?" Booly asked, his heart beating faster than it had been.

"Good question, sir," Winters put in. "How 'bout it, Reeger? Will the damned things work?"

Servos whined as one of the Trooper IIs came to sudden life, walked out into the center of the chamber, and came to attention. His voice boomed through external speakers. ''Ma'am! Yes, ma'am!''

Winters watched her commanding officer's face and saw everything she had hoped for. ''Happy birthday, sir, and many happy returns.''

Booly looked at Reeger, checked his wrist term, and started to laugh. It *was* his birthday! And there was hope.

Fort Portal was something far different from what the name seemed to suggest. More hospital than fort, it was home to hundreds of war veterans, many of whom had fought one battle too many and were waiting to die. Of their wounds, boredom, or old age. Nobody cared.

Lights twinkled from the low, one-story buildings, crickets chirped, and fireflies flitted through the soft night air.

It was a pleasant evening—and why not? Most evenings were pleasant at Fort Portal. The town, which was founded in 1893, was originally called Fort Gerry and then renamed for Sir Gerald Portal, an English adventurer. The rebel-controlled complex was located nearly two hundred and thirty miles west of Kampala about five thousand feet above sea level.

All of which was nice, or would have been, had Captain Horace Imbey been twenty years older, and ready for retirement. Such was not the case, however—no, not by a long shot.

Imbey stood six feet three inches tall. He had the body of an athlete, and a fire in his belly. He wanted—no, *deserved*—to be where the action was, where he could distinguish himself, and would settle for nothing less. That's why he had submitted no less than thirty-six SFM-690s, prayed twice a day, and roamed the grounds at night. He was antsy, bored, and generally pissed off. Not that it made any difference.

Imbey had just climbed out of the guard truck, and was about to stage a raid on Sergeant Hooly's kitchen, when he noticed a buzzing sound. A transport? No, not till the day after tomorrow. What, then? A giant mosquito?

The fly form looked like *all* fly forms, including those that belonged to the IWG. An inspection, perhaps? No problem, Imbey was ready.

That being the case, the officer wasn't too concerned until the *second* cybernetic aircraft appeared and started its final approach.

Later, when the locals discussed the matter, some gave the officer credit for drawing his sidearm and blasting away. Others, and they were in the majority, thought he was stupid.

Whatever the case, Hawkins, along with Neversmile and his Naa commandos, were able to liberate 1,021 "surplus" cyborgs. It took exactly forty-six minutes and twelve seconds to unhook their brain boxes from the coma-inducing life-support system, load them onto the fly forms, and haul ass. Or was it brain?

There was only one casualty. The locals, unable to decide what belonged to the truck and what belonged to Imbey, buried them together. The hole was bigger—but the result was the same.

19

Those who say that religion has nothing to do with
politics do not know what religion means.

Mohandas K. Gandhi
Indian spiritual and political leader
Standard year circa 1900

Somewhere beyond the Rim, the Confederacy of Sentient Beings

Every now and then, every other cycle or so, the Hoon liked
to tour the fleet. The easiest way to accomplish that was to
choose two or three hundred of the more than twenty thousand
surveillance devices at his disposal and spend a tenth of a
second on each.

Though once routine, the excursions had been more re-
warding of late, ever since the soft body had gone forth to
"preach the gospel"—the essence of which seemed to consist
of blocking thoroughfares, praising the supreme intelligence
known as "God," and seeking "converts," which is to say
semiautonomous units willing to listen to the human's rant-
ings.

The entire process seemed like a waste of time and resources except for one thing: Interspersed with the nonsense
regarding God was a good deal of anti-Thraki rhetoric. And,
like it or not, the artificial intelligence had no choice but to

support sentients that shared the same mission it had: Find Thraki and kill them.

Still, the Hoon had encountered a considerable number of soft bodies prior to the human, literally thousands of them, and knew many were disposed to *say* one thing yet *do* something else.

That being the case, the artificial intelligence decided that a test case was in order—a test that would either secure the human's position within the fleet, or prove he was lying. A finding that would remove the soft body from the protected classification and mark him for immediate disposal. It was a good plan, a *perfect* plan, as evidenced by the fact that the Hoon had conceived of it.

The Hoon switched perspectives, watched the soft body walk down a corridor, and noticed that his "flock" had grown. No less than six units of various shapes, sizes, and classifications had taken to following the human around. Why?

One was of Thraki manufacture. The rest were his. A quick check of their service records showed that at least some of them were overdue for maintenance. Others seemed normal enough, which made for inconclusive results.

A distant and rather minor member of the fleet noticed something of potential interest and sent a message to that effect. The Hoon went to investigate. The human, and those who served him, were of secondary importance.

His spirits buoyed by Henry's return and his steadily growing band of followers, Jepp felt happy, and knew that it was here, among heathen machines, that he had finally found his calling. Even his graffiti had a joyful quality, running as it did to "Rejoice in God!" "Kill the Thraki!" and "Love Thy Neighbor!"

And, thanks to his flock's ability to replicate such messages with machinelike precision, his sayings would soon occupy more and more of the otherwise blank bulkheads.

Also bolstering Jepp's spirits was the fact that his newfound respectability translated to additional freedom. Previously locked doors opened to his touch, shuttles obeyed most of his commands, and, with some minor exceptions, robots did his bidding.

And that was the only real problem he had. Except for Henry, the rest of his followers were nonsentient and bereft of souls. They were useful, especially within the context of his more grandiose fantasies, but not as satisfying as the kind of believers who have something to lose and *choose* to submit.

Ah, well, the prospector thought to himself, patience is a virtue. Time will pass, and God will show the way.

The caverns, some of which were natural and some of which had been carved out of solid rock, stretched on for miles and created huge reverberation chambers. The horn sounded, and the air vibrated in sympathy.

Keeta, a cub of less than eight solar rotations, skidded around a corner, bumped an elder, and yelled an apology over her shoulder. The youngster had a message for Dantha the priest—which meant that all things would be forgiven. The excitement of the moment, the pleasure of running full tilt, filled the youngster with joy.

The sound seemed to come from everywhere at once, and a stranger might have gone astray, but not Keeta, who was but an infant when the fleet had expelled the sect and left it to fend for itself. She knew every tunnel, every cove, and how music moved through each.

The youngster took a left, a right, and let her feet fly, for here was a long stretch, and, judging from the call of the horn, the procession lay just around the bend.

Adult voices called out, urged the cub to be careful, but there was no time to reply.

Keeta saw vestments up ahead, the story pole from which multicolored ribbons fluttered, and the slowly moving processional. And there, walking at the front, was Dantha, priest, uncle, and a friend.

The cub passed the horn player, came abreast of the priest, and tugged at his sleeve. "Uncle Dantha! I have a message! An *important* message!"

Dantha knew his niece—and knew it must be true. He stopped, the horn paused in mid-groan, and everyone strained to hear. The colony numbered barely five hundred souls, was cut off from all commerce with the outside, and was short on entertainment. A message, especially an *urgent* message, was something special.

Dantha knelt next to the cub. "Yes, little one? What is it?"

"The Sheen are coming!"

There was a hiss of indrawn breath as the members of the processional sucked air into their lungs, followed by something Keeta had never seen before. Her uncle was afraid.

For the first time since Jepp had boarded the ship, the Hoon sent a message to *him*, rather than the other way around.

The text came through Alpha and was translated by Sam. The human listened to it *three* times, and the syntax remained the same: "Thraki have been detected . . . let God's will be done."

Jepp began to panic. His heart beat faster, and sweat beaded his brow. Did the message constitute a comment? A suggestion? A commandment? What did it mean?

The prospector fed an inquiry back through Sam and Alpha, but there was no response. The Hoon had spoken—and there was nothing to add.

The human voiced his concern to Henry, who, knowing the human as it did, was quick to identify the critical facts. Since its present body had no vocal apparatus, it was necessary to communicate through Sam. "How did you represent yourself to the Hoon? As a lost prospector? Or something more?"

Jepp was offended. "I made mention of God's work, if that's what you mean."

"That's *exactly* what I mean," the computer replied cynically. "What else?"

"Well, there was some discussion about a race called the Thraki, and the fact that the Sheen are on a mission to find and eliminate them."

"Don't tell me, let me guess," Henry said disgustedly. "You signed on."

Jepp looked away. "No, not exactly."

"But close."

The human turned back. The tone was petulant. "So, what if I did? There was no other choice."

The navcomp would have sighed, had such a thing been possible. "I think the message is pretty clear: They found some Thraki—and the Hoon wants you to kill them."

"Why *me*?" Jepp asked desperately. "The Hoon could kill them himself."

"It's a test," the AI replied patiently, "to see what you'll do."

The better part of a minute passed while the human considered the matter. When he spoke, the words fell one at a time. "So it's kill or be killed."

"Essentially," Henry replied.

"Unless . . ." Jepp said.

"Unless what?"

"Unless I could *convert* the Thraki, and convince the Hoon to accept them."

"Dream on," the AI said simply. "The Hoon is a computer, and computers don't change. I should know."

"*You* grow," Jepp responded. "*You* learn. What about that?"

"Okay," Henry said levelly. "Have it your way."

"No," Jepp said sanctimoniously. "Let *God's* will be done."

In spite of the fact that Dantha had heard seemingly endless stories about the Sheen, and been forced to organize most of his adult life around them, he'd never actually *seen* one of the nearly mythical constructs. Not with his own eyes.

That being the case, the priest felt a sort of fascinated dread as the Sheen shuttle hovered over the moon's heavily cratered surface and lowered itself into the lock.

If one believed in Thraki lore, and as a priest it had been his job to do so, the Sheen were programmed to exterminate his race.

But were such stories true? Not having seen such machines themselves, many Thrakis had come to doubt such tales, in spite of battle footage to the contrary.

And that was one of the main reasons why Dantha's sect

had gone its own way. That, and the fact that violence solves nothing.

And now, as the shuttle landed on carefully planed volcanic rock, and the dome sealed itself closed, there was even more reason to hope. After all, why send emissaries if the only option was war? No, it seemed the stories were exaggerated.

Thus encouraged, the priest watched the hatch open and examined the being who emerged. There was no sign of weapons or other military paraphernalia. Though somewhat taller than the average Thraki, and less than pleasant to look at, the creature had two eyes, two arms, and two legs, all of which argued for at least *some* degree of commonality. Of equal interest was the fact that the visitor had a biological rather than a mechanical body.

There were machines, however, two of them—one of which looked familiar, as if it might be of Thraki manufacture. It transformed itself into a wheel and rolled across the surface of the laser-smoothed rock.

The other machine glowed the way the Sheen were supposed to, followed the biological off the shuttle, and showed no signs of aggression.

His fears alleviated by the low-key manner in which his visitors presented themselves, Dantha, closely followed by a delegation of elders, went to greet them. He held his hands palms outward. "Peace."

Sam transformed itself into communicator mode, made the necessary translation, and passed the reply back. "My master comes with peace in his heart—but with a warning as well. The Sheen wait in the blackness of space and are sworn to kill you."

Dantha felt his chest constrict and heard the elders start to moan. Hopes dashed, the priest fought to maintain his composure. "We are sorry to hear that . . . for it was our intention to live here in peace. Is that why you were sent? To tell us that the Sheen are going to kill us?"

"No," the human replied quickly. "I came because there might be a chance to save you and your colony. *If* we can convince a computer called the Hoon."

"The Hoon?" Dantha's ears flicked backward, the Thraki

equivalent of a frown. "The Way" included no less than seven demonic figures, each associated with a particular sin, but the worst of the lot was the terrible Hoonara, taker of souls, king of questions, and giver of lies. Coincidence? Or something more?

The priest chose his words with care. "*Why* does the Hoon wish to destroy us?"

The other being gestured with the upper portion of his torso. "I don't know. But it does tolerate *my* existence, and might tolerate yours, *if* you came to God."

Dantha listened to the translation, assumed the use of "God" singular was some sort of error, and asked the obvious question. "The gods dwell on a higher plane—how can we *go* to them?"

"Not 'them,' " Jepp corrected. "*Him*. There is only *one* God. You must go to Him in the spiritual sense, by believing that He exists, and is all-powerful."

Dantha was incredulous. "A single god? Who is all-powerful? We could never believe in such an aberration."

"But you *must*," the human said desperately, "or the Sheen will destroy your colony."

Dantha felt a great stubbornness rise from deep within his soul. The same stubborness that caused him to follow the non-violent way and to preach that philosophy to others. Even when the hierarchy objected, even when they threatened to expel him, even in the face of death. "Then they will destroy us . . . for our religion is the very heart of our culture."

They were strong words, *fateful* words, but the elders murmured their support.

Jepp felt anger mixed with sadness. "Then every single one of you will die."

Dantha thought of Keeta, of how short her life had been, and felt a terrible sorrow. "Yes, and so will you. Life goes on."

Jepp swallowed the lump that had formed in his throat, returned to the shuttle, and strapped himself in. The ship lifted, circled the tiny moon, and emerged from its shadow. The planet had a thick, gaseous atmosphere that roiled in response to hurricane-force winds, and knew no peace.

Attack ships, only two given the status of the target, awaited their orders. The Hoon projected part of itself into the more powerful of the two. What would the soft body do? The AI wanted to see.

Jepp bit the inside surface of his cheek. There was no choice. None at all. He could give the order, and destroy the colony, or withhold the order, knowing it would make no difference. Except to *him*. He gave the order.

Keeta, unaware of her fate, held her uncle's hand. The horn boomed, voices came together in song, and she was happy.

20

Like victory, defeat is but a moment under the stars.

Author unknown
Inscription north side, Building Two,
Temple Complex, Jericho
Standard year circa 30,000 B.C.

Planet Arballa, the Confederacy of Sentient Beings

The Starlight Ballroom was an enormous affair, capable of accommodating up to one thousand guests in microhab-controlled comfort, and protected by a transparent dome. It was like dining among the stars, and while most beings enjoyed the sensation, some found it uncomfortable. They sat within the embrace of specially designed screens.

The *Friendship*'s captain had positioned his vessel so that Arballa filled half the view, and, thanks to the slowly rotating deck, everyone could see.

Guests had started to arrive. Some relied on elaborate life-support systems, while others came under their own power.

The ceremonial meals were well attended in spite of the fact that they were a mostly human concept. Partly because of the status conferred on those who were invited, but largely due to the fact that the get-togethers represented a wonderful opportunity to consummate political deals, especially those that required some nose-to-beak contact.

This particular dinner was being held to honor the newly arrived ambassador from a little-known race called the Aaman-Du. But, for those in the know, which included everyone *except* the newly arrived ambassador, the meal was *actually* centered around Governor Patricia Pardo and "the Earth problem." Evidence of this could be both seen and heard as Pardo and her companions entered the vast, half-filled expanse.

Pardo was at her well-coifed best. She wore a stunning black evening gown, a matching armband to commemorate those lost during the "revolution," and some wicked high-heeled shoes.

The fact that the politician was accompanied by the highly visible Senator Alway Orno, and the less known but still interesting Ambassador Harlan Ishimoto-Seven, made her arrival all the more intriguing.

Pardo's not-so-subtle presidential campaign had started the day after she was sworn into office and included frequent appearances before the senate. That being the case, many of the politicos knew the human, and some even liked her.

Barely noticed during Pardo's entrance was the *actual* guest of honor's arrival and passage between well-set tables.

The alien was a comic figure by human standards. His small head boasted a birdlike beak. His saucerlike eyes seemed to bulge with pent-up emotion, the large, well-rounded tummy suggested a balloon about to pop, and his enormous three-toed feet looked like something a clown might wear. His oversized clothes, so loose that the fabric flapped all around, added to that impression.

But XTs can be and usually are deceiving. The Aaman-Du were no exception. Though provincial by Confederate standards, they had colonized three planets, and were said to be fierce warriors.

Moments later, while the ambassador from Aaman-Du was still settling onto his specially made roost, Sergi Chien-Chu and Maylo Chien-Chu entered the room and were escorted to their table.

The very sight of them raised the volume of conversation a

notch, especially in light of Chien-Chu's status as a past President, and his vocal opposition to Pardo's interim government.

Maylo attracted a certain amount of attention as well, partly because of her relationship to Sergi Chien-Chu, partly because everyone on the ship knew she'd been imprisoned by Pardo's government, and partly because she was breathtakingly beautiful.

Ambassador Ishimoto-*Seven*, his clone brother Senator Ishimoto-*Six*, and nearly every other human male turned to look.

She wore a high-collared, almost oriental red sheath dress decorated with just a touch of fantastically expensive stardust. She was beautiful and *powerful*—a combination that terrified some men and attracted others.

One such male was Samuel Ishimoto-Six, who had not only managed to keep his assistant Svetlana Gorgin-Three *off* the guest list, but had contrived to sit at Maylo's table in the chair to her right. He rose as she approached. "Good evening, Miss Chien-Chu. My name is Samuel Ishimoto-Six, senator for the Hegemony. It's a pleasure to meet you."

Maylo liked what she saw and felt an intangible *something* as he took her hand. "The pleasure is mine. Have you met my uncle? No? Please allow me. Uncle Sergi, it's my honor to introduce Senator Samuel Ishimoto-Six."

Chien-Chu had an excellent understanding of the Hegemony mind-set, as well as their on-again, off-again flirtation with the Hudathans during the previous war, and wondered where they stood now. The senator was attracted to his niece, that much was clear, which meant she would learn the truth. And what about the replica seated next to Governor Pardo? How did *he* fit in? Time would tell.

A party of exoskeleton-assisted Dwellers whirred into the room and approached the table. They were handsome by humanoid standards, having well-shaped heads, large, ovoid eyes, and long, sleek limbs.

It had been a member of their species, the now-famous Moolu Rasha Anguar, who had dragged Chien-Chu out of retirement during the second Hudathan war.

Now, at a time when every vote was critical, the industrialist hoped to solicit Dweller support. Though not fluent in their native tongue, Chien-Chu spoke enough to make himself understood: "I greet you with hands that are empty and a heart that is full."

Flattered by the unaided use of their language, the senior member of the party, Ambassador Tula Nogo Mypop, made the appropriate response: "Our people acknowledge and greet an old friend . . . the elder Anguar sends his regards."

"He lives, then?"

Mypop was a master of nuance and produced a human-style smile. "Lives *and* loves. . . . His vices remain intact."

Chien-Chu laughed. "I am pleased to hear it. Please send him my best wishes. May I introduce my niece?"

There was round after round of introductions, followed by predinner drinks for those who wanted them, and the usual small talk. Ishimoto-Six took advantage of the opportunity to begin a conversation with Maylo.

The meal began fifteen minutes later when President Nankool appeared at the room's center and a holographic duplicate popped into existence at each one of the tables. He "sat" in a chair reserved for that purpose.

The President's words were translated into a dozen languages, scanned for double entendres, racial slurs, or religious taboos, and edited accordingly. While something less than poetic, the results were nonoffensive.

"Good evening, honored guests. We gather to officially welcome the Aaman-Du to the Confederacy—and Ambassador Urulux-Green to our large and mostly functional family."

Many, though not all, of those assembled in the room were equipped with a sense of humor and made a cacophony of noises ranging from laughter to clicks, pops, whistles, and in one case a sort of honking sound.

Maylo thought the laughter was funny . . . and struggled to wipe the smile off her face.

The President's remarks were followed by a speech from the evening's official host, the senator from Arballa, who, though too large to attend in person, was visible via the centrally projected holo.

The speech was a long, rambling affair, which lasted

through the first two courses and well into the entree. All the guests were served something typical of their native cuisines, and, that being the case, some rather strange odors permeated the air.

Maylo, who had worn nostril filters rather than run the risk of embarrassment, strove to ignore some of the more disturbing sights and sounds. Ishimoto-Six was pleasant to look at, so it was easy to do.

The *Deceiver* was one of the few Hudathan vessels not quarantined in the home system. Built in secrecy beyond the rim, and crewed by the offspring of veterans from the last war, the ship was loaded with long-range sensors, highly specialized laboratory equipment, and the latest in stealth technology.

That being the case, Doma-Sa couldn't be sure the warship was even there, hidden among the slowly tumbling asteroids, until the identity of his shuttle was electronically confirmed and the *Deceiver* chose to reveal itself.

A proximity alarm sounded as the stealth ship suddenly appeared on the control screens, grabbed the shuttle with a pair of tractor beams, and pulled it in.

Pleased by the no-nonsense competency of the maneuver, the Hudathan placed the vessel's systems on stand-by, entered the somewhat spartan sleeping cabin, and assumed what he considered to be his *true* identity: *War Commander Hiween Doma-Sa.*

The title would have surprised those having dinner in the Starlight Room, but shouldn't have, since even the most superficial study of Hudathan culture would have revealed that there was no equivalent for the word "diplomacy" in their language, and that until their defeat at the hands, claws, and pincers of the Confederacy, their society had never included a class of individuals known as "diplomats."

After all, why maintain a staff of professional negotiators when you have no intention of negotiating? Victory included the right to annihilate the enemy, and by doing so, to protect the Hudathan race.

Defeat, unthinkable though it was, meant the Hudathans

would suffer the same fate. *Unless* their enemies allowed them to live—a mercy they were likely to regret.

Such were the Hudathan's thoughts as he buckled the belt and pulled the cross strap down across his massive chest. The strap bore a large green gemstone. It glowed with internal light. He wore the sidearm more for comfort than any particular need.

There was a noticeable thump as the shuttle's skids hit the *Deceiver*'s heavily scarred deck. Doma-Sa eyed himself in the full-length metal mirror, approved of what he saw, and headed for the lock. Had the mission been successful? He would know soon.

Senator Orno rather enjoyed the dinners, both as an opportunity to practice the fine art of politics, and as the means to enjoy a really fine meal. The ship boasted the best chefs in the Confederacy, one of whom was Ramanthian.

The politician smelled the platter of live grubs long before they actually arrived, reveled in the aroma of the carefully thickened hot sauce, and found it hard to follow the conversation.

Though malleable in the extreme, Governor Pardo was incredibly boring, and never stopped talking. Her current diatribe focused on the need for the Ramanthian government to recognize her administration, provide Earth with an interest-free loan, and send fifty thousand "peacekeepers" to deal with the insurgents.

That was an invitation the Ramanthians might have accepted, had more of Earth's surface been dominated by lush, green jungle.

Such was not the case, however, which meant that the Ramanthian government had no intention of granting even a tenth of what the human wanted.

There was a stir as the main course arrived. The humans, who preferred to eat dead food, tried to ignore the sauce-drenched grubs. The Ramanthian knew they were horrified as he used his single-tined fork to spear one of the large, worm-like creatures and shoved it under his beak. The knowledge pleased him.

The clean white napkin was large enough to flip over the Ramanthian's head. Rather than conceal what he was going to do, the action drew attention to the process. The grub, fattened for the occasion, was delectably ripe, which meant that its skin was tight and ready to burst.

Orno exerted the slightest pressure with his beak, heard the characteristic popping sound, and watched the mixture of blood and intestinal contents spurt outward, explode against the inside surface of the napkin, and form a circular stain. The taste was most memorable indeed.

There were six grubs in all, followed by a dip in the beak bowl, and a fresh napkin.

Patricia Pardo managed to last through all six of the grubs, waited for what she hoped was an appropriate interval of time, and excused herself. She was pale and a bit unsteady.

Orno was glad to see the woman go. Humans had been known to regurgitate in his presence . . . a truly disgusting sight.

Ishimoto-Seven looked bored, wished it were *he* who was seated next to Maylo Chien-Chu rather than his brother, and finished his food. He had consumed the same meat a thousand times before, and knew that like him, the chicken was genetically perfect.

The *Deceiver*'s commanding officer, Spear Commander Nolo-Ka, met War Commander Doma-Sa at the main lock. He wore the same uniform that his superior did—except that *his* gem was red. Though mutually respectful, both officers were wary as well, since no Hudathan truly trusts anyone else. "Greetings, War Commander. . . . We welcome your presence."

This at least was true, since Nolo-Ka had been waiting for two complete ship cycles, two *dangerous* ship cycles, and looked forward to leaving the sector as soon as he could. The cloaking technology was good, but so were Confederate sensors, and there were plenty of patrols.

Doma-Sa *assumed* subordinates would welcome his presence and ignored the greeting. "Did the torpedo arrive on schedule? Were you able to capture it?"

The questions were logical enough, especially in light of the ship's mission, but that didn't prevent Nolo-Ka from resenting the manner in which they were framed.

What? The War Commander thought nothing of the skill required to penetrate the Confederate defense zone? Of the courage required to wait through endless days? The cunning manner in which the Ramanthian message torp had been snatched out from under its owners' beaks? The clear answer was yes.

Careful to conceal his resentment, the Spear Commander gestured toward a corridor. "Yes, the mission was successful. The torpedo was recovered and awaits your inspection."

Doma-Sa was pleased, but saw no reason to reveal that fact, and delivered a human-style nod—a bad habit acquired during his time on the *Friendship*.

Metal clanged as the Hudathans made their way toward the aft section of the ship, passed no less than four labs packed with equipment, and entered the maintenance areas that adjoined cargo bay 3.

Three distinct shafts of light descended from above, mixed photons, and illuminated the long, slim missile. Though the torpedo was of Ramanthian manufacture, and marked with their curvilinear script, form follows function, and the torpedo looked the way most such objects did.

Approximately sixteen units long and two units in diameter, the tube was the logical result of a technological conundrum. In spite of the fact that many races had mastered faster-than-light travel, none had managed to come up with the interstellar equivalent of the nearly instantaneous com call. That forced them to send messages via ship or message torp, something most of the diplomats did on a regular basis—the Hudathan being a notable exception.

Doma-Sa knew that ninety-nine percent of the missile's considerable length was devoted to a navcomp, a miniature hyperdrive, a standard in-system propulsion unit, and the fuel required to make things go.

The other one percent, the part *he* had an interest in, consisted of a computerized payload. Though small when compared to the vehicle's overall size, the average torp could transport five hundred gigabytes of digitized information—information more valuable than the rarest mineral.

A panel had been removed to provide access to the electronics within. Multicolored wires squirmed this way and that, coupled with each other, and were connected to the ship's computers. "So," Doma-Sa demanded, "what, if anything, have we learned?"

"Quite a bit," a voice said, as Dagger Commander Hork Prolo-Ba stepped out into the light. Born into a colony on a world so distant the Confederacy didn't even know about it, the youngster had never seen the Hudathan home world or enjoyed Ember's slowly fading warmth.

Sad in a way, yet all too typical of the younger officers who crewed ships such as the *Deceiver*.

Doma-Sa liked the youth's brash confidence and met his eyes. "I'm relieved to hear it. Please proceed."

Thus encouraged, Prolo-Ba fingered a remote. A wall screen swirled into life. Ramanthian script appeared, morphed to Hudathan, and started to scroll. The text was supported by diagrams, photos, and video.

"It took our computers twelve point three standard units to break the Ramanthian code," Prolo-Ba said matter-of-factly, "but the task was accomplished. There is a great deal of content, much of which could be described as trivial, but certain items demand our attention."

Doma-Sa chose to ignore the rather presumptuous use of the word "our." "Yes, go on."

"You indicated that we should scan for any mention of non-Ramanthian planets," the intelligence officer said evenly, slowing the text to a virtual crawl, "and you were right. No less than *four* Hudathan colony worlds were included in this portion of the text. Not only that, but Ramanthian designators had been attached to each of them. The *same* kind they use to identify planets which *they* control."

Doma-Sa felt his fingers curl into fists. The words emerged as a growl. "Excellent work, Dagger Commander Prolo-Ba. Now, with your discovery in mind, how many of the worlds in question have a sixty-six-percent or better match to bug breeding requirements?"

"Fully one hundred percent, sir."

Spear Commander Nolo-Ka, who had been silent till then, said what the other two were thinking. "They mean to take our worlds . . . and keep them."

"Yes," Doma-Sa agreed, a jaw muscle rippling just below the surface of his skin. "They certainly do. Was there anything more?"

"Yes," Prola-Ba said, "there was. Based on what we've seen so far, it seems clear that the Ramanthians are in league with a human called Governor Patricia Pardo, a commercial enterprise called Noam Inc., and the Clone Hegemony."

"I want details," Doma-Sa said. "*All of them. You* forged the blade, and *I* shall swing it."

Now that the dinner was officially over, and drinks had been served to those that desired them, the crowd had started to thin. Governor Pardo, Ambassador Ishimoto-Seven, and Senator Orno remained at their table.

Pardo checked her image in a small compact, wondered where the little lines had come from, and allowed it to snap closed. "So, Senator, what's next?"

Orno rubbed his pincers together to stimulate the flow of gru and preened both sides of his face. "That depends. Your arrival supports our efforts, but ex-President Chien-Chu appears more formidable than first supposed."

"Assuming that Chien-Chu is something more than a mechanical fool, he will seek those sympathetic to his cause and urge them to support military intervention. Once such a resolution is passed, assuming they have the votes to do so, the President will approve it."

Pardo looked alarmed. "So, all is lost?"

"No," Ishimoto-Seven replied, "far from it. While Chien-Chu and his niece pursue *their* strategy—we shall pursue *ours*.

"The first step will consist of hearings. Hearings that will provide you with the opportunity to make your case, hearings that will buy us some time, and hearings chaired by a sympathetic being."

Pardo brightened. "Really? Who?"

Orno chuckled. It sounded like a series of corks being pulled from their bottles. "Why, by *me,* of course. Who else?"

• • •

The *Friendship* incorporated many wonders, some of which were advertised as such, and some of which were not. Ishimoto-Six was familiar with both, and, that being the case, had volunteered to show Maylo around—a strategy that succeeded in separating the executive from her uncle as well as everyone else.

The tour began with a trip to the observation deck bar, where the politician bought her a drink. They talked for more than an hour. Maylo observed the clone's technique with the wary detachment of a scientist monitoring an experiment, thought he was amusing, and waited to see what, if anything, would happen.

Then, at some undefinable moment during the subsequent conversation, the executive discovered that unlike most of the men who made moves on her, *this* one had something to say.

They shared a number of interests, one of which was marine biology. Maylo paid close attention as Six described the manner in which the Founder, Dr. Hosokawa, had sterilized Alpha 001's oceans and seeded them with what she called genetic "maxotypes."

It seemed that the indigenous species, few of which had survived, were a source of fascination for Six. He had established an extensive collection of native fossils and dreamed of bringing some back to life via the same science used to kill them. Genetic engineering.

Then it was Maylo's turn, and the politician listened in rapt fascination as the executive described the Cynthia Harmon Center for Undersea Research, the Say'lynt named Sola, and the plan to seed the southern oceans with iron particles. A plan that, like so many things, was on hold due to civil unrest.

It was at that point that Six looked as if he wanted to say something, seemed to think better of it, and shook his head. "I'm sorry so many were hurt . . . but glad you came here."

It was nicely said, *very* nicely said, and the tenor of the conversation changed. Maylo smiled. "Thank you, Samuel."

"Sam."

"Thank you, *Sam.*"

Six grinned, and a mischievous look came over his face.

"Would you like to *see* some of our marine life-forms?"

Maylo raised her eyebrows. "You have holos or something?"

The clone grinned. "No, better than that. The *real* thing. In a tank."

Maylo shrugged. "Sure, why not?"

"That's the spirit!" Six proclaimed as he thumbed the bar tab. "Come on, the fish await!"

It took the better part of fifteen minutes to make their way through a maze of corridors and down onto the bio support deck.

Six was well versed regarding the entire operation. He took evident pleasure in discussing the amount of food produced in the hydroponics vats, the manner in which certain diplomats could live off the "crops" produced within their carefully sealed biospheres, and last but not least the protein raised in marine tanks.

It was then, while the clone was speculating on what sort of organisms might dwell within the Aaman-Du tank, that a technician appeared and greeted the politician by name. "Senator Ishimoto-Six! How's it going?"

"Fine," the clone answered easily. "Just fine. When was your last break?"

The technician was a small man with sallow skin and the eyes of a ferret. He consulted a rather ostentatious wrist chron. "Well, I'll be! Time flies when you're having fun!"

"How true," Six said smoothly as he slipped some credits into the other man's shirt pocket. "Why not take your break *now*? The lady and I will keep an eye on things."

"That's right kind of you," the tech said, winking at Maylo. "Go ahead and enjoy yourselves . . . and I'll be back in an hour or so."

Maylo frowned as the man left. "Enjoy ourselves? What does he mean?"

"Sorry about that," Six replied sheepishly. "Malon knows his stuff, but doesn't have much class. See that tank down there? The blue one? It's filled with life-forms from Alpha 001. It's against the rules . . . but I swim in it from time to time. Want to join me?"

Maylo looked from the man to the tank and back again. "We don't have suits."

"Yeah," Six said unabashedly. "I know."

Maylo was amazed by the clone's effrontery, amused by his boyish charm, and surprised to find that she was tempted. It had been a long time since she'd done anything that crazy. "All right, Senator, you're on."

Six, stunned by the extent of his good fortune, turned and started to strip.

Maylo smiled at this strange manifestation of modesty, unzipped her dress, and wriggled free. Her slip, bra, and panties followed.

The clone shucked his shorts, turned, and took a sudden breath. She had smooth skin, dark-tipped breasts, and a narrow waist. "You're beautiful."

Maylo placed her hands on her hips. "Are you sure? I'm not a clone, you know. . . . My right breast is larger than my left."

"Beauty is in the eye of the beholder," the politician said sincerely, "and I've never seen anyone more beautiful than you are."

Maylo smiled and looked downward. "It appears that you mean what you say, Senator. . . . Thanks for the compliment."

Six looked down, realized he had an erection, and blushed bright red.

Maylo laughed gaily and took his hand. "Come on! The last one in is a Parithio tree snake!"

The clone spent a moment at a control panel and gestured toward a ladder. "Ladies first. . . . The snake will follow."

Fully aware of what the man would be able to see, and determined to ignore it, Maylo climbed toward the top. The grating felt cold under her feet. An inspection hatch was open, and blue-green water was visible below.

"Go ahead," Six shouted. "Dive in!"

Maylo took a deep breath, dove through the hole, and felt the water wrap itself around her. It was cool and soothing. She turned and looked upward as the clone entered the tank, his straight black hair streaming back from his head, bubbles escaping from the corners of his mouth.

The inside of the tank reminded her of the south Pacific. There was colorful coral, a thicket of slowly swaying kelp, and a multitude of quickly darting fish.

Then he was there, taking her hand and pointing toward one especially large fish. Maylo recognized it as an emperor snapper. She wondered if it was edible or there to support fish that were. Then it was time to kick toward the top, surface, and gasp for air.

"So," Six said, "what do you think?"

"You were right," Maylo replied, wiping water from her eyes. "It's beautiful. More than that . . . it looks like Earth."

"Not too surprising," the politician replied, "since that's where all of the Founder's seed stock came from."

"Including you?"

"Including me. Or a version of me."

The humans looked at each other for a moment, came together, and embraced. The kiss tasted of salt and ended when they sank. They kicked their way to the surface, took deep breaths, and tried the same thing again.

It had been a long time since Maylo had been with a man. She welcomed the feel of his hands on her skin, and the strength of his arms.

They surfaced after that. Maylo held onto the pipe that circled the inside of the tank, and opened her legs. Six allowed himself to be captured, searched for the opening, and nudged his way in. It felt wonderful . . . and they took their time. Enough time for Maylo to enjoy two orgasms before her lover allowed himself the same privilege.

And it was then, while the pleasure was at its height, that she remembered the cell, the door, and the man with the gun. How he had called her name, swept her off the floor, and carried her away. She screamed then, not in pain but in pleasure, and the sound echoed off the walls of the tank.

Malon, who returned early on purpose, discovered their clothes, grinned, and made himself scarce. Hey, so the senator wanted to have a little fun? Who the hell was he to object? Especially when the pay was good.

None of them, not the technician, the senator, or the executive, noticed the barnacle-sized machine that crawled out of the tank, inched its way toward the deck, and sent a half-second burst of code.

About a mile away, safe within the privacy of her cabin, Svetlana Gorgin-Three watched the video, ground her teeth, and wished it were her.

21

By making warriors of their misfits, criminals, and so-
ciopaths, the humans have purified their society and
strengthened it at the same time.

Grand Marshal Hisep Rula-Ka
An Analysis of the Legion
Standard year 2594

Legion Outpost NB-23-11/E, aka
Rust Bucket, the Confederacy
of Sentient Beings

The Thraki armada was more than five thousand ships strong.
They formed an enormous three-dimensional diamond, which,
when threatened, would morph into a globe with the arks at
its core and warships all around.

Consistent with the fact that the Thraki had no home world
beyond the one mentioned in ancient legends, and needed to
do everything they could to simplify the manufacture, repair,
and maintenance of their ships, they allowed themselves only
five types of vessels.

There were moon-sized arks, on which most of the civilian
population lived, worked, and eventually died; supply ships,
which carried the raw materials required to sustain the armada;

and three types of warships, including battleships, destroyers, and fighters.

The fleet had been traveling through space for more than a millennium and would continue forever. Or would it?

The Facers, so named because of their desire to put an end to the journey and ''face'' the Sheen, had become even more powerful of late, raising the possibility that things might change. Not that the Runners, who had ruled for so long, could be ignored.

Grand Admiral Hooloo Isan Andragna stood on the gallery that extended out from his private quarters and stared up past the hanging gardens and through the ark's transparent dome. The stars seemed especially thick in this sector—as if blown there by some cosmic wind. Very different from the wasteland the armada had traveled through only a hundred ship years before. But that had been many jumps ago—back during his father's time.

As he stared upward, Andragna knew that no less than 172 grand admirals had stood there before him. Most had died in battle, fighting the Sheen, or whatever race blocked the armada's path. A lucky few passed in their sleep.

What will *my* fate be? the officer wondered. The horn sounded, thousands of feet padded through the ark's labyrinthine passageways, and the stars wheeled above.

Legion Outpost NB-23-11/E had been a spaceship once, but those days were more than forty years in the past, when thousands of vessels had been decommissioned after the second Hudathan war.

Many had been scrapped, or sold into civilian service, but not the DE-507, an honorable hull that had seen action off Algeron and been credited with seven kills.

No, she had suffered the indignity of having her drives removed to enlarge the onboard living accommodations.

Then, as if *that* insult was insufficient, the one-time warship had been loaded onto a giant transport, carried out to the edge of the rim, and dumped into orbit around a world so hot, so shriveled that the crew called it Raisin. That in spite of the fact that the original survey team had deemed the planet too insignificant to merit a name.

Now, her globular hull marked only by the designator NB-23-11/E and a hand-painted sign that read *Rust Bucket,* the one-time destroyer escort turned endless circles around the planet below.

Angie Anvik waited for the hatch to open, aimed her miniscule spacecraft at the blackness outside, and fired the sled's jets.

Cybernetic bodies were expensive—*so* expensive that most borgs were limited to one. That being the case, Angie Anvik had selected the vehicle she believed to be the most versatile—a body that allowed her to work yet blend with human society.

That's why the woman who steered the space sled out of the lock *looked* human in spite of the fact that no mere bio bod could have survived hard vacuum without benefit of space armor.

Even more incongruous was the fact that she was dressed in a one-piece shipsuit, wore a ball cap with the Chien-Chu logo emblazoned across the front, and stood only five feet, five inches tall. Nothing like the hulking Trooper IIs and IIIs that the Legion favored.

Anvik eyed her instrument panel, compared the readouts to those provided by her onboard computer, and nudged the power upward. Thanks to the fact that there was no gravity to cope with, the otherwise overloaded sled was quite responsive and fun to fly. Yes, the cyborg reflected, I can't really say that I *enjoy* being a freak except during moments like this.

The technician aimed her tiny craft for the second of Raisin's diminutive moons and gloried in the moment. She had a purpose, the means to fulfill it, and a lot of elbow room. What more could your average dead person want?

Legion Captain Dal Nethro completed the second set of fifty push-ups, flipped over, and lay on his back. Physical training, or PT, was a daily ritual on the *Rust Bucket,* just as it was on any other outpost. The only person who enjoyed the process was Staff Sergeant Paula Jones, who led the drills and managed to look good while she did it.

The truth was that the sergeant was worth the price of admission. First came her body, which was damned nice to look at; then came her vocabulary, which other noncoms strove to emulate. Sweat gleamed on her dark brown skin as Jones grinned and eyed her victims.

"All right, you worthless, scurvy, odoriferous mounds of maggot-infested Dooth dung, let's see if you can do a couple of sit-ups." The count began, and all thirty-six of the legionnaires, Nethro included, groaned as the sergeant passed one hundred and kept on going.

The session ended not long thereafter. Nethro delivered the usual "Well done," saw Jones grin, and returned to his cabin. The shower felt good in spite of the fact that every ounce of water had been sipped, gargled, and pissed by everyone on board. Not just once, but *countless* times. But it was wet—and smelled better than he did.

He sang the last stanza of *The Stand,* which, like most of the songs associated with the Legion, focused on death.

The very tip of the Thraki formation consisted of a ship equipped with highly specialized sensors and protected by a swarm of two-seat fighters.

The purpose of the vessel was to probe the system ahead, locate threats if any, and warn the armada.

No less than forty-three ship cycles had elapsed since the vessel had last detected anything of substance, but that didn't matter to Basida Folo Ormoda, who never shirked his duties.

The electronic warfare section occupied an entire "slice," or deck, but one of the smaller ones, since it was topside rather than lower down.

The deck was split into four sections, each of which duplicated the others. The technicals spent each watch sealed into their own pod—an arrangement that made it virtually impossible to kill all of them with a single missile.

Ormoda felt at home in his U-shaped console—which made sense, since nearly all of the previous two years had been spent there. A single light blinked on and off, his right index finger tingled as a mild current passed through it, and a tone sounded in his ear. Electromechanical activity had been detected somewhere in the darkness ahead. The sort of activity produced by a Class III or better civilization. The Sheen, waiting in ambush? Or still another sentient race?

It made no difference. Activity equaled threat. Alarms sounded, messages flew, and fighters arrowed away.

The cloaking technology that protected the interceptors had been stolen from a race called the Simm, and, barring the possibility that the target had something even better, would allow the attack craft to approach undetected. Ormoda wished the pilots well.

The moon called Two Ball was not all that different from Earth's moon, to which humans compared all other moons, since it had been their first step to the stars.

Small when compared to the planet below, it not only lacked an atmosphere but was covered with overlapping impact craters. Anvik steered the utility vehicle toward a large depression. The surface dropped away and rose on the other side.

The prefab equipment blister had been erected with help from Nethro's legionnaires. It was nearly invisible against the dark gray background. A tone plus a single red beacon guided the cyborg in.

Anvik closed on the light, gauged the distance, and fired her retros. The sled slowed, hovered on its repellors, and settled into a cloud of dust. It was fine, like volcanic ash, and hung waiting for Two Ball to pull it down.

Anvik released her harness, kept her movements slow, and approached the blister. The shelter sensed motion, sent power to a pole-mounted spot, and lit the much-churned soil.

The cyborg stopped in front of the access door, punched her mother's birthday into the keypad, and waited for the hatch to open. She didn't need a lock, but the bio bods would, so the designers provided one.

That accomplished, the technician returned to the sled and released the tie-downs. The shrink-wrapped payload included a nonsentient computer plus the armor required to protect it. Because Anvik was extremely strong, and had gravity on her side, the load was more awkward than heavy.

Anvik carried the unit to the blister, entered the lock, and lowered her burden to the floor. Once that was accomplished, she thumbed a button, waited for the external hatch to close, and heard oxygen enter the lock. The inner door opened two minutes later.

Racks of neatly installed equipment claimed most of the interior space, while an emergency sleeping cubicle occupied the rest. Anvik slid the computer into the waiting slot, shoved jacks into the appropriate receptacles, and locked them in place.

Some people called the Early Warning System (EWS) a horrible waste of money, while others stared into the blackness of space and wondered who might come. *They* viewed the EWS as a form of insurance. *Life insurance.*

That was a postwar Hudathan sort of mind-set based on the premise that what you didn't know *could* hurt you.

Minds such as those appeared to be in the minority now, and, while Anvik hoped for the best, chances were that this particular blister, plus five more authorized as part of a beta test, would be the only stations ever brought on-line. So much for the company's contract—and so much for her job.

Anvik completed the last connection, summoned a wiring diagram from her onboard computer, and checked to ensure that everything was correct.

Then, positive that it was, but worried that it wasn't, she threw the main switch. Power flowed from the fusion generator buried six feet under the moon's surface. The computer spoke through an overhead speaker.

"Approximately four thousand individual targets have been detected . . . with a ninety-six-point-two-percent probability that there are more beyond the range of the system's sensors . . ."

Anvik shook her head in disgust, cut the power, and went to work. Something was wrong, and she would find it.

The *Rust Bucket*'s sit room was a multileveled affair. Nethro sat in the big black power-assisted command chair while the techs rode the next level down.

It had been a long time since the Inspector General (IG)

had swung through, so a variety of personal items had appeared, which was fine with Nethro so long as they didn't hinder operations, and could be "struck" in a hurry.

That's why Corporal Ivy was busy staring into his girlfriend's unblinking eyes, wondering what she was doing at that particular moment, when the computer whispered through his temple jack.

The machine could be programmed to emulate both genders, plus a wide variety of accents, but had come across as a soft-spoken female for the entire six months, twenty-two days, and sixteen hours of Ivy's stay. Everyone called her Sweetie Pie. "Hello, Corporal Ivy. . . . Please notify the OOD that my sensors indicate a class ten systemwide incursion."

Ivy switched his attention from his girlfriend's face to the monitors above. He couldn't believe his eyes. There were targets, *hundreds of targets,* and more appeared with each passing second.

And some of them were close, *so close* they couldn't be where the screens said they were, except that the screens never lied. Not yet, anyway.

Six of the incoming spacecraft were traveling faster than all the rest and constituted an immediate threat.

The tech flipped a cover up out of the way, hit the red button with his fist, and heard the klaxon go off. "Battle stations" had a distinctive sound—and the entire station came to life. Hatches were dogged, weapons came on-line, and the shields went up.

Nethro, who had been working on one of the endless reports for which he was responsible, switched his monitor to the same source as Ivy's, and felt something cold grab hold his stomach. The enemy ships, for there was little doubt as to what they were, were only minutes away.

Flight Warrior Hydranga Morak Nusu pulled one last check on her wingmates, verified that all were where they should be, and activated her weapons. Like everything else in her ship, they were controlled by the special gauntlets she wore. The words had been drilled into her from the age of five:

"Energy cannon—safeties off—accumulators on.

"Ship-to-ship missiles—safeties off—guidance on—warheads active.

"Electronic countermeasures on—shields up—max power."

They were like prayers, prayers said each night when she went to sleep, and part of who she was.

Nusu watched the target grow in her HUD and allowed herself to grin. Here was the moment that she and the other pilots had sacrificed their reproductive organs for—the opportunity to *give* life by taking it from others. Yes, some might die, but the armada would live, and so would her race. Nusu screamed. Not in pain . . . but in pleasure.

Anvik reconnected the final lead, ran the diagnostics one last time, and watched the results bloom green. The system was not only functional, but working flawlessly. What was wrong, then? Where had the false readings originated? From a one-time anomaly?

The technician flipped a series of switches and touched a button. The red lights reappeared, and the computer seemed to pick up right where it left off. "More than four thousand five hundred enemy craft have entered the system, and six have attacked Confederate asset NB-23-11/E. Repeat . . ."

Some rather sophisticated com equipment had been incorporated into Anvik's body, and she switched it on. The most commonly used military freq rattled with static. ECM! The *Rust Bucket* was under attack! The system had been right from the beginning. Shit!

Anvik tried to make contact, realized it was useless, and entered the lock. Oxygen was removed, time seemed to slow, and the tech started to swear. It was a long series of linked profanities that even Sergeant Jones would have been proud of.

But then, somewhere in the middle of it all, the words turned to prayer: "Please God, please God, please God," over and over again. It was all she could do.

The *Rust Bucket* lurched as still another enemy missile hit the shields, pushed them to the edge of failure, and dissipated the release energy. Lieutenant Commander Sena had responsibility for the station but not the legionnaires. He grabbed a console and yelled to make himself heard over the drone of Sweetie Pie's dispassionate voice, the constant rattle of static, and the bleat, bleat, bleat of the damage-control klaxons. "She won't take much more, Dal . . . my damage-control team is running out of chewing gum."

Most of the team had managed to slip into their emergency space armor, but Nethro hadn't found the time. The midships missile battery fired. Ivy yelled, "Tracking!" and one of the attack ships vanished from their screens. The smile was forced. "Your people did their best, Sam . . . we all did."

"So that's it? No surrender?"

The shields went down, the *Rust Bucket* rolled, and Sena fought to keep his feet. That's when the argrav generators failed and junk filled the air. A coffee mug sailed toward Nethro's face, and he slapped it away. Sena's feet came off the deck, and he grabbed a stanchion. "Damn."

The legionnaire pointed toward the monitors. They were filled with Thraki fighters. "Sorry, Sam. There isn't much point. Nobody tried to contact us. How 'bout the message torps? Did you get them off?"

"Gone," Sena replied. "All six made it out."

"Good," Nethro said grimly. "Here's hoping that one of the little bastards gets through. Maybe the brass will get off their collective asses and *do* something." They were the last words he ever said.

Hydranga yowled with glee as the enemy space station exploded. She pulled a high-gee turn and issued a new set of orders. Three aircraft and six lives had been lost during the attack. Their replacements were on station.

"The armada detected six, repeat six nontargeted missiles, some or all of which may contain enemy communications. Units four, five, and six will switch to channel seven, acquire tracking, and hunt them down.

"It would be nice to examine one or more of the units in question, but ensure that none escape.

"Units two and three will form on me. All enemy installations must be located and destroyed. Check the moon first. Questions?''

None were forthcoming.

The fighters split into two separate flights, curved away from each other, and sought their various targets.

Anvik left the protection of the equipment blister just in time to see the *Rust Bucket* explode. A miniature sun was born, lived to maturity, and died. All within the space of a few seconds.

The technician screamed the word "No!" But there was no air to transmit the sound . . . and no ears to hear it. Nethro, Sena, and Jones. All of them dead. It was impossible, inconceivable.

The fighter appeared out of nowhere, passed over Anvik's head, and fired a missile. The cyborg turned, saw the distant flash, and knew the antenna was gone. The equipment blister! That would be next!

Moving as quickly as she dared, Anvik hurried to the sled, threw herself into the seat, and fired the repellors. How much time remained? A minute? Three? The trick was to hide . . . and do it quickly.

The cyborg fired the steering jets, aimed for the blackness at the bottom of a nearby crater, and put the vehicle down. Then, working as quickly as she could, the technician pulled the emergency shelter out of its compartment, flipped the fabric shiny side down, and threw it over the sled. It took forever to fall. Maybe, just maybe the heat would be reflected downward, and escape notice from above. It was worth a try.

Determined to put some distance between the sled and herself, and determined to witness whatever happened next, the technician made her way up to the crater's rim. There were boulders at the top, some of which were big enough to hide behind, and Anvik ducked in and among them.

It wasn't until then, when the cyborg had a moment to reflect, that she thought to activate her recorders. Though intended to document each step of the installation process, the gear could be used for other applications as well. Like taping the strange manta-ray-shaped ship.

Not satisfied with the destruction already wrought, the warship cruised the moon's surface and probed the ground below.

The cyborg willed herself to disappear as the night-black hull passed not twenty feet over the top of her head.

Then, having located the equipment blister, the spacecraft fired its retros, hovered in place, and fired its energy cannons. The second shot was redundant. The facility was destroyed.

Nusu felt a sense of grim satisfaction as the enemy installation was reduced to a mound of half-slagged rubble. She extended the fingers of both hands, brought her palms together, and felt the fighter accelerate. Then, pointing to the right, she sent the vessel out and away from the moon. Her part of the mission was accomplished—but what of the others? How had they fared?

"Units four, five, and six, report."

The voice was that of Garla Tru Sygor, her second in command. His voice was tight with triumph. "One missile recovered—five destroyed. Returning to ship."

It was no small accomplishment, and Nusu said as much, so the entire squadron could hear. "Well done, Sygor. Congratulations."

The fighters landed, death songs were sung, and the armada swept on.

Anvik waited for a while, cautious lest the enemy ship return, and emerged from hiding. There was nothing on the radio—not even static. Should she send? It was risky, the technician knew that, but couldn't resist. "Anvik here. Does anyone read me?"

Silence.

The cyborg tired three times and finally gave up. That's when she wanted to cry. But cyborgs *can't* cry, not *real* tears, so the sorrow turned to something else. Something hard and cold.

Anvik stood there, Raisin hanging above, and sent her words raging into space. "Nice try, assholes . . . but no frigging cigar. You missed someone . . . and you're gonna *pay*."

22

When the enemy advances, we retreat.
When he escapes, we harass.
When he retreats, we pursue.
When he is tired, we attack.
When he burns, we put out the fire.
When he loots, we attack.
When he pursues, we hide.
When he retreats, we return.

Mao Tse-tung
Standard year 1937

Planet Earth, Independent World Government

The ship dropped hyper, a new set of constellations appeared on the screens, and the standard drives cut in. The destroyer's control room was small and cramped, but the CO had slotted Maylo into an empty seat and narrated each stage of the jump. Something she didn't require . . . but didn't have the heart to refuse.

The executive listened as orders were passed, marveled at the extent to which the military could turn even the most mundane activity into a ritual, and considered the task ahead.

Some progress had been made during her stay on the *Friendship,* especially where new alliances were concerned, but there was a long way to go. That's why she had begged her uncle to let her stay and help.

He had refused by pointing to the fact that *if* their efforts were successful, there would need to be some sort of interim government.

And that led to Chien-Chu's other main concern: the possibility that one branch of the resistance movement would dominate the rest, leading to some sort of dictatorship. The first fifty years of the industrialist's life had been spent under imperial rule, and he had no desire to repeat the experience.

To counter those threats, and ensure a democratic form of government, it was important to get involved now. *Before* the deals were done and the political concrete was poured.

Could Maylo pull it off? Her uncle thought so, citing her experience as CEO of Chien-Chu Enterprises, the extent to which her corporate connections would help, and the fact that her status as an ex-prisoner provided credibility where the resistance was concerned. Not to mention her relationship with General Kattabi and Colonel Booly.

Someone touched Maylo's arm. "Miss Chien-Chu?"

She turned, saw the boyish-looking CO, and realized he had repeated her name. "Sorry, Captain. My mind was elsewhere."

The officer thought his passenger was stunning and was willing to forgive almost anything. He smiled. "No problem, ma'am. Look at the screen. See that star? The one inside the green delta? That's Earth. Are you happy to see her again?"

Maylo looked, marveled at how small the planet appeared, and decided that she was.

The sun was high, the sky was clear, and the Imperial Coliseum was packed with human beings. Conceived by the long-dead emperor, and constructed as a monument to his empire-sized ego, it survived because people actually made use of it. The venue's size, plus the retractable roof, made it perfect for sports, concerts, and political gatherings. But not like this . . . never like this.

At least a hundred thousand people filled the surrounding seats, but unlike the normal crowds, this one was silent. So silent flags could be heard as they snapped in the breeze.

Colonel Harco stood toward the front of the governor's box. It was a large, balconylike structure that projected out over the seats below. The perfect platform from which to see and be seen. Food and drinks were available, but the officer wasn't hungry. What was going on? And why had he been summoned?

The arena was so vast that the people on the far side of the field looked like little more than specks of multicolored confetti. But they weren't bits of paper . . . far from it. Each was a real, live human being. Selected by computer, ordered to come, and afraid to refuse.

That was the kind of government Matthew Pardo ran . . . and the kind Harco had unintentionally empowered. Not for himself, but for the men and women of the military who had been used, abused, and left begging on the streets.

Some of them, including Staff Sergeant Jenkins and Sergeant Major Lopa, were with him now. They stood in positions reminiscent of parade rest, carried handguns under their jackets, and watched from the corners of their eyes.

No one knew why the crowd had been assembled—no one beyond Pardo, that is, and he was perennially late.

Maybe he planned to give one of the long, rambling speeches for which he was becoming increasingly famous, or—and this was what Harco feared most—the ex-legionnaire had something else in mind. Something crazy.

Harco found himself wishing that Patricia Pardo would return. Not because he *liked* her . . . but because she was sane.

It was then, as if summoned by Harco's thoughts, that the governor arrived. Not immediately, but behind a screen of security troops, all drawn from the militia.

They were heavily armed, wore black body armor, and seemed to know what they were doing.

Then, with the security troops in place, Pardo arrived. He wore the jet-black uniform of a general in the militia. It was a rank he had conferred upon himself, and, given the fact that Harco remained a colonel, rated a salute.

The usual retinue of sycophants, toadies, and suck-ups followed their leader onto the balcony and struck a variety of poses. Leshi Qwan was among them.

Harco, his jaw rigid with barely controlled anger, came to attention, delivered the salute, and saw the other man's smile. "Leon! Nice of you to come . . . not that you had a great deal of choice."

The entourage laughed, tittered, and giggled. This was the sort of entertainment they lived for.

Pardo ignored them. "I asked you to come because there are those who admire and take comfort from your stern military visage. About sixty percent of the voting public, give or take a point or two. They will note your presence and feel much relieved."

There was a humming sound as three ovoid-shaped robo-cams rose from the depths below and positioned themselves along the rail. Harco felt more lead enter his belly. It was a setup. But what kind? And for what purpose?

Pardo smiled sardonically. "Why, Leon, what's wrong? You look worried. What a silly thing to do! You're one of us . . . not one of *them*."

The last word was said with contempt—as if the still-silent crowd was inferior somehow.

It was at that particular moment that Harco realized that no matter what happened next, some of the responsibility would fall on *him*. Not because he had conceived whatever was about to happen . . . but because he had enabled it. Enabled it and lost control. Like a missile he couldn't recall.

One of the toadies offered Pardo a wireless microphone, whispered something in his ear, and stepped out of the way. Conscious of the vid cams, the entourage looked suitably respectful.

An announcer read from a carefully prepared script. Pardo stepped out where he could be seen and took a moment to admire the size of his audience. His image blossomed on three enormous screens. Halfhearted applause rippled through the crowd.

The odds were that the RFE's fly cams were covering the event as well, which was all to the good, since that would extend the breadth of Pardo's coverage. Dozens of black-clad troops appeared at the exits as he brought the microphone to his lips. The crowd stirred uneasily. "Greetings. Thank you for taking time out of your busy lives to attend this gathering.

"Most of you are law-abiding citizens. Thanks for your support. Others, and you know who you are, belong to the so-called resistance, or, if not active yourselves, persist in supporting those who are. *You will be punished.*"

There was a deep rumbling noise. Harco recognized the sound and scanned the horizon. The ship, which was too large to land within the coliseum, appeared from the west. It threw a shadow across the crowd. Twelve man-made cyclones held the vessel aloft. They destroyed a four-hundred-foot section of wall, sliced through a section of intentionally empty seats, and sucked debris into whirling columns of air.

People screamed, clung to each other, and surged toward the exits. The guards fired, people staggered, and the crowd retreated. The wounded called for help, and the dead lay where they had fallen.

The ship had completed its journey by then, and hung over the arena like an ominous lid.

In spite of the fact that the rebs controlled the upper layers of the atmosphere, they allowed government aircraft to operate below thirty-five thousand feet. So far, anyway—though that was likely to change. This particular vessel was about as large as a spaceship could get and still be able to land on a planetary surface.

The resistance had allowed the ship to exist because it was based so close to Los Angeles that an attack would cause civilian casualties. One of Harco's suggestions—and one he suddenly regretted. "So," Pardo continued solemnly. "It seems that some sort of example is in order."

The words were a cue. Six beams of bright blue light touched various parts of the crowd. There were screams followed by confusion as the targeting lasers swept the seats.

"Yes," Pardo said understandingly. "Scary, isn't it? Knowing that death can reach down and touch you. . . . But *only* if you're guilty—like citizen Deke Bayeva."

Three of the lasers converged on a single man. He stood, tried to run, and vanished in a flash of light.

The ash modeled the shape of his body for a moment, surrendered to a puff of wind, and dusted the seats beyond. Five people, all of whom had been seated near Bayeva, died at the same instant. A wooden seat back started to burn and was extinguished with a jacket.

"That's what happens to traitors," Pardo intoned. "And if you doubt that Bayeva was guilty, then watch the screens."

The crowd had little choice but to watch as the recently deceased Bayeva appeared on the screens, pried the lid off a public utility vault, cut the cables nestled within, and ducked off camera.

A new culprit was announced, and the torture continued. Harco watched in disgust as the targeting lasers swept the near-hysterical crowed, settled on their latest victim, and burned her down.

There were no apologies for those who died with the condemned, or the long line of blackened bodies that resulted when a burst of wind hit the hovering ship, sending an energy beam down row 123. The message was clear: Watch those around you, choose your friends with care, or share their fate.

Finally, after ten resistance fighters had been identified and executed, the assault ship was allowed to depart. Sunlight flooded the arena. Pardo, his eyes alight with emotion, scanned the crowd. "Remember what you saw, tell others, and obey the law. You'll live longer that way."

The security forces withdrew from the exits, people rushed to leave, and the governor turned his back. "So," Pardo said, his eyes locked with Harco's, "what do you think?"

The officer considered a political reply, knew he couldn't stomach it, and said what he truly believed. "I think you're insane."

A bodyguard went for her weapon, staggered as Staff Sergeant Jenkins shot her, and skidded across the floor.

The braver members of the entourage surged forward, hesitated when Sergeant Major Lopa aimed a machine gun in their direction, and stayed where they were. The militiaman to whom the weapon had been issued lay unconscious at the noncom's feet. The voice was little more than a growl. "If you want some . . . then come and get it."

No one accepted the offer. Especially Leshi Qwan—who had slipped out the door.

Pardo, the only one who dared to move, shook his head sadly. "I'm disappointed, Leon . . . *very* disappointed. I looked up to you, wanted to *be* like you, and believed you were strong. I thought you knew that political power, *real* political power, grows out of the barrel of a gun."

"The battle is for justice," Harco said hollowly, "not power."

Pardo laughed. "Speak for yourself, Leon. Now, if you and your men will step aside, I have a supper to attend."

Lopa, who could have killed the governor by exerting the tiniest bit of pressure on the machine gun's trigger, raised an eyebrow. Harco shook his head.

Pardo gestured to his entourage and led them out. All but the bodies, which remained where they had fallen.

Harco turned his eyes in the direction of the field. The cameras were gone and the sun had started to set.

The horizon seemed to shimmer as the sun-tortured tarmac released waves of heat. Rank after rank of troops stood at attention.

Thanks to the constant flow of volunteers, and the infusion of more than nine hundred "reactivated" cyborgs, the 13th DBLE was considerably over strength. So much so that they had been forced to muster at Djibouti's airport.

The ceremony was Kattabi's idea, a way to not only welcome the borgs back to active duty, but to show the once-demoralized 13th just how strong it now was.

The ground shook as the newly reinducted cyborgs marched past. Three had expired during the flight to Djibouti, six died while being transferred into their new bodies, and eighty-nine were declared unfit for duty.

The rest turned in response to an order, formed a column of twos, and marched the length of runway 1R.

Booly held his salute as yet another Confederate flag drew abreast of the makeshift review stand and felt a variety of conflicting emotions.

It was good to see these veterans, to have their strength to call on, but sad nonetheless. How many of these same cyborgs would die cursing his name? Wishing he had left them buried in the past? There was no way to know.

A bugle sounded, a flight of six fighters roared overhead, and the troops marched on.

The safe house was buried in south L.A. It belonged to a sympathizer who worked for the government. Water poured into the tub, and the bathroom filled with steam. It billowed, eased toward the window, and shivered as it passed through the opening.

Kenny had changed during the recent weeks and months. The acne-scarred face was the same, but *he* was stronger, more self-confident. And why not? He had founded the RFE, hadn't he?

Yes, there was the mysterious J.J., and the funds that greased the way, plus hundreds, no, *thousands* of underground correspondents who risked their lives to submit their reports, but he was the one who made everything tick, and lived with a price on his head. How many times had they come for him? Five? Six? He'd lost count.

He pulled the 9mm out of his waistband, laid it on the toilet lid, and shucked his clothes. They were filthy, and rather than wash them out he would throw them away. So much for laundry. A new set, tags removed, lay in a corner.

Kenny examined his body in the mirror, took pleasure in seeing how hard it was, and bent to brush his teeth.

That's where he was, spitting into the sink, when the girl entered. Her name was Jenny, and, like many of the women Kenny had run into of late, she was attracted to him. It was a new development—and one that he enjoyed.

Kenny turned. Jenny smiled, did an abbreviated striptease, and stepped into the tub. She had an elfin face, pert little breasts, and long, slim legs.

Kenny felt himself respond, saw her eyes widen in response, and grinned. He checked to ensure that the door was locked and crossed the room.

The water was hot. Some slopped onto the floor as he entered the opposite end of the tub. Her legs slipped up over his shoulders. He kissed one ankle, then the other. It bore a half-moon tattoo. Jenny giggled, found what she was looking for, and held it tight.

That's when something went thump, an intrusion alarm went off, and Kenny grabbed for the gun. "The window! Now!"

Jenny grimaced, brought something up out of the water, and pointed it at Kenny's chest. She screwed her eyes shut and sent a message to her right index finger.

Kenny shot her twice, saw blood tinge the sudsy water, and heard the gun thud against the bottom of the tub.

The teenager stood, grabbed his boots, and shoved them through the window. Clothes are nice but don't offer any protection from rocks, metal, and broken glass—just one of many things he'd learned during the last few months.

A voice came from out in the hall. "Jen? You in there? I heard shots. Did you nail the bastard?"

The bounty hunter hit the door with his shoulder, burst into the room, and took two slugs in the head. And a good thing too—since military-grade body armor protected his chest.

Kenny knelt on the back porch roof, peeked through the window, and wriggled back in. And why not? Government troops would have surrounded the place by now, and there was no sign of a backup. None except for Jenny . . . who floated face up. Damn. What a waste.

He retrieved the new clothes, switched weapons with the bounty hunter, and left the 9mm clutched in the other man's hand. Just a little entertainment for Pardo's police force.

That accomplished, the resistance fighter went out the window, found his boots, and jumped to the ground. Once there, it was a simple matter to run down the alley, duck behind a garage, and pull the clothes on. They felt stiff and scratchy.

A siren could be heard in the distance as Kenny took his bearings, waited for a cop car to pass over his head, and strolled away. A dog barked—but no one cared.

The command car circumnavigated the bomb crater, lurched through a drainage ditch, and growled onto the much-abused highway. A lizard raised its head, took exception to what it saw, and scuttled away.

Admiral Angie Tyspin felt her butt leave the seat and was grateful for the lap belt.

Colonel Bill Booly glanced in her direction and grinned. "Nice one-point landing, Admiral. . . . Sorry about the road."

"The name is Angie . . . and I'll settle for any kind of landing that I get to walk away from."

"So noted," Booly said cheerfully. "Now hang on—the road gets worse before it gets better."

The legionnaire's words proved prophetic. The vehicle topped a rise, granted a glimpse of blue, and plunged into a gully. It took the better part of twenty minutes to fight their way through a dry riverbed, up a series of ancient switchbacks, and along the side of a heavily eroded cliff. Tool marks left more than two hundred years before could still be seen.

But then, just as Tyspin was starting to regret the trip, they passed between a pair of graffiti marked boulders and out onto a gently winding road. The Gulf of Tadjoura shimmered below. The water was blue, the sun danced over the waves, and palms beckoned from the shore.

"That's where we're going," Booly announced. "Are you ready for a beer?"

Tyspin wiped the sweat off her forehead, decided that she was, and waited while the other officer climbed out of the rig, went to the back, and opened a cooler. There were two dozen cans nestled in the ice, along with a bottle of wine and a carefully packed lunch.

Someone—Fykes seemed the most likely suspect—had thrown a couple of assault weapons into the back. His way of nagging without actually being there. Booly grinned and left the weapons where they were.

Tyspin watched the infantry officer swing behind the wheel, thought how handsome he looked, and accepted the ice-cold beer. It hissed as she flipped the tab up and out of the way. The liquid was cold and tart. It soothed her heat-parched throat.

So, Tyspin thought to herself, should I keep it platonic? Or take a fling? Assuming he wants one. He's not in my chain of command, which certainly helps, but he *is* junior. Unless they jerk my star . . . which would leave us as peers.

The naval officer found the concept to be comforting, reminded herself that there was no need to solve nonexistent problems, and decided to focus on the moment. Something, she wasn't sure what, said, "Good idea," and faded away.

The road descended through some nicely engineered curves, passed a long-abandoned resort, and ended by the sea.

Booly drove the command car under the palms, turned the tailgate into a shelf, and opened a duffle bag. "Ready for a swim? There's three or four masks in here . . . see if one of them fits."

Tyspin wore a two-piece bathing suit under her shirt and shorts. She stripped down, examined the gear, and made her choices.

Booly, clad only in trunks, nodded toward the water. "Ready?"

Tyspin nodded and followed him across the sand. She'd been aware of the fur, but had never really seen it before. The silvery mane began at the base of his skull, flowed the length of his spine, and ended just above the waistband of his trunks.

Curious about her reaction, the naval officer checked, found that she rather liked it, and followed Booly into the water.

Protected as it was by the point west of Arta, the inner gulf was relatively calm and nonthreatening. Fine white sand shifted under Tyspin's feet, waves lapped at her ankles, and soon rose to slap against her waist.

Tyspin lay on her back, pulled the fins on, and adjusted her mask. Booly waved, and she followed him out. The bottom was mostly bare. The current pushed the sand into delicate ridges, bounced tiny bits of coral along the bottom, and tugged at the tiny, almost transparent fish.

Then, as the water grew slightly colder and the waves became more pronounced, the bottom fell away. Booly touched her arm and pointed downward. Tyspin pulled plastic-tainted air down through the snorkel, stored it in her lungs, and kicked with her fins.

Booly felt cool water close over the top of his head and checked to ensure that Tyspin was okay. She had a lean, almost boyish body. Her legs moved with the rhythmic surety of someone who had dived before.

Though she was not exactly beautiful, Tyspin exuded something the legionnaire liked. Intelligence, confidence, and competence. All sexy in their own way.

Rosy-orange coral heads rose to greet them, a school of blue chromis wheeled away, and a garden of sea anemones bloomed beyond.

Then, after what seemed like seconds but was actually minutes, the officer's lungs began to protest. Booly checked to ensure that Tyspin was aware of him, jerked a thumb toward the surface, and kicked his feet. The sky arched above.

The water, which was deep and blue, harbored many mysteries, including ancient wrecks, little-known life-forms, and volcanic vents.

The machine intelligence was aware of such things, but perceived them as variables, none of which meant anything in and of themselves.

No, what counted was the mission, the purpose to which the construct was presently dedicated. Its rather mindless gestalt was both a weakness, and, given the nature of the machine's assignment, a significant strength.

The machine *knew* it had limitations, just as it knew the enemy was sentient, and more than that, capable of sensing what bio bods thought and felt.

Not machines, though, which was why the three-hundred-seventy-foot-long attack submarine had been sent halfway around the world to intercept an even larger submersible, and then, as the people aboard screamed in pain, the artificial intelligence would assassinate the being that came to their aid.

It was a clever plan, far *too* clever for the attack sub to appreciate, not that it mattered.

Sound rumbled up ahead, the kind of sound made by twin screws, churning through the sea.

The attack sub checked to ensure that the sounds matched the correct computer profiles, loaded six AS-8 acoustic homing torpedos into its tubes, and prepared to fire.

●　　●　　●

Sola's extremities covered hundreds of square miles of ocean and, that being the case, could feast on nearly limitless sunlight. Wonderful, delicious sunlight, which was different from that available on her native planet had its own unique bouquet.

It was a dreamy existence for the most part, drifting with the currents, pursuing whatever thoughts happened along, and keeping the world at bay.

Well, *almost* at bay, since there was no way to ignore the surface vessels that did occasional damage to her delicate limbs, or the minds, thousands upon thousands of which planned, schemed, and plotted until the ethers were filled with the mental equivalent of static.

But there were others as well. Minds lost in deep meditation, surfing waves of creativity, or simply bubbling with joy.

Some of those, her favorites in fact, belonged to the dolphin people, who, though primitive in ways, had their own kind of intelligence, and lived in the ever-present now.

It was through them, while hitchhiking in their minds, that Sola had first experienced how wonderful if felt to slide along the crest of a wave, to dive for elusive prey, and to mate in the shimmery blue.

They called to Sola, begged her to come, and she went.

Designed to support the Cynthia Harmon Center for Undersea Research as well as similar facilities, the *Leonid* displaced nineteen thousand tons submerged, was five hundred seventy feet long, had a forty-five-foot beam, and was powered by two Norgo fusion reactors, each capable of developing forty thousand horsepower, and, when operating in tandem, of propelling the submarine through the depths at speeds in excess of thirty knots.

The sub contained two holds crammed with supplies, two hundred resistance fighters, and a crew of sixty, some of whom were in it for the money, and some, like Captain Mike Finn, who were true members of the Resistance.

Finn was a big man, *too* big according to his physician, and not all that tall. He had black hair, a matching beard, and a quick smile. His clothes, which were always the same, consisted of an excruciatingly loud shirt worn over immaculate white pants.

It was Finn's way of simplifying life, of reducing the number of variables one had to deal with, and generating peace of mind. Something he sought but wasn't likely to get. Not with a sub loaded with contraband, an ocean full of enemies, and a bad case of heartburn. The voice boomed through his earplug.

"I have a contact, skipper. She's dead astern, and closing fast. An attack sub, from the sound of her."

Finn swore, launched himself down the corridor, and exploded into the con center. He scanned the screens, confirmed the sonar operator's report, and chose a course of action. The *Leonid* had never been a warship, which meant she had no offensive weapons. "Prepare to launch acoustic decoys. . . . Launch."

"Prepare for silent running. . . . Execute."

"Sound the collision alarm. . . . Man damage-control stations."

The orders were executed quickly and efficiently. Evasive maneuvers were a possibility if the acoustic torps failed, but there wasn't much more that Finn could do. Nothing but pray. More than two hundred souls stared at the steel bulkheads and waited to learn their fates.

Sola was in the midst of a vicarious dive, rejoicing in the way that the water flowed across her supersmooth dolphin skin, when the fear jerked her back.

It took less than a second to locate the source, access a collection of minds, and define the problem: A submarine, loaded with volunteers, was under attack.

But how? Assuming that the humans were right, and there was no reason to think they weren't, a vessel was in the process of stalking them.

Yet how could that be? Especially since the Say'lynt was unable to locate the minds that such a vessel implied.

Then it came to her, *the fact that there were no minds,* that the enemy had devised a way to counter her abilities.

Sola wasted no more than a tenth of a second on self-recrimination before launching her intelligence outward. She found thousands of life-forms.

Most had very little intelligence, but that didn't make any difference to Sola, who was more interested in what they *felt*. The challenge was to sort through countless impressions, discard those with little or no value, and identify those that mattered.

A thirty-foot oarfish saw something considerably larger than itself but was too stupid to glean any meaning from it.

A lantern fish felt the backwash from the submarine's wake and dove to escape.

A shark sensed the presence of a large electric field, decided it was *too* large to be edible, and continued its search. And there were more, *many* more, all contributing tidbits of information.

Three seconds elapsed while the Say'lynt built what amounted to a sensory mosaic from the input she received, compared it to the information the *Leonid* had gathered, and knew where the attack sub was. Not *exactly* . . . but within a hundred feet.

That being the case, Sola shoved some instructions into Finn's brain, sent a summons down into the deep, and started to mourn.

The attack sub sensed the decoys, knew what they were, and stayed locked on its target.

Then, just as the computer was about to launch, the other submarine dove.

The defensive move made absolutely no difference. The AS-8s would follow. The attack sub fired.

Three bluish-gray Byde's whales all developed a desire to look for squid in the same place at the same time. They converged from different directions.

A sixty-five-foot-long sperm whale rose from the depths and wondered why.

Two humpback whales, one fifty feet in length, the other a good deal smaller, came as well. They had black tops, white bellies, and long, narrow flippers. Both used echolocation to find the *Leonid* and positioned themselves alongside.

And there were more, a dozen denizens of the deep, all summoned for the same task. More than half died as the lethal AS-8 torpedoes sought the *Leonid* and found their bodies instead.

The cargo sub shook as explosion after explosion blew its protectors to bloody bits and turned the water red with blood.

Confused by the uninterrupted sound of the other vessel's props, but certain that its weapons would carry the day, the attack sub fired again.

The second spread of torpedoes was no more successful than the first. They detonated one after another, but the target was fading.

The attack sub tried to follow, discovered that its prop was fouled, and lost forward motion.

A sentient might have experienced any number of emotions, but the machine was utterly calm. It launched a remote through tube one, waited for the device to reach the stern, and scanned the incoming video. Unlikely though such a circumstance was, it appeared as though two or even three *Loliginidae*, or giant squid, had chosen to wrap themselves around the propellor shaft and been torn apart. Sharks had been attracted to the scene and were starting to feed.

That was strange, but of no particular concern, since the problem would soon resolve itself. Or so it seemed to the machine.

Daggers flew regular coastal patrols now, and it was a relatively simple matter for Sola to summon two of the aircraft and point the pilots in the right direction. They located the attack sub, dropped two torpedoes each, and whooped as debris boiled to the surface.

Sola, who had experienced each death as if it were her own, floated in an ocean of tears.

Harco looked out across the vast mud flat to the rock on the far side. It was important to reach it, to reach the top, before the tide came in.

But how? The thick, glutinous mud was nearly knee deep, and clung to his boots like raw concrete.

He took a long, slow look around, realized there was no other choice, and started to slog.

Each footstep required tremendous effort—all of which would be wasted, since the water would sweep across the flats long before he was able to reach the rock.

"Colonel? Sorry, sir, but there's something you should see."

Harco raised his head, realized he had fallen asleep, and rubbed his eyes. The mud flats were gone, the desktop supported his elbows, and Staff Sergeant Jenkins was visibly upset. "It's on every channel, sir, even the RFE."

Harco nodded, wondered what "it" was, and pushed the desk away.

His living quarters, which consisted of a hotel suite about a block from the Global Operations Center, was strewn with stacks of printouts, half-eaten meals, military clothing, wall maps, and a corporal asleep on the floor. The officer had ordered his subordinates to deal with the mess on numerous occasions but it always came back to haunt him.

"There," Jenkins said, pointing to the holo tank. "Listen to what they're saying."

Harco recognized the reporter as one of the officially sanctioned "information coordinators" supplied by Noam Inc. She had blonde hair, perfect clothes, and a carefully modulated frown.

"Details remain sketchy, but it appears that thousands of citizens were forced to attend a gathering in the Imperial Coliseum, where Colonel Leon Harco addressed the crowd.

"Please be warned that the footage you are about to see is graphic . . . and not appropriate for children."

What followed was an exact rendition of what actually occurred at the coliseum, except for the fact that Pardo was nowhere to be seen, and it was Harco who summoned the spaceship, ordered Bayeva's death, and murdered innocent bystanders.

The technology had been around for a long time. Given enough sample footage, and there was plenty of Harco, the Noam Inc. technicians could create new images so seemingly real it was impossible to tell them from the real thing.

The citizens knew that, of course, and many would suspend judgment, but what of the rest?

Some—those who were naive, lazy, or just plain gullible— would believe Harco was a monster.

Yes, thousands of people had actually been there, and *knew* the truth, but what were they when compared to the billions who would see nothing except what was broadcast?

The soldier-cum-politician had not only played Harco for a fool—but succeeded in undercutting the officer's credibility as well. What had he said? A sixty-percent approval rating? Not any more. Pardo had seen to that.

That conclusion was underscored when the falsified sequence ended and the reporter segued into an interview with Pardo himself. The governor looked distraught, and wore civilian rather than military attire.

"I have no idea why Colonel Harco felt it was necessary to take such harsh measures . . . and wish he had consulted me first. This incident serves to illustrate the need for a unified command structure. The public can rest assured that I will investigate and take appropriate action."

Harco killed the broadcast but stared into the now-darkened tank. Now it was out in the open. Pardo wanted to control *everything*.

Jenkins looked anxious. "Now that you've seen it, sir, what should we do?"

Harco thought about it for a moment, then shrugged. "We'll do what we always do . . . we'll fight."

Maylo Chien-Chu stepped out of the shower, toweled her hair dry, and decided to allow the next stage to take care of itself.

The voyage in from the edge of the solar system had consumed three days, followed by some time spent in orbit, and a bumpy ride through the atmosphere.

Now, safely ensconced within Fort Mosby, she was ready for a good night's sleep. But first, while her hair continued to dry, a stroll on the ramparts. Would Colonel Booly be there? As when they first met? And why should she care, given what he had said?

But she *did* care, rational or not, and that in spite of the fact

that she already had a man in her life. Or did she? What was
the relationship with Ishimoto-Six, anyway? Something serious? Or nothing at all?

She didn't know, and more than that, didn't care to figure
it out. Not here . . . not now.

The parade ground was cool and, with the exception of the
usual number of sentries, empty. The sun painted the sky pink.
A bat swooped, snatched an insect, and flapped away. A mu-
ezzin called the faithful to prayer.

Pleased with the way the evening felt, Maylo ducked into
one of the towers, followed the spiral staircase upward, and
paused to catch her breath. That's when she heard voices . . .
and the scrape of footsteps.

Something caused her to step back into the relative darkness
of the stairs as the twosome passed. Maylo didn't recognize
the woman, but there was no mistaking Booly or the arm
around her waist.

The executive waited for them to pass, marveled at how
stupid she had been, and returned to her room. It felt dark and
more than a little lonely.

23

Men are so simple and so ready to follow the needs of
the moment that a deceiver will always find someone
to deceive.

Niccolò Machiavelli
The Prince
Standard year 1532

The Rim, Clone Hegemony, the Confederacy of Sentient Beings

The stars seemed to snap into existence as Jose Fonseca-Three
Hundred Forty-Six dropped hyper, switched his sensors to
max, and scanned the surrounding volume of space. Something that he, plus all 739 of his "brothers" had done countless times before.

In spite of the fact that the Clone Hegemony had joined the
Confederacy at the conclusion of the second Hudathan war,
they continued to maintain their own military forces and
placed little reliance on the Confederate Navy.

That being the case, the clones conducted regular patrols
along their section of the rim—mostly to control smuggling,
but to ensure their sovereignty as well.

A beeper beeped, data scrolled onto the scout's screens, and
the pilot felt his stomach lurch. The readings couldn't be true!
Nobody had a fleet that large! Not even the Confederacy.

Fonseca-Three Hundred Forty-Six ran the scans again, obtained the same results, and dumped them to memory. A swarm of fighters started in his direction. That was enough for him. The hyperspace jump occurred four seconds later.

Nine missiles, all fired by three supposedly cloaked fighters, raced through the space the clone had so recently occupied. Fonseca had no way to know it, but today was his lucky day.

The Chamber of Reason was lined with stone, *real* stone, said to have originated on the Thraki home world, though no one could be entirely sure of that, since all the records that pertained to the early years were missing. Or so the priesthood claimed.

Still, even though he couldn't be absolutely sure where the fossil-encrusted limestone had come from, Grand Admiral Hooloo Isan Andragna felt better while sitting in the stony embrace, as if protected by the very ancients who had launched the armada.

The chamber was shaped like a dome, the inner surface of which was pierced by thirty-seven narrow, slitlike windows, each arranged to admit a single ray of artificial light. They met on the table below and in doing so symbolized a convergence of worldly wisdom.

It too was made of stone, a circular stone that had a hole at its center and was divided into thirty-seven identical sectors, one for each member of the committee. The committee to which the admiral reported—and from whom his orders came.

That being the case, he sat at the table's center where an axle might have been, for he, or more accurately his position, was the point around which the armada rotated.

There was only one way to reach Andragna's position, and that was by ducking under the table's surface and crawling to the hole at its center. The journey was made slightly more tolerable by the runner laid down for that purpose . . . but it was humbling nonetheless. And that was the point, to remind admirals of their place, and to keep their egos in check.

Andragna completed his crawl, surfaced in front of his power-assisted chair, and took his seat. It was then and only then that committee members entered the room and sought their individual chairs.

At least half the representatives had small, hand-crafted robots with them. They set the machines loose to perform on top of the table. One did cartwheels, another juggled, and a third told jokes.

Though never formally acknowledged, there was fierce competition to come up with the most original, functional, or interesting "form," and considerable status attached to doing so.

Andragna waited for Sector 19 to take her seat and nodded toward the chamberlain. He lifted a cloth-covered hammer and struck a large metal disk. It was called the Shield of Waha. A single note reverberated between the walls, and the meeting began.

The forms walked, danced, tumbled, crawled, and flew to their owners, whereupon they were deactivated and returned to their custom-designed cases and carefully embroidered satchels.

Andragna waited for the overpriest to complete the benediction and for the meeting to begin.

No formal agenda had been established, and none was required. The sectors knew what the issues were, as did most of their constituents. In the closed community that was the fleet, it was hard *not* to know what was going on.

Still, someone had to get things moving, and Sector 12 liked to talk. She rose, checked to ensure that she had everyone's attention, and launched her attack.

"Thanks to Admiral Andragna's sloth, lack of initiative, and general incompetence the Armada is in danger. A scout ship dropped hyper, scanned the fleet, and made its escape. Even now the alien hordes may be gathering to attack. I suggest we strip Andragna of his rank and choose a new, more competent leader."

No one was surprised by Sector 12's pro forma attack, since she represented the Runners, and was playing to the cameras. There were catcalls, rude noises, and volleys of insults.

Sector 27 cleared his throat, stood, and looked around. He was a high-ranking member of the priesthood, a xenoanthro-

pologist, and a well-known wit. "I for one would like to thank
Sector 12 for the much-needed entertainment, and having done
so, move on to the business at hand.

"In spite of the high degree of technological match between
the space station that we destroyed seventeen cycles back, and
the scout ship that so recently escaped our clutches, the vessel
in question seemed to have more sophisticated systems than
the habitat did. A finding that suggests related yet disparate
cultures. A political schism, perhaps? If so, that could work
to our advantage."

"*Good*," Sector 12 said tartly. "The admiral will need all
the help he can get."

There was laughter followed by additional catcalls.

Sector 4 was a Facer, and, as such, never stopped preaching
her creed. She was a small thing, little more than skin and
bones, but her eyes were filled with fire. They darted around
the chamber.

"Consider what you heard. Here's a race with technology
approaching our own. Rather than destroy the savages, let's
befriend them, and form an alliance.

"Then, when the Sheen arrive, the aliens will help fight the
machines. Who knows? It may be possible to use them as a
protective shield. Later, at the conclusion of the conflict, we
can either continue the partnership or, if circumstances warrant, turn and destroy them."

Silence filled the chamber as the female took her seat. Sector 4's strategy was one of the most cynical, dishonest, and
downright diabolical proposals the sectors had ever heard.
Needless to say, they loved it.

Sector 18 was the first to stomp his right foot, Sector 32
followed, and the rest joined in. After years of waiting, the
Facers would have their day. Sector 4 looked triumphant. The
Runners scowled. All eyes turned to Andragna.

The warrior's mind flashed forward to the work that awaited
him. He felt a great weariness settle onto his shoulders, and
bowed his head. "The sectors have spoken . . . I will obey."

Jorley Jepp waited for the shuttle to settle onto its skids, adjusted the supplemental oxygen mask that covered his face,

and entered the lock. Sam, who never liked being left behind, sulked on a nearby seat.

The lock cycled the prospector through and provided access to the surface beyond. The Sheen assigned a number to every planet they encountered, but Jepp preferred names, and was quick to hand them out.

Paradise Lost, which was the name the human had given the once-lush world, was a testament to the downside of technology.

Like humans on Earth, the indigenous race had crawled out of the sea, climbed the long, uncertain ladder to sentience, and discovered the wonders of science—wonders they proceeded to exploit until the atmosphere was poisoned, the climate changed, and the world rendered inhabitable.

What then? Jepp wondered as he stepped onto the rocky surface, felt the heat embrace him, and scanned the once-verdant plain. Did they die? Or simply leave, taking their insanity with them? There was no way to know.

A specially equipped shuttle, its belly full of salvaged metal, rose from the pit ahead. It hovered while the onboard computer requested the necessary clearance.

Then, once the signal was received, the shuttle climbed into the orange-gray sky. The Sheen were hungry—and food was on the way.

Jepp heard gravel crunch under his boots as he walked to the edge of the depression and peered over the side.

Once the top of the ancient city had been stripped away, the Sheen realized that it had been constructed in millennial layers, starting at the bottom of a valley and growing over a period of fifteen thousand years.

In need of considerable amounts of metal, and happy to conserve the energy required to process raw ore, the machines took everything they could. Not in just *one* city, but in *dozens,* around the circumference of the planet.

The process had been underway for more than six local days by the time Jepp landed, and it would soon be complete.

Roads had been carved into the side of the now-restored valley. Machines, all controlled by a very minor aspect of the Hoon's intelligence, crawled like silver maggots through what remained of the once-proud city, fed on its flesh, and regurgitated their meals onto mile-long conveyor belts. Though huge, weighing many tons apiece, the robots looked like toys when viewed from above.

Jepp felt a sense of revulsion as he watched, knowing that priceless works of art had probably been lost, along with who knew what else? Libraries? DNA repositories? Valuable technology? And yet, repulsed though he was, the human had been a prospector and understood the morality of need.

More than that, Jepp had come to believe that the Sheen had not only been sent by God, but tasked with a divine purpose, a mission that he alone could understand.

That being the case, the rape of an ancient culture was thereby transmuted into something good and wholesome.

Another shuttle lifted from the pit, rose to eye level, and was cleared for takeoff. A second vessel, this one empty, approached from the east.

Jepp watched the machine depart, murmured a benediction over the dead city, and returned to the shuttle. It was *his* time in the wilderness . . . and there was much to learn.

The battle cruiser *Darwin* hung motionless in space. She was huge, one of only three ships of her class, but still less than a hundredth the size of a Thraki ark. The rest of the Clone fleet, some three hundred vessels in all, waited nearby. Not *all* their ships, but more than half. That was not many when compared to the thousands they might face.

Of course, "nearby" is a relative term—especially when applied to the vastness of space. Every person on board knew how vulnerable the *Darwin* was . . . and did what they could to ignore it.

But the Thraki had put themselves at risk too, by boarding the Hegemony vessel without so much as a single bodyguard. Or so Harlan Ishimoto-Seven had told not only himself, but the Triad of One, which consisted of Magnus Mosby-One, son to the notorious Marcus-Six and his free-breeder wife, as well as his half-brothers, Antonio and Pietro-Seven.

The scene outside the wardroom was tense, as everyone waited for the aliens to arrive, and wondered if they truly would. Magnus stood talking to Pietro. He had his father's black hair, his mother's tendency to put on weight, and a deep, commanding voice.

Their Alpha Clone's advisors, and in at least one case a lover, stood just beyond earshot. Though influential, Ishimoto-Seven was far too junior to stand shoulder to shoulder with the inner circle, and waited beyond.

That was something of a slight, given the fact that the strategy was his, but typical of the hierarchical way in which the Hegemony was structured.

The better part of two weeks had elapsed since the first, almost unbelievable reconnaissance report, the mass mobilization that followed, and the start of negotiations. Many of the government's most senior officials, up to and including Antonio-Seven, had opposed any sort of deal. Especially one that would be executed without the knowledge and consent of the Confederacy.

Others had seen the wisdom of such an alliance, however, especially those who happened to be privy to the secret agreement between the Ramanthians, the interim Earth government, Noam Inc., and the Clone Hegemony.

That was an alliance that Ishimoto-Seven had not only nurtured, but sold over the objections of fools like his brother Samuel, who spent an inordinate amount of time spouting outdated homilies about ethics, trust, and brotherhood.

Thank the nonexistent Lord for Svetlana Gorgin-Three, who not only slaved under his brother's rather uninspired leadership, but kept Harlan apprised of his sibling's peccadillos, the latest of which dealt with a water tank and a free-breeding executive. A rather useful piece of information, should he need to use it.

The only problem was that now, having sold two out of three Alpha Clones on the original concept, Ishimoto-Seven found himself busy trying to install a much-needed counter. What if the cabal was overwhelmingly successful? What if the Ramanthians grew too strong? Such questions had troubled the diplomat for months, until the Thraki dropped hyper and offered the perfect solution. The crowd stirred as the Thraki party was announced. Everyone turned to look.

Magnus Mosby-One wore a simple white toga secured by the double-helix pin bequeathed to him by his father. He produced a well-known official smile and stepped forward. Pietro was at his side.

Antonio, the doubter, remained with the fleet, ostensibly in case of treachery, but actually because he refused to participate and thereby endorse the meeting.

There were rumors about Antonio, people who claimed that his genetic material had been obtained directly from one of his predecessor's backup copies rather than the Hegemony's DNA banks, as if that might account for his independent ways. A seemingly silly theory—since there shouldn't be any difference—but who could know for sure?

Ishimoto-Seven watched with approval as the Thraki admiral entered the compartment, closely followed by an entourage of officers, priests, and a contingent who, in spite of the title "Sector," sounded suspiciously like the sort of politicians the diplomat was used to.

The two parties merged, exchanged greetings, and were herded in the direction of the *Darwin*'s wardroom—the only space other than the hangar deck that could accommodate such a large group. The Thraki spoke via small robots that rode on their shoulders, were carried like infants, and in one case walked on what looked like stilts.

The clones, by contrast, wore hastily programmed translators that hung around their necks and bounced as they walked. Magnus was uncomfortably aware of his . . . and the computer-generated voice that spoke through his implant.

The Thraki admiral was at least two and a half feet shorter than he was and looked sort of feline. Once the initial greetings were complete, he poured it on: ". . . So, imagine how happy we were when your envoy made contact and it was possible to . . ."

It was drivel, the same sort of drivel Magnus listened to all day and knew how to ignore—a strategy that provided more time in which to think his own thoughts.

Slowly, reluctantly, Magnus had allowed himself to believe that the cabal would make a useful counter against the sometimes inordinate amount of influence that the free-breeders seemed to wield where the Confederacy was concerned. A danger that he, as the product of a free-breeder union, must be especially sensitive to.

Now, the same advisors who had engineered the Hegemony's participation in the secret alliance wanted to align themselves with the newly arrived Thraki so as to counter the cabal. Where would it end? And why *him*? His father had been born to power—and his mother had married it. Both assumed he wanted the same kind of life they did. Both were wrong.

Doors parted, the leaders entered, and negotiations began.

Raisin hung huge and brown against the blackness of space. There, but no longer beautiful, not to Anvik.

It was lonely on Two Ball, *very* lonely, which came as something of a surprise to the cyborg, who had previously thought of herself as having fewer needs than bio bods did. It was bullshit, but *useful* bullshit, since it made her feel better. Till the aliens arrived, blew the *Rust Bucket* into small pieces, and left Anvik all alone.

But they would be sorry, the technician was sure of that, because in spite of their efforts to sanitize the crime scene, *she* had survived, and would live to tell the tale.

Maybe Sena launched some message torps, *maybe* one would get through, but *maybe* wouldn't cut it. No damned way.

Besides, Anvik had survived and, that being the case, was determined to get home. The only problem was *how,* since the sled was way too slow, and there was no telling when the next ship would come. In a month? Two? It didn't much matter, since neither possibility was acceptable.

That's why the tech decided to build her own ship—if the amalgamation of salvage could be dignified with such a term.

Her creation, which Anvik called the *Hybrid,* sat crouched at the bottom of a crater. Though strange and largely untested she was almost ready to go.

Powered by the fusion reactor salvaged from the equipment blister, and coupled to an engine removed from the wreckage of the *Rust Bucket*'s starboard lifeboat, the *Hybrid might,* just might, make the journey to Nav Beacon CSM-1706, which, if still intact, contained a tiny life-support module and—of more importance from the cyborg's perspective—an emergency message torp. Not what any rational being would consider a sure thing—but a helluva lot better than sitting on her plasti-flesh ass waiting for help to arrive.

All of which explained why Anvik was willing to launch the sled, enter the slowly orbiting debris field, and search for the necessary parts. That in spite of the fact that the activity forced her to confront bodies, or parts of bodies, some of which were still quite recognizable.

That's why she cried, prayed, and swore, mixing the three things together into long liturgies of her own devising. "I'm sorry, Nethro, sorry the bastards got you, sorry you died so hard. Look after him, God, he's one of the good ones, the kind you want to keep. Oh, Lord, whose hand is that? Damn! Damn! Damn!"

Anvik spoke with her friends as well, telling them about her plans and requesting their advice. "So, whaddya think? Should I go with eight steering jets? Or settle for six? Six would be easier. That's what you think, too? Glad to hear it. Sorry about your face."

And she *was* sorry. Sorry they were dead, and sorry she couldn't do better by them.

Yes, the technician might have gathered some of her former comrades up, parts in any case, and buried the remains on Two Ball, but survival came first. Survival followed by re-venge—which she knew they'd want.

That's why Anvik used a piece of conduit to push Sergeant Jones away, turned to hook some wiring, and pulled it in. Though frozen and somewhat desiccated, Jones still managed to look reproachful. Or was that the light? And the radiation that was starting to slow-cook her brain?

And that's how it was, day after bitter day, until the control interface was complete and the *Hybrid* came to life. There was no hull, just a frame, to which fuel tanks, the fusion plant, and the propulsion system had been strapped, bolted, and in one case wired, with no regard for anything other than function.

There were problems, small things mostly, but problems nonetheless. Three days passed while Anvik worked to fix them, and on the fourth day, she lifted off, broke free of Raisin's gravity well, and angled outward.

Nobody watched her go—nobody but the stars, that is, and they were mute.

Magnus accompanied the Thraki delegation all the way to the hangar deck, waited while they entered their shuttle, and retreated to the momentary privacy of the VIP lock. Pietro remained by his side. Like his predecessor, the other Alpha Clone was possessed of light brown skin, flashing black eyes, and perfect teeth. Unlike the previous version, he liked jewelry and wore more than he should have. Earrings on both ears, two gold pendants, and rings on every finger. A good sort in his own way—but ambitious, and far too trusting. "So? What do you think?"

Magnus shrugged. "They *say* all the right things. But talk is cheap."

"True," Pietro agreed, "but what have we got to lose? The planets belong to the Hudathans . . . or *did*, back before the war."

Magnus sighed. "Yes, dear brother, but ask yourself this: Why would an entire race board ships and roam the stars?"

"Admiral Andragna answered that," Pietro replied defensively. "Remember? Their native system had two suns. One became unstable, so unstable that they were *forced* to leave, and search for a new place to live."

The inner door opened, six identical guards snapped to attention, and Magnus felt tired. He placed a hand on the other clone's shoulder. "Yes, Pietro, that's what the admiral *said*. But what if the sonofabitch lied?"

24

Even the greatest wall is built one stone at a time.

Author unknown
Aaman-Du Rotes for Hatchlings
Standard year circa 250 B.C.

Planet Earth, Independent
World Government

The statue of Christ the Redeemer still stood over the war-ravaged city of Rio de Janiero, but little else looked the same. Great swaths of the once-attractive downtown area had been destroyed prior to when the Navy retook the skies. Now, having been victimized by repeated sub-launched missile attacks, the city lay in ruins.

The government tower lay where it had fallen, crushing hundreds of lesser structures, pointing toward Guanabara Bay. Sugar Loaf stood as it had for countless millennia, but the cable cars that carried people to the top lay crumpled where they had fallen, as did a row of three transmission towers.

Thousands of dispossessed citizens lived in the enormous soccer stadium, while an equal number camped in the streets. The citizens of Rio had paid a high price for their freedom and refused to let it go.

Farther toward the south, beyond the limits of the old city, the latest incarnation of the Hotel Intercontinental still stood, blackened by the effects of a five-hundred-pound bomb but defiantly vertical.

The aerospace fighters arrived first, checked for bandits, and flew cover while the fly forms landed. The long trip west had been punctuated by one inflight refueling, but all three of the cybernetic aircraft managed to complete the journey.

One of the insectoid-looking craft carried Kattabi, Booly, and Maylo, while the others were packed with troops selected by the recently promoted Sergeant Major Fykes. Half the security force was composed of bio bods, while the rest consisted of reactivated Trooper IIs. Not what the noncom wanted . . . but what the political situation would permit. Or, as Kattabi put it, "The idea is to make friends, not waste the city."

Still, it pays to be careful, *and* make an impression, which was why Fykes and his troops were allowed to deass the fly forms first and secure the recently cleared parking lot.

Brigadier General Cathy Cummings was big, about six-foot-six, with a personality to match. The marines called her Big Momma, respected her savvy, and loved her courage. She wore starched fatigues, boots she spit-shined herself, and a custom-made shoulder holster. The nonstandard .50 caliber recoilless was a lot of gun . . . but she was a lot of woman.

The Marine Corps officer watched with mixed emotions as the fly forms touched down. Legionnaires boiled out and secured the immediate area. Impressive, but redundant, given the fact that a full Marine recon company already occupied the hotel's grounds.

Come to think of it, that had always been the problem. The powers that be had assigned the Marine Corps and the Legion to much the same sort of missions—and forced them to compete for resources.

The Marine Corps had prospered back during the Empire but had fallen out of favor after the loss of *Battle Station Alpha XIV* at the start of the second Hudathan war.

Put it down to a regrettable defeat, lousy press relations, or suck-ass luck—the results were the same: The Corps was little more than a shadow of what it had been.

In fact, on the first day of the mutiny, the once robust force was down to only two brigades—the 6th, which she commanded, and the 2nd, which was off-planet.

So, much as Cummings might like to take Earth all on her own, she lacked the arms and legs to get the job done. That's why she was willing to meet with Kattabi—and he was willing to meet with her. They needed each other.

Cummings watched Kattabi jump to the ground, scan the area, and start in her direction. He was tall, not as tall as she was, but tall nonetheless. He had short, white hair, light brown skin, and a hawklike nose.

Three officers and a civilian female deassed the transport behind him but stayed where they were. No entourage. An excellent sign. She went to meet him.

The withdrawals started slowly, so slowly that no one noticed at first, not until the RFE raised the question on the six P.M. news.

Kenny didn't use human reporters, not on-air, and hadn't for weeks now. After all, why put someone at risk when there was no need to? Computer-generated simularcrums worked for free, never questioned editorial policy, and were impossible to capture and interrogate.

That's why Scoop Scully's lantern-jawed visage had become something of a pop icon. Nearly every graffiti artist in the land had mastered his cartoon face, and the Pardos had countered with a character of their own.

So, when Scoop suggested that the Legion had pulled out of major cities and was consolidating its forces in and around Cheyenne Mountain, people paid attention.

One of those people was Matthew Pardo. He killed the holo, slammed his fist onto the conference room table, and eyed his staff. "What the hell is going on? Why wasn't I informed?"

The senior officers looked uncomfortable, the junior officers looked confused, and a corporal blurted the answer. "You *were* notified, sir. I sent the intelligence summary via e-mail at 1530 hours yesterday and left hardcopy on your desk."

Many of those present grew pale and waited for the ass-chewing to begin. They didn't wait long. The words were tinged with disgust. "So, *that's* it. Nothing happens unless *I* do it. Harco pulls his troops, puts most of them into an underground fortress, and *I* get the news via the R-fucking-E! Are you people stupid? Don't sit there staring at me. . . . Go out and discover what the bastard is up to!"

No one had the courage to point out that Pardo rarely read the reports directed to his attention, had gone out of his way to crush individual initiative, and had intentionally forced Harco out.

That being the case, they rose from their chairs, shuffled out of the room, and set forth to document the obvious: Harco had chosen his ground and was ready to defend it.

Negotiations had been ongoing for the better part of two days now, and Maylo, who served as both an economic and a political consultant, had finally broken free. After talking about logistics for most of the afternoon, Kattabi, Cummings, and their combined staffs had finally recessed.

Maylo repaired to the largely abandoned beach, where, with the exception of a Trooper II who followed from a distance, the executive took a solitary walk. The Atlantic rushed in to swirl around her ankles, pulled sand out from under her feet, and drew itself back. She allowed her thoughts to flow with the water.

The military preparations were going well—perhaps *too* well, unless her uncle made some progress pretty soon. She, along with Kattabi and Cummings, could hold the coalition together for a while, but they wouldn't wait forever.

Something appeared up ahead. Maylo struggled to see what it was. A table? Someone sitting where the ocean met the beach? What in the world?

Curious, the executive continued her stroll. As the distance closed, Maylo confirmed her initial impression and saw that a man sat with his back to her. He stood and turned. It was first time she had seen Booly in civilian clothes. He wore a short-sleeved black shirt, white trousers, and no shoes. He smiled and offered a flourish. The table was covered with crisp linen, gleaming silver, and some of the hotel's best dinnerware. Coolers were stacked in the background. "Good evening, ma'am. Your table awaits. We have cold shrimp, a crisp garden salad, and a nice white wine. Madam approves?''

Maylo laughed. ''Why, Colonel Booly, you amaze me. What's the occasion?''

The legionnaire stepped forward to take her by the hands. He looked into her eyes. ''I want to apologize for what I said after the rescue. I was tired, and the words came out wrong. I hope you'll forgive me.''

Maylo smiled softly. ''Apology accepted . . . not that you owed me one. But why all of this?'' She gestured to the table.

Booly shrugged sheepishly. ''Because I think you're special, *very* special, and I hoped you would have dinner with me.''

Maylo searched Booly's face. ''Thank you, Colonel, but what about the woman in Djibouti? Won't she be angry?''

Booly looked confused, then brightened. ''Do you mean Angie? Admiral Tyspin? We're friends. Nothing more.''

''You had your arm around her waist.''

The soldier grinned sheepishly. ''True. We went skin diving, came back, and had a few drinks. Soldiers tell war stories. It went on for quite a while. The admiral required some assistance, and so did I.''

Maylo raised an eyebrow. ''Are you drunk now?''

Booly shook his head. ''No, ma'am. Stone cold sober.'' He gestured toward the table. ''So, will you have dinner with me?''

Maylo looked around, realized that no less than four Trooper IIs had taken up positions around them, all facing outward. She laughed. ''What choice do I have? You have me surrounded. Dinner it is.''

The officer grinned, offered a chair, and attempted to light the candles. The wind snuffed them out. Neither of them cared. The evening was theirs.

The aircar followed the highway toward Cheyenne Mountain. It was clogged with olive drab trucks, transports, and rank after rank of slowly plodding cyborgs, all moving at about ten miles per hour. Sitting ducks if Pardo or the loyalists had enough cojones to attack them.

Harco got on the radio, chewed some ass, and circled back. Three tank carriers pulled off the road, and the rest of the column started to pick up speed. Better, but far from perfect.

The aircar resumed its original course. Harco watched the mountain grow larger. It wasn't much to look at, just a big pile of granite with trees scattered along the top.

First established as a command post for something called the North American Defense Command, the semisecret facility had been closed for years, reactivated during the Hudathan wars, and sealed by the same budget cuts that put his troops on the streets.

There would be work to do, *lots* of work to do, but the facility was perfect for his needs. Other strongholds, five in all, would serve the forces abroad.

The engineers who had constructed the fortress hundreds of years before had drilled a 4,675-foot tunnel from one side of the mountain to the other. The purpose of the passageway was to relieve pressure in the event of a nuclear blast—and provide the cavern's occupants with a back way out.

The twenty-five-ton doors were reported to be in excellent condition and still capable of closing within forty-five seconds.

Beyond them, deep within the mountain itself, were fifteen shock-mounted buildings and everything required to support up to twenty thousand people for two years.

Six fusion generators, each capable of producing three thousand five hundred kilowatts of electricity, were up and running, the reservoirs held twelve million gallons of potable water, and the storerooms contained tons of food, ammo, and equipment.

The aircar circled, lost altitude, and settled toward the concrete pad. Yes, Harco thought to himself, we're almost ready. But ready for what?

Never one to tolerate excuses, especially from himself, the officer knew he had failed. Thousands of men and women *had* been rescued from the streets, but for what? Life in a cave? Rather than reconstruct the Legion, Harco had torn it apart.

The aircar landed, sentries snapped to attention, and Harco entered the command post. It felt cold . . . like the inside of a tomb.

• • •

The conference room was packed. Fully eighty percent of the
known resistance groups on Earth had sent some sort of representative. They were a motley group that included professional soldiers, underground warriors like the Euro Maquis,
criminal gangs such as the Jack Heads, and a significant number of corporations.

Booly called the meeting to order. Kattabi took the podium
and scanned the crowd. Some eyes were willing to meet his,
and some weren't.

"We came to build an alliance that will free Earth from
tyranny and restore the legally constituted government. Thanks
to you, and the agreements forged during the last few days,
we are ready to move forward.

"Many of you wonder *when* our day will come, *when* we
will strike, and find it difficult to wait."

"Yeah!" one of the Jack Heads shouted. "What the hell
are we waiting for?"

"A good question," Kattabi replied calmly. "The truth is
that we're waiting for a number of factors to fall into place.
It would be foolish to mention all of them, since one or more
of us may be captured, but some seem obvious.

"In order to succeed, we need buy-in from most if not all
of Earth's population, clear lines of authority, good communications, excellent logistics, off-planet military support, and
recognition by the Confederacy.

"Once all of those conditions are met, we will move and
move quickly. There isn't much more that I can say, except
to travel safely, tell your people to keep the pressure on
Pardo's government, and wait for the signal.

"We *will* rise, we *will* fight, and we *will* win."

Maylo joined in the applause, wondered how her uncle was
doing, and hoped that Kattabi was correct.

Booly found her from the other side of the room. He smiled,
and she smiled in return. Suddenly, much to Maylo Chien-
Chu's surprise, her life had changed.

25

He who plants lies and calls them food shall reap nothing but misery.

Author unknown
Dweller folk saying
Standard year circa 2349

With the Thraki Armada, off the Planet Zynig-47, the Confederacy of Sentient Beings

Grand Admiral Hooloo Isan Andragna stepped out onto his private gallery and looked up through the carefully tended gardens to the transparent dome beyond.

The planet called Zynig-47 hung there like a blue-green gem, beckoning the Thraki home.

Scouts had landed six ship cycles before, and were quickly followed by four teams of scientists, all of whom arrived at the same conclusion: The humans had been truthful.

The atmosphere was clean, some of the natural resources had been exploited by previous inhabitants, but plenty remained. The arks had assumed orbits that would allow them to function as fortified moons. Yes, their presence would result in tidal action down on the planet's surface, but so what? The indigenous life forms were not likely to be of much value anyway.

Though previously inhabited by sentients known as the N'awatha, the planet had fallen to another race called the Hudathans, who, though subjugated by a multisystem government called the Confederacy, still claimed sovereignty over the world.

And now, as if *that* history wasn't sufficiently complex, the Hegemony had introduced Andragna's race to the Ramanthians, who, though members of the Confederacy themselves, had designs on the Hudathan empire and wanted to use the Thraki annexation of Zynig-47 as an excuse to occupy more planets.

All of which was probably part of some larger plot that the admiral and his staff had failed to penetrate as yet. Not that it mattered much, since none of the species encountered up to that point had a navy that could challenge his.

Andragna gave the Thraki equivalent of a sigh. If this was an improvement over roaming the stars, the advantage was lost on him. Ah, well, annoying though they were, there was some comfort in knowing that most, if not all, of the factious aliens would be eliminated by the Sheen.

That was the plan, anyway, and, given how stupid their new allies were, it might even work. Who knew? Perhaps he, the first in many generations, would be interred as the ancients had been in a crypt made of stone. Perhaps the Facers were correct. Perhaps the race should put down roots and prepare for the Sheen. The thought made him feel better—and the admiral returned to work.

Planet Arballa, the Confederacy of Sentient Beings

Ambassador Hiween Doma-Sa looked in the mirror, checked to ensure that his ambassadorial robes hung straight, and cursed his fate.

To negotiate was bad enough, especially in light of the weakness that such an activity implied, but to negotiate with the individual known as Chien-Chu, the same human who played such a prominent role in defeating the Hudathans during the last two wars, amounted to the most exquisite torture he could imagine. Yet that was what duty demanded—so that was what he would do.

The Hudathan stepped through the hatch, checked to ensure that it was locked, and entered the flow of traffic. Lesser beings hurried to get out of the way.

The cabin was rather small, and, given the limited number of items the industrialist had brought from Earth, relatively uncluttered. There was his lap comp, a book titled *The Art of War,* and holos of his son, wife, and niece.

Sergi Chien-Chu read Maylo's report one last time—and fed it to his shredder. The meetings in Rio had gone well, an alliance had been formed, and the resistance was ready. Or as ready as such an unlikely group of allies was ever likely to be. *If* Maylo and the others could hold the allies together.

All they needed was continued air support, which was under attack from Orno and his colleagues; a few brigades of troops, who were stranded on a number of different planets; and legal legitimacy, which Chien-Chu had failed to obtain.

Not that he hadn't tried. The cyborg had stated his case in the *Friendship*'s corridors, over dinners he didn't need to eat, in steam baths he couldn't enjoy, deep under the surface of Arballa, and, in one case, in a certain lobbyist's chlorine-filled hab, all to no avail.

There were sympathizers, plenty of them, up to and including the President himself, but no one with the guts to take the bull by the horns. Each and every one of the senators had legislation to pass, legislation that required votes, and could easily be held hostage.

And then, as if to reinforce any concerns the politicians might have, there were Senator Orno's hearings—stage-managed affairs in which Pardo was allowed to deliver speeches during session breaks, while Chien-Chu and his allies were scheduled into the shipboard equivalent of evenings. All

of this was perfectly legal, and an excellent example of why
politicians like Orno wanted to chair certain committees.

A chime sounded. Chien-Chu glanced at the wall chron, saw
it was time for his next meaningless appointment, and rose
from his fold-down desk. It sensed the movement, collapsed
in on itself, and merged with the bulkhead.

Of all the meetings, both clandestine and otherwise, that
Chien-Chu had participated in of late, this one, with the Hudathan ambassador, seemed the least likely to deliver any sort
of benefit.

Everybody of any importance, and that included Chien-Chu,
had spent time with Doma-Sa, heard the Hudathan's story, and
written him off. More to the point was the fact that he couldn't
vote on legislation pertaining to Earth.

Still, the Hudathan diplomat had sworn that his mission was
of the utmost importance, and, lacking anything else to do,
the industrialist had agreed to see him.

Chien-Chu trudged to the hatch, checked the security
screen, and released the lock. The door hissed as it opened.
Doma-Sa nodded stiffly. "Greetings, Citizen Chien-Chu.
Thank you for receiving me." The words had a sibilant quality
but were understandable nonetheless.

The cyborg bowed, ushered his guest inside, and pointed to
a heavy-duty chair. "You are quite welcome, Citizen-
Ambassador. The privilege is mine. Please, have a seat."

Doma-Sa noticed that the chair had been placed in a corner
to ensure his comfort, felt a little bit better about the visit, and
accepted the invitation. "Thank you."

Chien-Chu sat on the bed-couch and gestured toward the
tiny galley. "Can I get you something?"

The Hudathan knew the question was a matter of form and
shook his head. "No, but thank you for asking. May I be
blunt?"

"Please," Chien-Chu replied fervently. "You can't imagine
how good that sounds. Tell me something—*anything*—so long
as it's true."

No wonder it was *this* human who beat us, Doma-Sa
thought to himself. He thinks as we do.

"It shall be as you suggest," the Hudathan said out loud.

"A cabal consisting of certain humans, the Clone Hegemony, and the Ramanthians is working to weaken the Confederacy, circumvent its powers, and confiscate worlds under its protection. Earth was first . . . others will follow. Some belong to the Hudathan people."

Chien-Chu sat bolt upright. "Can you prove that?"

"Yes," the Hudathan said grimly, "I certainly can."

It took the better part of two hours to review the data that the Hudathans had intercepted and decide what to do with it. When Doma-Sa left, Chien-Chu felt better than he had in weeks.

Senator Samuel Ishimoto-Six had a multifunction com implant located at the base of his skull. He felt the unmistakable tingle, noted two repetitions, and left his breakfast uneaten.

A variety of beings greeted the clone as he left the senatorial cafeteria and headed up-ship. He acknowledged their salutations, wondered why Gorgin-Three had paged him, and nodded to the brace of Jonathan Alan Seebos that stood in front of the embassy.

The hatch opened and closed behind him. They were waiting just inside. The thugs, all supplied by the Bureau of Internal Affairs (BIA), understood their assignment. Humble the senator, but leave him unmarked.

That being the case, two identical men grabbed the politician's arms, a third hit him in the gut, and a fourth used a baton on his kidneys.

Ishimoto-Six went down within seconds, was kicked exactly six times, and then jerked to his feet. The face that waited to greet him was the mirror image of his own.

Harlan Ishimoto-Seven grinned into his brother's shocked countenance. "Hello, Samuel, nice of you to show up. What? No cute comments? The kind you share with free-breeding sluts? Well, that's too bad. You have a job to do—and you'll damned well do it! Take him to room three."

The BIA agents lifted Ishimoto-Six off his feet and carried the clone down a sterile-looking corridor. His toes touched every third step or so. The politician caught sight of Svetlana Gorgin-Three's smug expression and started to put the pieces

together. She worked for Seven, and he had support from
above. But whose? There was no way to know.

They knew about his dalliance with Maylo Chien-Chu, that
much was obvious, but didn't explain the beating. Back in the
old days, maybe—but not for the last fifty years or so. An
entry in his personnel file, a letter of censure; either would be
sufficient. No, they wanted to intimidate him, but why?

Though ostensibly used for meetings, room three had other
purposes as well. That being the case, it was equipped with
sturdy easy-to-clean furniture.

They carried Six inside, dropped him into a chair, and
cuffed his hands—not because they were afraid of what the
politician might do, but to emphasize how vulnerable he was.
Then, so Ishimoto-Six would have time to worry, they left the
room.

A full hour had passed by the time the door opened again.
That was more than enough time for Six to imagine all sorts
of unpleasant possibilities and sweat into his clothes.

A number of beings entered the room. They included
Ishimoto-Seven, Gorgin-Three, Governor Patricia Pardo, Senator Alway Orno, and the BIA thugs. The latter stood with
arms folded while everyone else took seats at the table. The
Ramanthian used his tool legs to preen his beak. "Senator
Ishimoto . . . how nice to see you outside of chambers. We
should get together more often."

Ishimoto-Seven chuckled. "Please forgive my brother. His
sense of humor is somewhat impaired."

Pardo, her hair just so, and her legs carefully crossed,
glanced at her wrist term. "Can we get on with this? I have
a meeting at 1100 hours."

"Of course," Seven said smoothly. "Would one of you like
to brief my brother? Or shall I?"

"The idiot belongs to you," Pardo said harshly. "Please
continue."

"As you wish," the clone replied, clearly relishing his role.
"Well, dear brother, here's the situation. Listen carefully . . .
because *you* have a part to play."

Six listened as Seven described how the cabal had come
into being, the manner in which Earth's government had been

usurped, and how the Thraki had appeared from nowhere.

The politician forced himself to ignore the pain caused by the cuffs and concentrate on what his brother was saying. Saying and *not* saying, since Six knew Seven almost as well as he knew himself and could tell when the bastard was lying. Or, if not actually lying, then withholding critical information.

And that made sense, because the arrangement the diplomat described would provide scant benefit to the Hegemony. That fact hinted at darker motivations—ones Seven didn't want to discuss in front of the others.

One such motivation was obvious, to Six at least, and that was the desire to reduce the amount of influence that Earth exerted over the Confederacy—a trap into which Pardo had fallen like an overripe plum.

But what about the Thraki? Where did *they* fit in? And what of Orno and Pardo? Were all their cards on the table? Not very likely. It was a dangerous game that Seven was playing— and one that could pull the Hegemony down.

"So," Six croaked, "what do you want of me?"

"Very little, actually," Pardo said, glancing up from her compact. "All you have to do is give a speech."

"Yes," Orno agreed. "A speech in which you will reveal that the Thraki entered the Confederacy via Hegemomy-controlled space, that they seized the planet known as Zynig-47, and are well on the way to fortifying it.

"*Not* something our colleagues are likely to approve of, but will have to accept, since they lack the means to change it. That's when I will rise to announce that in an effort to shield nearby planets from a similar fate, the Ramanthian Navy has placed Jericho, Halvar, and Noka II under protective custody."

Six stared into the Ramanthian's compound eyes. "All three of which belong to the Hudathans."

"All three of which were *taken* by the Hudathans," Orno countered, "*after* the slaughter of their indigenous populations."

Six could almost see the events unfold. Ambassador Doma-Sa would protest, hearings would be scheduled, and the process would last for years. Meanwhile, the Ramanthians would colonize the worlds, and once in place would be nearly impossible to dislodge.

The situation was hopeless. He wondered if the Triad of One knew about these machinations, concluded that they must, and wondered why his instructions remained unchanged. Could there be a schism of some sort? A disagreement at the highest levels? That was the weakness of tripartite leadership—the need for eternal consensus.

Ishimoto-Seven saw the look in his brother's eyes and smiled. "So, Samuel, what will it be? Will you give the speech? Or take a fall down a ladder? The choice is yours."

The freighter, which was far too large to enter the *Friendship's* landing bay, lay a hundred miles off her stern, in orbit above Arballa.

The vessel's skipper, an ex-Navy officer named Ruxton, had spent fifteen frustrating hours talking his way through the fifty-thousand-cubic-mile defense zone that surrounded the ex-battleship. He might never have succeeded, except for the fact that he had served with the *Friendship's* XO twelve years before.

Now, with what felt like a cargo of lead riding in the bottom of his gut, the merchant officer stood next to the ship's main lock and waited for the legendary owner of Chien-Chu Enterprises to come aboard.

Had he made the correct decision? To ignore the itinerary he was supposed to follow and come here? And how much money would the company lose as a result? A quarter million credits? What if Chien-Chu fired him on the spot? His wife would be pissed, the kids would suffer, his creditors would . . .

The lock opened, and Sergi Chien-Chu entered the ship. He had never met Ruxton before, or even heard of him for that matter, but if the master of one of his ships had something important to say, and came all the way to Arballa to say it, then the least he could do was listen. Even if the ship was more than a million miles off course.

Chien-Chu looked around, spotted the man in question, and stuck out his hand. "Captain Ruxton, I'm Sergi Chien-Chu. It's a pleasure to meet you."

Ruxton took the hand, shook it, and tried to calculate how old the cyborg was. More than a hundred, that was for sure, not that it mattered. Unless the old fart was senile, that is—which would matter a lot.

"Welcome aboard, sir. Thank you for coming."

Chien-Chu smiled. "You're welcome. So, Captain Ruxton, what's so important that it brought you and *Big Bertha* all the way out to this corner of the Confederacy?"

Ruxton gulped. He was tall and very thin. His Adam's apple rose and fell. The crew called the freighter *Big Bertha,* but her official name was the *Beratha IV,* which indicated that Chien-Chu had fairly good data, and knew where she was *supposed* to be. Give or take a few light-years. The officer jerked his head toward the stern. "It'll be easier if I show you. Please follow me."

The industrialist followed the nearly skeletal officer down a well-maintained corridor, noted that his olfactory receptors had detected the presence of a highly spiced Martian curry, and knew people were peering at him.

Ruxton paused, gestured toward a hatch, and said, "Sick bay." As if that was all the explanation the industrialist would need.

Chien-Chu stepped through the doorway, eyed the pile of electronics that occupied the single examining table, and raised an eyebrow. "Okay, Captain, I give up. What is this?"

"Not 'what,' " Ruxton said carefully. "*Who.* Her name is Angie Anvik, she's a communications tech, and she works for Chien-Chu Enterprises. She has something important to say, something *real* important, which is why she pulled her brain box, loaded it aboard a message torp, and sent herself home.

"We happened across her transponder signal just shy of Transit Point WHOT-7926-7431, used a tractor beam to snag the torp, and listened to what she had to say. That's when we went looking for your niece. Couldn't find her . . . but latched onto you." Ruxton shrugged. "I reckon that's it."

Chien-Chu took a second look at the pile of equipment, recognized the brain box for what it was, and traced some tubing to the ship's life-support console.

He imagined what it had been like for Anvik to jerk her

own brain box, and then, assuming she had an implant, to view it through the sensors mounted on her disconnected body.

That would be bad enough, but to go for weeks without the ability to see, hear, touch, smell, or feel. That took courage. But why? "Angie? Can you hear me?"

Anvik felt relief mixed with pride. Finally, after the seemingly endless voyage aboard the *Hybrid,* her arrival at CSM-1706, and the decision to send more than just a message home, her moment had finally come. Not just for *her,* but for Nethro, Jones, Ivy, and all the rest.

She looked down from the surveillance camera mounted high in a corner, triggered the footage she had recorded on Two Ball, and told the story.

The industrialist stared into the wall screen until it faded to black, shook his head, and swore a silent oath. Now, just when the Confederacy was at its lowest ebb, when the military had been cut back to practically nothing, a new and clearly dangerous force had emerged. Nankool needed to know—and sooner rather than later.

"Angie, I can imagine how uncomfortable you must be, but I want others to hear your report. May I take you back with me? The company will pay for your next body—the best money can buy."

Anvik considered the offer, smiled, and wished she had lips. "Sir, you've got a deal, providing this one comes equipped with red hair, and I can keep my job."

"Done," Chien-Chu said willingly, "with a raise to boot. That goes for you, Ruxton—*and* your crew. Now let's get going . . . we have work to do."

The chamber was packed to overflowing with politicians, all happy to vote on something popular, all primping, preening and posing for the various cameras, eager to show constituents how effective they were.

He was originally slated to speak following eighteen of his more senior colleagues, but Samuel Ishimoto-Six suddenly found himself in slot number three, right after the representative from Arballa. Orno had influence, a lot of it, and knew how to use it.

Though known for his long and often convoluted oratory, the first speaker seemed unusually brief, as was the senator from Arballa. He participated via holo and extolled the virtues of low taxes, low unemployment, and low tariffs for manufactured goods. Especially *his*.

That's when Six heard his name, managed the walk to the podium, and looked out onto an ocean of snouts, tentacles, and a considerable number of optical organs—two of which were black and belonged to Senator Orno. Ishimoto-Seven, along with Patricia Pardo, sat nearby. Both looked expectant.

Slowly at first, then with growing confidence, the politician began to speak. Both heads and cameras turned in his direction. "Greetings, gentlebeings. My apologies for ignoring the subject at hand, but a rather urgent matter has come to my attention, and requires action by the senate.

"It seems that a heretofore unknown sentient race has entered Confederate space via our sector, taken up residence on Zynig-47, and fortified the planet."

There was silence for a moment, followed by complete pandemonium. The majority leader, enraged at the manner in which the session had been hijacked, bellowed in protest.

Other representatives gabbled incoherently and fought to make themselves heard. Six raised his hands for silence.

"Please, hear me out. The newcomers refer to themselves as the Thraki. They have five thousand ships. Some of these vessels are nearly as large as Earth's moon. I believe Senator Orno has more."

The Ramanthian had planned for this moment, had looked forward to it for more than two years, and had dressed accordingly. His robes shimmered with reflected light, there was a spring in his step, and he was quick to reach the podium.

Had a properly trained xenoanthropologist been on hand, he, she, or it would have noticed that rather than being concerned regarding the sudden arrival of a possibly hostile species, Orno seemed pleased. But no such expert was present—which meant that no one knew the difference.

"Thank you, Senator Ishimoto-Six. Greetings, friends and colleagues. As you can tell from Senator Ishimoto-Six's comments, we find ourselves in a difficult situation. What with the military cutbacks, and the troubles on Earth, the Confederacy's military assets are stretched rather thin.''

It was a clever gambit designed to strike the right tone, yet remind the legislators of how powerless they were. As if by magic, a carefully prepared star map blossomed over the stage. It showed two neighboring systems and the planets that comprised them.

"So, in light of scarce resources, it's my pleasure to announce that the Ramanthian Navy has moved to secure some of the more tempting planets in systems adjacent to Zynig-47, including Jericho and Halvar, which orbit NS-678-241, and Noka II, which, except for a single ice world, has NS-7621-110 all to itself.

"Those of you who happen to be familiar with this particular sector will remember that these are Trust planets, seized during the Hudathan wars, subjected to unspeakable atrocities, now guarded by orbital picket ships.

"While it's true that the Ramanthian Navy could not withstand a full-scale attack by the Thraki fleet, initial contact by representatives of the Hegemony leads us to believe that they are satisfied with Zynig-47. For the moment, anyway.''

The Ramanthian scanned the audience and savored his moment of triumph. "That's all for the moment. . . . Does anyone have any questions?''

Many of those present had questions, and didn't hesitate to yell, squawk, click, chirp, and squeak them till a highly amplified voice cut through din.

"Yes, *I* have a question. How can Senator Orno get up in front of such a distinguished audience and tell so many bold-faced lies?''

Most of the beings in the room were masters of indirection, subtlety, and circumlocution. That being the case, attacks, especially face-to-face attacks, were a rarity. Every head or similar organ swiveled toward the back of the chamber as President Marcott Nankool strode down the aisle. The chief executive looked confident as he took the podium.

Senator Orno, who had been shocked into silence, worked his beak. Nothing came out. The human turned toward the senate floor. His expression was grave.

"Anyone who cares to check section three, page five, paragraph two of the charter will find that the President can at his, her, or its discretion declare a state of emergency, and having done so, direct Confederate military forces as he, she, or it deems appropriate, given that the senate is properly informed."

The human consulted a card that he held in the palm of his hand. "There are three circumstances in which this power can be exercised. Invasion by nonsignatory sentients, treason by member states, or the gross violation of charter provisions."

Nankool looked up. "Unfortunately for both ourselves and the governments we represent, I'm sorry to announce that all three of these conditions have been met. Data supporting that conclusion will be available in a moment.

"First, however, it is my sad responsibility to instruct the master at arms to place Senator Alway Orno, Governor Patricia Pardo, Ambassador Ishimoto-Seven, and Senator Ishimoto-Six under arrest."

The President nodded to a thickly built human. "Chief Warrant Officer Aba, you have your orders. Carry them out."

There was gasp as those equipped to inhale the ship's atmosphere did so. Then came a roar of outrage as the War Orno produced a weapon he wasn't supposed to have and charged the stage.

This possibility had been anticipated, however, and the Ramanthian staggered under the combined force of four stunner bolts. He managed two additional steps and fell. His blaster skittered down the aisle. A pair of Aba's people lifted the warrior and dragged him away.

Orno was not only shocked by the manner in which his alter ego had been neutralized, he was stunned by the sudden reversal of fortune. Surely there was an error, a mistake, a miscommunication . . .

A pair of security guards fastened shock cuffs onto the Ramanthian's pincers and prodded him with their stun guns. Orno had just descended the stairs and started up the aisle when Governor Pardo screamed an obscenity and tried to break free. A baton caught the human on the side of her head. She dropped like a rock.

Ishimoto-Seven yelled, "Long live the Hegemony!" and Six went quietly. Yes, he was innocent, but they would never believe him, and it could be dangerous if they did. How much support did Seven have, anyway? The brig was preferable to a death sentence.

"Please consult your data terminals," Nankool said as the prisoners were carried or led from the room. "A considerable amount of data has been downloaded to your terminals. I would appreciate your full and undivided attention as we review the facts."

The presentation lasted the better part of two standard hours. It covered all the information uncovered by Hiween Doma-Sa plus that gathered by Angie Anvik. The senators watched in horror as the Thraki attacked NB-23-11/E and killed every person aboard.

Chien-Chu, with Doma-Sa at his side, stood at the back of the room and watched the presentation.

Though reluctant to act till all the cards had been dealt face up, Nankool was a master orator who knew each being present, including their cultures, personalities, and political agendas. That being the case, he better than nearly anyone else was able to find the words that would build consensus, avoid offense, and encourage the assemblage to act. "So," the President concluded, "while I cannot condone the means by which Ambassador Doma-Sa obtained some of his information, his actions were somewhat understandable.

"The question of censure is of course up to you, but I would remind the senate that like his peers, Ambassador Doma-Sa is protected by diplomatic immunity."

Nankool paused to scan the audience. "In spite of some evidence to the contrary, I choose to believe that with the likely exception of Governor Pardo, this conspiracy is the work of a few misguided individuals and in no way represents the official policy of their respective governments.

"Immediate steps will be taken to confirm that impression, which, if incorrect, will lead to serious consequences."

Chien-Chu glanced at Doma-Sa as the senators stirred in their seats and whispered back and forth. Was the Hudathan's face expressionless? Or was that anger in his eyes?

Yes, the cyborg decided, Doma-Sa was disappointed. But both of them understood the problem. Many members of the Confederacy had no military forces or their own, and, that being the case, the entire organization was dependent on the more warlike races, one of which was in total disarray, while a second was part of the problem.

All Nankool could do was to buy time, gather what forces he could, and hope the governments in question would disavow the actions taken by their representatives. His frown filled the holo tank. "Given credible evidence that Governor Pardo not only conspired to illegally extend her powers, but urged charter forces to mutiny, I hereby suspend her powers until such time as the senate can review my decision and name the honorable Sergi Chien-Chu to serve in her place.

"I think you'll agree that as a past President of the Confederacy, and a member of the Naval Reserve, Citizen Chien-Chu is highly qualified for this interim post."

Nankool looked for and found the being in question. Other eyes followed. "Governor Chien-Chu, I hereby authorize you to restore Earth's legally constituted government."

The President motioned toward the floor. "Others of you, including senators representing the Dwellers, Araballazanies, and Turr will be asked to advise my staff and I as we make contact with the Thraki. Please remember that this race destroyed one of our outposts without provocation, has taken possession of Zynig-47, and may have other territorial ambitions.

"I would ask that all member states suspend contact and withhold recognition of the Thraki until such time as our investigations are complete. Thank you."

A tone sounded, a light board flashed, and the majority leader struggled to reassert his authority.

"So," Doma-Sa hissed, "one battle is won . . . but another remains to be fought."

Chien-Chu looked at the Hudathan and nodded soberly. "Yes. Do you think we can win?"

"My people have a saying," the Hudathan replied. " 'Victory comes by blood alone.' How much are *you* willing to shed?"

26

Payback is a bitch.

North American folk saying
Standard year circa 2000

Planet Earth, Independent World Government

A front moved in off the Pacific, and rain fell on the city of Los Angeles. Not just a sprinkle or two, but a torrential downpour that flooded dry riverbeds, triggered mudslides, and boiled toward the sea.

Water thundered along the top of the bus, streamed down the windows, and turned the streets to black glass. Brakes screeched as the autobus came to a halt.

The other passengers didn't even look as Marcie stood and headed for the door. It hissed open. She descended the steps, tucked the purse under her coat, and dashed for home. It was half a block to her apartment, a ground-level unit with a door on the street. The palm plate felt cold. The eternally vigilant household computer unlocked the door, activated the lights, and waited for her to ask the question. "Messages?"

"You have *two* messages," the computer intoned. "One from your mother, and one from an anonymous caller."

"Caller ID?"

"Blocked."

"Play number two," Marcie said, as she draped her coat on a chair. She was tired, and *anything* beat talking to her mother.

There was a click as the computer switched to voice mail. A series of beeps preceded the message. Three short, two long, and three short. The gender-neutral voice made the words seem more ominous: "Let loose the dogs of war."

Marcie said, "Replay," and listened again. Both the beeps and the message were correct.

Her mouth felt dry. Here it was . . . the day so many had waited for. She swallowed, ordered the computer to forward the message to list six, and retrieved her coat. It was damp, but she hardly noticed. The cigarettes in her left-hand pocket were sealed in cellophane. She fingered the pack as she headed for the door.

Monolo felt his pager vibrate and checked the readout. "Let loose the dogs of war."

The Jack Head grinned approvingly, cloned the message, and sent it out. Other pagers, six to be exact, vibrated in sympathy.

A police cruiser appeared a block away, hovered over a low-rise apartment building, and dropped a recon bot onto the roof. It sniffed, caught a whiff of the DNA it was programmed to seek, and forced its way down an air duct. There were "incentives" for finding resistance fighters, and the cops were getting rich.

Monolo raised his hand, pointed his index finger at the cop car, and said, "Bang."

Marcie paused under an overhang and felt for the cigarettes, reassured herself that they were there, and remembered the instructions. Press the logo three times, leave the pack next to some paper products, and take a walk. Simple. Marcie remembered Deke and how they had murdered him. The memory brought tears to her eyes. She straightened her shoulders and headed for the corner.

Noam Inc. owned all sorts of business enterprises—not the

least of which was a chain of convenience stores such as the one across the way.

Marcie looked both ways, crossed with the light, and entered the store. She felt a sudden urge to pee. The lights were bright, the air smelled of plastic, and a holo blossomed next to an interactive display. The elf smiled beguilingly and motioned for her to approach. "Hey, lady! Over here!"

Marcie ignored the pitch, made her way to the back of the store, and left the device next to some toilet tissue. She felt guilty as she hurried down the aisle, exited through the front, and hurried away. That's when she remembered the security cameras, damned herself for a fool, and prayed the free forces would win.

The would-be saboteur was a half-block away by the time the cigarettes exploded into flame. A clerk noticed, and put the fire out. But other businesses weren't so lucky. Calls poured in, equipment was dispatched, and sirens wailed.

Lisbon was hot, *damned* hot, and there was no shade on the roof. Dom paused in the middle of his play pretend work, peered over the edge, and checked the police station. As with all such facilities, it was busy twenty-four hours a day.

Dom wasn't thrilled about the fact that it was daytime in Europe, but knew it had to be daytime *somewhere,* and was proud to be part of the Euro Maquis. He and his teammates had balls, magnificent balls, as the authorities were about to learn.

The freedom fighter looked at his watch, watched the seconds vanish, and checked his team. One of them really *was* a carpenter and made a show out of sawing some wood.

Dom looked back, saw two cruisers lift in quick succession, and heard the wail of sirens. Thousands of fire reports had started to stream in from Lisbon, Sintra, and the surrounding suburbs. Their opportunity would come very, very soon.

Monolo and his fellow Jack Heads had been watching L.A.'s 26th precinct for three weeks now. They knew how many cops worked there, plus the number of cruisers housed in the garage. They waited till every last one of the cruisers had been dispatched and then fired their shoulder-launched missiles. The first hit an exterior wall and exploded. There was a loud boom, and a flock of pigeons took to the air, but the damage was minimal.

Monolo swore, shoved another missile into Jorge's launcher, and yelled, "Ahora!"

It sailed through a window, struck the floor, and made a hole. The debris landed on the first-floor control center, killed the watch commander, and destroyed the com console.

The computer known as L.A. Central sensed the problem, routed the 26th precinct's voice, data, and video to the next station on the grid, and waited for an acknowledgment. None came.

Police, half of whom worked for a subsidiary of Noam Inc., and most of whom were data pushers, administrators, and ex-security guards, boiled out of the 26th and into the street. That was a mistake. The Jack Heads opened fire.

Satisfied that most of the *real* police had left the building, Dom keyed his radio. "Palo? You there?"

Palo looked down through dirty plexiglass. The yellow exoskeleton stood 125 feet tall and resembled a giant stick figure. He used an enormous grasper to place a half-ton pallet of electroactive wallboard on the third floor of the quickly growing office complex, straighted his durasteel spine, and turned the machine's torso toward the east. Tiled rooftops stretched into the distance.

The police station was two blocks away. He could see Dom and the others on the roof across the way. "I'm here. . . . Are you ready?"

"Ready and waiting," Dom replied. "Come on over."

Once in place, the cranelike exoskeleton rarely moved its enormous podlike feet. That being the case, they were locked into position. Palo released the safeties, assured the machine's onboard computer that he had done so intentionally, and stepped out onto the street. His right foot snagged the top of a steel fence, ripped fifty feet of it out of the ground, and sent workers running for cover. The machine operator grinned. Building stuff was fun . . . but so was tearing it down.

Palo stood in a web of sensors. They measured each movement his body made and furnished their findings to the onboard computer, which applied a series of algorithms. The results were delivered to servos that mimicked the operator's movements and waited for feedback. The result was precise, if a little bit jerky.

Palo moved cautiously at first. He didn't want to harm innocent citizens or damage the surrounding buildings. Three steps were sufficient to clear the area. The operator didn't even notice as a huge pod-shaped foot crushed an empty delivery van, a power cable snapped across his knees, and an aircar whizzed past his control module. The police station was ahead, and that was his goal.

Dom watched in open-mouthed fascination as his friend raised an enormous six-ton foot, dropped it through the police station's roof, and followed with the other.

Walls collapsed, a dust cloud billowed into the sky, and the giant continued to march. Wires, wood, and other types of debris rattled and screeched as Palo towed them down the street. The primary objective had been destroyed. There was no need for the missiles. The secondary target was only six blocks away.

It was nighttime in L.A., and much as Matthew Pardo wanted to turn off the lights and impose a dusk-to-dawn curfew, he had resisted the temptation to do so. And a good thing too, since to the extent that he still had any support, it was among corporations such as Noam Inc., which sold things and stood to lose money if people were confined to their homes.

That's why the lights were on, traffic flowed as usual, and Kenny continued to roam. The rain had let up by then, but the streets were wet and the air was unusually clean.

The delivery truck still bore the previous owner's sign, smelled of paint, and carried ladders racked to either side. Kenny, underground hero and founder of the RFE, rode in back while Mona, his newly acquired assistant, drove and kept an eye peeled for the police.

Though not especially pretty, she was intelligent and had plans for Kenny. *Big* plans. First she would have to keep him alive, however—no small task, given his reckless disregard for his own safety, and the extent to which the authorities wanted to find him.

Mona checked the speedometer and mirror prior to signaling the next random turn. The last thing they needed was a routine traffic stop. The truck leaned to the right as it rounded the corner. A red fire truck, lights flashing, arrived from the opposite direction. It slowed and blew through the light. There were a lot of fire trucks and police cars out and about, and Mona knew why.

In the back of the truck, blissfully unaware of the exterior world, Kenny prepared for the upcoming broadcast. He touched a sequence of keys, watched Scoop Scully's head rotate through a 360-degree turn, and decided that the effect pleased him. All he needed was a sound effect to create a surefire attention getter. Just the thing to open the next program with, and not just *any* program, but the most important segment he had produced. Time had run out for Pardo family . . . and they were going down.

Kenny chuckled happily, took the announcement the Free Forces had given him, and started to read. The sound of his voice was fed into a computer, altered, and rerecorded. Scoop Scully was about to speak, and when he did, everyone would listen.

The rainfall ended by six A.M., but a pall of gray smoke hung over the city. The sun was little more than a dimly seen glow.

Though not an active member of the resistance—he was too frightened for that—Hal Hamel was a sympathizer and watched the RFE on a frequent basis. He'd seen Scoop Scully's report the night before, knew the fires were part of a larger effort, and felt a wonderful sense of elation as he drove to work. Finally something was happening.

Hawthorne Elementary was a relatively new school, and Hamel, who had been principal for less than a month, had never tired of looking at it.

Designed to match the nicely landscaped beauty of the newly trendy Rialto area, it looked more like a park than a school, with lots of trees, grass, and recreational equipment.

There were no structures other than a bundle of what looked like steel-glass silos off to one corner of the property. That's where the elevators, escalators, and emergency stairs were located, along with the fiber-optic pathways that funneled sunlight down to the underground classrooms.

But this morning was different. Hamel turned the last corner and saw military vehicles, a cluster of black-clad bio bods, and two dozen robots. All dressed in the same pattern of camouflage green paint.

Something, Hamel wasn't sure what, was definitely wrong. But before he could turn the car around, a heavily visored military policeman waved the educator over and motioned him out of the car. That's when the nightmare began.

The militiaman, a human in this case, examined Hamel's ID, checked his name off a list, and led him onto the school's grounds. A group of smooth-faced robots stepped out of the way, and that's when the principal saw the fifty-foot lengths of chain, the small ankle bracelets, and realized who they had been made for. The MP gestured to the shackles. The tone was casual, as if a matter of routine curiosity. "How many children can we actually expect? About five hundred or so?"

Hamel started to answer, thought better of it, and closed his mouth.

That's when the military policeman stepped in close, grabbed the front of the educator's shirt, and jerked the smaller man up onto his toes. "Listen, you little shit . . . which would you prefer? To answer my question? Or have Ralphie shove a baton up your ass?"

Hamel had read about courage, had admired it from a distance, but never been able to find much. Not till he saw the chains. The principal brought the stylus up, stabbed the soldier in the neck, and watched the blood spurt out. The academic had been good at anatomy, very good, and was proud of his aim.

The MP released the civilian's shirt, grabbed the wound, and backpedaled away. He tripped, fell, and quickly lost consciousness. That was Hamel's cue to run, or should have been, except that he was so amazed by his accomplishment that he stood and stared.

The militiamen killed Hamel a couple of seconds later. They
fired one full mag apiece. Not for revenge, but because they
were scared of the little man, and worried there might be more.

The *Gladiator*'s wardroom had been turned into a de facto
command center and was littered with odds and ends left over
from a dozen meetings. The surface of the central table was
nearly invisible under hastily rigged computer terminals, printouts, and a tray of partially eaten sandwiches. Admiral Angie
Tyspin sat at the far end, face on arms, sound asleep.

General Mortimer Kattabi rubbed his eyes, yawned, and
took a sip of coffee. It was cold and tasted like the bottom of
a Naa mulch pit. He made a face, ate a piece of pastry to rid
himself of the taste, and looked across the table. "So, how are
we doing?"

Major Winters, who had been promoted to serve as Kattabi's adjutant, looked up from a screen. "So far, so good, sir.
The Euro Maquis and the Jack Heads report ninety-two percent of their targets destroyed."

"Do you believe them?"

Winters grinned. "Hell, no. The satellite intel suggests that
the *actual* mission completion rate is more like seventy-six
percent."

Kattabi allowed his eyebrows to float upward. "That's better than projected."

Winters nodded. "Yes, sir. The civvies are kicking some
ass."

"And Booly?"

The adjutant looked toward a tech sergeant, who provided
the answer. "The colonel is ten from dirt, sir."

Kattabi stood. He had an assault to lead. "I hope this
works."

Winters nodded. "So do I, sir. So do I."

Tyspin continued to sleep.

It was snowing in the Rockies, an early storm that would dump
a foot of snow on the higher elevations and dust the flatlands
below.

Visibility was so poor that the pilot had very little choice but to place the shuttle on autopilot and hope for the best. That was a nerve-wracking process in the best of times, made more so by the presence of a senior officer and the knowledge that people below had every reason to blow him out of the sky. Another radio message boomed through his interface.

"Shuttle Sierra Echo Bravo nine-two-one, this is Cheyenne Control. You have entered restricted airspace. I repeat, restricted airspace. Provide recognition codes or follow vector seven to the north. Over."

An indicator light appeared, followed by a tone. Cheyenne could fire anytime they wanted to. The pilot grimaced and looked at his passenger. Colonel William Booly looked back. If he was frightened, there was no sign of it. "Go ahead. Tell them."

The pilot hurried to comply. "Roger your last, Cheyenne Control . . . but I don't have the codes. Please inform Colonel Leon Harco that Colonel Bill Booly is aboard and would like to parley. Over."

There was silence. The pilot figured he would get five, maybe ten seconds warning before the missile hit and the shuttle ceased to exist. The altimeter unwound, snow swirled, and static rattled through his interface.

Five seconds passed, followed by ten, followed by fifteen. What the hell was taking so long? Suddenly Cheyenne was back. "That's a roger, Sierra Echo Bravo nine-two-one. You are cleared to land. Over."

The pilot looked at Booly, who shrugged. "You win some, you lose some."

That's fine for *you,* the pilot thought to himself, but what about me? *I* plan to win 'em all.

The children had been walking for hours now. From their schools, along the side streets, and out onto the expressway. It was closed to civilian traffic, which was good for the militia and bad for the resistance.

Nor had the maneuver gone unnoticed. Kenny received a tip, sent a fly cam to investigate, and couldn't believe his eyes. Thousands upon thousands of children had been chained together and marched onto the expressway. Some wore uniforms, some didn't. All were visibly frightened.

Hover bike-mounted militiamen sped the length of the column. They shouted orders to the robots, most of whom were armed with shock batons, and walked in among the children. Electricity arced between the sticklike weapons and anyone who cried, talked, or began to lag.

There was no need to ask who had engineered the march, or why they had done so. The hostages would shield Matthew Pardo's movements, slow General Kattabi's forces, and intimidate the general public. People were terrified.

Kenny sent a swarm of fly cams to cover the event and ran it live. Citizens not only saw the video, but made their way to the expressway, and lined both sides. Frantic parents responded as well. Many walked beside the road, or tried to, since abutments, on-ramps, and other obstacles made it difficult to do.

Others climbed the fences and ran out onto the expressway itself. The militia had been waiting for that. An aircar swept in from the east, braked, and hovered above. Machine guns rattled, the civilians fell like wheat before a scythe, and blood stained the road.

Children screamed, batons crackled, and the march continued.

Leshi Qwan stood at the center of the pit. The spotlights pinned him in place. The meeting had been called by old man Noam. ". . . And so," the industrialist continued, "not only have we failed to see much return from this arrangement, our expenses continue to soar. Please explain."

Qwan was standing there, wondering when the old fart would realize that things were even worse than he thought they were, when something seized control of his mind. It was strong, stern, and utterly alien. He tried to react, tried to warn those seated above, but couldn't control his mouth. The words formed themselves. "I feel ill. Please excuse me."

Then, like a puppet on strings, the businessman left the pit. Noam was screaming by then. "Come back here, you rotten sonofabitch! You're dead! You hear me? *Dead, dead, dead.*"

Qwan tried to reply, tried to scream, but nothing came out.

Sola, who was operating at the extreme limit of her range, struggled to stay in control.

Harco waited for the blastproof door to cycle open, felt a blast of cold air, and stepped into the snowstorm. Snowflakes planted kisses on his face, the cold found gaps in his clothing, and a white-clad sentry popped to attention.

There was activity around the heated landing pad. The lights were on, the crash team had mustered next to their equipment, and the crew chief stood with light batons raised.

Orange-red jets stabbed through the gloom as the shuttle lowered itself to the ground.

The crew chief extended her arms, skids touched duracrete, and the engines wound down.

Harco stood with hands clasped behind his back as a pair of orange robots pushed rollaway stairs into position. It was a strange, almost surreal moment.

Starting when he was a cadet, and extending through all the succeeding years, the officer had imagined how his career might end. There had been dreams of glory and the nightmare possibility of defeat. But none of his visions had captured the terrible sense of ignominy, of pointless waste, that defined this particular moment.

How exceedingly strange that after *all* the years, *all* the dangers, it would be one of his classmates that came to take his surrender. And not just *any* classmate—but one he had believed to be inferior.

No, Harco decided, not because of his mixed parentage, but because of an inherent lack of confidence. Something he had witnessed when they cocaptained the rowing team, then later on Drang.

Still, it was Booly who had won the battle for Dijbouti, Booly who had chosen the correct course, and Booly who had arrived to take him in. And all by himself. Now *that* took balls.

The robots locked the stairs into place, the hatch slid up out of the way, and Booly appeared in the opening. He looked older than Harco remembered him, *much* older, but then who didn't?

What mattered was *how* he stood, ramrod straight, the way

Harco had imagined that *he* would stand on the most important day of his life.

Booly looked out through the snow and wondered if it was one of the last sights he would ever see. But the attempt had to be made. The prospect of an all-out battle between two elements of the Legion was too horrible to contemplate. Did Harco share his concerns? Would the other officer listen? There was only one way to find out. Metal clanged as he descended the stairs.

A noncom met Booly on the ground, introduced himself as Staff Sergeant Cory Jenkins, and led him across the pad. They climbed a short flight of stairs and emerged onto a road. It was a short walk from there to the door.

Booly half expected to be met there, to see Harco step forth to greet him, but such was not the case. A cart waited. Jenkins gestured toward the passenger seat. Booly got in and waited while the noncom took the wheel. The vehicle jerked into motion, rolled through carefully maintained grounds, and out onto a huge parade ground. Newly painted yellow lines marked borders, pathways, and assembly areas.

The cart passed rank after rank of quads, Trooper IIs, and Trooper IIIs, all fronted by hundreds upon hundreds of bio bods standing at parade rest.

Was the display a matter of coincidence? Or Harco's way of telling him something? That his troops were ready? That they would never surrender? There was no way to know.

One thing was for sure, however: They might be mutineers, but the legionnaires looked as sharp as any he'd ever seen. Jenkins turned the wheel to the right, angled across the part of the grinder not occupied by troops, and stopped in front of a reviewing stand. It was large enough to accommodate five or six people, and, judging from the condition of the lumber, brand-spanking new.

Booly eyed the noncom, wondered why he looked so sad, and climbed the wooden stairs. *This* was where Harco had chosen to receive him, here, where his power would be most visible, and a request for surrender would sound absurd.

That's what Booly *expected*, but when the officer topped the stairs, there was no one to meet him. Not Harco, not his

XO, not anyone at all. The officer squinted into the lights, felt the weight of ten thousand stares, and wondered what to do.

That was the precise moment when a holo bloomed high above his head. Booly turned in time to see Harco appear, followed by additional images—one for each of the units stationed abroad.

Staff Sergeant Jenkins shouted, "Ten-hut!" Thousands of legionnaires crashed to attention, and Booly did likewise.

Harco's voice boomed through the cavern's PA system. "At ease. We are gathered here to welcome a *new* commanding officer. Colonel William Booly."

An audible gasp was heard, servos whined, and Staff Sergeant Ward bellowed into the mike. "You are at ease! No talking. Corporal, take that soldier's name!"

Nobody could tell who the sergeant had yelled at, and it didn't matter. What mattered was discipline, and it was intact.

Harco continued, and as he spoke, Booly realized the comments were prerecorded. "Some of you are angry. You were betrayed by society, by the Independent Government, and now by me.

"*Not* because I doubt our ability to win, or the quality of our cause, but because we were wrong. If the Legion is to be our country, it must be a *just* country, based on the rule of law and dedicated to more than its own survival."

Harco paused, his virtual eyes roaming the chamber, driving his purpose home. "Your commanding officer understands these things. His grandfather served the Legion, his parents served the Legion, and *he* serves the Legion. More than that, he is a warrior, one who stands by his word and supports his troops.

"Some of us, including myself, broke laws in behalf of what we thought was the greater good. We will be charged with our crimes and tried by a military court. We deserve no more and we deserve no less.

"I pray that the rest of you, the vast majority, will be allowed to serve. If anyone can lead you, can make that happen, it is Colonel Bill Booly.

"I have one last mission to carry out—one last task to take care of—then I shall return. That will be all."

Harco's image faded to black, the others remained as they were, and Booly looked out over the troops. *His troops. If* he could hold them. He chose his words with care.

"The battle for Earth has begun. Elements of General Kattabi's 3rd Foreign Infantry Regiment and the 2nd Foreign Air Assault Regiment will land during the next sixteen hours. Half of the 13th DBLE has been airlifted out of Africa, and the 3rd Marine Brigade is on the move.

"No one can promise you amnesty, not at this point, but I will fight for those who are deserving, and so will General Kattabi. So, what will it be? Do you plan to sit on your cans? Or go out and fight?"

There was silence for a moment—silence that stretched long and thin. The voice came from deep within the ranks. "Camerone!"

There was a pause, followed by a full-voiced echo from the cavern and all around the world. "CAMERONE!"

Booly smiled. The Legion was back.

The schoolchildren had been marching for more than a day now. They no longer filled the roadway from side to side but formed a five-mile-long column of twos. Those who had managed to survive hovered on the edge of exhaustion. Teenagers carried some of the smaller kids on their backs, shuffling forward, barely reacting when a robot poked them.

Matthew Pardo rode in the back of an enclosed command car that occupied a slot approximately a quarter of the way back. The bulletproof windows had been polarized, and Pardo sat in the dark. He felt numb. Partly because of the alcohol he had consumed . . . and partly because of the rapidity with which conditions had changed.

First came the report that his mother and her supporters had been arrested. Then, while he was still trying to absorb *that* news, four transports dropped out of hyper, all loaded with loyalist legionnaires. Not enough to retake Earth . . . but enough to shift the odds.

Kattabi demanded Pardo's unconditional surrender less than an hour after the fires, attacks, and riots began.

The ex-legionnaire's first thought was to ask Harco for

advice, but that option was gone, and he was on his own. Something he had worked hard to achieve and lived to regret. The truth was that he'd been happier taking orders, doing what he was told, and slacking when he could. Now *he* was in charge . . . and didn't know what to do.

A teenage girl collapsed three ranks ahead. The driver swerved but reacted too late. The command car lurched as it rode over her body. Pardo swore as his drink slopped onto his pants.

Maylo Chien-Chu stepped off the elevator and out into the reception area. This had been *her* office, or one of her offices, since there were many all around the world.

But that was before the so-called revolution, the Independent World Government, and Noam Inc.

Now she was back, and the time was ripe for some house-cleaning. The sign read "Noam Inc." rather than "Chien-Chu Enterprises." *That* was about to change.

An android sat behind the U-shaped reception desk. Maylo had never seen it before and didn't approve. Customers should be greeted by people, *real* people, regardless of cost. The machine smiled. "Hello. How may I help you?"

Maylo nodded politely. "I have an appointment with Citizen Qwan."

The receptionist frowned. "I'm sorry. There must be a mistake of some sort. Vice President Qwan is away from the office, and I don't expect him till sometime tomorrow."

Maylo listened to the voice inside her head and glanced at her wrist chron. "He'll be here within the next ten minutes. I'll take a seat."

The android opened its mouth, closed it, and used an onboard radio to call security.

Maylo smiled pleasantly, sat with her back to a corner, and kept an eye on the elevator. This was the part that Booly, Kattabi, and Tyspin had objected to. *Especially* Booly, who tried to talk her out of it.

Maylo smiled grimly. Men. Who could understand them? Distant one moment and protective the next.

Never mind the fact that Booly planned to drop in on Harco

unannounced—and probably get himself killed. *She* was supposed to wait till the danger had passed. Why? Because business was a secondary concern—a perception that showed how little *he* knew. It was money that made the world go round, and, assuming the counterrevolution was successful, the economy would be critical. Without commerce there would be no jobs, and without jobs there would be no taxes, and without taxes there would be no government services. Serious issues that couldn't be handled while sitting on her can.

A tone sounded, the elevator doors slid open, and a pair of security guards emerged. They wore burgundy jackets, gray slacks, and thick-soled shoes. The Noam logo was embroidered on their pockets. The larger of the two stopped in front of the receptionist, listened to what it said, and turned to stare.

Damn! Why couldn't they have been just a little bit slower? The executive opened her briefcase, placed her hand on the pistol, and waited for the twosome to approach.

The smaller guard had a fist-flattened nose. His name tag read "Linder." He showed some teeth but kept his eyes on the briefcase. "Sorry, ma'am, but you'll have to leave. I suggest you call Mr. Qwan's secretary and make an appointment."

The elevator sounded again. Qwan stepped off and looked around. The executive's movements seemed jerky, and his voice was forced. "Miss Chien-Chu! There you are. Sorry to keep you waiting. Let's use my office."

The android and the security officers watched in amazement as Qwan palmed the rosewood-sheathed door, ushered Maylo past people she'd never seen before, and led her into her old office. The personal effects were gone, but the furniture was the same. The desk against the wall, the circular table where she liked to work, and the enormous fish tank. It was empty and dry. She put the briefcase down. They turned to face each other.

Qwan gathered his strength and pushed the words through the screen that the other presence had placed in his way. "It's the alien, isn't it? The one with the mental powers."

Maylo nodded. "Yes. Sola offered her assistance, and I accepted."

Qwan pushed outward, detected a tiny amount of give, and worked to extend it. "So, what do you want?"

Maylo looked determined. "I want the financial records pertaining to Noam *and* Chien-Chu Enterprises . . . and I want them *now*."

Qwan struggled to free himself from Sola's grip, and the Say'lynt, operating from the far side of the world, felt the human wiggle free. She tried to contact Maylo, tried to send a warning, but it came to late.

Qwan threw himself at her, Maylo crashed into a floor-to-ceiling window, and her head hit the glass.

The fly form rocked from side to side as the antiaircraft shells exploded all around. Though driven from the air, the militiamen had plenty of ground weapons, and it felt as if most of them were aimed at the sky.

Still, there was some comfort in knowing that Tyspin had elected to lead the fire-suppression mission herself, and was kicking some butt.

General Mortimer Kattabi wished he could see through the aircraft's bulkhead, glanced at his wrist term, and touched a button. Half a dozen miniature holos appeared from nowhere. Some of the officers had been with him on Algeron, and some had been seconded from the 13th DBLE. There was Major Winters, Captain Runlong, Captain Hawkins, Captain Verdine, Captain Ny, and First Lieutenant Dudley.

All of the officers, plus approximately five hundred legionnaires, were headed for the militia base near Indian Springs, in the AR called Nevada.

The Free Forces couldn't attack the population centers, not without causing a great deal of collateral damage, which explained why the resistance was focused on the cities.

Kattabi's objective was the Noam Industrial Complex, the home of Noam Arms and the militia's main arsenal.

Some of the factories, warehouses, laboratories, ammo bunkers, and tank farms had been there prior to the mutiny, but some had been built since, and others remained under construction. With no competition to worry about, Noam Inc. had been working twenty-four hours a day to supply Matthew

Pardo's army with everything from combat knives to missiles.

Destroy it, and five similar complexes spread around the world, and the militia would be forced to capitulate. Noam Inc. knew that, of course, which explained why the factories were surrounded by weapons emplacements, all of which were determined to blow Kattabi's ass off. Or so it seemed to him. He killed the holos, forced himself to ignore the way the ship rocked back and forth, and remembered what the intel summaries had concluded.

For close-in stuff, the complex was defended by robot-portable, IR-homing, shoulder-launched Fang missiles having a range of six miles.

Those were supported by self-propelled antiaircraft platforms that mounted six-barreled Gatling guns, each capable of firing three thousand rounds per minute and engaging aircraft while traveling at speeds of up to forty miles per hour.

Then, to deal with medium-range targets, the militia had carefully sited mobile air defense stations equipped with long-range, over-the-horizon, back-scatter radars and highly effective Kaa surface-to-air missiles. Not a pretty picture.

Strangely enough, it wasn't a shell that disabled the aircraft, or a hostile missile, but debris from another fly form. A large chunk of metal was sucked into an intake, shredded by the rotating fan blades, and shoved into the compressors, where it destroyed the engine. Goya felt the equivalent of pain, lost fifty percent of his power, and looked for a place to land. The quad clutched beneath his belly was heavy, *very* heavy, and the fly form entered a glide similar to that of a rock.

It was tempting to release the payload, to let it drop like a bomb, but borgs take care of borgs. Not to mention the fact that General Kattabi was aboard and some bio bods, too. No, there was no *easy* way out, which left only one alternative: the *hard* way out.

Goya gritted teeth he no longer had, demanded full military power from the remaining engine, and chose the only possible crash site—smack dab in the center of the enemy complex. A tower whipped by, tracers floated up past his nose cam, and the ground rushed to meet him. Goya barely had time to yell

"Five to dirt!" before his skids hit, absorbed some of the impact, and failed.

The quad took the punishment after that, skidding fifty yards on her armored belly before the fly form hit the side of a building and finally came to a rest.

The quad, a borg named Obuchi, knew things were bad. Rather than land where they were supposed to, a mile short of the complex, Goya had dumped them right in the middle of the damned thing! It was time to move, and move fast.

Obuchi triggered the two-way clamps, or tried to, but found they were stuck. No problem—explosive charges had been provided to deal with that very possibility. She "entered" a code, blew all four of them, and "felt" the fly form shudder as 20mm cannon shells pounded the lightly armored fuselage. One of them found Goya's brain box and blew it open.

Obuchi felt a sudden surge of anger, extended her legs, and shrugged the wreckage off her back. A single missile would have been sufficient, but the borg was pissed, so the gun platform took two. The explosions sent shrapnel flying in every direction, ripped holes in a metal-clad building, and destroyed a fuel pump. The fire started with a pop, began to roar, and sent flames shooting into the sky.

Kattabi, along with the soldiers who shared the quad's cargo bay, were thrown back and forth. Harnesses held them in place. All eyes were glued to the overhead monitors. They saw the gun platform blow. Fykes, who had volunteered to lead the general's bodyguard, was the first to speak. "Damn! We're right in the middle of the bastards!"

"You took the words right out of my mouth," Kattabi said dryly. He turned to the others. "Check your weapons and prepare to deass the quad."

Major Winters was two miles to the west, standing next to a command-and-control bot, wondering where her boss was, when his voice sounded in her headset. "Hammer One to Hammer Two. Over."

Winters perked up. "This is Hammer Two . . . go. Over."

Kattabi watched the surroundings blur as Obuchi turned to her right and opened fire. The Gatling gun found the antiarmor team and tore them to shreds. The shoulder-launched Noam

Lancet was armed and still in the tube. It blew the remains into even smaller pieces. The general winced. "Sorry to be such a slacker, Two . . . but we're gonna be *real* busy for the next twenty minutes or so. The battalion is yours."

Winters frowned, took a look at the holo tank attached to the robot's back, and scanned for Kattabi's marker. There it was, centered in the middle of the enemy complex, blinking on and off. Shit. It would be hours before any kind of rescue could be mounted. He knew that . . . and she did too. The officer ran her tongue over parched lips. "Roger that, Hammer One. Watch your six. Over."

Kattabi gave her two clicks, felt the quad shudder as she took a couple of missile hits, and eyed the squad. "Get ready to bail!"

Obuchi collapsed as one of her legs was blown out from under her body. The deck tilted, and the quad went down. Kattabi released his harness, stood, and hit the emergency hatch release. It whirred open.

Fykes stood, waved the squad forward, and said, "What the hell are you waiting for? A frigging invitation?"

The noncom was the first one down the ramp. He turned right, ran forward, and climbed the cyborg's steel flank. His boots fit into recessed steps, there were handholds to grab, and the steel felt warm.

A platoon of green-clad militiamen left the shelter of a concrete storage facility and ran toward the quad. Kattabi tripped, rolled down the ramp, and came up firing. One of the legionnaires screamed, two of the opposing soldiers fell, and dirt geysered into the air.

Fykes made it to the top, felt Obuchi move, and heard her voice. "The Gatling is operational! Keep your heads down!"

Servos whined as the six-barreled weapon extended itself upward, tilted in the direction of the oncoming solders, and opened fire. The remaining militiamen were snatched off their feet, tossed backward, and cut to ribbons. A guard shack disintegrated, a hover truck exploded, and bullets tunneled halfway through a duracrete wall before the weapon fell silent.

Deafened by the noise, Fykes grabbed the T-shaped handle, jerked Obuchi's brain box, and jumped to the ground. Kattabi was waiting. "Well done, Sergeant Major. Let's get the hell out of here."

The general turned, saw the gate a hundred feet to the north, and waved his troops forward. "Vive la legion!"

They were halfway across the open area when a second armored car poked its nose around the corner of a building, paused, and opened fire. General Mortimer Kattabi, Sergeant Major Raymond Fykes, and a half dozen more died within seconds of each other.

One of the bodies fell on top of Sergeant Carolyn Obuchi's brain box, and four hours later, when the complex was liberated, so was she. A victory had been won . . . and the price had been paid.

Maylo felt her head bounce off the window, was stunned by the pain, and felt hands close around her neck. Qwan's face filled her vision; his features were contorted into a grim mask, and she could smell his expensive cologne. The pistol! She had to reach it!

Maylo brought her knee up, felt it connect, and heard Qwan grunt. His grip weakened. She twisted away and made for the briefcase. It was on the other side of the office, below the fish tank, what seemed like a world away.

Qwan swore, saw the case, and guessed what it contained. Maylo was four feet away by then, but he lunged forward and grabbed her shoulders.

That was the moment when Sola managed to reestablish contact, seized partial control of Qwan's mind, and squeezed with all her might.

The executive screamed, grabbed his head, and staggered backward. Sola felt the connection snap, sent a warning to Maylo, and tried to recover.

Maylo "heard" Sola's voice, rammed her hand into the briefcase, and felt for the handgun.

Qwan threw himself onto her back, felt Maylo collapse, and experienced a sense of triumph. She was his! The bitch was his!

The 9mm spilled out onto the floor. Maylo grabbed it and

tried to turn. Qwan straddled her, tried for the weapon, and felt the alien counter his efforts.

It was then, as Qwan fought for control, that Maylo rolled onto her back. She remembered how he had leered from the bottom of the tanklike cell, the way the water had risen around her shoulders, and squeezed the trigger.

The gunshot was loud, louder than Maylo had expected, and Qwan looked surprised. The first bullet struck his chest, the second tore a hole through his throat, and the third took the top of his head off. He tumbled backward.

Sola felt darkness close around her, broke the contact, and let the other being go. She wanted to run, wanted to hide, but forced herself to remain.

Maylo made it to her knees, fired two shots at the door, and heard the bullets flatten themselves against the fireproof metal. The executive made it to her feet, stepped over the body, and locked herself in. The resistance was on the way, or was supposed to be on the way, and she had things to do.

Someone hammered on the door as Maylo sat down at the computer terminal, entered the codes Sola had plucked from Qwan's dying brain, and went to work.

The fly form threw a cross-shaped shadow onto the land as it followed the ribbon of concrete toward the west. There were only two beings aboard: the pilot, who was a cyborg, and Colonel Leon Harco, who was tired. It had been three days since he had slept, really slept, and his thoughts flowed like thick syrup.

He looked back, searching for the exact moment when the first mistake had been made. The problem was that he couldn't identify it, which suggested that he had been going downhill from the very start, or that he was too tired to think properly.

The legionnaire allowed his head to rest on the window, felt the engines through his skull, and let gravity control his eyelids.

The column looked like a long, multicolored caterpillar as it followed the expressway into the mountains, gathered in the turns, and seemed to surge into the straightaways. Batons crackled, the smell of burnt hair hung in the air, and the children made a keening sound. There were no words, no cries of anguish, just a moan similar to a steady wind.

There were fewer children now, and the Free Forces were starting to hem him in, but Pardo was free. Well, sort of free, since he wasn't in custody. There weren't many options, though . . . not good ones. That's why he continued to ride in the car, and it continued to move.

A deal? Sure, if the Free Forces were willing to make one, but nothing so far. Nothing but threats.

Surrender? The thought had occurred to him dozens of times. But what then? The first prison sentence still awaited, and there would be more, many more, if they allowed him to live.

Suicide? Yes, if he had the guts, which Pardo knew he didn't.

What did that leave? An escape, if he could manage it. . . . Bail out of the car, let the Free Forces follow it east, and hide next to the freeway. But how? Every move he made was captured by the RFE, not to mention the clumps of people who monitored the column's progress.

What he needed was a diversion, something that would draw attention away from the car and allow him to escape. Kill a few of the children, perhaps? Up toward the front of the column? Yes! That would almost certainly work.

Excited now, and eager to implement his plan, Pardo stood. A servo whined as the roof hatch opened, and the ex-soldier stuck his head out.

The air was warm, but not *too* warm, and pressed against his face. The children moved slowly, heads down, slogging their way upward. The older kids were silent, but the younger ones, those who had survived, made a whining sound.

Pardo directed his eyes to the road ahead, gauged the terrain, and looked for the right opportunity. The Legion had taught him quite a bit about escape and evasion. This was the time to use it.

Then, as the ex-officer scanned his surroundings, something caught his eye. A fly form! Coming in from the east. The Free Forces? Or the rescue team he hadn't dared hope for?

His heart beating like a triphammer, uncertain of what to do, Pardo watched the aircraft grow larger, felt the air press down around him, and plugged his ears against the whine of the engines.

The fly form fell like a hawk, grabbed the car with a set of belly clamps, and snatched it right off the road. The engine revved, and the wheels spun as they lost contact with the pavement. The cyborg's belly was only five feet away.

Pardo drew his sidearm, realized how stupid that was, and put it away. Someone had him. The question was, Who?

Meanwhile, down on the ground, the column had stopped. Heads turned, eyes sought the fly form, and chaos followed.

Unsure whether their leader had abandoned them or had been snatched out of their midst, the militiamen fled toward the east.

The robots, still under orders, continued to march. But they could be dealt with, and would be, the moment the Free Forces arrived on the scene.

Frantic to learn what his fate would be, Pardo fumbled with the com set. That's when his driver opened the door to the passenger compartment, started to say something, and took two slugs through the chest.

Pardo restored the weapon to its holster, chose the most likely freq, and keyed the mike. "Who the hell are you? And what do you want?"

The response was calm and deliberate. "This is Leon Harco."

Pardo bit his lip. Harco had no reason to help, but who could tell? The asshole was an idealist and capable of damned near anything. A positive approach seemed best. "Harco! Thank God. Where are we headed?"

"To Los Angeles," Harco replied calmly, gazing out the window. "To turn ourselves in."

"Turn ourselves in?" Pardo asked incredulously. "Why would we do that? I have a ship. She's small but fast. We can break out, make a run for the rim, and live like kings. I have friends out there, lots of them, and we can start over. What do you say?"

"I say no," Harco answered laconically. "There are rules. We broke them. We have to pay. It's as simple as that."

"No!" Pardo shouted. "I won't go!"

"Really?" Harco inquired. "I think you will. Now shut up. I'm tired."

The following ten minutes seemed to last an eternity, from Pardo's perspective anyway, as the fly form flew toward the sun. Plans stuttered through his brain, dozens of them, but none were realistic.

Then something changed. The aircraft slowed, turned, and hovered in place. Were they preparing to land? Pardo looked out of the car's window, frowned, and climbed up through the hatch. The view was better from there . . . and he knew where they were: about five thousand feet over the Imperial Coliseum. The same place where he had put fifty-eight people to death. Something clicked, he knew what Harco intended to do, and the scream emptied his lungs.

Clamps sprang open. The car fell free and plummeted toward the ground. Harco didn't bother to look. He touched the intercom. "Take me to the academy . . . or what's left of it. I'll surrender there."

They cyborg obeyed, and the fly form banked away.

Meanwhile, down on the ground, a robot trundled out toward the center of the enormous playing field. Some sort of unauthorized structure had fallen out of the sky and buried itself in the turf. Standards had been violated, rules had been broken, and there was work to do.

The Chien-Chu executive jet left the city of Geneva in what had once been the country of Switzerland, turned to the southeast, and flew out over the Mediterranean.

Maylo had the passenger compartment to herself and enjoyed the privacy.

She worked for the first couple of hours, checking key indicators, monitoring the health of the business.

Then, well after the blue was replaced by brown, her thoughts turned elsewhere. Exactly sixty-two days had passed since the fall of the so-called Independent World Government. Things were better, not perfect, but better.

With Patricia Pardo off-planet, and her son safely buried, the previous government had no clear leader. Not only that, but Colonel Harco's surrender, followed by the militia's collapse, left no power base from which to rule.

Now, with the installation of her uncle as interim governor, and the restoration of military discipline, life was returning to normal.

Yes, there were odds and ends to be dealt with, not the least of which would be the investigations focused on those accused of war crimes. Colonel Harco's trial was sure to attract a lot of attention, as would Eli Noam's, and a dozen others. The process would be painful, but the planet would get through it.

All of which meant that the economy had stabilized, commerce had returned to something approaching normal, and the process of rebuilding the company had begun.

That being the case, Maylo had granted herself what she deemed to be some well-deserved vacation time.

That made sense. What didn't make sense, or *might not* make sense, was her spur-of-the-moment decision to join Booly in Africa.

Like her, the officer had been busy at first, assuming Kattabi's responsibilities and working to fold most of Harco's force back into the Legion.

There had been com calls—hesitant, sometimes awkward conversations that often seemed more painful than pleasurable. A natural outgrowth of the fact that they really didn't know each other all that well.

Booly had been attentive, though, going out of his way to see her on three different occasions, filling *all* of her offices with flowers, and once, when she was headed into an unpacified region of Europe, assigning a team of Naa commandos to accompany her.

So, while those things were nice, Maylo continued to worry. What if Rio's magic was just that? What if they weren't compatible? What if he snored?

"*You* snore sometimes, so why shouldn't he?" the voice asked, and Maylo felt a surge of joy. "Sola! How *are* you?"

"Better, now that I can go home," the Say'lynt replied. "Earth is a dangerous place."

"Yes," Maylo agreed. "It is. So, snoopy one, how 'bout it? Are Bill and I made for each other?"

"Such determinations are beyond my competencies," the alien answered carefully, "but I can tell you this. You aren't due for an hour yet—and he's at the airport."

Booly felt stupid in his civvies, glanced around to make sure that no one was looking, and consulted the badly cracked mirror. The man who looked back had two halves, one slightly larger than the other, both dressed in a short-sleeved blue sport shirt, khaki trousers, and casual shoes.

He heard the sound of a plane, forced himself to walk slowly, and made his way over to the open command car. It stood in the shade, so the seat was relatively cool. He started the engine, pulled out onto the apron, and watched the jet land.

The plane taxied toward the rather dilapidated terminal and came to a stop. Booly drove across the tarmac, got out, and waited while they opened the door.

Maylo ducked under the top of the doorway, squinted into the sunlight, and waited for her eyes to adjust.

Suddenly there he was, standing next to a military vehicle, grinning like an idiot. What he thought, what he felt, was plain to see.

That was when Maylo remembered the cell, the harsh, white light, and the man with the gun. What was it that Sola had said? "This is the beginning . . . not the end"? Maylo smiled and knew the words were true.

27

A prince being thus obliged to know well how to act
as a beast must imitate the fox and the lion, for the lion
cannot protect himself from traps, and the fox cannot
defend himself from wolves. One must therefore be a
fox to recognize traps, and a lion to frighten wolves.

Niccolò Machiavelli
Il Principe
Standard year 1532

Planet Arballa, the Confederacy of Sentient Beings

Sergi Chien-Chu stepped out of his cabin, paused to ensure
that the hatch was locked, and stepped into traffic. It was brisk
and carried him along.

Earth, and the restoration of a legal government, were yesterday's news aboard the *Friendship*, where most sentients
were focused on both the problems and opportunities posed
by the newly arrived Thraki.

Many of the passersby recognized Chien-Chu and said
hello. His elevation from historical curiosity-cum-lobbyist to
planetary governor had raised his status from the C list to the
B list, which he shared with other notable but nonvoting politicos.

There was a stir ahead, and traffic parted to allow someone

through. Chien-Chu spotted a Ramanthian war drone and knew who would follow.

Senator Orno, along with Ambassador Ishimoto-Seven and Senator Ishimoto-Six, had spent less than an hour in custody prior to being released on their own recognizance.

Then, in the wake of vaguely worded apologies from their respective governments, plus a slap on the wrist from the Foreign Affairs Committee, all had been reinstated.

That was not what Nankool had hoped for, and not commensurate with the crimes they had committed, but all the President could get. Orno had a lot of friends and the outcome was never in doubt.

Patricia Pardo was not so fortunate, however, and would stand trial for her crimes.

The Ramanthian delegation broke through the crowd, Orno speared Chien-Chu with his space-black eyes, and there was no need for a translation. The Ramanthian was and always would be an enemy.

The delegation brushed past. The cyborg felt the chill and continued on his way. Orno was a problem—but far from the most pressing one. Chien-Chu had just returned from Earth, where Maylo, along with countless others, had repaired the free market economy, restored civil liberties, and was starting to deal with the war damage, both real and psychological.

There was a lot left to be done, including the creation of a war tribunal, preparations for the upcoming elections, and military reforms. Reforms that would require senatorial approval, the kind achieved through intensive lobbying, all of which argued against his present errand.

Ambassador Doma-Sa had been insistent, however, *very* insistent, and was hard to ignore. Partly because of his size, partly because of his persona, and partly because of their history together. After all, it was information provided by the Hudathan that had broken the conspiracy wide open and provided Nankool with the means to boot Pardo out of office. That meant something, to Chien-Chu at least, which explained his willingness to come.

The clone spent the better part of fifteen minutes making the trip through the corridors and out into the landing bay where the Hudathan was waiting. The alien looked huge in his space armor. Chien-Chu heard the voice via his onboard com gear. "You came."

"Of course. I said I would."

Doma-Sa regarded the other being through his faceplate. "Many humans say many things . . . only some of them are true."

Chien-Chu looked up into alien eyes. "Just one of the many traits that our races have in common."

Hudathans don't laugh, not the way humans do, but the strange, grunting sound came fairly close.

The strange twosome crossed the busy deck, approached the Hudathan shuttle, and entered the lock.

Later, after Chien-Chu had strapped himself into the gargantuan copilot's seat, they were off. Traffic control cleared them out of the *Friendship*'s bay and onto an approved vector. "So," Chien-Chu said, "will you tell me where we're going? And more importantly, why?"

"Not yet," the Hudathan said stolidly. "It is better if you see for yourself. Someone is following. The Ramanthians, perhaps. We will take evasive action."

The evasive maneuvers, plus the trip to the asteroid belt, took the better part of eight hours. Chien-Chu didn't know he had fallen asleep until Doma-Sa touched his arm. "Come. We have arrived."

The cyborg looked at the viewscreen. It showed what looked a landing bay. "Arrived? Arrived where?"

But the Hudathan had gone, leaving Chien-Chu with little choice but to release his harness and follow. Doma-Sa waited in the lock. They cycled through together. A strange, manta-shaped shuttle crouched off to one side. It wasn't Hudathan— so who did the ship belong to? An officer was waiting. Doma-Sa made the introduction. "Governor Chien-Chu . . . Spear Commander Nolo-Ka."

The Hudathan officer came to attention as the cyborg frowned. "This looks a lot like a warship—the kind you aren't supposed to have."

"This vessel has the capacity to defend itself," Doma-Sa

admitted, "but the *Deceiver*'s main mission is to gather intelligence of the sort that freed your planet."

Though Chien-Chu had been already aware that the ship existed, *had* to exist in order for the Hudathans to intercept the Ramanthian message torp, the reality of it was something else. These were the beings who had murdered Chien-Chu's only son, who had bombed the N'awatha to the edge of extinction, and laid to waste entire planets. Something they would be only too happy to do all over again. So, insignificant as it might seem, the *Deceiver* hinted at a monumental threat. One that had been contained—but just barely.

Doma-Sa nodded. "I know what you are thinking, but believe me, my race is *nothing* compared to the threat that comes our way."

Nolo-Ka led the way. Chien-Chu was struck by how large everything was. He felt like a child forced to deal with adult-sized furnishings.

Gratings clanged underfoot as they made their way through a series of passageways and into a relatively small compartment. It consisted of little more than steel bulkheads, a pedestal-style table, and some throne-sized chairs. A single being sat under a cone of harsh light. She was small, much smaller than Chien-Chu, and looked tiny in the enormous chair. She had large eyes, catlike ears, and horizontal vents in place of nostrils.

"Governor Chien-Chu," Doma-Sa said formally, "please allow me to present Astria Parantha, also known as Sector 12, a title roughly analogous to Senator. She belongs to the Thraki leadership committee and represents a faction known as the Runners."

The Hudathan turned to the Thraki. "This is the human I told you about. Please tell him everything that you shared with me."

The female held a small robot in her lap. It translated her words into standard. It took the better part of three hours for the diminutive alien to describe the Sheen, the incredible power that they possessed, and their unbending determination to find the Thraki and destroy them.

And not just them, but any race associated with them, which meant the entire Confederacy.

It was a lot to absorb. Doma-Sa gave the human a moment to digest what he'd heard and turned back to the Thraki. "Thank you. Now, tell him about the Facers, and the plan to use the Confederacy."

Another fifteen minutes passed while Parantha laid out the plan first articulated by Sector 4.

Chien-Chu, already stunned by the magnitude of what was almost certainly coming their way, felt a terrible sense of hopelessness as the Thraki politician described how her race planned to sacrifice Confederate forces to the Sheen and then, if convenient, turn and destroy them.

But only if they fell for it. It was the sector's hope that once the Confederacy knew about the Sheen, they would force the armada to resume its nomadic ways—something that would make Sector 12 and the rest of her party very happy.

Chien-Chu listened, nodded, and asked the obvious question. "It's my understanding that you have approximately five thousand ships, all under Facer control. In addition to that, your race fortified one of our planets. How would we force the armada to leave?"

The Thraki hoped there would be a way, but wasn't sure what it would be.

The human looked at the Hudathan. Understanding jumped the gap. Nothing was safe. Everything was at risk. Death roamed the stars, and, sooner rather than later, it was going to find them.

Jorley Jepp had no idea what the space had been intended for, only that it was large enough to accommodate more than two hundred robots, all of which stood in orderly rows. They were clay, *God's clay,* needing only to be shaped, fired, and put to work. And that was *his* purpose, to give them the word of God, fill them with zeal, and send them forth.

The human raised his hands. "Repeat after me . . . there is nothing but the word of God . . . Jorley Jepp speaks for God . . ."

The Hoon listened with a tiny fraction of its overall beingness, put the fleet into a gentle turn, and authorized an additional expenditure of energy. All of the data points were in alignment. The Thraki were within reach . . . and the Thraki must die.

Praise for William C. Dietz's
Legion of the Damned
and *The Final Battle*

"A tough, moving novel of future warfare."
—David Drake

"A complex novel . . . scintillating action scenes . . .
A satisfying, exciting read."
—Billie Sue Mosiman, author of *Widow*

"Rockets and rayguns galore . . . and more than enough action to satisfy those who like it hot and heavy."
—*The Oregonian*

"Exciting and suspenseful . . . real punch."
—*Publishers Weekly*

Praise for Dietz's *Sam McCade* series

"Slam-bang action."   —David Drake

"Adventure and mystery in a future space empire."
—F. M. Busby

"All-out space action."   —*Starlog*

"Good, solid, space opera, well told."
—*Science Fiction Chronicle*